Acclaim for
THE STORY HUNTER

"A masterful conclusion to an entrancing trilogy. I couldn't put the book down. Couldn't stop thinking about it after I'd finished. This is the type of story readers everywhere crave."

— NADINE BRANDES, award-winning author of *A Time to Die, Fawkes,* and *Romanov*

"Written to perfection until the final page, *The Story Hunter* offers a stunning conclusion to a beloved trilogy only Lindsay A. Franklin could deliver. Fans will no doubt be both satisfied and devastated at once. Tanwen's journey is one I wish would never end!"

— SARA ELLA, award-winning author of The Unblemished Trilogy and *Coral*

"Lindsay A. Franklin's *The Story Hunter* is the perfect conclusion to the epic Weaver Trilogy. As always, Franklin's vibrant writing swept me away into the story with characters I already hold so dear, and her talented storytelling plunged me deeper into the rich world she created. The stakes are higher than ever, the raw emotion stronger, and the characters are just as real and brilliant as before. I highly recommend this tension-filled, beautifully written, captivating story with characters who will steal your heart."

— S.D. GRIMM, author of *Scarlet Moon*

The Story Hunter

The Weaver Trilogy
The Story Peddler
The Story Raider
The Story Hunter

THE STORY HUNTER

THE WEAVER TRILOGY

BOOK 3

LINDSAY A. FRANKLIN

Published by Enclave Publishing, an imprint of Third Day Books, LLC
Phoenix, Arizona, USA

www.enclavepublishing.com

ISBN: 978-1-62184-122-7 (print)
ISBN: 978-1-62184-123-4 (eBook)

The Story Hunter
Copyright © 2020 by Lindsay A. Franklin

All rights reserved. No part of this book may be reproduced or transmitted in any form or by any means, electronic, mechanical, including photocopying and recording, or in any information storage and retrieval system without prior written permission from the publisher.

This is a work of fiction. Names, characters, places, and incidents are products of the author's imagination or are used fictitiously. Any similarity to actual people, organizations, and/or events is purely coincidental.

Edited by Steve & Lisa Laube
Cover design by Kirk DouPonce
Interior typesetting by Jamie Foley

Printed in the United States of America

To my fellow survivors.

This one is for you.

CHAPTER 1
TANWEN

I STOOD BEFORE THE CAPITAL CITY OF URIAN, UNABLE TO breathe. Wispy strands of pearl-gray sorrow cascaded from my hands and pooled on the ground.

The city, the one I'd spent most of my young life dreaming about, hadn't been all I'd hoped for—that was true. It hadn't fulfilled me and my desires the way I'd once fantasized it would. But it had been my home for a while. It had been the place where I'd rediscovered my father, alive, after thirteen years apart. The place where we had triumphed over a tyrant, where Braith had rightly been crowned queen, and where I'd thought my future might lie.

And now, it was enveloped in chaos.

People poured through the cobblestoned streets and packed-dirt alleyways. Peasants, the merchant class, soldiers with uniforms in various states of disarray. Nobles, even. I watched as a lady in a fine dress stumbled over the rubbish strewn about the street. She cried out as she hit the ground. Half a moment later, three peasants were upon her, ripping at her fine clothing and jewelry.

Before she could scream again, my father stood over her, his sword drawn and his eyes ablaze. "You'll not harm her."

Surely the peasants didn't recognize him on sight—the former First General of Tir was famous by name, not looks, among the peasant class. But his sword spoke clearly enough.

That was a language we all understood. They released the fallen lady and took a few steps backward.

Father nodded to the rest of us, the knot of weavers from the Corsyth, standing frozen in shock or horror. I felt as though I'd sprouted roots into the street. I knew the lady needed assistance. The danger from the rioters pressed in on me like a black cloud of dark magic. And the heat from a nearby shop, awash in flame, warmed my back in the most unpleasant way.

Yet I couldn't seem to move.

Mor did instead.

He hurried to Father's side and bent beside the weeping, trembling woman. "Come on, now. Let me help you up."

She hesitated, and I could hardly blame her. We had traveled from the port city of Physgot to Urian at top speed, stopping only to tuck our injured comrade Aeron safely away in our Corsyth hideaway with Karlith as her nurse. And we'd been moons at sea. Though our ship was commissioned by the queen and we were all legitimate sailors in the eyes of the law, Mor looked every bit the ruffian pirate at the moment.

After a pause, the lady glanced at Father's blade, still poised protectively between her and the peasant attackers, then she accepted Mor's hand. He led her safely behind Father, toward the rest of us.

Father turned his attention back to the would-be muggers. "Now, what in the name of the queen has happened here?"

"We have no queen," one hissed. Her gaze wandered to the lady, who shrank closer to Mor's side, and her eyes lit up with greed. "There ain't no such thing as the nobility anymore. What's hers is mine!"

Zelyth stepped forward, his height imposing despite his thin frame. "That ain't how it works, last I checked. What's happened to this place? What's happened to Queen Braith?"

Another of the peasants, a lad no older than fifteen, sneered. "We don't answer to you. Or him," he said as he thrust his chin at Father. Though I didn't fail to notice he took several steps away from Father's blade before he decided to be so bold.

"Get out of here!" Warmil suddenly shouted, and the peasants scattered. To say the former guardsman captain was on edge was an understatement. Aeron was his lass, and he'd been none too pleased to leave her behind in the Corsyth, even though he knew she couldn't travel with us. She was still recovering from losing a leg in the battle that had sunk our ship, the *Cethorelle*.

Dylun's grip tightened on a wooden box in his hands. He shook his head. "I don't like this at all."

Father lowered his weapon, though he didn't return it to its sheath. He turned to the rattled noblewoman. "My lady, can you tell us what's happened?"

"Those beasts! Animals!" Her voice quivered as her pitch edged toward glass-splintering. I fought the urge to stick my fingers in my ears. "We were hiding in a shop for days. We were out of water, so I had to leave. I *had* to! The moment they saw me, they chased me!"

Father nodded. "Are you hurt?"

She ran her hands across the bodice of her dress and down her arms. "I . . . I don't think so." Her voice quieted as she checked her body for injuries. Then she began to cry again. "Have they no *shame*?" Back to glass-wrecking.

"Lady . . . ?" Father waited for her to answer his unasked question.

"Lady Gwan. Gwan Ma-Straychan."

The name didn't seem to spark any remembrance or recognition. "Lady Gwan," Father continued, "can you tell us what happened to the queen?"

"They took her!" Lady Gwan covered her face and sobbed. "They took Queen Braith off to goddesses know where and have done stars-and-moons know what to her." Her pale, thin shoulders heaved and rattled, and I wondered if this trauma would be the death of the poor thing.

Shrill though she was, I could only imagine how overwhelming this must be for her—for someone who had probably lived in relative peace and comfort her whole life.

"Why does she shake like that?" A young woman—my age but looking at least a few years younger—emerged from the shadow of an alleyway. Like a tiny female version of Mor—dark hair, piercing blue eyes, head cocked to one side curiously. "Why does she act like she's dying?"

Mor frowned at his sister over the head of Lady Gwan, who continued to weep in earnest. "Diggy, leave her alone."

Diggy shrugged, the curiosity dropping from her face. "Fine. Just wondered." She slipped back into the shadows a few feet away, to watch from a safer distance.

Father met Lady Gwan's watery gaze. "You said *they* took Queen Braith. Who are *they*?"

"The steward." Lady Gwan drew a halting breath. "Well, now he's the steward. Set himself up very well in the palace, I'm sure. Hosting fine banquets for his henchmen and fellow evildoers. Oh, why! Why has this happened?" She buried her face into Mor, apparently no longer concerned about his disheveled appearance.

Mor shot a wide-eyed glance between me and the tangle of blonde curls resting against his chest.

Under any other circumstance, I might have laughed.

But not now. Not with Urian ablaze and Braith kidnapped or dead and my mind running through a morbid list of names—those who had probably been in Urian when the peasants marched on it.

Cameria, Braith's maid and Father's lone ally during his long years in hiding. Ifmere, Zel's wife, and their baby son, Dafyth. I tried to calculate how old he was now. Half a year? We'd been at sea at least four moons. I had turned eighteen years old and hadn't even noticed on the day the *Cethorelle* sank. That was the day Wylie died, and I didn't think I would celebrate it ever again.

Almost three weeks had passed since then. Time seemed to slip away from me like an ocean current these days.

The names of about a dozen servants and guardsmen with whom I'd become friendly during my weeks living in the palace rolled through my mind now. Were any of them safe? Had everyone but Braith been unharmed?

Braith.

Bile rose in my throat. She was the kindest, goodliest soul I'd ever known. True, I hadn't known her long, but every time I turned around, she was fighting for what was right, trying to be a good leader to her people.

Why would they harm her? Why would they take her? She would be a good ruler. It was like a strand I couldn't quite grab hold of. It didn't make sense.

"Lady Gwan"—Father's voice carried into my thoughts—"we'll take you to safety. Then we must continue on to the palace."

"Oh stars in the heavens, don't!" she screeched. "They'll kill you! Absolutely *kill* you! If you were in the queen's service, they will treat you no better than me."

Father's eyes were kind, but his jaw hardened. "I'd like to know just who *they* are. And there's only one way to find out."

Lady Gwan's chin trembled, but she took Father's offered arm and allowed him to lead her away, back toward whatever shop she'd been hiding in, I supposed. I followed close behind, and after a moment, Father turned halfway around and lowered his voice. "Tannie, your strands. Get that under control."

"Oh." Those sorrowful, pearly strands were still spilling from my hands, and I had a proper cloud following me at this point. "Right."

"No need to draw attention. We don't know what we're about to face."

I looked at Mor. "At least the strands were gray. They kind of blend with the smoke. Sparkly purple would've been worse."

He lifted one eyebrow. "Yes, rather." He cast a glance over his shoulder, and I knew he was checking the shadows to make sure Diggy was staying close.

Until we'd plucked her from it—quite accidentally and against her will, if I'm honest—Diggy had lived alone on a tiny island for some years. The crush of people in Urian on its best day would have been a lot for her. This was . . . something else entirely. I was glad she'd chosen to stay and hadn't fled to the river or forest by now.

Lady Gwan nearly forgot about us once she crossed the threshold of the candle shop where the rest of her party hid. "Straychan!" She ran to a man propped against a barrel full of irregularly shaped candles. He had a wound in his side, and his shirt was stained with blood, but his color looked pretty good. It didn't seem he would be bleeding out any time soon.

Strange that I had any knowledge at all of bleeding out or of flesh wounds compared to mortal strikes.

How my life had turned sideways.

With Karlith in the Corsyth, Warmil was our most skilled in the healing arts, by far. Even when Karlith was around, Warmil dealt with the nasty work of stitches. I looked at him. "Warmil? Can we help him?"

He frowned. "I could, but I need supplies."

Father looked thoughtful. "Lady Gwan," he said at last. "We need to get to the palace. We will send help if we can."

"Yes." She rose and faced us again. "Thank you for your help." She patted at her hips as though searching for her coin purse. It wasn't there. "Oh, if only they hadn't taken it!"

A look of disgust settled over Warmil's face, but Father still had that steady, patient calmness in his eyes. "That's very kind of you, but we do not require a reward."

"But who shall I say rescued me? Surely I can give you your

proper due." Lady Gwan looked scandalized at the idea that she might not be able to attach our names to her harrowing story.

Father hesitated. "You may tell people you were rescued by servants of the queen."

"I know you," Straychan said suddenly. "I know you from the queen's council. I stood in the gallery once."

That was our cue. Father turned and swept his arms out as he moved toward the door, herding me, Mor, Zel, Warmil, and Dylun out into the street. Diggy had never followed us into the shop in the first place.

"He's Yestin Bo-Arthio!" Straychan fairly shouted. "The queen's advisor. I'm sure it's him!"

Father spun back to the man. "Perhaps we might keep that a little quieter?" Then he bowed once and fled the shop with haste.

WE WERE BARELY OUT INTO THE STREET WHEN SOMEONE grabbed my arm and yanked me sideways.

I screamed, then whirled around, ready to shoot strands of fire at my kidnapper.

Except I was face-to-face with a startled Diggy. "Oh," she said. "Sorry. Didn't mean to scare you."

The men thundered into the alleyway a second later. As soon as they saw it was just us, they lowered their blades.

My heart felt like a blacksmith might be shaping something on it. I willed the hammering to slow. "What is it, Diggy? Are you all right?"

"Aye. I just . . ." She glanced over my shoulder, through the rest of the group. "I think we're being watched."

Warmil spun, but there was no one there. In the street, people ran in all directions. A horse galloped by, eyes wild and body flecked with foam. With all the screaming and shouting, the chaos pressing in all around, I didn't know how Diggy could possibly sense we were being watched.

And yet I believed her.

Father had stepped away and now leaned against the stones of one of the shops beside the alleyway. His eyes fluttered closed.

"Father?" I ran to him. "Are you hurt?"

"No, Tannie girl. Just thinking. It's a peasant uprising. I would suspect Dray was behind it, but orchestrating such a thing from the dungeon is beyond even his capabilities. Could it be connected to Gareth's murder?"

He wasn't really talking to any of us, of course. Just thinking out loud.

He straightened. "Bo-Lidere, what were Commander Jule's plans when we parted at the river?"

"He said he was going to the queen's navy field office to see what he could find out." Mor paled. "That was probably a bad idea. I should have had him come with us. But he said he would send a runner—Sailor Bo-Cydrid—to check on us later. We have a meeting point set."

"None of us knew how bad it would be." Father's face was grim. "I pray they made it to safety. He and the crew are capable fighters, at least, but it would have been better if we'd stuck together. The more allies we have with us, the better. We'll have to make do."

"I'm sorry, General."

"It's not your fault, son. We'll just be ready to fight our way to the palace, if necessary. And *only* if necessary. I don't want to shed any more blood than we have to."

Mor nodded, his frown etching lines around his mouth. "Tannie. Will you—"

"Stay with Diggy. Of course."

A year past, when I was still living in the tiny town of Pembrone, nestled in the coastal cliffs of the Eastern Peninsula, I probably would have insisted on being in the thick of the fighting. I would have balked at the idea of being kept out of it, left behind, assigned to protect and guard rather than charge ahead.

But now I'd lost enough that I just wanted everyone to get across the city in one piece. If that meant I couldn't be in the middle of the action, that was fine as a fluff-hopper.

"Diggy," Mor said to his sister. "You'll look after Tannie?"

Diggy didn't respond with words, but her hands snapped toward two of the six throwing knives she wore strapped about her hips and legs.

I almost smiled. "You're asking each of us to look after the other, hmm?"

He wanted to say something, I could tell. But instead, he just lifted my chin with his hand. Gloved, so that when we touched, our weaver gifts wouldn't link and cause a spectacle of strands in the middle of Urian.

"Be safe, Tannie."

And then he, with my father, Zel, Warmil, and Dylun—a box full of priceless cargo tucked under Dylun's arm—slinked back into the street. Diggy and I followed in their wake.

We had barely gone ten feet before the men were parrying strikes and shoving people away from our group. We crept toward the palace in this way—so slowly, I could scream.

How much farther? I could see the towers, of course, but we wouldn't really be close until the perimeter wall came into view.

"Down!" Diggy's shout startled me, but I ducked without a second thought. The man who'd tried to grab me got a knife through his hand instead.

His screams nearly pulled up the contents of my stomach.

But Diggy didn't seem bothered. She bent over him and swiftly yanked her blade from his flesh. "I need that."

I swallowed hard, willing my revulsion away. "Come on."

The faster I could get her through the city, the fewer people would end up with knife wounds.

Two women barreling toward us might have become two more knife victims, but I got to them before Diggy did.

I thrust my hand in their direction and shot a strand that looked like flattened rope at one of the women, then turned slightly and launched another strand at the other. The first strand smacked into the woman just as she stretched out her hand toward my throat. It folded around her torso, pinning her arms to her sides. Then it coiled round and round her body until her screeches were cut off by my idea-strand gag.

In the space of a breath, the second peasant was bound up too.

I stared at them as they writhed on the ground. My strands wouldn't hurt them. At least, I didn't think so. That hadn't been what was in my mind when I'd imagined them. But why were these women attacking me in the first place?

"The whole world's gone mad," I said, mostly to myself.

Diggy appeared beside me. "Was it not already?"

Some distance away, Mor was shoving a thief away from Dylun, who was huddled protectively around the box in his arms. Dylun would die before he let anyone take the box—and the curse cure that lay inside it.

As I watched Dylun cradle the cure that had saved my life and cost Gryfelle's, I caught sight of a marble fountain. One of many scattered throughout the heart of the city. The whole core of Urian seemed to be carved of marble, after all.

But this one was familiar. I was almost certain it was *the* fountain I'd marveled at the very first time I came to Urian—bound with ropes not unlike those strands I'd just made. The king's guardsmen had dragged me through the city that first time, but the Pembroni farm girl in me couldn't help but marvel anyway.

All that smooth white stone. This one shaped like a perfect bowl.

Probably by an expert stoneshaper, I realized now, remembering the Meridioni weavers who carved stone with their fingers. I hadn't known such weavers existed before I'd seen them myself in Meridione.

And now, that pure, spotless fountain ran with blood.

I stared up into the vacant eyes of a man whose throat had been slit. His body was draped over the top tier of the fountain, and it seemed he'd been placed there on purpose. It reminded me of how Gareth would display the heads of his enemies around the capital when he had a mind to.

Or so I'd heard.

This man was one of Braith's guardsmen. He wore the black uniform of the palace guard. I wondered if that fact alone had sealed his fate or if he had done something specific to inspire such wrath.

It didn't matter. His blood splashed over the side of the fountain in a grim shower.

Blood and marble, marble and blood.

Diggy stood near me, her face a blank mask. "Come on."

I obeyed, and we caught up to the others at the palace wall without incident. They hadn't been idle while they waited. Already they'd agreed to approach the guards with weapons concealed but ready. As soon as necessary, they would draw and fight our way inside.

"And once we get in?" I asked. "We march to the throne room and demand to know what they've done with Braith?"

Zel's eyes were heavy with pain. "Or we look for my family."

That hit me like a punch to the gut. "Oh, Zel. We'll find them. We will. We have to."

He nodded, but that heavy look didn't lift. I knew it wouldn't until Ifmere and Dafyth were safe in his arms.

Mor and Diggy were fussing about something. "You can't walk in like that," Mor was saying. "Your knives are strapped all over your legs in plain sight."

Bare legs, I knew he was only just restraining himself from saying. He was rather scandalized by the grazer-hide shorts his sister insisted on wearing, no matter how cold she was. They had been comfortable for her on the island, and part of me wondered if she refused to put on trousers or a dress simply because she knew it nettled Mor so much.

"I'll stand behind that one." She pointed to Warmil. "He's big enough to block me, mostly."

Mor rolled his eyes, but we didn't have time to fight about this. "Fine."

And just like that, we were walking toward the guards standing at the front gate—soldiers who may or may not kill us on sight.

They dressed differently than the palace guards under Braith's or Gareth's rules—their uniforms were dusky green and deep red. I thought about the slain guardsman in the fountain. I guessed I wouldn't want to be wearing a black uniform right now either.

Father opened his mouth to speak, but one of the green-clad guards cut him off by raising his hand. Then the guard leaned a bit closer, squinting. He looked the rest of us over, one by one, settling for an uncomfortably long time on me.

"It's them," he declared finally. "Fewer than he said, but definitely them."

Everyone's fingers flexed near their weapons, though the guards didn't seem to be making any moves to attack. Instead, they pulled the doors open and nodded. "The steward's been expecting you."

CHAPTER TWO

TANWEN

MOR GRABBED MY HAND, THEN DIGGY'S. "STAY CLOSE," HE warned us quietly.

I noticed my father's strides were unnaturally long as he fought to keep some distance between the guardsmen leading the way and the rest of us. They had taken his sword, but I was sure he had at least one blade concealed elsewhere. He was a walking weapon, in any case. They couldn't very well take away his fists without some doing.

The guards bringing up the rear made me feel rather less confident than I might otherwise. However Father might be able to subdue the two guards in front of us, we couldn't make a clean escape from behind.

In truth, escape wasn't much on my mind at all. My thoughts whirled like violent wind strands.

Why was the steward waiting for us? How did he even know us?

The palace was nearly empty, and our footsteps echoed in a way that couldn't feel natural if you'd ever heard the bustle of the hundreds of servants and courtiers and nobles and advisors and ambassadors and guards who usually lived there.

Or . . . used to live there.

I fought the nausea again. Was that version of the palace at Urian a thing of the past? Was Braith's rule truly to be so short?

She could have ushered in a golden age for Tir. If only Tir had given her a chance.

Maybe this was what the palace would be now. A ghost of her former self. A shell—hollow and soulless.

I almost ran into Dylun when he stopped in front of me. Mor's steadying hand helped me regain my balance. I glanced up in annoyance, wondering why Dylun had come to such an abrupt halt. But of course. We were at the throne room doors.

My stomach churned at the thought of some usurper—why was it always a usurper?—sitting in Braith's throne room.

The guards paused at the doors, and one of them said, "He's asked to see you right away, so go on in."

"Don't try anything," the other warned. "You may have been important to the former queen, but you don't have allies here. The steward is well protected."

I imagined piecing together my story-strand halo-head that had devoured quite a few bad men in this very room when we brought Gareth to justice. Maybe I could summon that creature again if I thought about him hard enough, and he could rip this steward to pieces. Then we'd see who was well protected. They could take all our blades, but like my father's fists, they couldn't take my strands.

If they understood what that meant, these guards wouldn't be smirking right now.

Mor's fingers squeezed mine, and I glanced down at our clasped hands. My hand was lit up, white-hot, and his glove was smoking a little.

Oops.

I willed my anger to calm, my emotions to settle. *You have to control it,* Father always said.

A few long seconds passed, and my fingers dimmed. Mor's glove stopped smoking, and I squeezed his hand back.

The guards pulled open the doors and stood aside. I had seen this room with a poison-green carpet when Gareth ruled as king and a sparkling silver one when Braith was queen. But now, I frowned. The carpet wasn't really a carpet at all. And come to think of it, Braith's and Gareth's hadn't truly been carpets either. They were more like ceremonial runners that matched the story strands that unfurled in tales of each ruler. So the throne room carpets were more like banners, I supposed, than actual carpet designed for walking on.

But this was . . . strange, even by those standards.

A long piece of brown grazer-hide leather stretched from the doors at the back of the room to the dais on the opposite side. It had been stitched together in several places—I wouldn't want to meet the grazer big enough to make a strip of hide that long, thanks very much.

As I walked down it, my gaze pinned to each inch I passed, the leather pulled up a tempest of emotions, unbidden. We moved cautiously toward the dais, and the only thing I could guess was that it reminded me of home. Of my leather vest worn over my traveling dress and my satchel and—

"Don't be shy. Come on in."

I froze. That voice. So familiar, I'd never forget it.

But . . . here? My mind stuttered over it. Of all the things that didn't make sense today, this was the worst. The most upside down. The most impossible.

I couldn't bring myself to lift my eyes. I wanted to shut them tightly instead. To pretend I hadn't heard it and to will myself just about anywhere else in the world. But my focus stuck hard to the leather, because of course I knew now why it stirred my heart and kicked up a storm of conflict in my mind.

It was the exact grazer-hide leather of a certain farmer's floppy hat.

One awful moment passed, and finally, I looked up.

And there he was, clearly having just stood—from where he'd been seated on Braith's throne. The shock of straw-colored hair, the one that used to catch the Pembroni sunlight as it fell across his face when he walked me home in the evenings, was slicked back, and his beard seemed to have grown in a little thicker. His nose, for once, was not sunburned, and I supposed one didn't spend much time in the fields when one was staging a coup to remove the rightful queen.

But it was him, just the same, and the big, triumphant grin that split his face set my insides boiling.

"Ho, Tannie," said Brac Bo-Bradwir, my very best friend in the world.

I don't remember sprinting down the rest of the leather runner, and I don't remember deciding to throw a punch for the first time in my life.

But I well remember the satisfying *crack* of my fist against his jaw, and I remember Mor's and my father's voices, shouting for me to stop. Probably afraid I was going to get run through by a couple of Brac's guards.

In that moment, I couldn't have cared less.

"How could you?" I shouted. "What have you done? How? *How* did you do this? Why?"

Strong hands grabbed me under the arms and pulled me away from Brac. The fool stood there like a statue, mouth dangling open. Apparently, it had not been the reception he had been expecting.

That made two of us.

"Brac, how could you!" Fury doused me from head to toe.

"Now, listen here, Tannie." He rubbed his jaw with one hand and held his guards at bay with the other. "You don't understand. A lot happened while you was gone."

"I don't understand?" My voice pitched almost as shrilly as Lady Gwan's. "There is nothing—*nothing*—that could possibly make me understand this. You straw-headed, cheese-for-brains, dumber-than-rocks simpleton!" I had more where that came from.

But only one thought seared my mind.

I marched back onto the dais and stood on tiptoe to glare fire straight into his eyeballs.
"Where is Braith?"

CHAPTER THREE
BRAITH

BRAITH STARED AT HER MOTHER. IT *WAS* HER, WASN'T IT? Perhaps, in the flickering firelight of this dark place and still recovering from whatever drug she had been forced to inhale, Braith was mistaken about the identity of the figure before her.

But then the woman smiled, and there was no question. One does not forget her own mother's smile.

Frenhin Ma-Gareth pulled the black hood from her head, and her long pale hair tumbled out across her shoulders. "Braith, darling. Welcome."

Braith fought for her voice, fought to choose a question from the million tumbling through her mind. "Wh-what are you doing here? What is this place?"

The black-shrouded figure—so strange, since Braith was used to seeing the former queen in fine gowns with jewels and detailed embroidery—moved closer. "This is a little retreat of mine. I call it the Craigyl." She held out one hand as if showing off a finely appointed room. "Do you like it? Not quite as cozy as my chambers in the palace, I grant you, but I didn't exactly have the choice to stay, did I?" The false smile dropped. "You saw to that well enough."

Braith shook her head, clearing cobwebs from her mind. "I don't understand."

"You never did."

Braith eyed her warily. "What do you mean?"

"When I gave birth to a daughter, I had such hopes. Someone born in my image, cut from my cloth. Someone to lead alongside me. Instead, I got you."

"But . . ." Braith stammered. "But I did lead. I sat on Father's council. I tried to be a good leader for the empire."

Frenhin laughed. "Oh yes. Council. As though that's where the empire was conceived. As though that's where the hardest battles were fought and the true victories won. Foolish girl."

Braith spoke slowly as realization washed over her. "You were the one behind Father's reign. You were helping him rule . . . in secret."

Frenhin laughed again, hollow and mirthless. "The Master"—she bowed—"at your service. I did not have a right to the moniker when I chose it, many years ago. I hadn't been a master of anything yet. Not of my life, not of my gifts. Not even of my own future. But names can be aspirational, don't you think? I wanted to be like the marionette masters, in complete control of their stringed slaves."

"Slaves? Is that why you encouraged Father's land lust? So that your empire might provide slaves for you?" Braith pulled on her shackles—gently, so as not to make noise. If she could keep her mother talking, perhaps it would give her some space to think. Some time to devise a plan.

Frenhin snorted derisively. "No, silly girl. *He* was the slave. He, and a great many others. My marionettes needed to be powerful, and I made them so. I chose my toys carefully."

Braith stopped her clandestine investigation of her surroundings. She stared at her mother. "Father was not powerful when you chose him. He was just a soldier." She paused, churning over the bleak implication. "But you made him powerful by making him king. So . . . it was you who planned and executed King Caradoc's murder?"

Frenhin crouched low, dangerously close to her captive daughter. "Of course. You honestly thought your father could mastermind such an incredible coup? Or anything, for that matter? Your father was a talented captain with a hunger for adventure and riches and no love for our dark neighbors to the south and the west. I knew he would make the perfect conqueror. The perfect tool to win an empire. But if you think for a moment he had any capacity for plots or machinations, you are even more oblivious than I realized."

"You plotted all this when Father was a captain in the guard?" He had barely been a grown man then. Twenty, at most. Braith had always thought her father had worked his way through the ranks, meritoriously rising until he was a close advisor of Caradoc—a true member of the king's council. But now it seemed that position had been gained through other means altogether. That it had always been part of a larger plan.

"Of course," Frenhin said. "A masterful strategy, carried out with few hitches." Her gaze hardened. "You were one."

Defiance sparked in Braith's heart. "And Yestin Bo-Arthio was certainly another."

"Do not speak his name to me!"

The thunderous shout echoed about the chamber, and Braith winced.

But Frenhin's next words were calm—measured. "That man simply refuses to die. No matter. They all do eventually."

They all do eventually.

Braith's breath caught. "It was you? You murdered Father in his cell."

"*Murder* is an awfully strong word." Frenhin looked affronted. "It was a bit ruthless of me—I grant you that. But it was a necessary step. And when you think about it, his blood is on your hands too. All had gone according to plan for so many years. When the plan became corrupted, I was forced to take corrective action. You certainly had a hand in corrupting the plan."

Braith willed herself not to attempt to defend her actions to this madwoman.

"I have never understood where you get it from, Braith. Perhaps I ought to have educated you myself and not left you in the charge of so many tutors and advisors. I'm afraid they filled your head with things I'd rather they hadn't."

Braith's control over her tongue slipped. "Like honor? A concept of duty and caring for our people? What it truly means to be a leader?"

"Ah, there we are." Her mother smiled. "There's a little fire from you, darling. I can almost see myself in your eyes when you unleash it."

Braith tried to cool her temper. "I have always known I did not meet your expectations, Mother. Though to be frank, I no longer feel the need to apologize for that." She eyed her mother's black robes.

Frenhin sneered. "Amusing." She rose and swept back to the other side of the room. "No matter the disappointment you've been, you're here now. We may as well make the best of it, don't you think?" She held up her hands again. "It's been many years since I had this little hideaway made. Do you like it?"

"As lairs go, it's lovely."

"You will become well familiar with it before we're through."

"And when will that be, exactly? Why have you brought me here? Surely you know that, whatever you want, I won't do it."

"Oh, I believe you would do whatever I asked. But, truly Braith, I don't want anything from you."

"No?" Somehow this was worse.

"Not at the moment, at least. I have uses for you yet."

Dread swallowed Braith, but she remained silent.

"For now," Frenhin continued, "you're here as an observer. I thought to kill you first—do away with you, once and for all."

An icy dart pierced Braith's heart.

"But I couldn't bring myself to do it." Frenhin's voice

softened a touch. "You are still my daughter, after all. You deserve to see me take it all back. Everything you lost for me, for this family, will be reclaimed."

"You want me to watch while you destroy our kingdom?"

"Yes, dear, *kingdom* now, not empire, thanks to you. How long did you wait? Was it an entire moon before you gave back the land your father fought for?"

"It wasn't his to take."

Frenhin rolled her eyes. "Really, Braith. Are you still this naïve? This is how realms are formed. It's been the rule of the world since the beginning of time. Who are you to overthrow it?"

"I'm a queen who believes in a better way."

"Noble. Noble and foolish as ever." Frenhin tilted her head and regarded Braith. "What shall I do with you?"

"I will never help you."

"Oh, but you will, dearest. You will do whatever I ask. Trust that."

So many questions still begged for answers. How had this happened? Was her mother born with such evil in her veins, or had some trauma shaped her into this monstrous shell of a person who discarded the lives of others as if they were nothing? But one question shoved its way to the front of Braith's mind, propelled by Frenhin's insistence that, if she wanted to, she could bend Braith to her will.

Braith had spent enough of her life in politics to know why her mother would make such a claim. The only way she *could* make such a claim.

Leverage. The only way Frenhin could be sure Braith would bend was if she had some sort of leverage. And Braith knew exactly what it was.

Braith steeled her nerves. "What have you done with Kharn?"

CHAPTER FOUR

TANWEN

BRAC FLEXED HIS JAW AND SHOOK HIS HEAD. "SAKES, TANNIE. I don't remember you hitting so hard."

"That's because I've never punched you before, Brac, but believe me, I mean to make a habit of it if you don't start giving me some answers." I repeated my question, anger punctuating every word. "Where is Braith?"

Brac half shrugged in that sheepish way that might have been charming under entirely different circumstances. "She's safe."

"I rather doubt that!" I punched at him verbally instead. "Been outside lately, *steward*? Seen what's happening in Urian, that city under your care?"

He shrugged again. "She's well away from all that."

"You better tell me she's tucked away upstairs somewhere. Safe in her own bed. That better be the next thing out of your mouth, or I swear to all those rotten goddesses, I will pull every yellow hair off that stupid head of yours."

The tips of his ears tinged red. "Oh, calm down, Tannie." Then he quieted his voice. "You're making me look bad, you know. Could do with a little less shouting."

I lowered my voice to match his. "Could you, now? I could do with a little less epic betrayal."

Any hint of sheepishness or remorse disappeared from his expression. "You ain't one to talk about betrayal, Tanwen." His gaze shot pointedly to Mor.

My mouth fell open, and I knew I must look like a dolt standing there. "Is that . . . no. That cannot be what this is about. Please, Brac. Please tell me you did not betray all that is good and right in this world and commit an act so heinous I can barely look at you because you thought I left you for Mor."

A crease appeared between Brac's brows. "You did, though."

"No." I stared at the stranger before me. "I didn't. I did not, do not, and have not ever wanted to marry you, Brac. That's true enough. I never should have agreed to it, and I should have told you sooner. That I admit. But I jumped aboard the *Cethorelle* because I was sick. I had the curse, same as Gryfelle, and I needed to go with them if I was going to have a hope of being cured. I *did not* leave you for him. I left you to save my life."

He blinked. "Oh."

"Oh?" I gaped at him. "*Oh?* You staged a coup—and did stars know what to the only ruler worth trusting—because you thought I liked a different lad better, and all you have to say is *oh*?"

I wound up my fist to throw another punch, but Father was ready for me. He was on the dais holding me back before I could get myself in any more trouble with this imposter steward.

To Brac's credit, he looked a little sheepish again, but there wasn't enough remorse in the world to fix any of this.

"Now, let's calm down," Father was saying as he led me down the dais until Brac was well out of my striking range. "Everyone. Let's talk this through."

"She's not with you," Brac said suddenly. "The sick lass."

"No," I spat. "She died. She sacrificed herself for us. Thanks for noticing."

"I'm sorry for her," he said, and he actually looked it. "And the others? You're down a few." He looked at Diggy. "And you're new."

"How about you answer a few questions for us, lad?" Father interrupted. "Where has Braith been taken? Is she alive?"

Brac cast a glance over his shoulder toward the corner of the room. I followed his gaze, but the only thing I saw over there was a green-suited guard standing watch.

After a moment, he answered, "Aye, she's alive. And I'm told she's safe."

"You're told?" I narrowed my eyes at him. "You're working with someone." And as I said it, of course I knew it was true. Brac never could have orchestrated a coup—least of all a successful one—no matter how angry he was about Mor.

And so why was he here, sitting on Braith's throne, wearing the title of steward?

"Did you find the cure, Tannie?" Brac asked, ignoring my last statement. "Are you well now?"

"Not that it's any of your business, but yes, I'm fine, thanks. You have no idea what we've been through, what we've lost, or what we've been up against. The strands that we've—"

Mor stepped forward and grabbed my arm. "Best not, Tannie," he said under his breath. "Don't give him too much information."

"Hey!" Brac shouted. "Take your hand off her, pirate!"

Mor released my arm, but he glared back at Brac like streams of fire might shoot out of his fingertips at any second.

"Braith is fine," Brac said, firmly this time. "She's fine, and she's far from the dangers of the city. We have everything under control. You and your friends need to stay out of it, Tannie. Lest you cross me and I decide to throw your pirate in the dungeons."

Father blocked me before I could charge the dais again. He shooed me toward the back of the room. "It's wise for us to leave now."

True as a tumbleweed, that. But I still wanted to punch something.

All of us were through the doors, past the guards, and huddled in a deserted hallway before I realized what I'd almost done. I'd been about to tell Brac about the cure strands and how we'd collected an ancient artifact. About how evil strands had chased and attacked us, sinking the *Cethorelle* and murdering several of our comrades. I had been about to tell him all of that, because part of me still thought of Brac as my best friend.

But he had been responsible for all this. At least in some measure. And we had no idea who had put him up to it.

Brac was the very last person in the world I could trust.

CHAPTER FIVE
TANWEN

A PAIR OF BLUE EYES POPPED INTO MY LINE OF SIGHT. "You're not all right," Diggy said matter-of-factly.

"No." I sighed. "No, I'm not."

"You knew that boy. Man. Boy pretending to be a man."

I snorted. "You can say that again."

"Boy pretending to be a man."

A laugh bubbled up in my chest, and with it, tears spilled down my cheeks. I dashed them away. "I hate that. I hate that I cry when I'm angry. Why does that happen?"

"Because your feelings are too big for your body, so sometimes they spill out of your face." Diggy leaned even closer toward me, as if my eyes were windows and she might peer inside. "You have a lot of feelings in there."

"We need a plan," Dylun said suddenly, and I blinked. It was the first time I'd heard him speak since we entered the palace. "I don't feel at all safe carrying this around here." He nodded down at the box holding the ancient cure.

"True enough," Father said. "It would be prudent not to mention any details about our quest to anyone here." He glanced down the narrow corridor in both directions. "And perhaps we might do what we can to conceal our identities. I'm not sure how we made it out of that throne room without irons on our wrists, and I have no idea how long the good graces of the . . . ah, steward will last."

"He's not the one behind it," I said fiercely—partly because I didn't want anyone to think Brac would have sunk so low as to mastermind this and partly because I was so blasted angry with him. "He couldn't possibly have planned this. Or carried it out. And I don't know why he would. Or why he would work to do it for anyone else. I have half a mind to march back in there and ask him—"

"No," Father cut me off. "Tannie girl, please stay far away from Brac. We'll piece together what happened best as we can without him. He's too dangerous right now."

I opened my mouth to argue—to explain to them just how sunbaked and not-dangerous Brac was. But this time, it was Warmil who cut me off. "The general doesn't mean it's *him* who's dangerous, Tanwen. It's whoever he's working for."

"Oh. Right." I leaned back against the stone wall and closed my eyes. I needed to calm down. Anger colored my thoughts, making me reckless. If we were going to get out of this palace alive—and with the answers we sought—I needed to regain control.

As I willed the buzz of rage in my mind to quiet, a thought floated to the surface. "Braith isn't in the palace," I said. "They've taken her somewhere."

"Aye," Mor agreed. "Bo-Bradwir said she was far from the danger of the city."

"Right. And if she were here, he would have told me because it would have cooled me off." I looked at Father. "They've taken her and hidden her somewhere. Or else killed her."

"Would that boy-pretending-to-be-a-man lie to you?" Diggy asked. "I thought he was your friend."

"It's complicated." The bitterness in my own voice almost made me cringe. "I don't think he would lie to me, no. But he would believe whatever *they* told him. Whoever he's working for may have told him Braith is alive when she's not."

Father set his jaw. "We need to search the palace for

survivors and allies." He nodded to Zel. "We need to check on our loved ones. And we need to see what information we can gather. We may have to leave sooner than later."

I crossed my arms over my chest and rubbed my shoulders. "This place feels cold."

"Empty," Father said. "We might be able to escape notice better if we split up, but I don't want to risk it. Bo-Awirth? You agree?"

"Aye," Warmil said. "We stay together. Where should we start?"

"Nursery," Zel responded immediately. It was the last place he had left his wife and son—that wing of the infirmary where new mothers and babies stayed for moons so the palace nursemaids might be on hand at all times.

I thought of Ma-Bradwir back in Pembrone, of how she cooked supper over the fire with an infant on one hip, a toddler on the other, and three little ones zipping around her legs like harried hedge-nibblers. Quite a different picture than the ladies tending their wee ones in the palace.

"Yes, of course." Father led us to a staircase at the far end of the hallway. "Infirmary is in the west wing. This way."

If we had to creep around the palace like rope-tails, hoping to avoid discovery, I supposed the man who had lived in the palace walls for thirteen years would be a decent guide.

The rest of us followed after him up the stairs. A knot of seven people traveling around the palace together might not have attracted notice six moons past, but now the halls echoed with every step. Every breath drawn, every word spoken seemed like a shout.

Where had everyone gone? It seemed they had just . . . vanished.

But as we reached the landing to the next floor up, Father jerked to a stop so abruptly, Warmil bumped into his back.

Father held out his hand. "No. Don't go farther."

My heart fell. "Father?"

"Don't come up here, Tannie."

But Diggy wasn't having that. She slipped past me on the stairs, then ducked around the men and slid beneath Father's arm before he could stop her.

Her shoes skidded on the stones at the top of the stairs. She placed her hand against the wall. "Bodies," she said at last.

Our party exploded with motion as Zel shoved his way to the landing. I waited in the stairwell. They would tell me if it was anyone we knew. Whether it was or it wasn't, I didn't think I wanted to see.

"Guardsmen," Warmil said. He crouched out of my view. "These are stab wounds, but the weapon was not sharp. A pitchfork, perhaps?"

"Farmers." I frowned. "Farmers like Brac."

"Fitting for a peasant rebellion, I suppose." Father's eyes were troubled. "We must find the queen."

Mor, a couple stairs above, offered his gloved hand to me. "You don't have to look if you don't want to."

I took his hand and let him lead me as I focused my gaze on the ceiling. My stomach turned over when he moved me to the side, obviously directing me around a body. I swallowed. "Is it bad?"

"I count six in this hallway."

We trailed the others. Warmil paused every once in a while to bend down and look for signs of life, but we were too late to help any of these men.

"They've been dead several days," he said quietly to Father. Not quietly enough. I could still hear every word. "None of these wounds appear to have been made by a skilled hand. They are haphazard. Not targeting vital organs or major arteries."

"They must have had quantity," Father ventured. "To overrun the trained men of the guard, they must have numbered in the hundreds. Maybe thousands."

How many thousands even live in Tir? Then I remembered that Physgot had been almost completely deserted when our new ship, the *Lysian*, docked there three days past. They'd all marched on Urian, the old man left behind had said. If the Physgotians, all the way on the coast of the Eastern Peninsula, had gathered to march on the city, maybe Brac and his goons had managed to collect just about every peasant in Tir old enough to hold a farming tool.

"Why weren't there dead bodies downstairs?" Diggy asked.

Dylun clutched the cure box tighter to his chest. "They must have started cleaning on the lower level first. When people commit unspeakable acts, I find they want to remove reminders as quickly as possible."

I thought of Brac in the throne room. He had found time to replace Braith's silver carpet with his leather runner while bodies rotted on the upper floors of the palace.

Next time I saw him, I was going to sock him. Again.

We made it up one more level, and as we turned a corner, Mor murmured, "Oh."

I forgot myself and looked at the ground.

A servant girl, younger than Diggy and me, and a guardsman I recognized. He had stood watch outside the dining hall doors during meals. He always nodded as I passed into the room to take my seat at Queen Braith's table.

A slit gaped across the girl's throat, and the guardsman's stomach was slashed open.

Warmil knelt to examine the wound. "Their attackers had blades."

Surely he was right, but I had no thought for such practical matters. My mind spun. Who were they to each other? Had he died protecting her? Was this his lass? His sister? Had they merely happened to be in the same place when a flood of rebels spilled into the palace?

What was his name? I had never asked, and now I would never know.

Grief swelled inside me until I felt there wasn't enough room in me to hold it all.

"Tannie, don't look." Mor pulled me gently.

"I know him," I choked around my tears and the smell of rot. "He guarded the dining hall."

"Aye, that's right." Mor tugged me again. "Come on."

"I didn't know his name." My voice rose, and I knew I was practically shrieking. "Mor, what was his name?"

He put his arm around my shoulders and led me away. "I don't know either. Maybe we can find out."

Somehow, I couldn't cry. The swollen grief tamped down my tears, stoppered them as if I were a bottle.

Father paused before a door at the end of the hall. "The infirmary is here." He turned to Zel. "Son, are you—"

But Zel didn't even wait for him to finish. He pushed through the door.

And the rest of us followed him into a bloodbath.

CHAPTER SIX
TANWEN

"I<small>FMERE</small>!" Z<small>EL SHOUTED</small>.

Silence answered him.

I covered my mouth with both hands. I wanted to cover my eyes, but somehow, I wasn't able to.

Splashes of blood spattered everything. A place of healing—usually clean, white, crisp—was painted as if by a murderous child.

Braith's physicians and their assistants—people who had helped Karlith care for Gryfelle when she'd stayed here—lay crumpled on the mattresses where patients usually reclined. Broken glass was scattered across the floor like fallen leaves. One patient remained in bed, white as the sheet beneath him, but his face was still peaceful. As though he had been unconscious in his final moments and hadn't known to be afraid. Hadn't known to scream.

I caught a flicker of movement out of the corner of my eye, then Diggy appeared from behind me, sprinting across the room and drawing a knife. Before anyone had time to say *stop*, she'd dived behind a bed at the far corner of the room. She reappeared a moment later, yanking a girl up with her.

Diggy's fingers laced through the girl's ashy-blonde hair as she pulled her head back to expose her neck. The knife, unsurprisingly, rested blade-first against the girl's throat.

The lass's eyes popped wide, and she looked too terrified even to scream.

"Diggy!" Mor shouted. "Don't hurt her!"

"I won't." Diggy tilted her head to one side. "Not yet."

The girl whimpered.

"Diggy, be careful," I said, struggling to keep my voice calm. "Don't nick her."

"She was hiding. Sneaking." Diggy squinted. "She'll know something."

Father took a step toward them, one hand out. I wasn't sure if he was trying to calm the girl or Diggy. "What's your name, lass?"

"L-Lany," she squeaked, leaning away from Diggy's dagger.

"Lany, can you tell us what you're doing here?"

"Cleaning up. Steward's orders." Tears rolled down her cheeks. "I didn't mean to do nothin' wrong."

Father still held a hand toward Diggy and Lany. "You didn't, lass. Can you tell me what happened here?"

"Rioters. The steward's rebels came and took the castle. I didn't do nothin' with that." She glanced down at Diggy's blade. "They rounded up some folks to help clean."

"Where do you live, child?"

"I ain't a child. Just turned eleven!" But she sucked in a breath as Diggy tightened the distance between the knife and her throat again.

"Diggy!" Mor pleaded. "She's just a child."

Diggy frowned. "I didn't stab her."

I bit back a sigh. I knew she wouldn't hurt Lany unless the girl gave her a reason to. But *Lany* didn't know this. And Diggy didn't seem to see the cruelty in frightening the lass.

Was that the kind of thing you could teach someone? Someone who had gone feral in a Spice Island jungle?

I hoped so.

Lany flinched. "I live in the city. In a pub with my mam. Mam runs the bar, and we live upstairs."

"Does that mean they've killed all the servants?" I wondered aloud. "If they're recruiting from the city . . ."

"Digwyn, she's just cleaning up the room she's assigned to," Father said to Diggy, his tone soothing and as fatherly as it was when he spoke to me. "We can let her go, don't you think?"

Diggy considered this. Then she released Lany with a small shove. "Watch yourself, though. It's dangerous around here."

She didn't seem to see the irony, and Mor sighed—mingled relief and exasperation.

Lany looked like she might have a few choice words for Diggy, but she clamped her mouth shut.

"They ain't here," Zel said suddenly. He had been checking the bodies, apparently, searching for his wife and son. The comfort of not finding them among the dead was not enough to blot out his panic. "I need to check the other rooms in the wing."

Now that I thought about it, I was sure Ifmere and Dafyth had been moved to the private rooms before we left. They shared a room like the one Gryfelle had spent most of her time in.

Zel and Mor disappeared, Warmil close behind them.

But Father focused on the peasant girl. "How long ago did the rebels come?"

"Five days past, I think. Maybe seven."

"And what did they do to the queen?"

The girl's eyes lit—more with the novelty of such a thing than malice, I thought. But still it made me ill. "They took 'er, right out of the palace gardens. I saw it, even."

She had Father's full attention. "You saw her?"

"Well . . ." Lany bit her lip. "*I* didn't see that part, exactly, but one of the other girls who lives at the pub did, and she told me." She looked at me knowingly. "My mam doesn't like her mam."

I could tell Father was fighting to keep his voice even, exercising every ounce of his considerable patience. "Lany, I need you to tell me everything you know about what happened to the queen. This is very important."

"They took her. Her and that one noble. Sir somebody."

Helpful.

Father's brow furrowed. "Sir Dray?"

"No, not him." Lany laughed. "Haven't heard a thing about him since the trial."

Blast. We had missed a lot. Had Dray been executed at last?

"Who, then?"

"The queen's suitor."

Stars.

"Anyway," Lany continued, "they dragged them through the streets of Urian—and that part I did see with my own eyes—then they stormed the castle. Took it over. No one was ready, and it wasn't that hard. Once you get past the walls and all. And if the guards ain't expecting you and ain't organized and there's no leaders because you got to them first, well, you just run down the halls and kill people, I guess."

Brilliant.

Father paused for a long moment. "Lany," he said. "This is the most important part now, so I want you to think very hard about what you saw. When they dragged out Queen Braith and the nobleman . . . were they alive?"

Lany pursed her lips. "I think so. They had cloth tied round their eyes, and I don't see as why you would do that if they was dead. They wasn't awake, though. And the man was bleeding."

My breath hitched. I didn't know who this man was, but if he truly was Braith's suitor, I certainly wanted him to be alive and well.

"Bleeding from where?" Father asked.

"His head. Like he'd been hit."

"And the queen?"

"We're not supposed to call her that anymore." Lany brightened. "I seen her once before, you know! When she wasn't knocked out and being dragged away. She was so pale. Like a cup of grazer milk. I never seen a person so pale. Mam would think I was sick if I was so pale."

Father and I shared a glance, and I could tell he was thinking what I was. She had told us all she knew, and the rest of what we would get would be the random musings of a child.

"Thank you, Lany," Father said. "This was very helpful."

Lany beamed, then glared at Diggy. "*She* was not helpful, thanks much. I could do without seein' her again."

Couldn't say I blamed her on that one.

Mor's, Zel's, and Warmil's voices carried in from the hallway, and I supposed we should go face whatever they had found.

The rest of us turned to leave, then I stopped. "Lany?"

She glanced up from where she was already kneeling beside a bucket of bloody water, rinsing a rag. "Aye?"

"Did you see which direction they took Lady Braith and the nobleman?"

"North," she said immediately.

"You're sure?"

"Aye. I remember. Because Rae—that's my friend—Rae said they was taking them to the river and heading north, and I remember Rae's mam saying it would be cold this time of year if they went too far north. Then she said she'd like to go south to Meridione for the winter, if only it weren't full of Meridionis."

I cringed. Dylun stood right beside me. He seemed not to notice the child's careless comment—or else he was so accustomed to hearing such things he didn't react anymore.

At least not on the outside.

W<small>E MET UP WITH THE OTHERS IN THE HALL</small>. I <small>MADE EYE</small> contact with Mor, silently begging him to give me good news.

"They're not here," he said.

Best news we could hope for at the moment, short of finding them safe and alive right where we had left them that balmy summer morning.

A chill late-autumn breeze whispered across my shoulders, as if to whisk away the memories. I shivered. I hadn't noticed how drafty a castle could be. I guessed I'd only lived in one during the spring and summer moons.

Zel looked twice his age, lines of concern creasing his face. "Where could they be? There were no bodies. No babies and no mothers or nurses. It looked like someone grabbed a few things from the chest in Ifmere's room before they left."

"Could have been somebody ransacking the room afterward," Dylun mused, then looked pained. "Forgive me, Zelyth. I didn't mean to be unfeeling."

Zel's face pinched tighter. "I don't know where to look."

"They might have gotten out," I said. "Would she have gone back home? Back to Hauplan? She could have blended in with the peasants easily enough. Perhaps she made her escape."

"I don't know that she would have had the presence of mind to get away. She's . . . innocent. Kind. Like a light-foot. If danger came, I'm afraid she'd—" His voice caught. It took him several moments to collect himself. "I'm afraid she'd just freeze. And not know what to do or how to fight back or flee."

"But she had her son, didn't she?" Diggy looked at Zel.

"Aye, I believe so."

"Then she would know what to do. She's a mother. She would protect her child."

I spun to look at Mor. "She's right. I once saw the sweetest woman you'd ever met beat away a pack of hungry fluff-hoppers with a stick because they were coming for her wee twins."

His eyebrows rose. "A whole pack of fluff-hoppers? By herself?"

"Yes. With only a stick. Ifmere would do the same for Dafyth."

Diggy shrugged. "It's just nature."

I glanced at Father. He was staring intently out a window. "Father?"

He jumped.

"What is it?" I asked.

"I believed . . . that is, I assumed that wherever Queen Braith had been taken . . ." Uncertainty filled his words.

Realization clicked in my mind. "That Cameria would be with her."

"Yet Lany didn't mention a maid or servant or advisor."

"Only the suitor nobleman."

I closed my eyes. Cameria was anything but a light-foot. She most certainly would not freeze. Or shrink. If she had been with Braith at the time Braith was taken, she would have fought. That meant Cameria was most likely dead.

And if that was the case, there was nothing we could do to help that now.

But if she hadn't been with Braith—if they had been separated at the time the palace was stormed—where might she be?

Anywhere.

If she heard trouble, what would she do?

Fight back? Maybe. But that would be hopeless with so many peasants and legions of Brac's goons running roughshod through the halls.

My eyes popped open. "She would protect others," I said. "She would have tried to protect those who needed help. People who were vulnerable or unable to defend themselves."

"Like infants and mothers." Hope kindled in Father's expression. "She might have come here."

"Here or any of a hundred other places," Dylun said. "How will we know?"

"Father," I asked, "if she *had* come here or somewhere others needed help, what then? Where would she go next?"

"She would take anyone she was protecting to safety."

"Aye."

His eyes went wide. "She would hide them."

And in the same breath, Father and I both knew exactly where she would have gone if she'd had the chance. We turned and ran for the staircase that led to our old apartments.

I COULD TAKE THE STAIRS THREE AT A TIME IN MY TROUSERS. I didn't know if I'd ever wear a dress again.

We stumbled across a few more peasants from the city who had been assigned to clean up the carnage of Brac's coup. And we skirted around far, far too many bodies. But we didn't meet any of those green-suited soldiers on our way to the place that had been my family's home in the palace.

The hallway that led to our apartments was like a graveyard. I tripped over a noblewoman in a fine dress and forced myself to look at her face.

Though the unseeing eyes and blue skin altered her appearance, I recognized her. A woman who ate at the queen's table most meals. Someone Braith had known from childhood, maybe?

I couldn't remember now. But we had spoken several times. Just niceties over our wine at dinner. But that was enough to make bile rise in my throat at the sight of her lifeless body.

Mor didn't need to pull me away this time. I wanted to run and never look back. To get to our private chambers and search for them. Any of them.

Please, Creator. Let someone be alive.

We burst in through the door—unlocked.

Zel looked crestfallen. "If she were here, she'd have bolted the door, surely."

But I had been expecting this. "Follow me."

I moved toward the bookcase, but as I took a few more steps into the front room, the stench of blood and death nearly knocked me to my knees. This wasn't like the drafty hallways or the large, open infirmary. This was a close space, the small windows shut tightly.

And someone had died in this room.

I scanned the ground, the furniture, everything. There was a spray of blood across Father's writing desk. Books and papers shoved to the ground—signs of a struggle.

But no body.

Father and I both darted to the bookcase behind his desk—the one with the open back. Father could reach the false stone hiding the lever without standing on a chair the way I had to. I slipped my mother's necklace over my head and handed it to him. He pressed the twisted knot of metal into the hollow on the false stone.

A *click*. He wiggled the false stone from its place to reveal the lever. Then he pulled.

The whole bookcase budged away from the wall and swung outward on hidden hinges to reveal a pitch-black hallway—the darkened secret tunnels in which my father had lived for thirteen years.

Father pulled back the bookcase to allow more light to flood the passage. I didn't wait another moment. I bolted into the darkness.

And was met with the tip of a sword.

CHAPTER SEVEN
TANWEN

MY BOOTS SKIDDED AGAINST THE STONES JUST IN TIME. I stopped a hairsbreadth from the point of a blade I vaguely recognized.

It was one of Father's swords. The one he kept in his bedroom.

"What the—"

"Halt," a lady's voice commanded from the darkness. "Take one step further, and I will run you through faster than you can spit."

I believed her. I lifted my hands in surrender. "Don't spear me, please."

A long pause. And then, "Tanwen?"

"It's me."

The sword lowered, and a woman stepped into the light—the woman who belonged to the softly accented voice. The woman threatening to run me through. Her silky black hair fell over her shoulders, disheveled but still beautiful. She blinked in the light like it assaulted her eyes, and I wondered if she had been back here all five days.

But it was definitely her. No mistaking it.

"Cameria." Father rushed to her.

His sword fell from her hands and clattered to the stones. "Yestin, my lord." Despite the formality, she threw her arms around his neck. Her shoulders wracked with great, heaving sobs. "I knew you would come. I knew, if it was at all possible, you would come for us."

Us.

As she spoke, figures emerged from the shadows behind her. So many I wondered how they all fit, how deep these tunnels must run throughout the palace, and what number of people were, at this moment, jammed inside. They were women and children, all of them, and it seemed everyone had some sort of battle scar. A hastily bandaged wound, a torn shirt or skirt, dirt or blood smeared on their clothing.

A child of about five appeared around Cameria's skirt. He cradled an arm that appeared to be missing its hand. The stump had been wrapped tightly, a tourniquet applied at the wrist.

I gasped. "Cethor's tears. What did they do to him?"

Cameria's eyes brimmed. "It was chaos. They just . . . ran through the halls, hacking away." She looked at Father. "At children, my lord. Women and children."

"Whoever is behind this is not honorable enough to observe the rules of engagement." Father's voice was ice.

"Arystia." Cameria gestured to someone. "The boy."

A young woman with honey-blonde hair appeared a breath later, gently pushing around the silent group huddled behind Cameria.

I recognized the fire-haired boy on her hip immediately. "Dafyth!" I cried out as my tears welled. "Zel, he's here!"

The young woman's eyes widened. "Zelyth? Ifmere's husband is here?"

Zel was in the passageway in a heartbeat. He let out a strangled sob. "Dafyth!" He scooped the little boy into his arms. "He's alive." He pressed the baby to his chest.

The baby looked slightly startled, then he babbled softly. "Ba. Ba-ba."

Zel soaked up one long moment, then his attention darted to the gathered women. "Where's Ifmere?"

No one responded.

My mind froze. My gaze stuck on the little boy with the maimed hand. He looked up at me with shocked, hollow eyes, and for some reason, he reminded me of Diggy.

Finally, Cameria spoke. "Zelyth, I'm so sorry."

I moved to take Dafyth, afraid Zel would drop him, but he didn't. He held the baby tighter. "No—no, that can't be. The baby is safe."

Cameria put her hand on Zel's arm. "Arystia is Dafyth's nurse. She and Ifmere fled the infirmary with Dafyth when it was attacked by peasants."

"Cameria saved us," Arystia added. "She had your sword, my lord, and she scared them off. Brought us here. But it was—" Her voice faltered.

"Perhaps it is kinder if you do not know," Cameria said to Zel.

"No, please." His voice was ragged. "Tell me what happened."

She studied his face, then continued, "I brought them here, but soldiers fought their way in." She turned to Father. "They do have some soldiers, my lord. Former guardsmen. Those who defected and led riots when Gareth fell, I suppose. Or perhaps just Braith's guardsmen who were willing."

The green-uniformed goons.

"We had just about gotten everyone into the passageway, but we couldn't get the door closed fast enough from the inside. It was the only place I knew to take everyone where we might be safe and hidden until someone came for us or we could escape." She turned back to Zel. "And she knew that. Ifmere knew that if they broke into the room while the passageway was open, it could no longer be used as a hiding place. They would know of its existence, and everyone would be in danger, our only chance to remain hidden lost for good."

She pressed her fingers to her temples. "I've gone over it a thousand times in my mind. How did I end up in the tunnel and she did not? How was she the one who thought to stay behind to close it from the outside? Why didn't I have her go before me?" Tears streamed down her cheeks. "It happened so fast."

Arystia placed a hand on Cameria's back. "Ifmere closed and locked the passageway just as they broke through. Before she closed it, she told me to look after Dafyth. I think . . ." The nursemaid's voice shook. "I think it was fast."

The blood in the front room. The stench of death. It was Ifmere.

"How did I end up in here and she out there?" Cameria repeated, looking at Father as though he might be able to answer the question that would probably never stop tormenting her.

"It's only nature," Diggy said, her voice soft.

"She fought," I said to Zel, half smiling through tears. "She fought back the only way she could. She fought to protect your boy. *Her* boy."

Zel was holding his son close to his face. "Where—" He cleared his throat. "That is . . . did they take her away?"

"They left her body," Cameria said quietly. "I couldn't let her stay out there like that. I—" She closed her eyes. "The day after the coup, I waited a bit. Then I went out there to move her. I wrapped her in a sheet and put her on the couch in your room, my lord." She gazed at Father. "I just . . . I didn't know where else to lay her. But I couldn't leave her like that."

Diggy stepped up beside Zel and held out her arms. Surprisingly, Dafyth's chubby little arms stretched out to her. "You can go to her," she said to Zel.

Dafyth was halfway in Diggy's arms. I nodded at Zel—I would make sure Diggy didn't do anything odd or dangerous with his son. He relinquished his hold and allowed Mor to take him into the other room.

A fresh wave of tears hit me when I heard Zel cry out a few moments later.

"Ifmere . . ." His voice was strangled by harsh weeping.

I could barely stand it. A knot of cold rage tightened in my stomach. I pushed past Diggy, who was bouncing a giggling Dafyth on her hip, and burst into my family's front room.

Mor was there, standing by Father's bedroom door and listening to his best friend's heart breaking.

"Mor, I feel like I'm going to explode." No sooner had I said it than my hands lit up white.

"Tannie—"

"No. I don't want to hear it. I will have no fellowship with this . . . evil."

"I know, Tannie, but just—"

"No!" Beams of white light shot from my palms, slammed into the stone floor, and ricocheted around the room.

Mor ducked, and a strand blasted against the wall behind him half a second later. He rose and shot me a look. "Are you finished?"

"I will never be finished. There aren't enough strands of white-hot anger in the world for me to ever be finished."

He crossed the room to me, and I buried my face in his shoulder. He rubbed my back as sobs shook me.

When the tears subsided, I pulled back. My face was set, my voice hard as flint. "Mor, I will never, ever forgive Brac."

CHAPTER EIGHT
TANWEN

Warmil guarded the door, standing watch by the newly repaired deadbolt. He held Father's sword, a vacant, hardened expression on his face.

The others were talking, but my mind wandered. I wondered what Warmil was thinking about. Was he worried about Aeron and Karlith hiding in the Corsyth? Of course he was. Did that occupy his mind while he stood there, protecting the door? Or did he have a special soldierly space in his mind—like an empty chest he went into when it was time to fight or defend or guard—where there was no worry for his loved ones, no thought for anything except his mission?

I wished I had one of those empty chests. Instead, I had a whole castle full of thoughts, and every chamber spilled over with anger and dismay.

"How many are you?" Father asked Cameria.

Only some of the survivors had ventured into our front room, blinking in the afternoon light slanting through the windows.

"One hundred sixty-two souls," Cameria answered.

Mor sputtered into the cup of water he was drinking. "One hundred sixty-two? But . . ." He looked around at the dozen or so who had come into our apartment to wash their faces, use a proper chamber pot, or remember what sunlight looked like. "How?"

"The tunnels run throughout the entire palace," Father said.

"In places, they open up into proper rooms, almost. Caverns the size of a room, anyway."

"You'd never know it," Mor said.

"No. They were crafted for a paranoid king centuries past, legend has it."

"By stoneshapers," I said suddenly, and I realized it had to be true. "They would have had the skill to craft such tunnels and caverns."

"And the genius to keep it secret," Dylun added.

"Still . . ." Mor shook his head. "One hundred and sixty-two. How are you feeding them all?"

"I've been stealing food from the kitchen in the middle of the night, and I'm not ashamed to say so." Cameria lifted her chin. "But supplies are running low. I have some of the kitchen servants in here with me, and they say the steward and whoever he's working with have no idea how to run the palace properly. It's no small feat. The pantries were nearly bare on my last trip."

"You can't stay here." Father's eyes were grave. "The food will run out, and even if it doesn't, you're not safe."

"Forgive me, my lord, but if you are asking me to abandon them"—she nodded to a couple children who had wandered into my room and discovered a crystallized fluff-hopper I'd made—"I'll have to refuse." Her black eyebrows arched. "And you would not be half the man I thought you were."

Father looked startled. "Peace, Cameria. Of course I don't mean you should leave them. I meant everyone. We have to get the survivors somewhere safe."

"Nowhere is safe." Zel's voice rang hollow. Dead and empty. "Ifmere and Dafyth were supposed to be protected here. What could be safer than the palace nursery under the care of the queen's physicians and nurses? But look what's happened. Nowhere is safe."

Father didn't speak for a moment, perhaps allowing Zel's

grief a space to breathe without contradicting it. "You're right, lad. They should have been safe here."

"What should have been a fortress has become a tomb," Dylun observed.

I sighed. "Yes. They should have been safe. But they weren't, and that's because some evil greater than even Gareth has entered this place. So where? Where can we go *now*?" I watched the children giggle over the sparkling fluff-hopper. "We have to do something."

"We could stay here," Cameria said slowly, "if we had the supplies. But with so many to care for, I'm not sure it's possible."

"The Corsyth?" Mor suggested.

"No," Dylun said. "Their numbers are too great, and our allies in Bowyd could not supply them with sufficient food, no matter how much gold we promised. One hundred and sixty-two would be too great a strain."

Cameria shook her head. "It seems impossible, no matter where we go."

"Pembrone," I said suddenly.

Everyone turned to face me. Heat crept into my cheeks. But there was no time for that.

"They can go to Pembrone," I said again. "Some could stay in our cottage, Father. There's no shortage of barns, and maybe some would even open their homes."

Father's expression grew thoughtful, and I could practically hear his mind turning it over. "But the Steward of Tir is Pembrone's own son. Would those fleeing the palace be received?"

"Well, we don't have to send a crier to announce that they're from the palace, or anything," I said. "They can say they're refugees displaced by the riots. That's true enough, anyway." I went to Cameria, who looked uncertain. "I've said a lot of unkind things about Pembrone before—how it's poky and ordinary and dusty. Those things are true, I guess, but the people there are good, solid folk. Loyal. Decent. Kind, even, most of them. They wouldn't turn away hungry women and children." I looked at my father. "Would they, Father?"

"I don't believe they would."

"There's room for a hundred sixty-two souls in Pembrone," I told Cameria.

"But how would we get there?" she asked. "That is quite the traveling party, and the Eastern Peninsula is no short distance away. How would we make it there with no protection?"

Mor popped up from his seat at our dining table. "Commander Jule. If we can get to the meeting point and connect with Sailor Bo-Cydrid, he can get us to Jule and the crew. Perhaps they would be willing to serve as a guard for the refugees."

"For us but not you?" Cameria turned to Father. "Would you not be coming with us?"

"We must find Braith," he said simply.

Of all that had been revealed, of all we had discussed, nothing had such an effect on Cameria as this.

She clutched her hand to her chest and gasped. "Braith? The queen is . . ."

"Alive," Father affirmed. "At least we believe it's possible. She was alive when they took her from the city, or so they say. They went toward the river."

"The river?" Cameria paled. "Then she could be anywhere."

"We're told a nobleman was taken with Braith."

"Kharn Bo-Candryd." Cameria blanched whiter. "They were to be engaged."

Father put his hand on Cameria's shoulder. "I have an idea about how we might find them, but I can only proceed if I know you and the survivors are protected and on your way somewhere safe."

Cameria searched his face. "My lord, I would do anything

you asked if it enabled you to find Braith and Kharn. But . . . there is something you are not telling me. I see it in your eyes."

"Aye. Some pieces have been coming together in my mind."

"Pieces, my lord?"

"And I don't like where they are fitting."

I shared a glance with Mor. Then my gaze wandered to Diggy, who was huddled in the corner, completely still and silent. "What pieces, Father?"

His eyes were far away. "What if . . . what if there is one person behind *all* the coups?"

"One person?" I tried to understand. "One person who overthrew Caradoc, Gareth, and Braith?"

Father chuckled. "Tannie girl, *you* were the ones who overthrew Gareth."

Oh. Right.

"But what if," he went on, "the one who plotted to depose Caradoc also worked to rid Tir of Braith?"

"This person would have an aversion to good rulers, it would seem," Dylun said.

Father nodded. "Indeed. This person would have selfish motives, yet undetermined. They would have been close to Gareth and to Bo-Bradwir or those who control him."

"And you think you know who this is?" Mor asked, brow furrowed.

"Not yet." Father's face was grim. "But I think I know who might be able to help us find out."

Cameria seemed to turn to stone, her uneasiness so thick I could almost taste it. "And you do not like it," she said.

"No, I do not. But I'm afraid we have no choice. I must speak to him."

I looked between the two of them, both their expressions intense and filled with dread.

Then I asked the question hanging in the air. "Who?"

CHAPTER NINE
TANWEN

WE WATCHED FROM BEHIND A CORNER AS WARMIL STRODE like he meant business toward the two guards at the entrance to the dungeon. "Step aside, soldier."

One of the green-suited goons narrowed his eyes. "And you are?"

"Captain Arathew Bo-Orweth. Here on official business from the steward. Need to perform a few cell inspections."

The false name and the lie rolled easily off Warmil's tongue. I sometimes forgot how long the Corsyth weavers had lived in hiding.

The guard didn't look convinced. "Where's your uniform?"

"Sakes, man, we staged the coup not a week ago. You expect the steward to be able to suit and arm and feed his men in the blink of an eye, do you? You have any idea who you're speaking to?"

The guard frowned. He turned to his fellow, who was staring silently at Warmil. "Bo-Thyd, you stand watch. I'm going to go confirm his story." He turned back to Warmil, eyes narrow. "You wait here until I get back."

Warmil looked to be stifling a yawn. "Enjoy. See how that goes for you."

The guard looked troubled a moment, but then he scurried off to consult his superiors.

Now what? How would we get past the other one? I knew

Father and the others didn't want to resort to violence, but how else would we get into the dungeon?

But as soon as the first guard was out of earshot, the second turned to Warmil. "I recognize you, Captain."

Thoughts of capture and torture and death flashed through my mind. But he hadn't sold us out to his fellow guard. So maybe . . .

"You served in the guard, didn't you?" Warmil asked, studying the green-suited soldier's face.

"Aye." He looked down at his new uniform. "Things have taken quite the turn."

Warmil lowered his voice. "Are you still loyal to the queen?"

Bo-Thyd paused, and who could fault him? It was a dangerous question. "Aye. If Queen Braith is alive, I am loyal to her still."

"Then please help us." Warmil nodded our direction, and we slipped from our hiding spot.

Bo-Thyd's eyes widened. "Yestin Bo-Arthio."

I didn't know that I would ever get used to that—all these soldiers who knew my father.

"And Braith's weavers!" he added as he caught sight of me, Mor, and the others.

Well, that was even stranger.

"Soldier," Father began, "we need to speak to one of your prisoners."

Bo-Thyd looked uneasy, but he nodded. "It will take Bo-Hunfed some time to confirm your story, I'd imagine. But you'll have to hurry." He pivoted to unlock the door, then handed Father another key. "This unlocks all the interior doors, though not the cells. I can't help you there. The steward doesn't have the manpower to keep every interior door guarded the way it was under Gareth and Queen Braith. You should not be bothered until Bo-Hunfed returns."

"Thank you, Bo-Thyd," Father said. "If he returns while

we're still down there, tell him we overpowered you. Chase us like you mean to capture us. Understand?"

He nodded.

No sense in this man losing his life for trying to help the rightful queen.

I took Diggy's hand—as much for her peace of mind as mine. It was dark as deathberries down here, and the torches flickering in brackets on the wall didn't do much to make it homey.

Per Father's instructions, Cameria had remained hidden in his shadow. The last thing she should do was show her face around the palace just now. But she knew the exact cell we needed, the precise location of the prisoner Father believed could help us.

She took the lead now, past several interior doors, each of which led to a row of cells. Then she stopped short of one particular door. "Here," she whispered. "This is the row, first cell, closest to the door. I shan't let him see me."

Father nodded. "Wait here. We will make this as quick as possible and get you to the meeting point with Sailor Bo-Cydrid."

"One hundred sixty-two souls," she murmured. "It weighs heavy."

"Indeed." Father fitted the key into the lock. "Ready?"

"Aye," Mor said, and he put a hand on Zel's shoulder. "You ready, mate?"

Zel's features hardened, but he nodded, steeled for whatever met us.

Cameria waited in the hallway, and the rest of us pushed through the door into the row of cells. Diggy melted into one shadowed corner to observe, as she always did.

He stood in the first cell, just as Cameria said, and it almost looked like he had been expecting us.

But, of course, that was impossible. It was just his way.

Always needing to appear calm, in control. One step ahead of everyone else.

He had lost weight, and he wasn't as neatly trimmed and well dressed as the last time I saw him. But there was no mistaking the cold glint of his gray eyes and his fine-featured, handsome face.

Dray Bo-Anffir—Gareth's closest advisor, traitor to King Caradoc, and Braith's one-time suitor. Much against her will.

"Well," he said, his smile full of mockery, "this is a merry traveling party." His gaze roved over me, then skimmed Mor, Dylun, and Warmil before settling on Father. "To what do I owe this great honor?"

Father's jaw flexed. "I assume you know what's happened, Dray."

Dray shrugged. "As much as one might be expected to know when trapped like an animal in a cage. They don't send the criers down here, you know, and my news is no longer delivered by pigeon. Pity, that."

"Braith has been kidnapped." Father was in no mood to mince words, apparently.

"I gathered as much."

"A steward has control of the palace now."

Dray's smile grew. "And yet you still managed to find your way down here. Teach me your ways, wise one."

Father glared. "We don't have time for this. Tell me what you know."

"Now, now. Why the haste? Surely we have time for some niceties. I don't get much company down here, and I've rather missed it."

Father took one step toward Dray's cell and looked straight into the man's eyes. "You once said you cared for Braith. And now, when her life is threatened, you want to play games and make jokes?"

"Quite the contrary. I want to help you."

Father's eyebrows rose. "Oh?"

"Yes." Dray smirked. "Let me guess what you already know. You know the steward is a dolt and could not have possibly staged a coup." He glanced at me. "I believe he is *your* dolt, as a matter of fact."

My face ignited. "He is not *mine*." But I supposed he *was*, in a way.

Dray ignored me. "You know someone else is behind the overthrow and kidnapping of Braith." He studied Father's face. "And you must suspect the person pulling Bo-Bradwir's strings to be the same person who pulled Gareth's, or else you would not be down here speaking to me."

Father's jaw twitched again, but he didn't say anything.

"Well, if you think it's me, you're dead wrong. My first act as puppet master would have been to have my tired bones released from this wretched cell."

"No, not you," Father said. "But you worked closely with this person once, did you not? You know who it is."

"Define *know*." Dray shrugged. "We never sipped tea together, if that's what you mean."

"And yet you must have been in his employ for years."

"In a manner of speaking. But you're too confined by your own experiences, General. You assume that a group of people working together know each other, when that is not at all the case. We did not have planning meetings and debriefings in the throne room, if that's what you're imagining. We shared common goals and used each other accordingly."

Mor huffed. "Noble."

Dray's gaze shifted to him. "The pirate turns legitimate for a couple moons, and look how judgmental he's become."

A noise sounded somewhere far away, and I jolted. We had to hurry.

"We need to find Braith," I said. "Are you going to help us or not?"

"I am helping. I'm giving you information." He turned to Father again. "I believe you're right. I think the person behind Gareth's coup is behind the steward's."

"Names." The word was ice on Father's lips.

"He's not the mastermind," Dray said, "but Naith Bo-Offriad is surely involved. Though I must say I'm impressed by how low a profile he has been keeping."

"And the true mastermind?"

"I couldn't tell you even if I wanted to. Which I don't."

Mor rolled his eyes. "Of course you don't."

"I need to use all the bits of leverage at my disposal, son."

Hearing him call Mor *son* the way my father did made me want to vomit.

But Father looked entirely unsurprised. "What can you give us, and what do you want in return?"

"I can lead you to the place where I believe the Master would take Braith."

For a moment, I thought he had only answered one of Father's questions—what he could offer us. But then I understood. That one statement contained both answers.

He could *lead* us. He wanted to come with us.

He wanted us to break him out of the dungeon.

Insanity.

But Father was already examining the hinges of the cell door. Eyeing the lock. Frowning at the bars.

I took his elbow and spoke quietly in his ear. "Father, you can't be considering this."

"Not sure we have a choice, Tannie. I wouldn't even know where to begin to search for Braith."

"We can't trust him."

"Of course we can't. But we must work with him."

My mind clawed for more arguments—more reasons why we couldn't possibly take this man anywhere with us.

But before I got any of those brilliant rebuttals to come out of my mouth, Diggy had moved out of the shadows toward the cell.

"Well, well," Dray said, one eyebrow quirked. "I don't recognize you."

And then, almost like it was an involuntary reflex, a habit he couldn't resist, his gaze raked over her body.

Her strong, golden-tan legs, her dark flowing hair.

A spark of hunger, tinged with amusement, lit Dray's eyes. Like a great game was about to ensue.

Diggy stopped examining the cell bars and turned to him. "I'm called Digwyn."

But then she looked into his eyes, and though I was fairly sure their paths had not crossed before, I knew she recognized the lust in his expression all too well.

Before I could do anything to stop her, she pulled a dagger from her thigh and lunged toward Dray.

CHAPTER TEN
DIGWYN

You can always tell by the way they look at you.

Maybe you don't notice it at first. Maybe in the beginning, when there's still some sort of innocence left in your soul, you don't see that ravenousness—like a slavering mountainbeast denied a kill for too long.

But as the innocence is chipped away, like flecks of paint peeled from an old ship, one flake at a time, you begin to recognize the look.

You know you're being watched with unnerving keenness. You know you're being violated, even though no one is laying a finger on you.

You know, beyond a doubt, that you are being hunted.

I pull my dagger from its scabbard, spin it between my fingers, and slam the flat of the blade into the bars, just in front of that man's smug face.

He flinches away. Satisfaction burns in my heart.

Now he'll think twice about hunting me.

"Diggy!" Tannie hisses.

I turn to her. Her big blue eyes are wide with concern, like always. I'm not sure why. I didn't stab the man, though I thought of that first.

I understand we need him. I understand he will lead us to the queen and that the queen matters to Tannie and Mor and Yestin.

The man is staring at me, his mouth agape. I lean close to him, through the bars. "Take a good look now. Because if you ever look sideways at me again, the tip of this blade will be the last thing you see before I run it through your eye."

The blade spins in my hand again, and I replace it on my leg. Then I step away, holding the predator's gaze with mine.

He turns to Tannie. "Well, isn't she charming?"

A noise sounds down the hall. The Meridioni woman is waiting out there. This is taking too long.

Tannie steps close to the bars. "Dray, you leave her alone, or I swear, I'll—"

She doesn't finish her sentence. Her hand lights up with that glow, and I realize how we can get the hunter out of his cell.

I grab Tannie's wrist. As my fingers wrap around her, strands like fire shoot from her hands. The strands arc above my head, and I reach for them. I snag one, draw a quick breath, and will the strand to increase its power. Then I hurl it at the cell.

The hunter stumbles away, and the crackling strand blasts through the bars. A hole opens up—large enough for a man to walk through.

Once again, everyone is staring at me. I wish I could shrink away. Melt into the floor. Disappear.

I don't understand what I've done wrong this time. Or if I *have* done something wrong.

I aimed to solve a problem. Think I've done so. Don't they want the hunter freed? Why do they stare?

Life was easier on my island. Without other people and their confusing expectations and scandalized gapes.

The hunter scans the hole I've just made in the bars, then trains his gaze on me. "Does the Master know about her?"

Tannie's face pinches. She looks uncomfortable. Doesn't want to answer. "That's none of your business."

The hunter steps through the hole, his eyes still fixed on me. I force myself not to squirm—or flinch the way he did when I slammed my dagger at his face.

"The Master would be very keen on this one."

I meet his glare. Meet, match, surpass.

But inside, I wonder . . .

Who is this Master, and what would they want with me?

CHAPTER ELEVEN
TANWEN

THE HOLE IN DRAY'S CELL BARS GAPED AT ME LIKE AN OPEN mouth. It may as well have been mocking us, that open mouth, because Dray's words were true enough.

If the Master—whoever that was—had seen Diggy's gift, they would stop at nothing to have her. To use her for their evil ends.

I thought about how those dark strands had targeted me and Mor because we shared linked gifts. Diggy's gift was twice as powerful and a lot less predictable.

Perfect to use. Perfect to exploit.

What if this Master that Dray spoke of—this madman overturning the kingdom—was the same person who had chased us? The same person who had murdered Wylie, sunk the *Cethorelle*, and attacked us on the beach of Kanac? If it were so, then they *had* seen Diggy's gift.

The urge to protect her grew ever greater. I wanted to make sure nothing and no one ever had the chance to use her in that way—to take this broken creature and make her a tool of evil.

A crash pulled my attention from my troubled thoughts. A moment later, Cameria appeared in the doorway, her eyes grave. "My lord, they are coming." Her gaze landed on Dray, who was standing outside his dungeon cell, and her features lit up in rage. "What is this?" She rounded on Father. "My lord?"

"There's no time to explain now." Father took her elbow. "We have to run."

Without waiting for her reply, he darted back into the main hallway, then took off in the opposite direction of the door where we'd left Bo-Thyd.

Deeper into the dungeon.

"Digwyn," he called over his shoulder as we all ran after him, "can you create another explosion for us?"

Diggy's hand was clasped in one of mine, and I got the feeling she was slowing her pace so she didn't drag me too much. "Aye. I suppose."

"I know a hidden back door that leads up into one of the gardens, but it's bound to be locked."

We reached a niche in the wall that appeared to be nothing more than an inconsistency in the stones. But one moment, Cameria and Father were in front of me, and the next, they'd disappeared.

I realized that they had slipped into a narrow gap between two walls. Mor stood in the gap now, his hand extended out to us. I spared one glance back the way we'd come.

Six green-suited guards sprinted toward us. Bo-Thyd was not among them.

I grabbed Mor's hand, and he pulled me and Diggy into the alcove. But surely the guards would find the niche and figure out where we'd gone.

"Hurry." Father squeezed through the narrow passageway, and the rest of us followed.

He didn't need to tell me what I would have to do once we reached the door. As soon as it was in sight, I imagined a ribbon of fire pouring from my hand.

What came out instead was a strand of molten metal that looked far too much like the one that had killed Wylie.

But Diggy snatched it from the air and somehow turned it explosive, then threw it at the door.

The wooden door splintered before us. Father and Cameria turned their backs just in time to shield themselves from a shower of wood chips. Cameria's face tilted up and registered dismay when she realized she had turned directly into Dray. He stood inches from her now. She scrambled away, nearly tripping on the hem of her dress in her haste to put some space between them.

I could picture him smirking, enjoying her anger.

"Halt, traitors!" a rough, unfamiliar voice sounded within the narrow passageway.

"Move." Another one-word command from Father.

We all obeyed and stumbled into the dank air of a path dug down into the earth like a cellar, then toward the stone steps on the other side. Mor paused before following the rest of us up the stairs. He yanked off one of his gloves and created a web of strands, then he plastered them across the opening Diggy had blown in the side of the wall.

It looked like a giant, eight-legged night-trapper had been there.

He replaced his glove and helped me up the stairs. "They can slice through them with their swords, I'm sure, but it should slow them down. Those strands are sticky as boiled honey."

The cry of surprise that followed told me Mor's plan had been a success. At least for the moment.

Once we had all reached the top of the stairs, Father ducked into a nearby velvet-petal garden. He lowered his voice. "Cameria, can you get to the meeting point undetected?"

She looked around, collecting her bearings. "Now that I'm out of the palace, yes. I believe so. I shouldn't draw much notice."

"I doubt that's true," Dray said wryly.

Father ignored him. "Give Sailor Bo-Cydrid my letter. Jule will see you and the others safely to"—he paused and glanced at Dray—"your destination."

Best not to give Dray more information than we had to.

"Thank you, my lord."

"Ma'am," Zel said to Cameria, his voice strangled. "Will you make sure Arystia looks after my boy?"

"Of course, Zelyth," Cameria assured him kindly. "We will all look after him."

"And when we've found the queen, I'll return for him," Zel promised.

"Of course you will."

Then Cameria stretched up on her tiptoes to kiss Father on each of his cheeks, as Meridionis sometimes did. "Send word to us. Please."

He nodded. "I will. Be safe."

After one final glower at Dray, Cameria slipped from the garden and hurried along one of the shadowed walls.

Father turned to the newly freed prisoner. "Where to now?"

"Out of the gardens, for a start."

Father glared at him.

"To the river," Dray said.

I didn't bother pointing out we'd already known that much.

"Won't they know we'll head that direction?" Mor asked.

"Doesn't matter," Father said. "We'll hide for a while if we have to, but it's the fastest way to get out of Urian. We don't have a choice."

"I know a less-traveled route." Dray inclined his head toward a different archway than the one Cameria had just used. "Follow me."

And we did, because we had no choice.

"Father . . ."

"I know, Tannie girl. I don't like it any better than you do. I feel as though I've made a deal with a fiend."

And that was probably true enough.

But as the guards' shouts carried over from an adjoining garden, the realization struck me hard.

If we wanted to find Braith, we truly had no other choice. We had just broken that man out of the dungeon, and there was no turning back now.

CHAPTER TWELVE
BRAC

If you ever have reason to sit on a royal throne, I don't recommend it in the least. They ain't comfortable, and that's the truth.

The flowery carvings on Braith's fancy chair poked into my back as I stared at the guards standing in front of me. "What do you mean *they escaped?*"

Bo-Hunfed shifted his weight. "They overpowered Bo-Thyd and forced their way to Sir Dray's cell. It looks like they have some kind of . . . weapon that can blast apart anything they want. That cell is ruined, and they blew a hole in the wall by a hidden back passage."

"Hidden back passage?" My enemies knew this palace better than I did, and that didn't sit too well.

Not enemies, I tried to remind myself. This was Tannie we were talking about. Tannie and her father.

And the pirate. He was an enemy, anyway. And Dray? Wasn't Dray supposed to be the enemy of *all* of us?

I couldn't make fluff nor fuzz of that one. What was she playing at, breaking that man out of the dungeon?

"Sir?" The guard stared at me, a question all over his face.

"Sorry, what did you say?"

He cleared his throat. "They blasted a hole through a wall by a passage we weren't aware of. Then they put some sort of substance over the opening. Like a web. By the time we cut through the strands, they had escaped."

"Blazes."

"I've ordered some men after them."

"Good. That's good." At least I guessed it was. I had no idea what I was doing.

I turned to look toward the shadowy corner where the high priest sat, concealed by a cloud of darkness he'd asked me to conjure for him. Still wasn't sure how I'd done it, but it seemed I could do just about anything Naith asked me to these days.

Except make bread. That one had stopped working for some reason.

And none of the powers worked unless Naith was near. I asked why once. He said the goddesses often used him to help others channel their powers.

He nodded to me now, and that was the signal to pull back the cloud of darkness. I screwed up my face and waved my hand as if drawing a curtain to the side.

Naith rose from his chair and strode toward me.

"Your Holiness," I said quickly, "I'll send a hundred guards after them, so don't you worry. We'll get them back. Them and that prisoner."

"No, my son." Naith lifted his hand to acknowledge the guard kneeling in respect. Then he sat on the throne next to mine—Gareth's old seat he'd dragged out of some royal storage closet.

"No? But they can't have gone far, and sure as sugar they're headed toward the river. We can still catch them. But I don't want *anyone* else hurt."

My mind tripped over what I'd seen on that first day. On my way to the throne room and the private apartments Naith had ordered prepared for me. The bodies scattered across the floor like hay inside a barn. I'd protested. At least, I think I had. When I tried to recall the memory, it was like seeing it all through water. Blurred and distorted.

"There is no need, my lord," Naith said. "All is well." He nodded to the guard. "See to it that repairs are started straightaway, and that the perimeter of the dungeon is once again secure. If it is possible, seal up the hidden passageway so that it cannot be exploited again."

"Yes, Your Holiness."

"And have that Bo-Thyd interrogated. Make sure he is not working for the rebels." Naith looked at me knowingly. "We can't have spies and subterfuge, now can we?"

"I don't reckon." Whatever *subterfuge* was.

The guard bowed and left. Naith and I were alone. His formal manners disappeared, and I knew he wouldn't be calling me "my lord" or any such thing now. But the pleased smile remained, so that wasn't an act.

But I still didn't understand why.

"See, my son," he said. "All is well."

He said that so often the words were probably carved on the insides of my ears by now.

But I guessed that was probably my fault. All I ever did was tell him I couldn't do this, that I didn't know what I was doing and didn't understand how we were making anything better for Tir. And I asked him about forty times a day if Braith was still alive.

They had promised. *Promised* they wouldn't hurt her. But something in my gut—something wiggly as a waterworm—told me some people's promises didn't mean a whole bunch.

Tannie sprang to mind.

She had promised to marry me, hadn't she? And the first thing she did after returning home was punch me in the jaw.

"Don't be troubled, my son," Naith said, and I guessed he took my sour expression to mean I was upset over the rebels' escape.

"No offense, Your Holiness, but why aren't *you* troubled? You didn't want them to escape, did you? You told me to keep a close watch on them."

"True enough. It was rather shortsighted of me, I suppose, but I did not anticipate that Yestin would think to go to Dray. It was clever, really." He chuckled.

I didn't understand this man at all. The things he found funny . . .

"But it works out perfectly," he went on. "Dray will lead them straight to the Master."

The Master? The waterworms in my gut set to wriggling again. "Who?"

Naith's smile faded. "I . . . that is . . ."

"You mean the goddesses?" But I could tell he didn't. He'd made a mistake.

I just didn't know how or why or what.

"Yes, my son. My masters, the goddesses."

My face screwed up in confusion. How could Dray take Tannie and the others to the goddesses? They were but carved statues.

Didn't matter. Naith wasn't giving more—least not at the moment. "Where Dray's taking them . . ." I trailed off, and it almost felt like my tongue was tied in a knot. I tried again. "They won't be hurt, will they? I don't want more bloodshed. There's been enough of that already."

Naith smiled pleasantly, and a sense of peace wrapped around me. "Don't worry, Brac. Dray will lead them exactly where they need to be, and all will be set to rights. I swear it."

CHAPTER THIRTEEN
BRAITH

Frenhin smiled down at Braith, who was still tethered helplessly to the wall. "Ah yes. Kharn."

"Where is he?" Braith repeated. "If you have harmed him, I swear, I'll—"

"You'll what?" Frenhin laughed. "I'm sorry, dear, I don't mean to mock. But really. Look at yourself. You are quite literally chained to a wall in a cavern in an unfamiliar secret hideaway. You have no allies, no hope of escape. And yet you still seek to threaten me." Her smile changed—warmed, somehow. "I hadn't thought it possible, truly."

Braith glared. "Hadn't thought what possible?"

"You have actually fallen in love."

Braith forced every muscle to obey so that nary a twitch of pain, a shred of emotion, showed.

"It won't change things, darling," Frenhin said, leaning back in her chair. "It's only . . . it amuses me that the ice princess is capable of some human emotion."

"I am capable of many. I have displayed them often. Perhaps they are simply feelings you cannot understand."

The smile dropped from Frenhin's lips. "Enough." She snapped her fingers.

A pair of soldiers dressed in uniforms not unlike the palace guardsmen, except of the deepest gray instead of black, entered the room. They dragged a man between them.

"Kharn," Braith choked. She couldn't will the tears away now that she actually saw him, doubled in half, bloodied and unconscious.

Frenhin pointed to Braith. "Bring him there," she ordered the guards.

The thick, metallic scent of blood filled Braith's nose. A sticky, coagulated mess covered half of Kharn's face. Braith's eyes searched him for the source of the wound—there, just along his hairline. Where they'd hit him with the hilt of a sword, she now remembered.

His eye had swollen shut. Bruises, some fresh and some healing, covered every inch of his exposed skin. They spoke to a beating far worse than the single blow he'd endured in the palace garden as he tried to protect her—tried to give her time to escape.

"Bring him closer, please," Braith begged.

The guards glanced at Frenhin, and she nodded. Her smile glinted in the firelight.

The guards dragged Kharn beside Braith, and she pressed her cheek against his. Warm.

He was still alive.

"Take him there," Frenhin commanded. She pointed to a set of irons identical to Braith's, driven into the same wall where Braith sat chained, but in the far corner. Well out of her reach.

"Please, no." Braith cast a desperate glance at Kharn. "He needs a physician. Don't chain him there."

"And what would you give to have him chained closer? Or to receive the care of a physician?"

Braith stilled. Leverage. These were lessons in politics her father had tried to teach her. Lessons, she now realized, he had probably learned from her mother.

Find what your enemy loves most. Find the thing they value above all else. Then threaten that thing. Use it. Exploit it. Kill it, if you have to, in order to force your enemy to surrender.

Frenhin's laugh pierced Braith's thoughts. "You see, darling? If I want anything from you, I will be able to extract it."

Fire snaked through Braith's veins, through the veins of the ice princess, threatening to melt her resolve and render her a quivering puddle. A puddle willing to do whatever Frenhin demanded, as long as no further harm came to Kharn.

But she could not give up. Kharn needed her to be strong. And so did the people of Tir.

She lifted her eyes to meet her mother's. "Then you had better keep us both alive, hadn't you? You cannot use us if we are dead."

"Romantic."

Braith ignored her. "Bring us food and some water."

Frenhin paused a moment, considering her daughter. "Very well, then." She snapped her fingers, and the guards responded.

They placed the slumping Kharn against the wall in the corner and locked him in place with shackles around both his wrists. Then they brought a tray of bread, cheese, and some kind of dried meat—though barely enough for one person, let alone two. Cups of water were next. Kharn's was placed on the floor beside him.

"Wake him," Frenhin ordered.

Braith held her breath. It would have been kinder to let Kharn remain unconscious, perhaps, for the time being. But a guard was already shoving a cloth soaked in something pungent under Kharn's nose.

He sniffed twice. His eyes flew open. He coughed, and blood sprayed from his lips. "Not a good nap." Kharn cleared his throat, then coughed again. He glanced up at the guard crouched before him. "Ready to go another round already?"

How often had they wakened him just to beat him again?

"Kharn?" Braith said gently. "I'm here."

He jerked his head around—too fast, and he winced.

"Braith?" Relief flooded his face, followed by alarm. "No. What are you doing here?"

"Do not worry." Braith smiled. "All will be well."

Kharn raised the one eyebrow that wasn't caked in blood. He glanced at Frenhin and the guards, then back at Braith. "I hope you won't think me a terrible pessimist if I disagree with you, my love."

Braith almost laughed.

"How long have you been here?" Kharn asked Braith, casting a withering glare at Frenhin.

"I don't know. I was drugged and brought here."

Kharn swore under his breath. "But they have not harmed you otherwise?"

Braith paused, unsure how to answer.

"That's enough catching up for now." Frenhin smirked. "Let us move on to something more entertaining."

Kharn shook his head. "Why are you doing this? What could have happened to you to corrode your soul so thoroughly?"

"Corrode? You sound like my dear daughter. She believes all people are good if given the chance to be. No one acts less than nobly unless some catastrophe corrupts them or some opportunity eludes them."

"You think me very naïve, indeed." Braith looked away.

"Is it not so? I thought that was why you always advocated for the utter dregs of society."

Braith turned back to her mother's cold smile. "Of course I do not suppose all people are good and noble. I believe every person, no matter their class or heritage, is capable of both the utmost nobility and deepest evil. Most of us live in the space between, choosing one or the other every moment of every day." She paused, considering Frenhin. "I fear you have found an unfortunate extreme."

Frenhin placed a hand to her chest. "That was truly stirring, Your Majesty. Moving and profound. If only your courtiers were here to listen." She smiled coolly. "You always did have a weakness for impassioned speeches."

"Most politicians have worse vices."

True amusement danced in Frenhin's eyes. "Don't I know it." Braith fell quiet for a moment. "Do you deny it, then? That something happened to set you on this path? Because truly, Mother, even you must see the evil of your deeds."

"Ah, Braith. You do not understand. My deeds are not *evil*. I am not corrupted. It's not as simple as all that. I am merely committed—willing to go to great lengths to make things right."

Braith glanced at Kharn. He kept his head low, but the keen light in his good eye told Braith he was absorbing every word. He knew as well as Braith that Frenhin's answers could hold the key to getting them out of captivity.

"And what needed to be set right?" Braith asked. "For surely you can see that this is madness—that what you have done has made everything truly and terribly wrong."

Frenhin's tone turned as sharp as a blade. "You know nothing of which you speak. Your grandfather had to be avenged."

In all Braith's years, her mother had barely spoken of Braith's grandparents. Both died before Braith was born. She knew neither had been of noble blood—that her mother was the daughter of a middle-class merchant. But nothing more had ever been said about either of them.

Now Braith was curious. "What do you mean? What happened to him?"

"Not just him, dear." Frenhin's voice was controlled again. "Our family. It was always supposed to be for our family."

She rose and began to pace. "My father had been due to receive a rather important appointment. Steward of Trade. It would have changed everything for us." Tendrils of smoky-gray story curled from her fingertips as she spoke, and Braith tried not to show her surprise.

She hadn't realized it before, but it made sense. The strands of fire, these streams of smoke that seemed to come automatically as Frenhin spoke—Braith's mother was a storyteller.

"Our family would have been provided for," Frenhin said. "The cares of the middle class would have been removed from our lives at last. It really is the cruelest position to be in, the middle class. To be so close to wealth, so near a life of ease, and yet unable to grasp it. Always striving for prizes just out of one's reach."

Braith's mind filled with images of starving peasants. Those who had not enough to feed their children, let alone themselves. She thought of the enslaved farm laborers in the southern part of Tir, along the Meridioni border, and of the Haribian servants who worked the docks along the western coast, little better than slaves, desperately hoping to provide a life of better opportunity for their children.

But she did not argue. She let her mother continue on.

"I was fifteen years old, and Father's appointment would have changed everything for me too." Frenhin lifted her chin, and in the firelight, Braith could almost imagine her mother as a fifteen-year-old girl—pale, beautiful, and proud. "I would have been courted by the noble class. I could have become the wife of a duke or a governor. Perhaps even one of Caradoc's lesser nephews might have noticed me. There were so many of them, you remember."

Braith heard Kharn draw a long breath. Of course he remembered. These were his elder cousins she spoke of—his own flesh and blood.

"But instead, do you know what Caradoc did?" Frenhin's smoky tendrils flared with fire. "He gave the position to some Meridioni. Said it would strengthen diplomatic relations. Said that my father, born and bred of Tirian stock, was less qualified to serve as Tir's Steward of Trade."

"It ruined him. He was a laughingstock." Her features hardened, uglier and angrier than Braith had ever seen them.

"The Tirian merchant passed over for a dirty foreigner. He was crushed—destroyed—and his business never recovered. Not only did we not obtain the position we sought, we lost whatever wealth we'd had. We were ruined. When he saw that he could not offer the better life he dreamed of to me and my sisters, he went mad with grief."

"What sisters?" Braith had never heard of her mother having sisters.

"You can be rather simple sometimes, Braith. Do you think I could have ever gotten close to Caradoc's court again carrying my own disgraced family name? Thankfully I had never met the king face-to-face, so all I needed was a new name—a new identity that did not carry the shame of being Wallyth Bo-Ashgoff's daughter."

"So you picked a new name for yourself."

"Of course. But surely you understand. My real family would have known the truth. And my sisters and mother would have noticed if I was suddenly a courtier. And certainly if I became queen."

Braith's heart stuttered. "You murdered them too."

"Disposed of. Yes."

Braith stared at her, unable to comprehend her detachment—and the dissonance of her actions. "In order to avenge our family, you killed them."

"It sounds rather silly when you phrase it like that. But it was the only way."

"It was . . . a position in the government." Braith fought to control her shaking voice. "He was merely passed over in favor of another. And all this for that one simple act? All this death and pain, sorrow and destruction?"

"You didn't see what it did to him!"

Columns of fire sprang toward the ceiling from Frenhin's hands. Braith and Kharn shielded their faces from the heat.

"You weren't there! You can't imagine what it was like,

watching my father descend into madness, driven there by the selfish whims of a foolish king."

"Perhaps not." Braith spoke into the fire. "But I do know what it was like to watch my father go mad with greed. I know what it's like to watch him speak to people who aren't there as though he hears voices in his head. And what it's like to know that my own mother killed my father."

Frenhin let the pillars of fire die and considered Braith. "Fair enough, my dear. I suppose we have both suffered." She sank onto her chair again. "No matter. That is all in the past."

Braith fought to tamp down her horror. How could her mother's tone be so dismissive? So casual?

"And what of the future?" she finally asked.

Frenhin smiled. "Well, darling, before this recent upheaval, my list was about complete."

"List?"

"My revenge list. It seems a tad childish now, but I was still a child when I made it. Every person who crossed my family, every person who mocked my father, supported the king's decision, or welcomed that Meridioni trash into what should have been set aside for us. Each of those names made my list. And it took me thirty years, but I had just about done it."

"You said it *was* just about complete. And now?"

"Now, sadly, the list is growing again. For a while, Yestin Bo-Arthio was the only name left. If I'm being honest with you, my dear—and believe me, I have been honest with you lately—I thought one day I might find his bones somewhere and cross his name off at last. I did not truly believe he was still alive until I saw him in the flesh. But no matter. He is alive, and I shall remedy that eventually. Him, and the others who have crossed me.

"I think it might give me even more pleasure to watch these troublesome rebels die than it did to eliminate the courtiers around Caradoc's table."

Braith pressed her lips together, afraid to draw fire toward her weaver friends.

Frenhin laughed suddenly. "You know, it feels good to tell you all of this. You would not believe how heavily it weighs to hold such secrets for so long.

"No one knew until recently." Frenhin's eyes lit up. "Except the handful of servants and contingent of guards who live here in this secluded place—my Craigyl staff. But with the rest of my allies, I kept my identity secret, even from my closest advisors. My closest confidants. Even your father did not know."

And she was proud of the fact. Proud of her cleverness. Her deception.

"You were the voice Father heard in his ear all the time," Braith said.

"Yes." Frenhin shook her head. "His belief in the goddesses was rather easy to exploit." She apparently misread Braith's expression of disgust. "Yes, he was a fool, I know. I didn't marry him for his brains, after all."

"No, I don't suppose you did."

"And now that Gareth is gone, it is time to pursue the throne more openly. I would offer you a seat at my right hand if only you weren't so very *you*."

Braith remained silent.

"My marionette is in place in Urian," Frenhin continued. "Soon I will step forward and reclaim the throne. And finally, once and for all, I will make sure I am too powerful ever to touch again."

Braith looked at her mother for a long moment. "When you say *touch*, you mean hurt. You want to be so powerful that no one can ever hurt you or take anything away from you again."

Silence swallowed the room.

Frenhin's icy stare dripped with venom, but only briefly. A controlled mask slipped back over her face. "It does not bother me to have you make such observations, Braith," she said calmly. "You always did see things I wish you weren't able to." She glanced at Braith's chains, almost as though to confirm they were still there, holding this dangerous young queen in her place. "I'm almost ready to strike, but I must be invincible first. My plan was brilliant last time. This time, it must be unstoppable."

"And how do you expect to gather such power?" Braith asked. "Every ruler has weaknesses. Everyone can be touched—hurt, if you will. No army in history was ever as invincible as you describe."

"No army in history had the weapons I am gathering."

"There is no amount of steel that will—" But Braith stopped short because suddenly she realized what her mother was after.

She wanted others like herself.

"You sought to suppress the weaver gifts when Father ruled, not because you believed they were intrinsically wrong but so that you might be the only one to control them. And now you wish to . . ."

Frenhin waited a moment, but Braith couldn't bring herself to finish.

"Yes, Braith. I wish to build an army of strand-wielders."

Captain Bo-Lidere. Captain Bo-Awirth. Zelyth, the farmer. Karlith, the colormaster healer. The poor, sick girl they had hoped to cure—Gryfelle. The Meridioni scholar, Dylun. The former guardswoman who had called Braith a princess, even when Braith had not felt she deserved it—what was her name? Yes, Aeron.

And, of course, Tanwen En-Yestin, daughter of Frenhin's most frustrating opponent. Tanwen would be quite the prize.

"They will never help you."

Frenhin chuckled. "Oh, I believe they will. I will offer them power deeper and stronger than they have ever imagined. They won't be able to resist. They may be brave to the point of stupidity, but they are still human. As you said, everyone can be touched."

Braith closed her eyes and leaned her head back against the wall.

Leverage. Personal weaknesses.

If Frenhin knew the weavers' personal weaknesses, Braith could only pray that they *weren't* human, somehow. That they would be able to resist when few others could. That they would be able to fight all their natural instincts and every selfish desire.

And for the first time since Braith had found herself chained to this wall with her world turned upside down, she despaired of hope.

CHAPTER FOURTEEN
TANWEN

During all my mornings heaving my breakfast over the side of the *Cethorelle*, I never imagined myself longing for a ship. Back then, those few moons ago, I'd only yearned for dry ground beneath my boots.

But as the men paddled two riverboats against the current of the Endrol River, that is exactly what I wished for. A ship with sails I could fill with wind strands so it might bring us up the river faster. Every moment we battled the current in broad daylight was a moment we risked discovery, and that knowledge set my nerves on edge.

But Father didn't seem to believe we would be captured.

We had slipped away from the docks along the north side of Urian without being noticed. We had made it to the Endrol, following Dray's step-by-step directions, and about that time, one of the palace pigeons had tracked us. Cameria and Jule had found each other. They would be leaving the next morning with any of the refugees who wished to travel to Pembrone. Jule and his men vowed to protect the refugee party and stay with them as long as they were able.

I watched Father as he read the note. I could tell he was trying to figure out what their chances were. How would they get the survivors from the palace? How would they escape from Urian? How would they travel all the way to the Eastern Peninsula?

"We made it out," I'd offered to try to bring a little hope to his worried expression.

Father had looked at me. "I think we made it out because the steward allowed us to."

That idea sank to the bottom of my stomach like a basket of river stones.

It made sense. And it meant we had a little freedom to move without Brac's goons at our heels. For whatever reason, Brac and whoever was helping him didn't mind if we slipped away from Urian and went on our quest to find Braith.

Which meant she was either dead or we were walking right into a trap.

Probably both.

And still, we continued on up the Endrol, because that seemed to be how we lived. Tiptoeing to the edges of cliffs that sane people avoided and diving right off, headfirst.

"We could stop at Ashton for supplies," Father said from the other boat.

Dray shrugged. He sat on the bench across from me, apparently unconcerned that Dylun and Mor were doing all the work of pulling our boat upstream. "Ashton is fine, if you like. Pick a river city. Any river city."

Mor grunted from his place at the oars, but he didn't comment. It wasn't worth it. Dray was revealing the information we needed one tiny piece at a time—wisely, if you asked me. I would have had no qualms about throwing him overboard if we got all the information we wanted out of him.

"I'd like to go to the Corsyth," Warmil said. He was in the boat with Father, but we were traveling close enough that we could hear each other speak.

"The Corsyth?" Father hadn't been to our forest hideaway, but naturally I had told him all about it.

"Yes, sir. I would like to see Aeron."

Of course. Aeron was there with Karlith.

"Aye." Father furrowed his brow.

"And I'd like to give Karlith the chance to come with us, if she likes. We've never left either of them behind on a mission this big before, General. It doesn't sit well with me."

"Karlith is as expert a folk healer as I've ever seen. And En-Howell is a fine soldier." Father stopped rowing and turned toward Warmil. "But do you think she will be able to travel with us?"

The stitched-up stump where Aeron's leg used to be came to mind, and I brushed away the gruesome memory. It was a wonder she hadn't bled to death when they cut it off on Kanac.

"I don't know, sir," Warmil admitted. "But I would like to give her the chance to refuse."

Father nodded.

"Though I am uncomfortable with some of our present company," Dylun interjected with an irritated glance in Dray's direction, "I would not turn down the opportunity to—ah—deposit some things in the Corsyth for safekeeping."

The cure box, of course. I tightened my feet around the box that rested between my boots at the bottom of the boat.

Dray couldn't know what was inside. But if he had half a brain, he would realize it was important to us, the way Dylun had barely been willing to part company with it.

And Dray certainly had at least half a brain.

I looked up to find him watching me, a smug little smile tugging one side of his mouth. "I don't care what's in there. I assure you."

"I didn't say anything," I shot back. He had practically read my thoughts, but I knew I was no genius at hiding them.

"You don't need to trust me," Dray said to Dylun. "Just remember that we have a common goal at the moment. I have no desire, nor reason, to hinder you."

"We could blindfold him," Mor suggested.

Dray shrugged again. "Whatever you wish."

"Then we can get supplies in our usual place," Zel said from the other boat.

He meant Bowyd, the town just on the edge of the Codewig Forest where the Corsyth was hidden.

"Whatever you wish," Dray repeated. "Though I should remind you there are no secrets between us now."

Diggy snorted. "I'm sure that's not true." She scooted closer to me on the bench and glared at Dray. "You tell a lot of lies."

He laughed like he truly was amused. "Frankly, my dear, I hardly notice anymore. You get used to it after a while."

"I'm sure *you* do," Diggy retorted.

But his smile only grew. "You really despise me, don't you? That hardly seems fair. We just met, little one."

I put my arm around her shoulders, as if I could shield Diggy from his smugness.

But she didn't shrink away. "You're a taker," she said. "I've known men like you—too many to count. You don't know how else to be, just like your lying tongue doesn't know how else to speak. You take and take and take because that's all you know. That's who you are." She looked toward the water. "If we're smart, we'll smother you with a pillow in your sleep."

Dray glanced at me for half a moment, then studied Diggy as if trying to dismantle her mind.

Good luck, Sir Creepy.

We passed the many docks of Ashton on our right just then. Not much looked different than it had any other time I'd passed this way. It seemed incredible to think that Brac—my Brac Bo-Bradwir of poky Pembrone—sat on the throne in Urian and the docks of Ashton couldn't even be troubled to look different on account of it.

It wasn't too much farther to the little spot along the north bank of the river where we usually pulled our boats ashore and hid them in the bushes, then hiked to the Corsyth. Half an hour, maybe. So Dylun and Mor wrapped a strip of cloth around

Dray's eyes, though if he was good at tracking time, he could work out where we stopped.

I hoped he was telling the truth about not wanting to hinder us, though I had to wonder how long that would hold out, even if it were true.

My heart fluttered when I saw that spot on the bank come into view. A lifetime had passed since I'd first been to the Corsyth—at least it seemed so. It was the place where I'd begun to find myself. Where I had figured out who I wanted to be. Where I had begun to learn what mattered to me.

The men, except blindfolded Dray, climbed from the boats and started to pull them onto dry land. Once our boat was fully ashore, Mor pulled the strip of cloth from Dray's eyes—a little roughly, perhaps.

Then Mor removed his leather gloves and rubbed his palms, wincing. "That rowing isn't kind to my hands, no lie." His smile flickered as he extended his hand to help me over the side of the boat.

I took it. Immediately, our gifts linked.

Gold ribbons snaked from his fingers across my hand and wrapped around my forearm. The strands lifted me from my feet. I glided up and over the side of the boat, then the strands set me gently ashore, about a breath from Mor. Brisk-leaf paste and shave oil and the slight scent of sweat glistening on his forehead invaded my senses.

I stepped away and nearly fell back into the boat, except that my hand was still firmly clasped in his.

He helped me find my balance, looking sheepish. "Oops. I forgot." He released my hand and replaced his gloves.

Dray snorted. "Cethor's tears."

I expected him to mock our awkward—yet painfully obvious—attraction to each other, but he didn't. Instead, his observation brought back the fear of what we already knew.

"No wonder the Master wants you two," he said. "You'd be

terribly useful. Pray you don't fall into that iron grip. If you do, I promise you'll regret it."

Diggy cocked her head to the side. "Well, that's the truth, at least."

CHAPTER FIFTEEN
TANWEN

I PAUSED JUST BEFORE WE REACHED THE EDGE OF THE Corsyth. It couldn't be seen yet—the location had been selected too carefully. You couldn't see it until you were in the middle of it.

But I could feel it. I could sense the magic of a thousand strands, the art of half a dozen weavers I loved like family.

I stood there, soaking it up for just a moment, and I could swear a gloved hand brushed mine.

Then came Father's beckoning. "Come, Tannie girl."

I followed him and the others through the curtain of moss and into the forest wonderland.

And there was Karlith. She gasped when she saw us. "Thank the Creator!" Then she burst into tears. "Oh, you're here! Thank the Creator above."

She hurried toward us but came up short at the sight of Zelyth leading a re-blindfolded Dray by rope-bound hands.

"What's happened?" she breathed. "What is this?"

"I'm not a *what*, I'm a *who*, thanks." Dray frowned. "Kindly take off this blindfold now, if you don't mind. I've caught quite enough brambles in my trousers for one day."

Karlith looked at Warmil. "Captain?"

"We had no choice. I'll explain everything after . . ." He trailed off as Aeron emerged from behind a cluster of trees.

She stood as tall as she ever had. On two legs, somehow, though her movements were a bit halting and jerky.

Warmil stood rooted to the spot, unable to speak.

Aeron smiled, a little pained, but mostly proud. "What do you think?" She bent over, her dark hair falling across her face. She lifted the leg of her trousers to reveal . . .

I leaned closer. "It's wood."

"Aye." She grinned. "We had it made in town."

She lifted the fabric further to reveal beautiful flowers carved into the wooden leg. Either she or Karlith had painted them, for only a colormaster could have brought wooden flowers to life in such glorious detail. As Aeron rolled her trousers just a bit higher, she revealed active strands swirling around the place where her stump met the false leg.

"It hurts a little still," she said, lowering her trouser leg again. "But I'm getting better walking on it."

Warmil uprooted himself and caught up Aeron into his arms, clearly restraining himself from twirling her around. But only just.

"Um, excuse me?" Dray again.

I fought the urge to roll my eyes. He was as trying as a tattlebird.

I yanked the blindfold away while Zel untied his hands. "There," I said. "Happy?"

"I wouldn't say that's the word for it." His gaze landed on Warmil and Aeron. "Well, isn't that precious." Then he looked around at the color-smattered trees and twinkling lanterns. "This is . . . different."

"Warmil," Aeron said, eyeing Dray, "what's going on?"

Warmil took a few moments to explain to Aeron and Karlith all that had happened—and how it had come about that we had Dray Bo-Anffir traveling with us.

Of all people.

"I'm coming with you," Aeron said as soon as Warmil had finished.

"Aeron, I don't think—"

"I'm coming," she said firmly. "Why do you think I had this made?" She tapped her leg. "I'll not be left here, Warmil. If you leave me behind, I may as well have died on that island."

Warmil and Father shared a glance. Father relented. "If you think you are able. And that you will not slow us down," he added, but his voice was kind.

As far as Braith's life was concerned, time was probably not on our side as it was.

"I will not slow the group down." Aeron nodded once. "We only got the leg this morning, and already I'm improving my speed."

"We will be glad to have you back, En-Howell." Father clapped her on the shoulder. "We'll need to gather supplies in town before we travel to"—he gestured to Dray—"wherever he is taking us."

"Yes, supplies." Dray rubbed his hands together. "Excellent. I shall provide a list."

Father's brows rose. "A list?"

"Yes. I require a decent set of clothing—two, preferably. And a proper razor to maintain my beard. Beard oil, a tooth-cleaning cloth, brisk-leaf paste, soap. I suppose these would be considered necessities, even for you people." He pursed his lips. "See if you can't find a decent waistcoat. I rather doubt you'll be able to. I prefer fine grazer leather, but I'll take the best of whatever you can find." He flashed his over-white smile. "I'm flexible."

"Anything else?" Father snapped.

"A looking glass. A traveling cloak—fur-lined, please. Mountainbeast fur, if you can find it, though I don't know that you can this far south. I suppose you would know what small-town merchants in these areas stock better than I, so do your best. Lined gloves wouldn't be a bad idea either. And my boots could use repairing. Is there a good cobbler in Bowyd? That is the town in question, is it not? I rather doubt they have a decent cobbler, but any provincial dolt ought to be able to deal with these soles. Half a year in the palace dungeons has been murder on my wardrobe."

I couldn't listen anymore.

I spun and stomped deeper into the forest, wondering how Father would stand it. Listening to that vain, pompous man make his demands for fine clothing while the queen was kidnapped or dead.

This was supposed to be a rescue mission, but far be it from Sir Dray Bo-Anffir to travel in anything less than high style.

"He may not wear frills and lace like some of the noblemen, but he's no less foppish," I muttered to myself as I climbed over a boulder. "'Fur-lined, please,'" I mimicked. "Ugh. What a puff-prowler he is."

I slid down the other side of the boulder, then stopped and leaned against it. I held a hand to my chest, affecting Dray's pompous demeanor. "'I'm flexible.' Are you now, Sir Puffy? Shall we test the limits of that flexibility?"

Even over my grumbling, I heard it—the sound of a twig snapping nearby.

And then another. I whirled, my hands thrust out, strands ready to meet the threat.

CHAPTER SIXTEEN
TANWEN

IT WAS MOR.

He held his hands up in surrender, a corner of his mouth upturned. "Don't shoot. The others left for Bowyd, and I wanted to make sure you were safe out here. I'll leave if you like."

I lowered my hands and breathed out a laugh. "No, don't. You just startled me is all. Don't leave."

Say it again, Tannie, just in case he didn't hear it the first seventeen times.

My face flushed, and I looked down. But he didn't respond right away, so I did say it again. "Don't leave, Mor."

"All right. I won't."

I dared a glance. He was leaning against the boulder beside me, looking into the forest. He seemed deep in thought.

"Care to share?" I asked.

"Huh?" He turned to me. "Oh. I don't know. I'm just . . ." He looked away again. "I'm sorry about Brac."

I swallowed. "Aye. I am too. I don't understand how he got mixed up in all this."

"You will get the chance to ask him someday." He said it surely, as if there were no doubt.

But of course there was doubt. We were floating down a river of doubt at the moment, and nothing was sure. Not tomorrow, and certainly not *someday*.

"I have a feeling this is much bigger than he is," Mor said. "I don't mean to minimize Brac, only that—"

"Please, make him as small as you like." Betrayal simmered hot in my gut.

"Tannie." Mor frowned at me, like he disapproved.

"Don't defend him. Don't defend that sunbaked sack of rocks that got Ifmere killed and Braith kidnapped and Urian thrown into chaos."

Mor hesitated. "I just think there is a good chance he didn't know what would happen. That someone has used him terribly."

I wouldn't allow the possibility to take root. The risk of hope cut too deep.

Because if I hoped Brac had not been as guilty as he looked and it turned out he *had* known exactly what he was doing and who would be hurt, I didn't think I could bear it. I couldn't bear the devastation of that disappointment.

"I hope I never see Brac again."

"Just think about it, Tannie." Mor, gloves on, took my hand. "Maybe not now. But after the hurt fades a little." He squeezed and released my hand.

We stood like that for what felt like a long time. The forest sounds soothed my buzzing mind. I could set aside thoughts of Brac and Braith and the Master and just listen to the wind rattling through the dried-out gold and orange leaves. The last of them would fall soon, and winter would be upon us.

But for now, birdsong still filled the woods, as if the birds called all the forest wildlife to hunker down and prepare for the white days to come.

One bird's twittering caught my notice, and I briefly closed my eyes. It tickled something in my memory.

Ah yes. That was it.

"It sounds like Gryfelle," I said aloud.

"Aye."

He had noticed too.

"It's strange," I said. "She was barely awake most of the time at the end. I knew her longer that way—sick, sleeping, just barely hanging on for us. But I miss her. I only got a handful of conversations with her before she left this world. But she has left a hole in my heart."

"And mine."

Our conversation that night on the ship—the one where we had said we could figure out *us* later—came flooding back. I hadn't had much chance to think about it since then. It seemed we were always running for our lives.

"There might not be a later for us," I said quietly.

I didn't need to say anything else since I knew he remembered our conversation as well as I did—that he had maybe been thinking of it in this moment too.

"Aye."

"There might never be a later where we can figure everything out—where we can figure out if there's a place for us to be happy, even after what happened with Gryfelle. And Brac. I don't know if there's a way to climb out from under the shadow of that." I brushed away a few tears.

"I don't know either, Tannie."

"Will this be our life forever, Mor?" I faced him. "Will we always be on the run, our lives in danger? Chasing cures and queens and quests?"

Mor was quiet. He wanted to assure me that this wouldn't be our life forever. That we would find a slice of peace and a little bit of space to decide what we wanted. I could see it on his face—the struggle of wanting to say it but knowing it wasn't true.

"Sometimes there is war and strife for a person's whole life," I said for him.

"Aye. Some lives are filled with unrest and there never is a tomorrow."

The tears fell a little harder now—frustrated, exhausted. And in that moment, I allowed myself to set Braith aside. To imagine that the quest to save her was fruitless. That she was already dead, and even if she weren't, we were up against too many enemies to overcome them all. And that maybe it wasn't our job to find her.

I even allowed myself to imagine that Brac and his allies, whoever they were, would run Tir at least as well as Gareth had. That life would go on. People would return to their farms and villages and towns and taverns. That crops would grow and taxes would be paid. Ships might even sail, and stories would be told and sold.

"We could stay here," I said with difficulty. "We could stay in the Corsyth and be safe."

"We could have all the tomorrows we wanted here." He took my face in his bare hands—no gloves. He had taken them off and I hadn't noticed. His fingers heated and began to glow. Then he leaned forward.

I lost myself in his blue eyes, so like the crystalline waters along the Meridioni shore.

He paused for a heartbeat—hesitating.

I didn't wait. I stood on my tiptoes and closed the space between us.

Our lips met, and a cyclone of multicolored light encircled us. I closed my eyes, but I could still feel the rainbow beams swirl around us, lifting my hair and ruffling my blouse.

I resisted the urge to wrap my arms around Mor's neck. I wasn't entirely sure what would happen if I did, and I wasn't keen on the idea of an explosion of rainbow shooting into the sky just now. I didn't want to give away the location of the Corsyth.

And I didn't want to have to explain it to my father.

As if my thought made him appear, suddenly I heard my father's voice. "Tannie?"

"Mor?" That shout had come from Warmil.

Mor and I broke away from each other. He looked as flushed as I felt, and to my horror, the beams of light lingered around us, even though the connection was broken.

Mor pulled his gloves back onto his hands just as Warmil and Father appeared around the boulder.

Father scanned the scene, taking in the strands of light and our mortified faces. He was pale.

I hoped not from anger.

But in the next moment, I knew for sure it was not anger or embarrassment that had caused the blood to drain from Father's face. He held a piece of parchment, and as soon as I caught sight of it, he thrust it into my hands.

CHAPTER SEVENTEEN
BRAITH

"And again."

At Frenhin's command, a guard balled his fist and delivered another blow to Kharn's face.

Braith shut her eyes. But it did not block out Kharn's groans, and it did nothing to ease the ache when Frenhin's voice sounded again. "Another."

Braith squeezed her eyes tighter. "Please!" she begged. "Enough. You're going to kill him!"

The dull *thud* of another punch.

"Please stop."

Silence wrapped the room, and Braith dared to open her eyes. Frenhin was holding one hand up, stilling the guards. She regarded Braith, amusement twinkling in her eyes.

"Surely there is some sort of agreement we might strike." Kharn's voice, faint but solid.

Braith turned to him. Kharn was dragging himself to a seated position, wiping blood from his forehead onto the shoulder of his filthy shirt.

"Ah. He speaks." Frenhin arched an eyebrow. "Tell me, blood heir—what makes you so sure there is a deal to strike?"

Kharn shifted and winced. "Braith is Queen of Tir. I am blood heir to the throne, last of Caradoc's line. Whatever you asked for, we would be able to get it."

Frenhin pursed her lips, considering. "It's not entirely

untrue. You do hold a certain amount of power. Or did, some days past."

Braith studied Kharn's face. She knew him well enough to know that this must be a play. He would not hand anything of import over to Frenhin, even if it cost him his life to resist her.

But what might he give if he thought it would save Braith? Leverage.

"What could you offer, blood heir?" Frenhin took her seat—the chair stayed in the room at all times now, as though Frenhin held court in this cavern. She looked down at Kharn. "What could you possibly give me that I might want?"

"You want control. So we could give you an important council seat. A title."

"And would it be better than *Queen of the Tirian Empire*?" Frenhin pointed a long finger at Braith. "She made sure to strip me of that title."

It wasn't completely true, and it certainly wasn't fair. But there was no use arguing the point. Not with a woman who kept a list of enemies and crossed them off as she murdered them.

"No," Kharn said carefully. "We could not offer you the title of queen. But how did you use it when you had it? You were always in the shadows, exerting your power behind closed doors. Hidden and in secret."

Frenhin's eyes lit.

Kharn had found a weakness—Frenhin's pride.

"That is true, blood heir," she said, pursing her lips. "There would be something rather glorious about having a political career in the open. I engineered Gareth's rule—built his empire with my own two hands—and it was the men who took the glory. Gareth, the heroic conqueror. Dray Bo-Anffir, the great strategist. Naith Bo-Offriad, the faithful spiritual guide." She laughed. "It was all me. Always me."

Braith held back the words that sprang to mind. If she knew Dray at all, he was at least half as good a strategist as her mother.

A thought struck her. "Did he work with you?"

"Who?"

"Dray Bo-Anffir."

A flicker of cruelty crossed Frenhin's face. "You sound . . . disappointed."

Braith could see in her periphery that Kharn was looking at her, but she didn't care. Her relationship with Dray had never been romantic, whatever he had tried to make of it.

But the possibility that he'd worked with her mother did stir something in her—something akin to disappointment, tinged with disgust. She had thought Dray was changing, and maybe he was. But just how far into darkness had he descended before that change began?

She allowed a long moment to pass. "I suppose I am disappointed."

"Why?" Frenhin tilted her head to the side. "You saw how he grabbed for the throne—grabbed for *you*. You knew how he was."

Even in the distance, Braith could see Kharn's muscles tense.

"Yes, I knew how he was," Braith conceded. "But I thought . . ."

"You thought he had changed," Frenhin supplied. "Well, darling, you're certainly not the first foolish woman to be taken in with the idea that men can change. I doubt you will be the last."

"It was not like that," Braith said, more for Kharn than her mother. "I was concerned more for his soul than anything."

"Of course you were." Frenhin sighed. "Dray was a useful, though unpredictable, pawn. One might think, with his levelheaded manner and cool temperament, that he would not have caused such trouble. But, oh, he did."

"Did he?" It gave Braith strange satisfaction to imagine Dray bringing trouble to her mother's plans.

"I did not appreciate his little grab for the throne. He didn't consult me on that play."

Braith thought about this for a moment. "But he didn't know you could see his every move. If he did not know your true identity, he would assume he could act somewhat secretly in the palace and the Master would not know about it. He didn't realize you were there the whole time."

"I told you my plans were brilliant. It was all by design." Frenhin paused. "Dray was unpredictable and troublesome because he was never truly loyal to me. He was loyal to his own desires, and those desires shift often, believe me. When our desires aligned, he was a perfect ally. When they did not, he was a nuisance."

"I'm honestly surprised you were not the one to orchestrate the failed attempt to marry me off to him," Braith mused.

"That was all his own doing, my dear." She looked at Kharn. "But you found a preferable option. Preferable for us all, actually. Because this one has somehow won your heart, and Dray would never have managed that, no matter how reformed he became. Yes, this is very much my preference."

Because to Frenhin, love was just one more weakness to exploit.

Frenhin clapped and rose. "Enough of that. Forgive me, blood heir, but I'm afraid our negotiations have come to an end. There is nothing you could grant me. When I execute the final phase of my plan, I will be queen again. I will have more than what you offer me now. Besides, everything you have to give is temporal. Fleeting. Less than what I seek."

"Which is?"

"I've told you. Ultimate power. Not the kind that can be gained on a council seat. I have my sights set on something that is . . . not of this world."

Something supernatural. Power that could not be touched by

the sort of forces Braith or any other earthly ruler might have access to. What might Frenhin do with such power?

Kharn spoke up again. "And what makes you so sure these weavers will join you?"

"Oh, it is startlingly simple. I will offer them what I seek—what all men seek. I will offer them power."

"But they are the ones with the power here," Braith protested. "They have what you need, not the other way around. You want to use their gifts. *You* need *them*."

"I don't expect you to be able to understand this, Braith. You are not, much to my disappointment, a weaver. You don't understand what it feels like to have that sort of magic running through your veins. It's heady. Addictive, one might say."

"They don't need you in order to use their gifts."

"No, but I'm offering them something greater than the version of their gifts they have previously known."

Apprehension gripped Braith.

"I will offer them magic deeper and more powerful than they could have imagined a few moons ago." Frenhin inhaled deeply, as if she were drawing in the power. "They have had a taste of it now. That their little seaward quest involved hunting such magic works to my advantage. Now they will understand that what I offer them is real, for they have seen and tasted it themselves."

"What magic do you mean?" Braith asked guardedly.

"Oh, it's a power more ancient and sacred than anyone has a right to touch. But that has not stopped me before."

She glided over to Braith and stooped so they were at eye level. "What you cannot understand, darling, is that weavers are born with their gifts, and we are compelled to use them. That is why Dray's plan to suppress the arts for your father's sake failed. It brought an ancient curse upon the weavers who tried to obey the law. I knew it was a possibility but did not see much alternative at the time. Art reveals truth, you know, and we needed to quash truth just then. It was an interesting experiment, that ban."

Braith's mind went to the sick girl—the one her friends had traveled around the world to save. Gryfelle En-Blaid. An experiment? The destruction of life was an experiment to this woman.

"Interesting but unsuccessful," Frenhin continued, "because weavers must weave. We must not only use our gifts but nurture them. Stoke them from tiny, inborn flames to wildfires beyond imagining. I will offer the most useful of your weaver friends the fuel to feed their wildfires."

"The most useful?" Braith regarded her mother with dread. "What do you mean?"

"I do not plan to use them all. There are three I want, in particular. They have shown certain . . . promise. I would like to help them grow into that potential."

"How?" Braith whispered hoarsely. "How will you offer them ancient magic and fuel this wildfire?"

Frenhin snapped her fingers to call one of her soldiers. "Bring me the prisoner." She smiled at Braith and Kharn apologetically. "The other one, I mean."

A few moments passed, and the soldier reappeared, dragging a man beside him. The man was old, and Braith did not recognize him. He wore the draped garment of a Meridioni senator, or perhaps an *atenne* scholar. Shackles bound his wrists and ankles, and he stumbled as he walked.

The soldier shoved him to the ground before Frenhin. She kicked him. "Don't be rude. Introduce yourself."

The man lifted his head and smiled through the many bruises on his face. "It is an honor, Queen Braith."

Frenhin kicked him again, and he collapsed to the stone floor.

"Stop it!" Braith cried. She bent down as best as she was able to look the old man in the eyes. "What is your name, sir?"

"M-Master Insegno, Your Majesty." He coughed, a trickle of blood on his lips. "At your service."

CHAPTER EIGHTEEN
TANWEN

I LOOKED AT THE PARCHMENT IN MY HANDS, FULLY EXPECTING to see what I had the last time someone brought such a piece from Bowyd: a wanted poster with my face, or perhaps the faces of some of the other weavers. Something else to put a big fat target on all our backs and make our quest to rescue Braith—or else our dream of a simple life hidden here in the Corsyth—all the harder.

But it wasn't that at all.

I stared down at it. "I don't understand."

"It's an advertisement," Warmil said.

Thanks for the help, War. "I can see that. But . . . an advertisement for a *Story Hunt*. What's a Story Hunt?"

I turned to Mor first, then to Father, then to Warmil. They all looked grave as they studied the flier, and I didn't understand why this was such serious news.

Or why it concerned us at all, except that we had some storytellers among us.

"Tannie," Father said, pushing the advertisement closer, "read it."

"'Story Hunt,'" I read aloud. "'Looking for an adventure? Join us! Wealthy benefactor seeking brave, talented crews to join the Hunt. The first team to recover at least three of the missing treasures will be handsomely rewarded. Details below.'"

I scanned the parchment. "It's strange, to be sure. But—" I stopped short as my eyes landed on one phrase.

Buried strands.

I backed up. Tried to understand what I was reading. Some "wealthy benefactor" was calling for teams of adventurers to retrieve three buried strands. And promising huge rewards in return.

"A thousand gold pieces?" I spluttered. "Stars, who has that kind of coin in the first place?"

"A wealthy benefactor, it would seem." Father's tone was somber. "Tannie, look at the team requirements."

I skipped ahead. "'Each team should have those with combat experience. Mining experience a plus.' Mining?" I raised an eyebrow at Mor, who was reading over my shoulder.

He pointed. "Look."

"'Each team must have at least one storyteller to call forth the buried strands.'"

Memories flashed through my mind—our quest around the world to find and retrieve the cure strands, pulling them up from various rock monuments in Meridione, Haribi, Minasimet, and Kanac. How we had to use a variety of weaver gifts to beckon the strands from their ancient hiding places.

I lowered the parchment. "They . . . they are searching for ancient strands."

Father nodded. "Aye."

"At least three of them. And only a storyteller can pull them out."

"Aye."

"If this person—this benefactor—knows how to pull out the strands they're after, it means they already have at least one," I said. "And that the others they want are identical. We were always guessing at how we would be calling up our next strand for the cure."

"Not guessing," Mor reminded me. "Dylun knew how to get each of them."

Yes. My memory sharpened at the reminder. "Because he had researched the ancient texts. Of course. With Master Insegno." Some of the memories I had lost to the curse and reclaimed through the cure were fuzzy around the edges.

"So," I asked slowly, "are we saying there's someone out there who not only knows about these incredibly powerful ancient strand artifacts but who also knows where some of the strands to build one might be buried?"

"It looks that way," Father answered.

"And they're trying to build the artifact, just like we tried to build the cure." I frowned. "But why 'at least three'? If they want to build an artifact, they'll need all the strands."

I thought of the cure strands curled in the box, awaiting their fellows, while we hunted each in turn. The strands wouldn't form an artifact unless they were all brought together.

"Maybe they don't realize that?" Warmil suggested.

An unwelcome voice cut in. "Not possible."

I whirled to find Dray standing behind me. When had he slithered around the boulder? I would have to remember that he was quiet as a fluff-hopper when he wanted to be.

"What do you mean?" I asked sharply.

I tried to gain control of my tone. Dray knew things we didn't. If we wanted to make the best use of this uneasy alliance, I should at least try to be nicer to him.

I fought for a smile and arrived somewhere south of a grimace. "How do you know it's not possible?"

"This is the Master." He nodded to the parchment advertisement. "I'm sure of it."

Father took a step toward Dray, and it looked like a threat. "How are you sure? Tell us what you know."

Dray didn't look ruffled—at least not on the surface. But he took a small step back. "Because the Master is a weaver." His gaze shifted between us. "You . . . didn't realize this already?"

And then, of course, when he said it like that, all the pieces of the puzzle snapped together. The force behind the dark strands that had chased us all through the autumn—the one that created the strands of fire and smoke and night and death that had sunk our ship and murdered Wylie and maimed Aeron and killed Gryfelle. Of course it was a weaver. And Dray had erased the last question mark, confirmed it for sure: the person staging the coups and chasing us with clouds of strands across the world were one and the same.

The Master.

But something about this verification made my stomach roil. It seemed we were constantly battling attacks from four sides at once. The thought that one person was powerful enough to orchestrate it all was unsettling.

Dray seemed to be biting down on a smile. "You mentioned being chased by some dark strands. I've been telling you there is a dark force behind all the troublesome happenings in Tir. I guess I thought you would have connected these things and recognized your own gifts in the Master's tactics." He cast a condescending glance at Father. "That you might, at least."

Father glared. "I always have my theories. But the confirmation is helpful. Thank you."

Dray bowed. "I live to serve."

Mor took the parchment and shoved it at Dray. "Tell us what this is."

He read it carefully, then handed it back. "It looks like the Master wants ancient strands for some reason."

"Helpful." Warmil rolled his eyes. "What would that reason be?"

Dray shrugged. "What are the uses of the ancient strands? You would know better than I."

I tried to recall everything I'd heard about them. "We know

they are used to build artifacts. Cures and other objects with strong powers. We should ask Dylun." I hesitated. "Or send a message to Master Insegno? He would know best."

"Oh, so that's what is in that box the Meridioni was burying a few moments ago." Dray grinned. "I told you I didn't care, but that doesn't mean I'm blind."

Would it be bad form to shoot fire strands at this man? He was technically our ally, but surely it wouldn't have been the worst thing I'd ever done.

"We know the strands are very powerful," Father ventured carefully, avoiding Dray's mention of the cure we had built.

Dray leveled his gaze at us. "Then you should be very concerned that the Master wants them."

I thought back to Father's epiphany on ship—that the force chasing us wanted to capture me and Mor and turn us into a weapon. The strands of this story were coming together with sickening clarity.

"Dray . . . do you think the Master might want something more than the strands themselves?" I asked. "Do you think he could be after the storytellers pulling them up?"

He took the parchment from Warmil once more. "It says three strands. That's rather specific. But it appears to be a wide call out to anyone who might respond. The Master is more exacting than that when choosing pawns and allies. I have no direct knowledge of this plan, mind you, but my guess is the Master actually wants strands. And when the strands are delivered, the teams are likely to be disposed of."

"Killed?" My voice came out as a squeak. But truthfully, I preferred that to the casual way Dray spoke of Creator knew how many people being murdered.

"I don't see any benefit to softening this truth for you," Dray said. "The Master will have no problem disposing of any person who poses threat, obstacle, or annoyance. As long as doing so doesn't create a larger threat, obstacle, or annoyance.

You should all begin to think of your lives in this way. If you don't, you will never survive an encounter with the Master."

"I'm sure you survived many." Father's tone was terse.

"And that makes me useful to you." Dray pointed to the bottom of the advertisement. "I don't suppose there's any harm in telling you now. This is where I've been taking you."

I looked at the sentence and read it aloud for the others. "Teams will report to the huntmaster in Ir-Golyth." My eyes widened. "In the Highlands?" I looked at Father. "That's in the Highlands, isn't it?"

"Aye," he answered wearily. "And we've scarcely a moon before winter begins."

"Sorry to inform you," Dray said, not sounding sorry at all, "but I believe the Master will have taken Braith to a particular point near Ir-Golyth."

Another strand of the story crystallized.

And the dream of a safe, quiet life tucked away in the Corsyth with tomorrows stretching before me and Mor and the others shattered.

Because, of course, we would go to Ir-Golyth. Or the highest peak in the Highlands. Or to the stars, if we had to. Whatever this Master was playing at, it was bigger than our lives. Bigger than our personal happiness. To use that ancient magic we had just barely brushed against for anything resembling evil was . . .

I couldn't even imagine. It would spell disaster for Tir, disaster for everyone we had ever loved who was still alive.

And disaster for Braith, if she endured still.

We had to try. Even if it was a lost cause, we would *always* try.

Father's hand twitched near the hilt of his sword, and Dray held up his hands. "Now, now, General. None of that. You only know where to go in the vaguest sense of the word. If you have any hope of getting close enough to the Master to rescue Braith, you still need me."

Father's jaw tensed, but his hand relaxed.

Dray smiled and turned to me. "Unless you don't care to rescue Braith. And if that's the case, by all means, let that fool sit on the throne all you like."

CHAPTER NINETEEN
BRAC

I STARED DOWN AT A BUNCH OF PAPERS—DOCUMENTS, NAITH called them—and they might as well have been written in Minasimetese for all I could read them.

"My son. Your thoughts?"

What was I supposed to say, exactly? He knew I couldn't read. "Your Holiness, it ain't gonna make more sense to me the longer and harder I stare at it. I told you, I can't read the words."

Two of my aides, seated on the other side of the table, looked at each other, and I could see what passed between them, plain as pickles.

What a fool.

Stupid farm boy from Pembrone.

What kind of watta-root-for-brains have we appointed steward?

But Bo-Fergel, the aide sitting next to me, leaned over and picked up the paper on top of the stack. "Shall we work through it together, then, my lord?"

Naith sighed.

I scowled at him, in spite of myself. "Apologies, Your Holiness. Did you have more important business tugging your tail?"

His gaze turned sharp, but he didn't dare rebuke me. Not in front of the others. He would wait for later, I knew. He would wait until we were alone, and then he would scold me and tell me he was only there to help and that he only had my best interests—and the best interests of the people—in mind.

I'd heard it a hundred times before, and I was right sick of the refrain.

But now, in front of the aides seated around the old council table with us, he plastered on a pleasant smile. "Forgive me, my lord. I confess my heart is not here at the table this afternoon."

I glanced at the aides. "Give us the room for a moment, will you?"

Bo-Fergel rose. "We will order something from the kitchens, then return. Perhaps refreshment will help revive us all. Tea, my lord?" He inclined his head to Naith. "Your Holiness?"

"Fine, fine." Naith waved his hand.

The aides went out, and Naith and I were alone.

The pleasant smile dropped from his face. "You can't behave that way in front of the others, Steward. It doesn't present the correct image. Those around us must see your regime as seamless and unified. It must look altogether different from the messy politics the people remember under the royals."

"But it isn't different, is it?" I looked down at the papers. "We have all the same problems."

"Well, you're running a kingdom."

"Am I?" I slapped the stack of documents. "How, exactly? I only got into all this mess because I thought I could help people. But I haven't even been able to make bread for them to eat lately." I held my hands in front of my face and wiggled my fingers. "It's like the power is gone, and I don't know where it went."

"You have freed the people from Braith's rule, and that was help enough."

As soon as the words left his mouth, I could see Naith knew it had been the wrong thing to say to me.

I rose from my chair. "You know I don't hold nothin' against the queen. Or *former* queen," I said before he could correct me. "And I don't know what you have against her neither." I plunked back into my seat. "Nothing makes sense anymore. I just . . . wanted to help people."

"Son. May I remind you why you joined this cause? As I recall, you weren't so concerned with helping people as you remember."

Shame ate at me like a root-snacker on a watta.

Because he was right, of course. I hadn't been interested in helping people. Not at first. He had to talk me into all that *chosen one* nonsense. Blazes, I didn't even really believe in the goddesses.

No, that wasn't what had pulled me into this mess. It was because I was jealous—jealous of Tannie and her pirate. Jealous and brokenhearted and despairing. She had left me for him, no matter what she said.

Her words pricked me like a thousand briars.

She said she'd been sick. If she had been sick, she would have told me sooner. *Wouldn't she?*

I tried to shove memories to the corners of my mind—memories that had been bothering me since Tannie and her friends burst in here like a spate of blight three days past.

Ever since she'd said it, new remembrances had been creeping up. Like little hedge-nibblers, their heads popping up in the middle of the garden at the worst times. The memories poked out, and I tried to smash them down.

But they wouldn't stay down, those memories. Those moments when I thought maybe Tannie had been trying to tell me something. Maybe she did try to tell what was going on and I hadn't been able to listen.

Or willing. I hadn't been willing to listen.

I closed my eyes and rubbed my temples. "Whatever the reason, we're here now." I opened my eyes and looked up at Naith. "And what good are we doing, exactly? This ain't . . . well, this ain't how I pictured it would be."

Naith lowered himself into his velvet-padded chair—extra cushioning for His Holiness's backside. He seemed to like rich things an awful lot for someone who was supposed to live a life dedicated to the goddesses.

"Brac," he said more patiently, "we will help the people. We *are* helping the people. But I confess . . ." He turned and looked toward one of the high windows on the north wall. "I confess I grow weary of government work."

I tried to stop my jaw from falling. "Weary?" I looked at the mess of papers again. "I can't afford for you to be weary. We only been here a week!"

"I long to return to the Master." He was still staring out the window with a faraway look.

"You . . . you what?"

He started and came back to himself. "My masters, the goddesses. I miss my work at the temple."

But his ears tinged pink, and then the flush spilled all over his face and his bald head.

I eyed him. "Well," I began slowly, "the way I see it, the city is worse than ever. I can't seem to make bread anymore, and the people will begin to go hungry before long. Maybe we could just undo it all? Just take back what we've done?"

I knew it sounded doltish. And I knew this was why people thought me simple. And maybe I was simple. To even suggest we might just erase all this was woefully simple.

But I wasn't as dumb as all that. I knew we would have to pay for it. Even if we were somehow able to undo things, we wouldn't be able to walk away, easy as you like, and go back to whatever our lives had been before.

I understood that. And still . . . I wanted to undo it all, restore Braith, and let her see to the business of running the kingdom. She was built for it and I wasn't. It didn't take a whole hour on the throne, let alone a whole week, for me to see that.

Naith snorted. "Take it back? No. We cannot and we will not take it back."

I gathered what courage I had. "Well, even so, maybe I don't want to do this anymore."

"You no longer have a choice." Naith's mouth curved as if it was filled with sting-tail venom. "Son."

Just then, Bo-Fergel returned, carrying a tray with tea and cakes. He hesitated as he drew near, almost as though he could feel the ill will between me and the high priest. "Refreshments, my lord. Your Holiness?"

"None for me." Naith moved toward the door. He paused and caught my eye. "I shall consult with the goddesses about your—ah—feelings. We will see what's to be done."

I gave half a stiff nod as he swept from the room.

Bo-Fergel set the tray on the table. "The others will be along in a bit. They decided to take a stroll and get some fresh air."

"Fresh air sounds nice. I miss it."

He smiled a little.

"I used to be a farmer," I said, although he already knew that. "Then I was in the guard. Got plenty of air and sunshine doing both those things."

"Yes, I suppose you would, my lord."

"Ugh." I grimaced. "When the others ain't around, can you just call me Brac? *My lord* was fun for a few days. It's starting to poke my ears like prickle-back quills."

He smiled again in that tight, thoughtful way he had. "If the others aren't around, I will submit to that."

I knew a little of his background—he was the son of one of the royal library keepers under King Caradoc and Gareth. He had to be older than me by five or ten years, but not much more. He was kind and serious, steady and clearheaded.

And, more than anyone else in my life at the moment, I felt I could trust him.

Though it was just a feeling in my gut, and stars knew my gut had been wrong more than once.

Still. I needed someone to talk to.

"Bo-Fergel?"

He paused in the middle of pouring hot water. "Yes?"

"What's your given name?"

"Hysgrifenyddion."

"Sakes."

Bo-Fergel chuckled. "My friends call me Eny. You may, too, if you like."

"Eny, you ever feel like maybe you accidentally jumped off a cliff?"

CHAPTER TWENTY
BRAITH

Braith looked up sharply from the bruised, bleeding Meridioni to her mother. "What have you done to this man?"

Frenhin gave a delicate shrug. "Only . . . interviewed him."

"With your fists, apparently," Kharn muttered.

Frenhin smiled. "I do whatever is required, blood heir. I understand how that might make someone as weak-willed as you uncomfortable."

Braith took in the pitiful old man before her, and her heart twisted. "Why have you *interviewed* him? If that is what you wish to call it."

"Oh, I have your weaver friends to thank for this gem of a man." Frenhin bent and caressed the man's face as though stroking a beloved pet. "He has been most useful."

"Forgive me, Your Majesty," he croaked to Braith. "She abuses her gift in the most shocking ways. She used her strands to pull things from me."

"You see, blood heir?" Frenhin said to Kharn. "I did not lay a hand on him. My strands did all the work for me."

"Your strands and your guards, I wager," Kharn shot back.

"Trifles."

"Sir," Braith asked the man kindly, "what did you say your name was?"

"Insegno, Your Majesty. Master Insegno."

"He was the tutor of the Meridioni colormaster," Frenhin

said. "They led me straight to him. Bordino was the first stop on their quest, and it was all so the Meridioni could catch up with his old teacher."

Insegno shook his head. "You listened to conversations you had no right to."

Frenhin moved to kick him.

"Stop it!" Braith demanded. "Do not hurt him again."

Frenhin regarded her. "Or else what? It is truly incredible you do not recognize you are in no position to barter, my dear. Always the princess, aren't you?"

Braith met her mother's eyes. "Do not hurt him again, or else you might kill him. He is old, and you have abused him enough already. If you kill him, you cannot use him."

Frenhin moved away from Insegno. She sat back in her chair and laughed. "It pains you to set aside principle and appeal to my basest desires. To beg for a man's life on the basis of his usefulness."

Braith did not dignify that with a response. Of course she hated to reduce any human being to a game piece.

But this woman standing before her could not be appealed to on any other basis.

Frenhin shrugged. "Whatever works, right, darling?" She produced a small fireball in one of her palms and began to bounce it up and down. "In any case, without Insegno, I would not have learned all I needed to know for the next phase of my plan."

"And which phase is this?" Braith asked. "I've lost track."

Frenhin's eyes narrowed, and the fireball stilled. "Don't get haughty. You are here to listen and to watch. If you refuse to do these things, you are no longer entertaining and I will dispose of you." She glanced at Kharn. "And him. So I suggest you mind your tongue."

Braith pressed her lips together.

"I had sought the storyteller girl—Yestin's daughter—because she was young and impressionable. Ambitious, too, and I can use all of these things. There is also a certain amount of talent that is inborn for a weaver. There are some things you can't teach. She has them in spades. I wanted her from the moment I saw her crystallize a story.

"When that farm boy begged your father for her life and insisted she was truly loyal to Gareth, not to be counted among the rebels, it was easy enough to convince the king to keep her instead of executing her. I thought, perhaps, I might one day make her like a daughter to me."

She looked at Braith expectantly.

"Mother," Braith began, the word like acid in her mouth, "I have always known I was a disappointment. And we were never close. I used to wish I was not beneath your notice. Now I understand why I was, and I count it as a credit."

"Fair enough, I suppose." Frenhin resumed playing with her fireball, directing it as it swirled through the air before her in lazy circles. "I thought Tanwen might be a better fit for my plans."

"Then you have misread her."

"Possibly. I lost the opportunity to find out." She glared at Braith. "I have no trouble delaying satisfaction, my dear. I was married to your father for fifteen years before he became king. I am a patient woman. One step at a time, I execute my plans. It would have been the same with the storyteller. I would have worked on her slowly, and then I would have had someone to—"

Frenhin's voice cut off. She turned toward her fireball, and Braith could see emotion swimming in her eyes for a long moment.

Then Frenhin composed herself. "I would have had someone to take over when I'm gone. At my age, one must think of such things, and you certainly would not continue my work. Don't you see? This has grown bigger than mere revenge. I have built something. Something worth preserving. I wanted to pass it down to someone. I still do."

Kharn shook his head. "You're mad."

"Perhaps." Frenhin shrugged. "But Braith stole that chance from me with her betrayal."

Braith did not bother pointing out it was actually Tanwen and the other weavers who conquered Gareth, not she.

"So I thought to simply steal the girl. Force her into my service. Or perhaps slowly work on her from afar, though I did not have the power or resources of a queen any longer. But then, to my dismay, she jumped aboard that ship with the others."

Yes, Braith had received word of this from Yestin. When Tanwen did not return after seeing off the ship from Physgot, Braith had assumed at first that she had chosen to return home to Pembrone—back to her family cottage to await the return of her friends. The girl had not been entirely happy in the palace.

But then Yestin had sent news from Bordino that Tanwen was afflicted with the weavers' curse and in need of assistance. Braith had been concerned for her young friend, of course, but Tanwen was in her father's capable hands. If a cure was attainable, Yestin would find it for his daughter.

"It was a good thing she did jump aboard," Frenhin remarked. "Or else I would not have followed the weavers quite as closely as I did. I would not have heard all I needed to know."

"How could you have followed them?" Braith frowned. "Surely they would have noticed the former queen sneaking around Meridione."

Frenhin sighed. "This is why we can't communicate about anything, darling. You always have your sights set on the temporal, whereas I exist in the supernatural. That is my dominion, and you know nothing of it."

"What you have done is dangerous." Insegno pulled himself to a seated position. "You have twisted your gift and misused power that does not belong to you. You meddle in the supernatural, but you do not understand or respect it."

Frenhin leaned forward and slapped him across the face. "Silence!"

She took a moment then—regained her composure and her malicious smile. And Braith realized something. Her mother did not like those occasions when her emotions took over. She did not like it when she was out of control.

Interesting.

"I did not literally follow them," Frenhin continued. "One of my strands did."

"One of your . . ." Braith blinked. "What?"

"I told you I play a long game. I have been honing my skills for a great many years. My strands can do things you can't even imagine."

Kharn stared at the fireball hovering above Frenhin's left hand. "I might believe it."

Insegno held his palm to the cheek Frenhin had slapped. "You are not honing *your* skills. You are using power that does not belong to you. You will pay dearly for your transgressions. Turn away before it is too late."

Frenhin kept her composure this time. "Or else what, old man? What do you think you can possibly do to me?"

"Not I," Insegno said. "Do you think these ancient strands appeared from nowhere? Do you think the weaver gifts have no origin? They merely reflect the Source. I tried to tell you." He shook his head. "I tried to tell you."

"I have not experienced any consequences like you describe." Frenhin ran the fireball across her fingers. "So, I appreciate the effort, but you will not frighten me into submission."

"I tried to tell you," the old man said again. "Your destruction, however it comes, will belong to you and you alone."

A shadow of fear eclipsed Frenhin's face. But only for a breath. She turned back to Braith. "Yes, I suppose they might have noticed the former queen skulking through Bordini alleyways. But they did not notice my invisible strands trailing them, transmitting sound back to me."

"You can just throw a strand after someone and hear whatever they say?" Braith asked in disbelief. If it were so, would anyone be able to mount a plan to stop Frenhin? She could listen to any conversation she wished, overhear any plan to take her down.

"Oh, it's not as simple as all that. It's safe to say I'm the most powerful weaver in history—right, Meridioni?—but even I have limits."

Master Insegno did not respond to her question, but Frenhin did not seem to care.

She forged on. "The closer I am to the strands, the better I can hear. I had to launch a ship from the Eastern Peninsula quickly to stay within range of the rebels. To hear in Bordino from Physgot or some other peninsular town would have stretched me too thin. At least, without someone with whom I had a strong connection. In any case, I had other strands working for me elsewhere at the time." She flashed a twisted smile. "I am only one person, after all."

Braith tried to keep her tone even. "What special knowledge did you gain that you had not yet possessed? It seems you have been at your business for a very long time. What did Insegno have to teach you?"

"Do you want to tell them, Meridioni, or shall I?"

Insegno looked at Braith. "Forgive me, Your Majesty. I did not wish to tell her anything at all."

"I understand," Braith assured him. "Do not trouble over that just now. This is not your fault."

Insegno's head was bowed. "I helped my former student—you call him Dylun—complete his map and his plan to rebuild an ancient cure to save his two friends. One was too far gone.

That was plain to everyone except those who loved her. Such is often the case, isn't it?"

Braith smiled sadly. "It is, indeed."

"But there was hope for the other *ragizzi*. I taught them about the ancient weavers—how the weaver gifts had been more powerful in days past, how the gifts had been exploited, and why the artifacts needed to be broken apart and their strands hidden. I warned them to be careful. This is power from the Source, and one does not interfere with such things lightly." He glanced at Frenhin. "At least, not if one is wise."

Frenhin flicked her fireball toward Insegno. It hit the floor just beside his filthy garment.

He flinched. "I have tried to warn—"

"Anyway," Frenhin cut him off, "as they began to follow their map and as they drew that first ancient strand out of the rock monument, I recognized the feel of it."

Braith's brows rose. "You recognized the feel of it?"

"I was surprised when they said it was vivid blue. Not quite the same strand after all. And the others were not right either. Gold, purple, and red. But the unseen waves that pulsated from those strands reached me, even at my distance. I knew I had felt that power before. I knew I *had* that power."

Braith fought to control her voice. "And what power is that?"

"I possess one of these ancient strands, and from it, I draw my strength."

Braith stared.

"You don't believe me?" Frenhin pulled back the edge of her sleeve.

There, wrapped around her forearm, was a white strand so bright it flashed like lightning. Braith blinked against the brilliance.

Frenhin smiled at the strand. "It was an accident, really." She glanced at Insegno. "One might say it was destiny."

He turned his face away.

Frenhin replaced her sleeve, and the light of the strand winked out. "Many years ago, before I was queen, in the early days of the plan, I had this place, the Craigyl, carved out for me. I needed a retreat. Somewhere I could go to practice my weaver skills and not be seen. Somewhere to meet with those loyal to me. Somewhere to be alone and think. So I had a fortress built into a mountainside."

Braith scanned the carved stone of deepest gray. "Where in Tir are we?"

"I don't suppose there is harm in telling you. You are inside a mountain in the Mynyth Range."

"The Highlands?"

Even her father had always held a healthy fear of the Highlands. Highlanders were perhaps the toughest of all Tirians, bred in harsh conditions, cut off from the rest of the country unless they ventured south to trade pelts. And besides, mountainbeasts dwelt among the cliffs. And in the caves.

Braith shrank into the wall behind her.

But Frenhin did not seem bothered. "Yes, in the Highlands. It was the perfect remote location, I thought at the time. And it turns out my inclination could not have been more fortuitous. As my builders drilled and mined and carved, they stumbled on a curious streak. They said it was like a thick ribbon of white light snaking through the rock. But they could not seem to take hold of it, move it, or do anything with it. It repelled their tools, burned their hands, and thwarted all their attempts to remove it. They called me to investigate.

"I knew immediately it was a strand. Any weaver would have known. And, as I was a weaver and none of them were, it responded to me in a way it did not to them. I was able to coax it from the stone. I took it, and it has been mine ever since."

"It is not yours." Grief edged Insegno's words. "It does not belong to you."

"So you've said. And yet, here we sit. I have used this

strand for twenty years. Manipulating it has enabled me to do things other weavers could only dream of. So if you want me to apologize for my deeds, I will not. I am who I am and I have what I have because of that strand. And now I understand why—I understand how it works in a way I did not before."

Insegno turned back to Braith. "She had seen Dylun's map. She knew where they planned to travel. So she waited until they restocked at Bordino and were on their way to Minasimet before kidnapping me."

"Now, that isn't quite fair, is it?" Frenhin tsked. "I did try very hard to procure some company for you, but those weavers are so slippery."

"You tried to kill Dylun." Insegno's voice trembled. "You tried to murder him in front of me. I watched as you sank their ship."

"Oh, right. I had forgotten about that. As I have told you before, the young scholar is not useful to me. He is a colormaster, and I need storytellers."

"Why?" Braith asked. "Why only storytellers?"

"These strands—the ones buried in the mountainside—must have been created by an ancient storyteller. They will only respond to storyteller commands."

Braith's heart sank. "There are other strands buried in the mountain?"

"Yes." Frenhin patted Insegno's cheek, and he cringed. "This one confirmed what I had suspected since I first became aware of the blue strand in Meridione. I had thought my white strand was unique, you see. But once I knew it was not, I wondered if it, like the blue strand, was part of a greater whole. Turns out it was."

Insegno looked ever-more miserable. "I am sorry, Your Majesty."

"Don't mind him." Frenhin waved a hand. "Let him sulk.

It was he who told me there are eleven others just like mine, hidden in these rocks."

"They were part of a great whole once," Insegno said to Braith, the scholar's eyes lighting just a bit. "Once it was a grand story, the history of this country before it was called Tir. This artifact brought prosperity and peace to the land—prosperity that was promised by the Source, part of a covenant agreement. But the covenant was broken, and this artifact was destroyed, just like the others."

"And truly," Frenhin said, "what difference does it make? I don't care why they exist, only that they do. And that I find them."

"You want to rebuild the artifact?" Braith was puzzled.

"No, no. I'm only after three. At least for the time being."

"Three?" Understanding settled over Braith. "There are three storytellers—Tanwen, Captain Bo-Lidere, and Zelyth, the farmer."

"Very good, dear. And you are correct. That was the plan for a while. Capture the storytellers, kill the rest."

Braith caught her breath.

"Oh really." Frenhin flicked something from her sleeve. "Don't be so easily scandalized, Braith. We must do what is necessary to reach our goals." She spread out her hands. "I had this place built before I had the royal resources at my disposal. Do you think I could have done such a thing if I weren't willing to endure a few losses along the way? Being willing to do what is necessary was a choice I had to make long ago, back in the beginning."

Kharn's utter disdain showed on his face. "What did you do—promise the workers chests of gold you didn't have, then murder them when the work was complete?"

"More or less. But if you try to make me feel remorse over this, you will be wasting your breath. They were frightfully late and tried to charge double what the job was worth. Renovations are just the worst."

Braith shot a glance at Kharn. He clamped his mouth shut, though it looked like it cost him to do so.

She turned again to her mother. "And now your plan has changed. How?"

"The Tanwen girl has fallen in love with your sea captain." Frenhin seemed amused. "And if you wonder about her farmer boy, don't worry. I haven't let that situation go to waste either."

A fuzzy memory of Bo-Bradwir restraining her in the garden came floating back to Braith. "What did you do to Guardsman Bo-Bradwir?"

"A broken heart is easy to exploit. But still, he was a bit stronger-willed than I cared for. In the end, I had to use my strands to manipulate his emotions. Once we finally crossed that bridge, he became a perfect game piece.

"And, by the goddesses, this new little romance has caused Tanwen's gift to link with Bo-Lidere's. They are thrice as powerful together as either could be on their own."

"And so you wish to harness that power." Braith's voice was dull.

"Yes."

"And you will use the ancient strand to make them and their linked gifts ever-more powerful."

"Yes."

"And the third strand? Zelyth shall become a regular evil strand-wielder, I suppose?" Braith's sarcasm was reckless, and she knew it.

"No, actually." Frenhin trailed her fingers through the air, painting fiery designs. "I don't particularly want the farmer anymore." She shrugged. "If someone will deliver a fourth strand to me, then sure. But he is not a primary target any longer."

Braith's eyebrows rose. It was the first thing her mother had said in a while that was unexpected. "Who, then?"

"Oh, darling. Wait until you meet her. She is the most fascinating of them all, and I know now that *she* is the one I've been waiting for. She is the one who will carry on my work." Frenhin's smile sparkled. "Tir will tremble in her hand."

CHAPTER TWENTY-ONE
TANWEN

I STARED AT THE PILE OF TEN MOUNTAINBEAST-PELT CLOAKS Warmil had plunked before me.

"How? How did you find ten mountainbeast cloaks?"

War shrugged. "I know a dealer in Bowyd, and we paid him handsomely."

"Hey," I realized aloud. "I never thought about that before, but how do you afford such things? Or supplies at all? I know you have friends in Bowyd, but surely they haven't footed the bill to keep the Corsyth running all these years out of the kindness of their own hearts. Who could afford to?"

Zel snorted. "No one from our neck of the peninsula, anyway."

That was true enough. "Surely you must have gold somewhere," I said.

Mor grimaced. "Best not to ask where it came from."

Father glanced up from where he was rolling a traveling pack, but he didn't say anything.

Ah.

If I was a gambling lass, I would wager whatever chests of gold lay hidden in the Corsyth had been procured through piracy, and maybe it wasn't the grandest idea to bring that up in front of my father, former First General of Tir.

He didn't fault people for finding ways to survive under the iron fist of Gareth, mind, but something told me the straight-arrow military man would be annoyed by theft of this magnitude.

Mor looked uncomfortable. "We donated a lot to help people," he whispered to me. "Always bought food and things when we could."

Diggy stepped between us, frowning at the furs. "Is it very cold there?" She had been struggling to adjust to the late-autumn weather here by the river. The north would not suit her at all.

Karlith wrapped an arm around Diggy's shoulders and handed her a mug of steaming tea. "Aye, lass. That's why the Creator gave mountainbeasts such pelts."

Diggy shuddered, and I didn't think it was on account of the mountainbeasts.

"It would help if you would wear trousers," Mor pointed out. He held up a small pair that must have been made for a young boy. "Please?"

"But how will I reach my knives in those?"

Dray picked dirt from beneath his fingernails. "Personally, I'm quite comfortable with the idea of you *not* being able to reach your knives." He examined the other hand. He had washed himself, shaved his face, and re-sparkled his teeth as soon as the others had returned with supplies.

"That's because you're afraid I might stab you," Diggy remarked.

I had to bite my lip to hide my laughter. Though in truth, I wasn't sure why I was worried about offending that man. I supposed a farm girl could turn the world upside down, shake everything up until it barely resembled reality anymore, but in the end, she'd still worry about offending the king's councilor.

"So," I said, turning to Dray, "what else can you tell us about this Master of yours?"

"Not exactly mine. Not anymore, and maybe not ever. We had . . . mutual loyalty."

"But only as long as you were mutually beneficial to

each other," Father said, and his voice was cutting. "That's not loyalty."

"I don't suppose it is. But it worked profitably for us for many years."

"How many years?" I asked. Didn't know what might be helpful down the road.

"About eighteen, I guess."

Same age as me. I shuddered when I realized that Dray was probably living in the palace, working with the Master, when I was born there.

Father seemed agitated suddenly, like a swarm of stripe-jackets had descended on him. He hopped up and sheathed a blade at his hip. "We will travel north in the morning. I think it best if we register for the Hunt."

"I agree," Dray said, and I was pretty sure it was the first time they had shared an opinion on anything.

"And if we can actually find the strands," Dylun said, "all the better. I am not keen on the idea of this Master getting hold of any of them."

"Right," I said. "Should be easy. The only thing standing between us and the strands is Creator knows how many mercenaries working for an unknown person of boundless evil. No problem."

"Unless the huntmaster has been told to watch out for us—and that is a possibility, bear in mind—this is our best chance at slipping into the fray unnoticed and rescuing Braith." Father looked at Dray. "You will get us close to the Master."

"Of course."

"I don't know why the Master let us escape from Urian, but I guess we'll find out when we meet him."

"Her," Dray said.

"Excuse me?"

"When we meet *her*."

We all stared at him as shock washed over the Corsyth.

I recovered my voice first. "The Master is a woman?"

"Aye."

"I thought you didn't know the Master's identity!" Somehow, I was deeply offended that he had lied to us.

But truly, what had I been expecting?

Dray held up his hands in defense. "I don't know the Master's identity. But, unlike that idiot Naith, I'm well familiar with the female form and recognize it when I see it. Even if it is wrapped in a hundred yards of black fabric."

Dray's gaze wandered, trailing its way over to Diggy and her leather shorts.

Without a word, she snatched the trousers from the spot where Mor had set them and stalked over to a tree.

Dray smirked unpleasantly. Until Father stepped up to him. Then the smirk fell, and his throat bobbed as he swallowed.

"Here." Father shoved the bedroll into Dray's arms so hard that he nearly toppled from the rock where he sat. "Go to sleep. We leave at dawn."

Father strode away, and if Dray knew what was good for him, he would keep his mouth shut for a good long while.

But instead, Dray turned to me, holding out his bedding as if it were distasteful. "No pillows?"

CHAPTER TWENTY-TWO
DIGWYN

THE SHIP SWAYS.

Back and forth, left and right. Up and down over the waves. I rise and fall with them.

Wind slices through the planks of the hull, somehow, and cuts me to my bones. My fingers lace through my threadbare blanket, and I pull it tighter around my shoulders.

And still, I'm cold.

A knock. The sound of a large fist pounding against wood.

The blanket wraps tighter.

The fist pounds again, and I pull the blanket over my head as though I might hide from reality.

I don't answer. I never say come in. I wait under my blanket, swaddled in darkness, eyes closed. And the door swings open.

I'm cold.

THE MOUNTAINBEAST FUR ISN'T ENOUGH. I WRAP THE CLOAK tighter. Turn my face away from the wind. "I'm cold," I tell Tannie.

"Me too," she says, and draws nearer to me.

We hike alongside each other, through the forest north of the Codewig. What's the name of this one, and how many days have we been gone?

I couldn't tell you. All I can think of is the cold. Like it pulses from within and batters me from the outside at once.

"We should stop for the night," the general says, and I see him watch a few flakes of snow drift through the air. "It's going to be a cold one. Let's build the fire."

My only consolation is that Dray looks at least as miserable as I am. He shudders and drops his pack. It's easily half the weight of the one on Mor's back.

Mor stands beside me, frowning into my face the way he does. Like my thoughts might be written across my forehead, and if he only peers hard enough, leans in close enough, he might be able to make out the words.

"You all right, Dig?" he asks.

"I'm cold."

"Aye." He rubs my arms through the mountainbeast fur.

Tannie joins in, rubbing my back. It doesn't work. I shiver.

"I think I'm turning to ice," I say, and Tannie's mouth twitches.

"My father is building a fire. We'll get you defrosted in no time."

The general is already striking flint toward a pile of kindling. I'm glad Tannie's father is here. That *someone's* father is here to look after us.

I shiver again.

Mor is still peering at me, and I roll my eyes. "My thoughts aren't there," I huff.

He seems confused. I've said something else that doesn't entirely make sense, because he can't read my thoughts. Can't follow the thread. Much as he tries.

Would it be better or worse if he could?

The crease between his brows is there again. I wonder what it means. Anger? Disappointment? But he only says, "Would you like some tea?"

"Spike-fruit," I answer immediately. "If Karlith has it."

Karlith's grin answers me from the other side of the new

fire. "I wouldn't leave without plenty of spike-fruit for Diggy, now would I?"

I let a little shadow of a smile through, then curl into Tannie so we might shiver together.

Mor nods, the crease deepening even as he smiles. "I'll see to that. You two try to get warm."

Tannie and I ease down to the ground. I arrange my cloak around me so that it creates a sort of tent to keep in the warmth. Then I pull out a knife and my small sharpening stone and set to work.

I feel Tannie's eyes on me. She doesn't say anything at first. But she's Tannie, and she can't stay quiet for too long. "How do you know when it's sharp enough?"

I nod to Dray, huddled and shivering nearby. "When it looks sharp enough to slice off his nose, it's done."

Dray glares and Tannie snorts.

"You don't want it too sharp," I say after a moment. "A blade that's too sharp will nick when you use it." I look up and Dray is still watching us, so I add, "But that's unlikely if you're cutting through the soft flesh of a politician."

He finally takes my hint and turns away from us. Now I can sharpen in peace without his penetrating gaze watching, dissecting, assessing. He unsettles me at least as much as I unsettle him. And he can never know that. The less he watches me, the better.

"I hope she's still alive," Tannie says.

"The queen?"

"Aye. You would like her. She's a good person."

"Surprising, considering her father."

"I suppose. Though you have to wonder how much of that sort of thing passes down." Tannie glances at the general, and I know she's once again wondering how she can be his daughter. She truly doesn't see the many ways they are alike.

Tough. Resourceful. And kind.

"I couldn't say." I pull out another dagger and check the edge. "I know nothing of family."

We both glance at Mor as he crouches beside the fire next to Karlith.

"I don't think that's true," Tannie says softly.

I swallow, my mouth suddenly dry. "He's . . ." But there's no end to that sentence, and I fall silent.

"He loves you."

My blade sings across the stone.

"He has always loved you."

Sing.

"Families who have been broken apart are still families, Diggy."

"Are they? I thought that was kind of the point of a family."

"There are a lot of points to families."

"How would you know?" I regret it the second it leaves my mouth. But that's the thing about words. Once you've spoken them, they're out there, and you can't pull them back in, no matter how much you might wish to.

Tannie flinches, and I feel even worse.

"I mean . . ." I begin, trying to figure out exactly what I *do* mean. "We are both from broken-apart families. Maybe neither of us knows anything about them."

"Aye, that's true." She glances at the general, who's warming his hands over the fire as he talks to the captain and the Meridioni. "But we've found some missing pieces, haven't we? Besides"—she smiles—"you lived a lot of years with your family whole before . . ."

She trails off. Who in their right mind would want to say the rest?

Before your father was murdered.

Before your mother died of grief.

Before you became a slave.

Before you were broken.

Before they killed you without ending your life.

"Aye," I say after a moment. "I did have my family once."

"So, then, you tell me what's the point of them." Tannie's voice offers a gentle challenge.

I watch Mor wince as he singes his fingers trying to pull the cloth bag of tea leaves from a steaming mug of water he's preparing for me.

My mouth twitches. "Family is there to hold you together in the places you're weak." I close my eyes and remember Mother and Father, Mother's long black hair dancing on the wind as she leans against the ship's rail and laughs at something Father has said. "Family is there to teach you right from wrong. To take care of you. To let you know you belong somewhere in a world that might want to chew you up and spit you out."

I open my eyes and catch Mor's gaze. He grins sheepishly, then blows on his tender fingers.

"Family is supposed to be by your side forever."

I scowl, hoping it will push the tears away. It doesn't work. A moment later, Tannie's hand is on my arm.

"He loves you," she says again.

And I want to believe her. I want to believe her so much.

I shrug off her hand and pull out another knife. "Family is dangerous. If anyone can hurt you, it's family."

Mor approaches, his hands wrapped around the steaming mug.

I sheathe my knife and rise, ignoring the bite of the wind. I glance down at Tannie. "It's safer to be alone."

Then I stride away into the trees, leaving Mor with that crease between his brows growing deeper and a mug of spike-fruit burning his hands.

CHAPTER TWENTY-THREE
TANWEN

Is it possible to grow a second layer of skin if you make your first one cold enough? Because I was fairly sure that was happening to me. We'd been trekking through the northern wilderness of Tir for the past two weeks, and I wasn't sure I would ever feel completely warm again.

But somehow, though we traveled farther and farther north and the last moon of autumn waned, welcoming winter's icy breath and snow-drenched days, my bones shivered less each night. Diggy, Karlith, and I still huddled together under all our cloaks every evening, as close to the fire as we could manage without igniting our hair. But each night seemed easier than the last.

At least for me.

"Make a strand of fire, Tannie." Diggy rattled within her cloak as we walked.

Whatever second skin I was growing, the same wasn't happening for Diggy. At least I was used to a little snow and the ice-cold breeze off the Menfor Sea back in Pembrone. She had turned islander to her core, and I wasn't sure she would make it through to the end of our quest, to be honest.

"I can't, Diggy. I think my story strands are frozen somewhere by my elbows. Besides, the fire only seems to come out when I'm angry."

"Then get angry about something. Where's Mor?"

I laughed, and my teeth chattered a little.

"Did I hear my name?"

I glanced to my right, and there he was. Maybe we could make fire strands if we kissed again . . .

My face suddenly wasn't cold anymore. In fact, it felt like I had just stuck it into our nightly campfire.

What was wrong with me? I had spent the past two and a half weeks trying to scrub that kiss from my memory. The last thing I needed just then was a distraction so vast and wiggly.

And those blue eyes, the dark beard beginning to fill in after several weeks without shaving, and that smirky smile were definitely distracting.

"Tannie?" He was watching me with a question mark on his face.

I had been staring.

My cheeks flushed hotter.

"I . . . nothing. I don't know. What?"

Diggy rescued me. "I thought you might be able to make Tannie mad so she could make a fire strand to keep us warm."

Mor's curious gaze lingered on me for an extra second. Then he turned to his sister. "No need. We'll reach Ir-Golyth shortly."

I glanced around at the thick evergreens surrounding us on every side. "Is the town in the forest?"

"Just on the edge. We're almost there, if Dylun's calculations are correct."

"They usually are."

And sure enough, within the hour, the trees broke up ahead of us, and I could see shingled roofs and buildings constructed of logs.

Diggy frowned. "Those houses are made of trees."

"From the girl who used to sleep under a palm frond." I nudged her. But I knew what she meant. It was a bit strange to see buildings made of felled logs like this.

Up ahead, my father stopped walking and paused, staring out at the town before us.

I hurried to catch up with him, as quickly as I could with the heavy cloak wrapped around my shoulders.

"Father?"

He turned toward me. "Yes, Tannie?"

"Is everything all right?"

He didn't answer. He turned back toward the town, his lips pressed into a line.

I tried again. "What's the plan? Do we just march in?"

"I don't think we will be as recognized here as we were in the Midlands." But he was obviously concerned.

"What is it?"

"It's nothing."

"We might be on the steward's wanted list," Warmil said. "And if we are, the news would certainly have traveled this far north."

Father faced him, not looking entirely pleased.

But Warmil didn't flinch. "All due respect, General, but she's not a child. She is of age by all standards, and she's seen enough life to warrant telling her the full truth."

Well, after that vote of confidence, I couldn't show a shred of the panic opening up like a gash inside me.

"All right," I said. "We might be on the wanted list. What would that mean?"

"A bounty on our heads," Father said grimly.

Yes, that would be bad. The famine hadn't ended when Gareth fell, and heading into winter, there would be a lot of peasants desperate for food. And if you had enough gold, you could usually afford food.

"But they let us go," I reminded them. "They let us leave Urian." I looked at Father. "Isn't that what you said?"

"It certainly seemed so at the time."

"But now," Warmil said, "standing here at the edge of

Ir-Golyth, it seems a big risk to assume the steward doesn't want to see us captured. Or killed."

"Brac wouldn't order that," I responded. But then I wondered . . .

Would he? Did I even know Brac anymore? The boy I knew—the one who chased fluff-hoppers with me and shared his hathberry pie and was my family when I had none . . .

Did he even exist now?

My thoughts shifted to Zel's face—to Cameria's face as she broke the news about Ifmere. I tried to remember every death Brac had been involved with, directly or not.

"Well, maybe he would," I said at last. "Or someone he's working for might."

As we stood there, looking pensive and worried, Aeron strode by, limping slightly. She went past the trees and into the open, then turned back to us.

She reached inside her cloak and adjusted her sword belt. "We knew the risks. If we want to find Queen Braith, we better get a move on." She spread her hands wide, a glint of challenge in her twinkling eyes. "Well? Are you coming?"

MAYBE SOMETHING ABOUT THOSE LOG BUILDINGS BLOCKED the thrum of the town from reaching the outside world. Maybe the forest swallowed up the buzz of humanity before it reached us. Whatever it was, if I had thought Ir-Golyth looked to be asleep for the winter from the outside, I knew I was dead wrong the moment we entered it.

We rounded a corner and stepped onto a cobblestoned street. I was met bodily by a mountain of a man.

"Watch it!" he shouted, shoving me away with his forearm.

Father appeared beside me in an instant. He gripped the man's wrist. "You'll want to get your hands off my daughter."

The man winced but managed to wrench himself away. He

rubbed his wrist and glared as he backed up. "She ran into me, after all."

"An accident." Mor helped me regain my balance, throwing a sharp look at the burly, bearded stranger.

"She ran into me," he said again before disappearing into a crush of people.

Diggy shrank into my side as she looked around at Ir-Golyth. "Tannie . . ."

Truly, the streets ran like streams—a continuous flow of human bodies moving with the current.

Aeron and Warmil sidled up beside Father. "All here for the Hunt?" Warmil asked quietly.

"Probably so," Father replied, his eyes watchful.

A trill of laughter drew my gaze to a knot of people nearby—one woman and four men. They all wore clothes that somewhat resembled the uniforms of the queen's navy, but it was like the garments had been patched, pieced together, and adorned with baubles and trinkets from the four corners of the world. They all wore their hair in rows of tight braids tracing along their scalps and then swinging free down their backs. Feathers, charms, and beads were interwoven through the braids.

The lady winked at Mor as she passed, though she had to be at least fifteen years his senior, flashing a smile that revealed more than one gold tooth and somehow still managed to be pretty. She turned back to her fellows and laughed again, then placed a tricorn hat over her braids before she and her comrades disappeared into the stream of people.

Pirates.

I turned to Mor. "Do you know them?"

"Because I know every pirate who sails the five seas of the world?" he asked, one brow raised.

I shrugged. "Thought maybe you had a guild, or something." I glanced at Father. "Definitely here for the Hunt. They said *adventurers*, right?"

"Aye." Father scanned the crowd, and I was sure he saw what I did.

An assortment of muscled warriors, all with multiple weapons strapped to their bodies. Those in sailing garb, both of the navyman variety and the pirate persuasion. Men who had the same hardened, gaunt look as Warmil and those who were dressed almost entirely in leather—grizzled Wildlanders from western Tir.

I even saw one group comprised of what looked to be Meridioni sailors, and they appeared to be shivering half to death.

And there we stood—three legitimate soldiers, one former pirate, a scholar, a farmer, a healer, a story peddler, a crooked politician, and . . . Diggy.

"Would you mind terribly if we didn't stand here all day?" Dray's teeth chattered. "I'm a moment away from an icy death, I'm afraid."

"Shall we find an inn?" I stood on tiptoes, trying to see over the heads of the crowd to read the shop signs.

And then I found I couldn't read them at all.

"Father? The words look foreign."

"Highlandish uses different characters." He craned his neck and sighed. "And I'm not fluent. In the northern Wildlands, they speak a Highlandish-Tirian blend, using Tirian lettering. I'm competent in that, but this is pure Highlandish."

"You *only* speak Highlandish-Tirian blend? Father, I'm shocked and disappointed."

"Well, I'm fluent in a few other languages but none that would hel—" He stopped as he caught my grin. "You're jesting."

"That one over there is an inn," Dylun said, pointing. "We might try there."

I stifled a giggle. "Of course you actually *do* speak pure Highlandish, Dylun."

Father and Warmil took the lead in trying to forge a path through the crowd toward the building Dylun had indicated.

"Not exactly." He grunted as he took a stray elbow to the gut. "But if you are familiar with the logographic system that predates Old Tirian and from which Highlandish characters originate, it isn't too difficult to—oof!" Someone stumbled into him, and he went sprawling into Zel's back.

"Oh yes. If only you're familiar with those." I helped him regain his footing.

"Almost there!" Father called. In the next moment, I was tripping over a threshold, clutching Diggy by my side.

"Oi, can I help ya?" a woman with two long yellow braids asked in thickly accented Tirian.

I looked around. It was less an inn and more just one big room with a hard-packed dirt floor and two dozen cots lined up along the walls.

"Do you have any beds available for the night?" Father inquired.

"We 'ave one left, but there's room on the floor. Full price, though."

Dray nudged his way to the front of the group. He unleashed that too-white, sparkly smile of his. "Full price? Now, surely there's something we can do about that. What's your name, lass?"

She narrowed her eyes at him, but her lips twitched just a little. "Oosta."

"That's beautiful."

I snorted. Mor pinched my arm, and I tried to recover with a false cough.

But Dray acted like he could only hear and see the lady in front of him. "Oosta, surely you could give us a little break since we'll be sleeping on the floor. It will pay off handsomely, I assure you. We are well connected all throughout the empi—that is, the kingdom. Your lovely establishment will become *the* place to stay in all of Ir-Golyth."

She folded her arms. "Most places is full up. You ain't got much choice but to sleep on my floor and pay what I ask, ya know."

"There are always choices in life, Oosta." Dray took her hand, flashed his smile again, and kissed her fingers.

She laughed and pulled her hand away. Then she grinned. "Oh, all righ'. Stay on the floor for free, but ya pay for the bed, mind. And ya tell everyone about my place, got it?"

"Of course." Dray stepped back and ushered Dylun toward Oosta to take care of the rest of the arrangements.

As Dylun loosened the strings of the coin purse, Dray reached in and plucked out a silver bit. Before anyone could object, he slipped it inside a pocket in his waistcoat.

I must have been wearing my indignation plainly, because he smirked at me and shrugged. "I just saved us ten times as much."

"But cost us double that savings on your fancy clothes," I grumbled.

"No matter. I intend to find a stiff drink in a dirty pub somewhere." The smile again, at me, then Diggy. "You lasses should join me."

"Actually, we'll all join you," Father informed Dray. "We're not splitting up. Not in this crowd with this chaos."

Dray shrugged. "Suit yourself. As long as I have a decent drink in my hand shortly, I don't care what you do."

Mor had shed his heavy pack and held out his hands for ours. "Oosta says the place is secure. Her father and brothers are guarding the perimeter." A shadow of unease crossed his face. "Our belongings will be safer here than on our backs, I'm afraid."

"Aye." Diggy shrugged out of her pack and handed it to him. "It's all these blasted pirates running around."

Mor and I shared the quickest glance. She was teasing

him—like a sister might. I could practically see the achy place inside Mor's heart warm.

"Dylun," Father said, "make sure you keep the coin purse close. There are some supplies we'll need to pick up for the Hunt. I want to find the huntmaster first thing in the morning."

"I think I shall take the cot," Dray drawled as we left the inn to find a pub he deemed acceptable. "It was I, after all, who secured the floor for free."

Karlith looked scandalized. "Would you really do that? With an injured lass in our party?" She nodded to Aeron. "I thought a little better of even you, Dray Bo-Anffir."

He shrugged. "Then perhaps I'll share Oosta's bed. Surely you wouldn't object to that. I'm fairly certain she's half mountainbeast, but a warm body is a warm body."

Karlith looked like she had been slapped. "As a matter of fact, I—"

"Karlith," I cut in gently. "He's only saying it to upset you." I glared at him. "Leave her alone, and sleep wherever you feel like. No one here cares."

He chuckled and gave me a slow, appraising scan. "I doubt that's true."

I made a mental note to make sure Mor, Father, Warmil, and at least fourteen weapons within easy reach were between Dray and me that night.

"Here." Father stopped in front of a shop. He peered in the front window. "Yes, this is a pub." He gestured Dray inside. "Go on. Get your drink."

I looped my arm through Mor's as we followed the others into the pub. Diggy pressed up close to my other side.

We walked into what looked like a light show.

Strands like the sunset—pink, yellow, orange, red—sailed through the room to the gasps and cheers of the crowd. The strands formed wide splashes of color from one end of the room to the other.

A glowing orb in the center of the pub hovered for a moment, then dropped to the floor and made a sound like shattering glass.

"Never fear!" An ashy-haired young man dressed in Wildlander leather raised his arms, a smug grin on his face. "It's all part of the show."

He waved one hand with a flourish, and the story shards that had once represented the sun re-formed into an orb—one that was a bit wonky and didn't glow quite as well as the original.

"Wait until you see it crystallized, folks," the Wildlander bragged. "My stories are costly but worth every bit and more!"

Diggy rolled her eyes. "Yours are better, Tannie."

"Hey, don't say that too loudly"—Mor grinned—"even though it's true. We don't need to make more enemies, if we can help it."

"Yours are better, too, Mor." Diggy glared at the storyteller. "I don't like this guy. He's a braggart, and I hate braggarts."

"Don't bother over it." I glanced at the Wildlander and those around him, some already reaching into their pockets to bid on the story once it crystallized.

A young lad in patched woolen clothes looked up at the sunset story in delight. "It's brilliant! Wish I could buy it."

The Wildlander paused. "Do you have coin, lad?"

The boy shook his head. "Nah, not me. If I did, I'd hafta buy more bread and leave the story behind."

"Then what are you doing here?" The Wildlander stared down his nose. "Go on. Get out of here. The show is for paying customers only."

The boy's smile fell.

My insides turned hot, then cold. Memories flooded through me—traveling around to peddle stories with Riwor. How the eager children had always gathered first. How I'd assessed the young men I was willing to speak with based on the state of their worn clothing and calloused hands. How Riwor had taught me to cater to the customers who looked like the highest bidders.

But also how I would, almost without fail, tell a story to one child after most of the others had left. How I would share a secret fairy story or whisper a thinly veiled yarn about my own ambitions in life or recite the tale of the pink fluff-hopper granting an ill-fated wish.

Because I *was* that child, too poor to buy a story or any other trinket. I was the little girl worrying too much about where my next meal would come from to indulge in something so frivolous as art.

Frivolous, yet the lifeblood that kept me going.

As I stared at the cocky Wildlander, my hands warmed. He was everything I hated about story peddling and everything I hated about myself.

But before I could force my hands to cool off—or foolishly let strands pour from them—Diggy brushed past me.

"Enough of this," she said.

I watched her in mute shock.

The Wildlander storyteller regarded her with a superior air as she approached, then his eyes darted to the tattoos snaking down her fingers. His eyebrows rose. "Well, well."

"Dig—" Mor started, but it was too late.

Diggy reached into the air and grasped one of the storyteller's strands in each of her hands.

"What the—"

The strands of light turned solid in her grip, and she spun them until they obeyed her commands. They wrapped around the Wildlander, a cocoon of sunset-colored strips.

A muffled shout sounded from within the cocoon.

Mor cursed under his breath and pushed his way toward the captive storyteller, but the crowd had knotted up, everyone peering closer to see what the crazy little lass was on about.

It might have been less noticeable if the floor had opened up and swallowed us whole.

After a long moment of watching the Wildlander struggle,

Diggy rotated her hands the other direction and collected the stolen strands between her fingers. The storyteller stumbled as he tried to regain his legs beneath him.

Diggy raised the strands above her head, then threw them to the ground. The strands crashed to the floorboards with an impressive splat. The floor turned every shade of sunset, and I wondered if Diggy had somehow turned them into colormastery strands. But as I looked closer, I could see the color wasn't caused by paint-like colormastery. It was as if the wood had absorbed the pigment of the strands and they'd become one with the boards. There was no scrubbing that off.

And I had no clue how she'd done it.

"There." She glared at the storyteller. "Sell that, braggart."

His mouth dangled open. Every mouth in the pub dangled open, except my father's. His eyes said everything.

We need to leave. Now.

"How'd she do it?" an onlooker asked.

"Never seen anything like it in me life!"

"Who is that?"

"What's your name, lass?"

"Can I buy you a drink?"

"Can I buy you a cage?" That was the storyteller, finally having recovered his wits. He glared a million daggers at Diggy, and I almost wished I could warn him about her real ones.

Almost.

"My brother could tell stories in circles around you." She nodded toward me. "So could Tannie."

"Tanwen En-Yestin?" The voice came from the crowd, though I didn't recognize it.

A hand gripped my arm, and I turned to find Father there beside me, his gray eyes filled with urgency. "Go now. Quickly."

I slipped toward the door, keeping my head low and praying he would get Mor and Diggy out of this somehow.

Just as I reached the door, Mor appeared at my right elbow, and seconds later, Diggy turned up at my left.

"Go, go, go," Mor whispered.

Over the ruckus of the crowd, I could hear the storyteller shouting something. Then came a booming voice I assumed belonged to the barkeep. "You'll need to be payin' me for this mess, *now*."

"But I—"

"Your show, you pay."

"But she was the one who—"

Mor shut the door on the rest of the storyteller's protest and led us back to the inn. "Diggy, I swear, it's like you're trying to get us killed." He stopped before the door of the inn and looked out at the teeming streets behind us. "Both of you stay here for the rest of the night. General's orders. We don't need to attract any more attention."

He slipped inside and beckoned us to follow.

Diggy turned to me and shrugged. "Well, he deserved it."

THE NEXT MORNING, I PULLED THE HOOD OF MY CLOAK LOWER over my face and huddled close to Mor. Carefully, our group made its way through town toward the meeting point just outside Ir-Golyth where all Hunt teams were supposed to register with the huntmaster.

"I can't see," Diggy said from Mor's other side.

"Should have thought of that before you made a spectacle of yourself in front of everyone in Ir-Golyth."

"Really?" Diggy pushed her hood back an inch and looked up at Mor. "I should have thought about the annoyance of hoods before I did that?"

"And to be fair," I added, "it wasn't *all* Ir-Golyth. Just those gathered in that pub."

Mor rolled his eyes. "You'll be the death of me. Both of you."

Diggy gave her typical shrug, and I grinned.

But truthfully, the results of Diggy's display weren't particularly funny. Rumors and gossip had swirled throughout the town all night, according to Warmil, Karlith, and Zel. Father had sent them out to keep an ear open for the chatter. They were the least conspicuous of our party.

Dray had insisted he be allowed to explore Ir-Golyth, and Father begrudgingly allowed him to do so, only because it seemed chaining him to a bed in the inn was the only other option. But he set Warmil to watch Dray, and somehow, they both managed to make it back alive. Which rather surprised me, honestly.

Now we crept along the outskirts of Ir-Golyth, cautious in the early-morning darkness. Aeron leaned against Warmil, and he helped her negotiate the bumpy terrain. Karlith walked near them, ready to help.

"It hurts her," Diggy said. She'd apparently seen me watching the three of them up ahead.

"What?"

"The soldier lass. Aeron. Her wooden leg hurts her, even when it's not dark out and the path isn't bumpy. She just tries to hide it."

I bit my lip. I supposed she must be right, and a pinprick of guilt pierced my heart. I hadn't thought about it or paid attention near as much as I should have.

"I guess we often try to hide the things that hurt us," Mor remarked.

Before anyone could answer that, we reached the registration tent.

Father looked at me, Mor, and Aeron. "You three with me. Stay close," he said in a low murmur. "The rest of you, wait here. We are less conspicuous if we split up."

He nodded to Warmil—it would be his duty to guard the others in Father's absence.

Father held back the flap that served as a door, and Mor, Aeron, and I followed him inside.

My mouth dropped open.

I had expected the huntmaster to be a bookish fellow—like a Tirian Dylun, perhaps, with stacks of parchment and rules and checklists, tracking all the details and making sure everyone was behaving properly.

Instead, the huntmaster looked like one of the mountains of the Mynyth Range come to life.

He stood as tall as Zel, but he was twice as wide. The braids in his thick red beard stretched all the way to his chest. Though he wore a mountainbeast-fur waistcoat, his arms were bare, as though defying the wind to prove itself stronger than he.

My eyes stayed wide and my mouth agape until Mor nudged me. "He's a Highlander, Tannie. Don't stare."

My mouth snapped shut, and I tried to wipe the wide-eyed look from my face.

The huntmaster leaned against a wooden table, his arms crossed as though he'd stand there like that all day, just waiting for Hunt teams to enter the tent and gawk at him.

Father stepped forward, unruffled as always. "Greetings. We're here to register."

"I figured." He pushed off from the table and stepped aside, gesturing toward a smattering of papers and a couple pens. "Rules are here. I'll read 'em to you. You'll listen."

I raised my eyebrows at Mor. "Well, all right."

One corner of his mouth lifted.

"Rules are as follows," the huntmaster said as we gathered around. "You're hunting for strands. These things is precious, apparently, so you will treat them with care. If you don't, you'll answer to me. You can dig, blast, chip away to heart's content, but don't even think about holding me responsible for cave-ins. Don't blast if you don't know what you're doing."

I swallowed hard.

"On that score, me and the boss isn't responsible for death or dismemberment." He glanced at Aeron as if he could see her wooden limb through her trousers. "You enter the Hunt at your own risk."

"And the reward?" Father asked. "What is the offered reward should we accept this great risk and succeed? Hardly seems worth the thousand gold advertised."

The huntmaster let a slow grin spread across his face. "The boss has wealth to spare, that's all I'll say."

"And exactly how badly does your boss want these strands?"

"Quite." He squinted and leaned back as if sizing up Father. "If the boss is happy, you will be too. Trust me on that."

"Oh, I don't know . . ." Father motioned vaguely to the rest of us. "It takes quite a lot to make some of my companions here happy."

I knew he was trying to wiggle information from the huntmaster, but I almost snorted. His statement was true enough about Dray, in any case, though he was standing outside.

"A thousand gold might be enough to satisfy some teams. But if we find these prized strands, perhaps your boss is willing to negotiate. So, how much are we talking here? How high will the boss go, in your estimation?"

"Well . . ." He glanced over our heads as if checking for eavesdroppers. "I ain't saying this to most. Wouldn't want this getting around. You understand my meaning?"

"Aye," Father assured him. "We'll keep it to ourselves."

"At one point, the boss mentioned a thousand crowns per strand."

Mor choked on the sum. "A thousand gold pieces for *each*?"

"For each."

"And how many are out there?" Father asked. "The advert said at least three were required to win the Hunt."

"Boss thinks eleven."

Stars. Eleven. Chances one of the other teams would find a strand were pretty good. And if they did? And if we were right about these strands being the same ancient, insanely powerful ones we had used to build the cure?

And the Master got hold of them?

I tried to push it from my mind, but all I could imagine was the total destruction of Tir—of the world as we knew it.

Father folded his arms across his chest. "If we find all eleven, your boss will pay us eleven thousand gold crowns. Is that what you're saying?"

"I think you could squeeze that much." The huntmaster grinned. "But since I told you this, I expect a little kickback for my trouble."

Father returned the grin. "If the boss is happy, we'll be happy. And if we're happy, you'll be happy."

"That's how the world turns over."

Father and the huntmaster shook on it, and I couldn't help but wonder how he would feel about breaking that promise later.

But all Father said was, "The rest of the rules?"

"Right." The huntmaster returned to his parchment. "You interact with me at all times. The boss wishes to remain anonymous. You bring the strands to me. I deal with the boss. Got that?"

"Aye."

"First one to the finish with three strands gets the reward. You want to search for eleven? Go ahead. But don't be surprised if someone else beats you to three while you're eyebrow-deep in the caves."

"Understood."

"You're supposed to have a storyteller among you. For pulling up the strands. Got one?"

"We've got three."

Plus one Diggy—whatever she was.

"Three?" The huntmaster looked genuinely surprised. "Well, that's a first."

"Did the others only bring one?" Father sounded casual as could be.

"Aye, that seemed to be the way of it."

Father shrugged. "Pity for them."

"Maybe you *will* get all eleven." The huntmaster shook his head and laughed. "And your name? For my records."

I held my breath. But Father didn't hesitate. He picked up the pen from the table and scrawled the name *Esgusod Bo-Dyn* on the parchment. I tried not to notice that at least ten teams had already entered the Hunt.

Because stars knew there were at least a dozen more sleeping in Ir-Golyth and fixing to register today.

"Right, then," the huntmaster said. "You're set. Entrance to the caverns is a hundred paces due west." He pointed. "Bring the strands to me, if you find 'em, and we'll work out our special arrangement after the boss pays you."

Father nodded. "Thanks."

"Nice doin' business with you, Bo-Dyn."

Father offered a tight-lipped smile, then turned and exited the tent. The rest of us followed in silence, rejoining our group outside and beginning our journey to the cave entrance. In hushed tones, Aeron and Mor began to relay what the huntmaster had told us.

When we had taken about twenty of the hundred paces toward the entrance, I caught up to Father. "Esgusod Bo-Dyn?"

"One of my aliases."

Better not to pull at that thread . . .

"So, what did we learn?" Warmil trudged at Father's other side.

"Well, I can be absolutely sure of a few things." Father ticked them off on his fingers as we continued westward. "One, the huntmaster has made an arrangement for kickbacks with every single team that has entered the Hunt."

My brows rose. "But he said—"

Father's glance cut me off. "Tannie girl, a man of such mercenary sensibilities doesn't put all his hedge-nibblers in one barrel."

Aye, he was probably right about that.

"Which means," Father continued, "it's likely at least some of the teams know there are eleven strands out there. And that the boss, who we know to be the Master, is supposedly willing to pay up to a thousand gold for each."

"Can't imagine such wealth as all that." Karlith shook her head. "How would a body ever spend it all?"

"Oh, that's the second thing." Father stopped walking and looked at us. "The Master has no intention of paying out such a ridiculous sum of money, though the huntmaster seems unaware of this. He seems to truly believe he'll get his big windfall when his boss pays out the winning team."

"And the third thing of which you're so sure, General Bo-Arthio?" Dray inquired, a lazy smirk on his face.

"Third," Father went on, "the Master has put this Hunt coordinator between the Hunt teams and *her*"—here he glanced at Dray, acknowledging that bit of information he had revealed to us—"and it is therefore unlikely that following these Hunt rules will help us achieve our second goal, finding and rescuing Queen Braith."

"And that's where I come in." If a smile could be cold as the weather, Dray had mastered it. "You hunt your strands, do your thing." He waved his hand as though our mission was a buzzing blood-sucker to be shooed away. "But don't return anything to that avaricious oaf in the tent. I will lead you close to the Master's lair so we might achieve our common goal—saving Braith."

"You know where the Master is in here?" Zel motioned with his chin toward the vast range before us.

I could only imagine the network of tunnels and caves buried within.

"It's been a fair few years since I visited," Dray admitted. "This is something of a retreat for her. Not her usual dwelling. But I remember the landmarks well enough."

The Corsyth weavers shared glances, mistrust scribbled all over their faces. Mine surely looked just as skeptical.

Dray sighed. "Why would I have come all this way with you if I didn't think I could actually find Braith?"

"To escape prison," Dylun said.

"To avoid execution," Mor added grimly.

Dray shrugged. "All right, yes, I could have had ulterior motives. I admit it." He approached Father, who had been silent for several moments.

Dray knew Yestin Bo-Arthio was the one he had to convince.

"Braith believed in me," Dray said. "She believed that people could change. My sentencing grieved her. She didn't want to see me executed."

"That's because she's kind and decent," I cut in. "It doesn't mean she believed in you."

"True, but she did. She told me so herself. She believed my heart had changed—that I was learning to become a better man." Just for a moment, the arrogance and self-assuredness dimmed. Something vulnerable and small flickered in his eyes. "I want to prove to her that she was right to put her trust in me."

I watched his face. Watched my father's face. Observed their silent standoff. And wondered at Dray's words.

Could people change like that? Was it possible?

My gaze drifted to Diggy. Dray had chosen to act in his brokenness, to give himself over to dark, selfish deeds. But Diggy had been broken by others. She hadn't had a choice. And still she struggled to find her way out of it—to be a person who reached for the light.

If I condemned Dray in my mind, was I also condemning Diggy?

"Fine." Father's voice startled me from my thoughts. I

looked up and saw him shaking hands with Dray. "We have an accord. We will follow your lead and trust you mean what you say. But I swear to you, Dray Bo-Anffir, if you betray us or harm any one of these people—"

"Yes, yes. Big, scary fighter will do big, scary things to me."

I could practically see every one of Father's muscles tighten, and I wondered if Dray had any idea the mountainbeast he was poking.

"It will save us time and effort if we dispense with the posturing," Dylun said. He turned to Dray. "I am speaking mostly to you, to be clear."

Dray smirked. "Then shall we get to your precious strands? We will need them if you hope to strike a bargain with the Master."

"And will she not kill us on sight?" Aeron leaned against Warmil. "If we have the strands, it seems the easiest thing for her to do would be to kill us and take her prize."

"Perhaps," Dray said. "We must be cunning so that she will not have the opportunity. Bargaining—that's how you might rescue Braith while sparing your own lives. The Master only destroys those who are of no use to her."

His gaze turned toward Diggy, and his smirk blossomed into a grin that sent frost through my veins. "Make yourselves useful, and you will not be destroyed."

CHAPTER TWENTY-FOUR
DIGWYN

Some people are built to take.

I have become convinced of this fact over and over again until I can no longer reasonably deny it.

Everyone *wishes* to take. That is human nature. But some... some are built to seek out, to take, to use.

To prey.

Like wolves, they stalk and pursue, chasing what they might gain from you. What they might take. What they might use.

Until they have devoured your very flesh.

Then they find it brings but momentary satisfaction, and they must seek another. And another, and another.

They hunt. They prey. And they will never be satisfied. They will never stop.

They will never repent.

Some people are built to take.

"That's why the Master will be awfully keen on you, you know."

That blasted man is speaking to me again—looking at me like he's removing my clothing—and my fingers twitch. I long to draw my knives and end the speaking and the looking.

Instead, I turn to him.

"Because she can use you," he finished, as if I didn't know his meaning all along.

"No one can use me." I glare. "Not anymore."

He shrugs, but the smile doesn't drop. Condescending mud-snuffler.

The general leads us forward again, and I try to edge closer to Tannie and my brother—away from Dray. But he seems to shadow me, to haunt my steps.

We all pause before what looks to be an entrance designed for a small child. The gap in the rock meets me mid-thigh and sits lower on everyone else.

"This can't be it," Tannie says, her eyebrows raised high as she looks at the tiny cave mouth.

Karlith chuckles. "Not sure I'll fit through there, General."

"Ah, child-birthing hips." Dray gestures. "The downfall of many a woman."

"Shut up," I say, and I elbow past him. "I can fit." I turn to the general. "Shall I squeeze through and let you know what it's like? Maybe it opens up inside."

Mor steps forward as if he might object. My eyes warn him off. He keeps tighter watch on me now that I'm eighteen than he did when I was eight.

Yestin glances at my brother but then turns to me. "Are you sure?"

"Are *you* sure you want to find those strands?" I shoot back. "Then someone has to."

To avoid further discussion—because Cethor's tears, do these people like to discuss everything into oblivion—I shrug out of my cloak, hand it to Tannie, drop to the ground, and begin to crawl through the opening.

As predicted, the small cave mouth belies a larger chamber just inside, like the foyer of a house. I check the height of the ceiling—tolerable—and stand. I don't have to stoop, though

Zel the farmer will. But when you're tall as a tree and poking around caves, what do you expect?

"It's all right," I call back. "The inside is bigger."

I hear the sounds of argument and plunk down onto a rock to wait in the near blackness. This could take a while, if I know this crew.

A few moments later, a golden head appears, then blocks out the little light from the entrance. There's a bit of struggle, then Tannie is in the entryway with me.

"Well!" she says, and I can see her vague outline turn this way and that, sizing up matters. "This is not what I expected."

"It's dark."

"Yes, quite. I hope Father brought a lantern, or something."

"I doubt he would have forgotten."

"No, only that maybe he couldn't—" She cuts herself off, and I'm confused.

Then I realize she was about to say maybe he couldn't gather the supplies he had hoped to because my little display in the pub made it impossible for him to move about the town last night.

I didn't mean to ruin things. I never *mean* to ruin things, exactly. It's just that I often seem to.

Whatever Karlith's concern about fitting was, it proves to be unfounded when she crawls through without much trouble and helps Aeron in after her. Aeron has it worst because she can't bend in the way the rest of us can.

Then the men follow, and I say, "You'll want to watch your—"

Zel stands and crashes his head into the ceiling. "Oof!"

"Heads."

Mor finds us and stoops in front of where Tannie sits on the rock. "You all right, Tannie? Everything good?" He searches her face and glances over her shoulders and arms like the act of crawling for five seconds might have bruised or injured her.

As if he could make out any injuries in this light, anyway.

Tannie meets his gaze, and her eyes are glowy and filled with warmth. "I'm fine, Mor. Stars, you do fuss."

He stares back at her, all melty, like he wants to wrap her up, pull her close, and stay there forever. I have to bite my lip to keep from laughing at these two. Laughing or vomiting, one or the other.

They should just get married already. Maybe they will if we find our way out of here alive.

"Hey," I say, rising to my feet, "maybe we can just use the heat between the two of you to light our way. That should work."

I see Mor's eyes go wide, but I don't linger to enjoy their embarrassment.

"I have several lanterns." The general, slightly annoyed, and I realize he's heard my jest.

"But limited fuel, I'd guess," Tannie says, recovering herself and approaching her father. "What if we try something else first?"

A ribbon of light unfurls from her palm, and we all blink against it.

"Dimmer, Tannie," the general says quietly. "We won't want to announce ourselves to the others."

The strand dims, and Tannie produces another from her other hand, identical to the first. "How's that?"

"Good." In the light, I see Yestin frown. "But can you keep it up?"

"I'm not sure. If I can fill a ship's sails with wind for an hour at a time, I can do this for a while, at least."

I step toward her. "And if we need to stop, we could do this."

And I take one of Tannie's light ribbons in my hand and toss it at the cave wall. The strand crashes, shatters, and scatters into tiny bits of light sprinkled all over the wall. That section of rock now glows softly, pulsating with gentle light bright enough to illuminate the surrounding area but not so bright as to attract much attention. At least not more than a lantern might.

"Wow." It's Aeron. "It's amazing what you do, Diggy."

But Mor is frowning. Displeased, as always. I wonder why. Does he hate my gift? Is it jealousy? Disgust? Not sure. Won't ask.

"There is only one way forward," the general tells us, "though I'm sure that won't remain true for long. We will have to choose our course carefully. And be ready for surprises."

"Then they won't be surprises anymore," I say, immediately realizing I'm probably not helping.

Yestin ventures into the tunnel, Tannie and her light strands close behind him. Mor wraps my cloak back around my shoulders and gives me a squeeze.

"Stay close, Diggy."

And I do, but not close enough to deter Dray Bo-Anffir from finding me.

"That lass is right," he says. "What you do is amazing. I've never seen anything like it."

"A popular sentiment." My voice is clipped. Irritated. I wonder why this man won't leave me alone.

"Possessing you would make the Master more powerful than ever—more powerful than she could hope to be without you."

I stop walking. "I thought she wanted ancient strands. And Tannie. And Mor."

He smiles in the waning light. "Oh, she'll want it all. I assure you of that. She will want it all." Then he rounds the corner after the others.

I stand still, alone, until I am in darkness.

Chapter Twenty-Five
TANWEN

"Everyone, stop." Father held up his hand. "Listen."

We all stilled, though I made sure to slip my arm through Diggy's. Last time I got distracted, I had to backtrack and collect her. I'd found her standing like a statue by herself in the dark. She wouldn't tell me what she was thinking, and I had learned long ago it was best not to pry.

"What do you hear?" Father asked us.

Warmil frowned. "Absolutely nothing."

"Exactly. If you're not used to it, the thickness of true silence can drive you mad. You think you have silence during a quiet moment in the garden, perhaps, or when you read alone in your study. But no. That's not silence. Always there is the hum of humanity, the thrum of nature."

I thought about falling asleep alone in my cottage in Pembrone, listening to the sound of the Menfor's waves kissing the cliffs below. I would have thought those nights the stillest, loneliest, quietest in the world. But Father was right. They were not silent. Not like the silence of the caves.

"Spend much time cave-dwelling, General?" Dray quirked his eyebrow.

Oh. Dray still had no idea how my father had hidden from Gareth for thirteen years, only to appear suddenly when his bow and sword and presence mattered most.

Dray didn't know about the passageways in the palace, and it was best kept that way.

"I know a fair bit about a lot of things, Dray." Father turned away from him. That was clearly all he would say on the matter. He addressed the rest of us instead. "The caves will play tricks with light too. Bo-Ino. What do you see up there?" He pointed at the ceiling.

Dylun looked up. "Nothing. Just stone."

Father put his hand underneath mine and lifted, angling the light in a slightly different direction. The strand came closer to the ceiling, and all of us gasped. The beam of light revealed an intricate carving in the spot that had, most assuredly, looked blank a moment before.

"How is that possible?" Mor strained to get a better look.

"Light and sound don't behave as we expect them to in here." Father released my hand and turned to Mor, smiling. "Like underwater."

And somehow this made sense to Mor, though I still stood there with my mouth open.

Dray indicated the marking. "This is one of the Master's inscriptions. We'll need to watch for these."

"Excellent." Diggy's gaze flared at him. "Now that we know what to look for, can we dispose of you?"

"Only I know what the inscriptions say, love." Dray tweaked Diggy's chin.

In a flash, she gripped his wrist, spun around so her back was to him, and yanked his arm down over her shoulder. Dray cried out and reached for his elbow.

"Diggy!" Mor forced his way between them and broke Diggy's hold. He pulled her into his arms. "Stop. You're all right. You're safe." He glared at Dray over Diggy's head. "Back away from my sister."

Diggy allowed Mor to hold her a moment. Then she pushed away and whipped toward Dray. "Don't touch me!" she shouted, and the sound echoed off the cave walls. "Don't ever touch me!" Furious tears poured down her face.

But she allowed Mor to pull her back into his arms. "I have you," he said softly.

I could see Diggy's thin shoulders shaking beneath her cloak. Her voice came between ragged gasps. "Don't—don't let him. Don't let him touch me."

Mor embraced her more tightly. "I have you."

Dray was rubbing his elbow, looking equal parts furious and bewildered. "She's insane! You think I'm the loose cannon." He jabbed a finger at Diggy. "That one is your problem."

Father closed in on Dray. "I warned you not to bring harm to anyone in this group."

"I didn't harm her!" Dray protested. "I merely—"

"Stop." Father held up his palm. "Keep your hands to yourself, or I will remove them for you. Understand?" He flashed a mirthless smile. "Big, scary soldier making big, scary threats. But I promise you, I mean them."

Dray sulked, still rubbing his elbow. "Fine."

Warmil cleared his throat. "Perhaps we ought to leave our cloaks here. The air in the caves is warmer than I expected, and this carving on the ceiling would at least give us a shot at finding them again."

"Agreed," Father said as he took his off and folded it up.

The rest of us followed his lead. I hadn't really noticed, but Warmil was right. The caves were downright temperate compared to the icebox outside. We didn't need mountainbeast fur in here.

After that, we were able to move a bit more freely. Until my hand started to go numb and I decided it was time for someone else to take over lighting the way.

"Mor?" I gestured to my strand. "Could you for a bit?"

He was still keeping Diggy close by his side, and my heart wrenched when I noticed tears trickling down her cheeks.

He nodded and moved to the front of the pack. I sidled up next to Diggy at the back of the group.

"Are you all right?" I asked her, knowing the answer already. She sniffled.

We picked through the semidarkness carefully for a while, following the paths Dray indicated and discovering two more carvings on the ceiling when Mor held the light just right.

"He won't leave me alone," Diggy said.

My heart sank. "He's your brother, Diggy. He just wants to make sure you're all right."

"Not him. The other—Dray."

Oh. "Aye, well . . ." My voice took on a savage tone I hardly recognized. "He's pond sludge."

"But the queen doesn't think so?"

I paused. "I don't know what the queen thinks," I said finally. "We only know what Dray *says* she thinks. But I do know Braith a bit. And I know she wants to believe the best about people. She wants to believe in goodness."

"Do you?"

"Believe in goodness? Of course. I just don't know if I believe in goodness from him." I pointed at Dray's back up ahead.

We walked a few moments.

"I don't know why he cares so much about my gift."

"Well, he's not wrong about it. Your gift is definitely . . . unique. Everyone seems pretty interested in it."

"Yes, but he . . ." She faltered. "I just steal things. I steal things and twist them. That's all. I don't see why it's such a big deal. I used to be like Mor. I used to be able to make strands when I was younger."

My eyebrows rose in surprise. "Did you? Mor never said."

"I hadn't told him yet. I wanted to be sure before I said anything. I was so old for it to be happening. It was just starting to show up right about the time—" She broke off.

I had heard of that before. Most weavers showed their talents as young children. Others saw their gifts show up in earnest during their teen years.

"But then it changed after," Diggy said. "Like my gift broke, or something. If anything, I should be ashamed. I'm a . . . strand thief."

"No," I said right away, because I knew it had to be wrong. Untrue. It didn't feel like a fair description of what Diggy did.

I mean, technically it was true, I supposed. But her gift was so much more than theft.

"Diggy, you don't steal strands. You take something someone else made, and you make it better."

She seemed to consider this. "Still sounds like stealing."

"Fixing, maybe."

"But they're not broken to begin with."

True. "Improving, then."

She didn't respond, but the furrow between her brows deepened.

"Stop." An unexpected voice—Karlith's. She held out both her hands and stared hard at the ground.

She closed her eyes and stood as still as death.

After several moments, Warmil went over and placed his hand on her arm. "Karlith? What is it?"

She opened her eyes, turned to him, and smiled wide. "Do you not feel that?"

Without waiting for his reply, she moved toward a narrow passageway we had already passed. "Through here."

Warmil turned to Dray. "Have you been leading us astray?"

He looked miffed. "I don't know what the lady's on about, but the Master's hideaway is this direction." He pointed the way we had been traveling.

"Not the Master." Karlith moved toward the narrow offshoot and felt along the stone wall. "A strand." She smiled again, and then it blossomed into a laugh. "Do you not feel that?" She put a hand to her heart. "Like . . . hope."

Dray raised an eyebrow. "Is she serious?"

Father didn't respond. He followed Karlith. "You're sure it's through this passageway?"

"Aye. I'm sure."

"Very well." Father looked at me. "Do you think you could make a light strand to go ahead of us?"

I nodded and lifted my hand to let the light unfurl into the tunnel. Then an idea struck. "Diggy? Would you mind?"

Her uncertainty showed plain, but she stepped forward and grabbed my strand. Then she threw it against the wall, and it scattered into glowing bits on the rock.

"Lighting our way," Karlith said with a smile.

"Improving," I added, nudging Diggy.

She didn't respond to either of us, but I hoped she'd heard. And believed.

We filed through the narrow passageway—squeezed, more like. There was hardly room to breathe, but after what seemed like half a league, we all popped out, one after another, into a large chamber—the largest we had yet seen in the caves.

I created another strand of light, and Diggy cast it onto the walls. Still, the light from the glowing rocks was completely lost before it reached the ceiling. The cavern was so large it seemed only a small portion was illuminated by Diggy's work.

Somewhere nearby, water trickled.

"Tannie girl, we're going to need another strand." Father looked up at the endless darkness. "A bigger strand, if you please."

"Right." I created a beam of light, then looked at Mor.

He removed his leather glove and extended his hand. I took it, and our gifts linked. My beam expanded to thrice its size, then rainbow bands appeared on either side. My face went hot. Couldn't look at a rainbow without remembering that kiss in the Corsyth.

But the next second, all thoughts of the Corsyth, kisses, and even Mor fled from my mind. Because our strands lit up the entire vast cavern around us so that every corner was visible.

And from one of those corners, a creature uncurled itself as if waking from a long, deep sleep. It rose on hind legs, up and up until its head scraped the ceiling where it stood—nine feet tall, at least. Its chest swelled with one great inhale, then a roar to shake the mountains issued from its wolfish mouth.

Creator help us. We had found a mountainbeast.

CHAPTER TWENTY-SIX

TANWEN

I used to tease Brac about being slow to react, slow to respond. Just a little slow in general.

And yet, for all my teasing, it was me who now stood frozen while everyone else around me seemed to know to move.

Diggy scaled the stone wall at the tallest part of the cavern, out of the beast's reach, within the space of a few seconds. And I knew Father could do the same but wouldn't.

All around me, swords sang from their scabbards. And still, I stood there openmouthed. For though my mind knew the danger and my heart was seized with fear, I couldn't help myself. I couldn't control my wonder.

I had always wanted to see one.

"Tanwen!"

Mor's shout brought me back to myself, and I saw one of the swords belonged to him, the other four to Warmil, Father, Zel, and Aeron. Dylun held a stream of fire in his hand, and I vaguely recalled my first day in the Corsyth when his temper had exploded because I had thought there were only two songs.

Dray and Karlith stood behind a web of watery colormastery strands. No surprise that Dray would duck behind the safety of Karlith's protective artistry. He was quite the coward when it came down to it.

"Tannie, move!" That was Diggy, high above us all, clinging to the wall like a night-trapper.

I tried to shake off my shock because that terrifying creature I'd always wanted to see was now thundering across the cavern on all fours.

Straight toward me.

I stumbled backward. Then regained my footing and ran.

But where? Back into the passageway?

I scrambled toward the tunnel, then turned and tossed a strand back at the beast.

There had been no time to take a breath and put any sort of intention behind the strand. I'd just sent whatever had come out.

I glanced back in time to see a sunshine-bright rainbow smack the mountainbeast right in its eyes. Not what I would have picked, no mistake, but it did cause the beast to stumble. The creature tripped, then stood a moment, blinking.

The problem with shooting rainbows into the eyes of angry mountainbeasts is that they recover their wits and their sight shockingly fast, and then they're twice as livid as they were before the rainbow.

The beast loosed another roar.

Surely it would catch me in another breath or two, then tear me limb from limb.

Did mountainbeasts actually eat people? The fairy stories said so, but fairy stories could embellish. Storytellers do that sometimes, you know. We have to keep it lively for the crowd.

"Hey!" Father's yell didn't seem to faze the beast. But the rock he threw with his next shout did. "Hey!"

The stone bounced off the mountainbeast's head, and the massive paws slid to a halt. Then the animal changed direction to face the offending rock-hurler. It reared up on its hind legs.

"Captain, now!" Father hollered.

Warmil appeared from nowhere, so near the beast, my breath caught. But before the monster had a chance to notice the new presence, Warmil dragged his sword across its side. It seemed he was aiming higher—for the armpit, perhaps. But the blasted creature was so tall.

The ground shook with the beast's bellow of pain. Its head whipped toward Warmil.

But Father had drawn his bow and nocked an arrow. He loosed it, hitting the creature in the shoulder just as Warmil ducked beneath a swipe of a front paw the size of a dinner plate.

Father nocked another, but I grasped the truth with a sinking heart. It would take a great many arrows, a great many strikes, to bring this thing down.

We would all have to work together to make it happen.

An idea struck. "Dylun, together!"

He let his ribbon of fire go, and I created a stream of oil to meet it in midair. The two strands collided, and a ring of fire exploded like a halo around the head of the creature.

Its paws slapped at the burning fur on its face and shoulders.

"Diggy!" I called out, wondering if she would catch on quickly enough. I hoped so, because if I hit her with this strand . . . well, best not to think of it.

I thought the word *blade* as I created a strand and launched it toward her perch high on the wall. She kept her grip with one hand and reached out with the other. As she caught the strand, she turned it into a wicked sword and hurled it toward the beast.

The creature twisted, putting out the last of the fire in its fur, and the blade missed by inches. Diggy cursed.

The beast pivoted back to me as if it knew I was to blame for its singed eyebrows and smoking face fur.

"Stars." I froze again, struck by panic as it thundered toward me once more, angrier than ever.

Father loosed two more arrows that found their marks, and still it kept coming.

I tried to think of something I could turn into a strand, but nothing would come. My mind was a blank slate of panic. In a moment, it would be over. I closed my eyes, ready as I'd ever be.

The beast slammed into me, and we rolled together across the cavern floor. And then—it stayed huddled over my body like a shell.

I peeked up and found two wide, very concerned, very blue, decidedly human eyes staring back at me. "Mor?"

But he didn't take time to respond. He turned and thrust his sword into the chest of the creature that had just about overtaken us.

The mountainbeast roared and reared up. It drew back one of its forepaws to slash at Mor, and Mor pulled out his sword and took another strike.

Both Mor and the beast found their marks.

Mor buried his sword in the creature's chest, but the animal slashed its dagger-like claws across Mor's shoulder and up his neck.

"No!" I pushed off the ground and lunged for Mor.

A strand like a shield flew from my hand and filled the space between Mor and the beast. I pulled Mor back, out of range.

That horrible war cry I had heard more than once sounded nearby. I turned back toward the chaos to see Aeron thrust her sword in the spot beneath the armpit where Warmil had aimed before. The beast was doubled over this time, and Aeron stabbed true.

It was enough. Praise the Creator, it was enough.

The beast, Mor's sword still buried in its chest, stumbled back and fell. A river of purplish blood spilled from its many wounds. Some small piece of me pitied the creature. It had only been napping in its own cave, after all.

But then I turned to Mor and saw the gashes stretching from the top of his shoulder, up his neck, and onto one side of his face—that precious face I rather adored.

"Oh stars." I pressed my hands over the wounds in his neck. "Karlith! Warmil!"

They appeared beside me in a flash.

Warmil knelt beside us. "Oh, lad." He started pulling things from a pouch at his hip.

Mor seemed to have finally recovered his voice. He winced. "How bad?"

I watched his blood ooze between my fingers, and a sob escaped my throat.

"That bad, huh?"

"We'll fix you up." Warmil pulled his curved needle and fine thread from his pouch, and my stomach roiled.

A pair of tattooed hands appeared next to mine over Mor's wounds. I glanced up at Diggy. I wasn't sure I'd ever seen so much fear on her face, so much panic in her eyes.

"He'll be all right," she announced to Warmil, almost like a threat. "You'll make him all right, won't you?"

Warmil threaded his needle and didn't answer.

"Won't you?" she nearly shouted.

"Lass, please." Warmil tied off a knot. "If you want to help, get me some better light."

Karlith crouched beside me and wrapped her arm around my shoulders. "I have a gethweed tincture here. You put it on." She handed me a tiny glass bottle.

My hands shook as I tried to remove the miniature cork. "Blast. Was this made by wood fairies, or something?"

Karlith helped me pull the cork from the bottle. "Just a few drops where the bleeding is the worst."

I remembered watching her and Warmil work on Brac when he had been injured in the battle in Gareth's throne room. Karlith had shoved the untreated gethweed plant into Brac's stab wound to stem the flow. Surely this would work even better.

I carefully allowed one drop from the bottle onto Mor's neck.

He jumped. "That stings."

"Don't be such a baby."

He shot me a look.

My response was somewhere between a laugh and a sob as

I dripped a little more over his neck, face, and shoulder. I'll be blazed if the bleeding didn't slow to a faint trickle.

"Good, Tannie," Karlith said. "See how it's helped?"

I knew she was coddling me. Calming me by making me feel like I had some sort of control over what happened to Mor—like *I* could make sure he didn't die right in front of me. As if it wouldn't have worked just the same to have had anyone else drizzle gethweed tincture onto his wounds.

But I loved her for it.

"Aye, Karlith." I rested my head on her shoulder for a moment.

Then I turned back to Mor. Warmil had already stitched part of one of the scratches on Mor's neck. I forced my gaze away from that, so as to hold on to my breakfast, and focused on Mor's face.

"Does it hurt much?"

"Nah. Feels lovely." He gritted his teeth as Warmil's needle pricked in again. "The gethweed helps."

"I thought it stung."

"After the sting, it numbs it a little."

"I'm so sorry. I just . . . I was so scared, I couldn't seem to move."

"You know that saying on the peninsula?"

I gave a shaky laugh, despite my tears, because I knew exactly which one he meant. "I'd fight a mountainbeast for you?"

"Now you know I mean it plainly."

"It is well and truly dead now," Father proclaimed as he strode toward us, wiping purplish blood from his hands with a rag.

I decided not to ask for particulars.

Warmil was nearly halfway done with Mor's stitches, and I replaced the tiny cork and turned to hand the bottle of gethweed to Karlith.

But she wasn't there.

"Karlith?"

I scanned the cavern and found her in the corner where the mountainbeast had been sleeping. She knelt and placed her hands on the cave wall near the floor. She glanced up, and our eyes met.

"There?" I asked.

"Aye. I think so." She smiled sadly. "The beast was lying right by it."

"To guard it?" I swallowed hard. Did that mean there would be a mountainbeast by each strand?

"I don't think so. I think . . ." She trailed off and pressed her hands against the wall a little harder. "I think it liked the warmth."

She beckoned me closer. I glanced back at Mor. Warmil and the others had him well in hand. Besides, I couldn't bear to watch Warmil stitch him up. Not that I didn't like a good scar as much as the next lass. But heavens. We had come that close to a mountainbeast tearing off Mor's face.

Why had I always wanted to see one? Some things were better left in fairy stories.

I made my way over to Karlith, and she took one of my hands. "Feel here."

She pressed my palm against the wall. Warmth met my fingertips. And the wall . . . pulsed somehow. Very slightly. Not anything you would see, even if you were looking for it. But something you could feel. And now that I thought about it, ever since we'd entered the cavern, there had been something. Like a slight humming in my spirit. That must be what Karlith felt when she sensed the strands.

I glanced back at her. "How do we pull it up?"

Dylun appeared behind us, sighing. "I rather wish we had a map and plan for these."

"Any guesses for this one, Dylun?" If Dylun didn't have an idea, we were all but sunk.

He studied the wall. "We know the Master has one strand—that it must have been brought up some time ago. I suspect if she has waited this long to seek out the others, the first was not collected through much study."

"You're saying she stumbled on it by accident."

"That seems reasonable, given the circumstances."

"Then maybe . . ." I ran my hands along the wall, trying to will the strand to speak to me. "Maybe it's not as complicated as all that."

A tremor quivered beneath my palm. Without thinking about it, I pushed as hard as I could into the stone.

I half expected a broken wrist for my trouble—and distantly wondered if Karlith had a tincture for it.

Instead, the rock swallowed up my arm to the elbow.

"Ack!"

I almost yanked my arm back, even though this was what I had been hoping for, somewhere in the back of my mind. But I took a breath and forced myself to calm. To remember the sort of power that these strands held and that the rock must not be truly solid—or else the strand had somehow changed the nature of rock in its resting spot.

Who knew?

I ran my fingers along the stone until I felt a change. A subtle zing along my fingertips, and I knew I had found it—one of the ancient strands we were searching for.

"I . . . I found it." I glanced up at Dylun, my arm still pinned in the wall. "Now what? I'm not Diggy. I can't just grab a strand and force it to come with me."

"Can you coax it out?" he asked. "Draw it toward the surface of the rock?"

I could try.

I closed my eyes and tried to concentrate. Tried to send my thoughts toward the strand as if it could hear me.

Please, come with us. We need to keep you safe.

My heart hitched. Was I lying to it? We did want to keep it safe—to keep it from landing in the hands of the Master and to protect it from all the ways she would abuse whatever power lay inside this ancient creation.

But would we have to use the strand as leverage to rescue Braith? Would we have to turn it over to that madwoman anyway?

Best to sail that strait when we came to it.

After a moment, the strand responded. I could sense it wriggling closer to me, fighting its way through the stone.

My hand withdrew slowly, beckoning the strand to follow, and before long, I had pulled free of the wall.

Then the tip of the strand emerged.

"Oh my." Karlith exhaled. "Look at that."

Bright white and shining, like lightning. Like the white fire whose flames flickered around the outside of the cure we had built.

Definitely an ancient strand. Definitely created from the same Source as our cure that broke the weavers' curse.

I used my hand to direct the strand out of the cave wall until it was completely free. It lit up the entire cavern. I knew the others must be watching by now, but I tried to block out all other sounds until the strand waved before me, turning lazy, brilliant circles in midair.

Then I nodded at Dylun and repeated the phrase that seemed always to be on the tip of my tongue. "Now what?"

But he was ready for me. He opened his traveling pack and pulled out a medium-sized jar. He removed the lid and held it out to the strand. "If you please."

The strand continued to twirl in front of me.

I had a thought. "Karlith, let's try something. See if you can get it inside."

Karlith waved her hand toward the jar. "It's all right. You'll be safe in there."

The strand shuddered in response as if her words tickled it somehow. But it didn't obey.

I looked toward the others across the cavern. Mor was sitting up now, a patchwork of stitches across his body.

"Zel?" I called. "Can you try?"

He cleared his throat, looking awkward. "Er—that jar there looks right nice. Maybe try it out?" He moved his hands toward the jar.

The strand paused as if unsure, then slithered into Dylun's jar and curled up.

Only storytellers. The Master had gotten that part right, anyway.

I watched as Dylun tucked the jar into his pack.

And silently I prayed I had not just sealed the fate of this beautiful, terrifying ancient tendril of lightning. If the Master got hold of it, it would be worse off than the departed mountainbeast whose carcass lay on the floor behind us.

CHAPTER TWENTY-SEVEN
TANWEN

I was none too pleased to leave the hulking mountainbeast carcass as we squeezed our way back through the passageway and onto the main path.

Or what seemed to be the main path. We had only Dray to guide us, and I still wasn't convinced he wouldn't lead us right off the edge of a cliff.

"Does it hurt?" I asked Mor for the fortieth time as we followed Dray and Father, who seemed to be bickering about something. Again.

Father had lit one of the lanterns to give us storytellers a break from making light strands, and I'd spent all of my free energy fussing over Mor.

"Aye, it hurts," he acknowledged with a half smile.

"I'm sorry."

"Stop apologizing."

"It's all my fault," I said, also for the fortieth time.

"Not unless you planted the mountainbeast in the cavern."

"I should have moved faster."

"I'm not having this conversation again."

"Or not shot rainbows into its eyes."

"I agree with you there."

"What was that, anyway? Of all things!"

"Maybe you were thinking about the Corsyth."

I looked at him. "Aye. Because that's what I think about

when anything beastly and hairy is moving toward me—kissing you."

Diggy pushed past us, her nose wrinkled. "*Akē*. Everyone can hear you, you know."

My cheeks warmed, but I found myself not caring. Mor's stitches were a solemn reminder of how close the mountainbeast's claws had come to the veins in his neck.

A shudder skittered down my spine. Had I truly almost lost him? An inch to the left, a little deeper, a little more force and Mor's throat might have been slit.

My fingers found his palm in the semidarkness.

No glove. He must have left them off after the mountainbeast attack.

I took his hand anyway.

A beam of light shot from our connection and vaulted straight toward the ceiling. It found solid rock and pinged back toward us before hitting the ground with a *pop*.

But I held tight. Because as long as I didn't let go, it probably wouldn't happen again. At least I didn't think so. There didn't seem to be any rhyme or reason to what happened when Mor and I touched except that *something* happened each time.

"Tannie, we are going for stealth," Warmil tossed over his shoulder from up ahead. "You could try to keep things under control."

I looked up at Mor. "As if we had any idea how."

Mor's face seemed to redden in the dim light as he returned his concentration to the path in front of us. But he didn't let go of my hand.

Don't think I didn't notice.

A few long, silent moments passed as we worked our way through the caves.

I sighed. "If I never see the color slate gray again, it'll be too soon. Do you think this is what it's like to be a root-snacker, tunneling through the earth, the ground the same as the ceiling and same as the walls?"

Mor chuckled. "Couldn't tell you."

"What a boring life."

"But there are all those roots to snack on, and that's something."

Snacks. I grimaced. "Why did you have to mention food?" My stomach rumbled on cue.

"Sorry." But he didn't really look it.

"If you thought you'd turned me into a hardened, seaworthy sailor, you're wrong, you know."

"Truly? I couldn't tell. You seemed downright hard-boiled."

"Shocking, I know. But no. I need a hearth, a bed, and three warm meals a day to be truly settled. Oh! And pillows! Preferably three."

"What in the world would anyone want with three pillows?"

"Two under my head, one at my side."

"Forgive me, Your Highness."

It was a little funny to think about, since I couldn't actually remember the last time I'd had such comforts. Before we left on our quest for the cure, I supposed. Truly, my brief weeks in the palace were the only time I'd had such things in all my life.

And that was some moons ago. Maybe I'd become hard-boiled by accident. I glanced down at my fingers, interlaced with Mor's, and my stomach did a backflip.

Scrambled, more like.

"So . . ." He slid a sideways glance at me. "You really need a hearth on solid ground to be happy?"

"No, actually." I grinned. "Wouldn't mind a bunk on a ship right now, to be honest."

Suddenly, Mor yanked my arm back, and I nearly stumbled to the ground.

"Hey, what—"

He put his hand over my mouth before I could say anything else. Then he held a finger to his lips and gestured up ahead.

I had been so lost in my thoughts that I hadn't noticed everyone in front of us had stopped. Father held up one hand to signal us to halt, and then he covered the lantern box partway with a cloth to block out the light.

He must see something up ahead. Or someone.

It was then that I could just make out the muffled sound of voices. They seemed far away, but it was probably the cave playing its tricks on us. They were obviously close enough that Father could see them.

After what felt an eternity, Father pulled back the cloth a bit and allowed more light to illuminate the path. He gestured to Warmil, then nodded down one passageway.

Stars. They were going to get closer.

I took a step forward to . . . do something. To stop them from approaching whatever lay beyond.

The Master, perhaps?

But one glance at Dray told me that wasn't likely. True to form, he was hanging back behind several others. He did have a knack for keeping himself out of danger. If we were approaching his former Master, he would have placed himself front and center, surely, to be our mouthpiece.

It had to be a competing team up ahead, and that could be just as deadly.

Father and Warmil moved away, taking the light with them. For several awful moments, we stood in complete darkness. I listened to the sound of my blood drumming in my ears and prayed my father and Warmil would make it back alive.

The lantern light shimmered toward us again.

"Come," Father whispered. "I want you to see. All of you."

We tiptoed after him and Warmil, whose sword was drawn.

After a quick right turn, then a left, we found ourselves by an archway of stone. Beyond the archway was an open cavern like the one where we had discovered the ancient strand—and the mountainbeast—except this one was about a third the size, if I judged right.

Since we didn't have the benefit of light strands or Diggy's rock sparkles, I wasn't sure I *was* judging right.

But there were three men huddled near the far wall.

One had his hand pressed to the stone. "I think it's back here. I feel something."

"Well, get it out," another said. "We don't have time for this."

"I'm just not sure how to begin . . ." The man pulled his hand away from the wall.

The third man drew a tool from his pack. "I'll get it."

The first began to object. "I don't think—"

A pickax slammed into the stone.

The second man rose and rolled his brawny shoulders as if working out the kinks. "Let him. That's why he's here."

The first man stood too. "Not sure if this is the best way to go about it, is all."

"He's the digger, and you're the weaver. Let him do his job so you can do yours."

The weaver shot a look at the brawny one. "And what's your job, exactly?"

"I'm the leader," he said with a smirk in his voice. "And the muscle, obviously."

Father studied the digger. Probably gathering information. And also watching to see if they succeeded in collecting a strand.

A terrible thought struck me.

What were we supposed to do if they did collect one of the strands? We hoped to find all eleven so another team could not deliver them to the Master. So what would we do if this team collected one while we stood here? Surely Father wouldn't hurt them . . .

I glanced at his right hand, resting on the hilt of his sword.

Stars. Maybe he would.

But in the next moment, those thoughts fled from my mind. All my thoughts were crowded out by complete and total horror.

I stood frozen as Diggy pushed past all of us and strode straight into the cavern, in full view of the other team.

The weaver saw her first. "What the—"

The pickax stilled in the digger's hands, and the brawny one's eyes popped wide. "Hey, what are you—"

"Do you know me?" Diggy interrupted. She stared up at the brawny one as she stalked ever closer.

"No, who are—"

"I know you. You're Lasech Bo-Camdrine. You sailed under Captain Bo-Gallogwyr three years ago."

I saw nothing about the big one to indicate he was a sailor, and I wondered if she might be mistaken. But then I saw his boots—so like the sharkskin ones I had noticed on Mor when we first met.

Diggy stepped closer to him. "You were my friend at first. Do you remember? You liked the way I brewed the bitter-bean. Said it reminded you of home." She paused. "But then you started visiting me at night, and you weren't my friend anymore." Diggy's voice was deathly calm. "Do you know me now?"

My insides finally melted, my feet unfroze, and I sprang to life. "Diggy, no!" I sprinted into the cavern after her.

But I was too late. Many years too late.

The recognition dawned on Bo-Camdrine's face as he finally seemed to recall the young girl whose innocence he'd helped steal. How could he not have known her on sight? How could her face not be etched into his memory?

It didn't matter. For Diggy was within striking distance now.

"Diggy, stop!"

She drew the dagger from her left hip and plunged it into his stomach. Quick as lightning, she withdrew it and thrust it into his armpit and left it there. She spun a half-turn, pulled another knife from the scabbard on her left thigh, and stabbed backward—straight into the man's inner thigh.

Three wounds in the space of a breath.

I reached her just as she yanked both blades from Bo-Camdrine's body.

He stared, his hand clutching the abdominal wound. Then he dropped to his knees.

Karlith rushed into the cavern, up to the bleeding man. "Oh, Creator." She turned. "Warmil!"

He was already halfway there, as were Father, Mor, and everyone else. The two other men from Bo-Camdrine's team stood immobilized by shock at what had just happened.

The only person in the whole cavern who didn't look shocked was Diggy. Her face was calm, but boiling just beneath the surface were four years of rage and pain and horror and heartbreak.

Bo-Camdrine collapsed to the floor. Warmil crouched beside the bleeding man. He didn't reach for the pouch at his hip. Didn't examine the wounds closely. Just shook his head.

"She knows anatomy," he said finally, glancing at Diggy, then back to Karlith. "There's nothing I can do."

Before he even finished saying it, Bo-Camdrine's blood spilled its last. One of Diggy's many tormentors lay dead on the floor of the cavern.

She took a step back from him, then turned. Her brows rose, almost as though she had just realized she wasn't alone—that she had a horrified audience. She looked around at each of us in turn.

Only Karlith moved or spoke. She muttered prayers under her breath as she closed Bo-Camdrine's eyes. Then she looked up at Diggy, tears brimming on her lashes. "Oh, my dear girl. What have you done?"

Diggy took another step away. Her chest began to heave.

"Diggy," Mor began. But there was no end to his plea. What else could he say?

Nothing could take back what had just happened, same as nothing could take back what had happened to her four years past.

Diggy's gaze darted around the circle—between her friends and companions, across the still body, then to his fellows, whose faces began to register fear and anger. And then her focus landed on Dray.

He was staring at her, wide-eyed. And then that snake opened his mouth to speak. "Yes. The Master will be *very* keen on you."

A shadow crossed her face—something I couldn't decipher. Something too deep and too painful for me ever to understand.

Without a sound, she turned and bolted into the darkness.

"Diggy, wait!"

Mor and I both ran into the passageway after her. A ribbon of light from my hand raced one way, and a strand from Mor flew ahead in the other direction.

But there was no sign of her. She had vanished.

And just like that, in every way that mattered, I lost Digwyn En-Lidere.

CHAPTER TWENTY-EIGHT
BRAC

Eny Bo-Fergel pressed his lips into an invisible line as he looked down at the piece of parchment in his hands. I had scribbled a few figures on there, like I had done in the dirt with a stick when my father and I would puzzle through the matters of acreage and seeds and projected yield at harvest.

I couldn't read or write words, but the hash marks and symbols we used to deal with numbers for the farm were as familiar to me as the scent of fresh-turned soil and the feel of a flail or harrow in my hands.

"It won't work, will it?" Defeat billowed around my words like a cloud of dust.

Eny paused another moment. "I did not say that, Brac."

I pointed to one set of scribbles. "I thought if we could get fifteen hundred good, solid farmers, it might work. Surely there are fifteen hundred farmers in Tir who would be willing."

Eny nodded. "Farms are failing on both coasts. The Wildlands have it even worse than the east, if you can imagine. And you're right—the land in the middle of the continent has not dealt with drought and blight to the same degree."

"Then could we do it? Could we cultivate that land and turn it into some sort of . . . communal farmland, or something? If that's where the soil would produce, that's where we should go."

Eny's lips pressed tighter. "But the cost." He looked at me. "The cost to feed and house the men working the land. It would be a massive undertaking, and I'm not sure the royal treasury could support it."

I flopped into the chair behind my desk. This study and the rooms attached to it had once belonged to one of Gareth's councilors. Naith had chosen them as my apartments because they were close to the throne room.

I couldn't quite stomach the idea of moving into the queen's rooms, though those were suggested first. I had ordered them left empty and her things untouched for the time being. But I knew eventually Naith would demand I do something with them.

"I don't see another solution," I said to Eny. "This is all I have to offer the people. I'm a farmer, so I—" A lump rose out of nowhere in my throat. A big fat lump of failure.

I took a breath. "This is all I have to offer Tir, and it's a whole lot of nothing."

Eny sat across from me and placed the parchment on the desk. "It's not nothing. This is a good idea. We just have to take a very close look at the royal treasury."

"You know, it's funny," I said bitterly. "When I was a peasant, I thought there must be a pile of money in the palace somewhere. A roomful of it. And that the king could just do whatever he wanted with it."

Eny smiled faintly. "There is money enough. But not a roomful. And it is a delicate balance, income versus expenses. We must be careful not to drain the treasury all at once on one large project. This is why wars so often bring financial ruin." His gaze returned to my scribbles. "Perhaps if we implemented it in phases . . ."

"I wonder what Tannie would say," I said without meaning to—without thinking about it, really.

It was habit to wonder what Tannie would think about my ideas and plans. Those plans had always been small when we were younger. And hers had always sounded so wild—traveling around the world, selling stories, living life out of her satchel and meeting new people every day.

Mine were simple. A new crop next planting season. An idea about how to set up my farmhouse on the land my father had set aside for me.

For us. For me and Tannie. That had always been part of my plans.

But now, when I thought about the future, I didn't see Tannie by my side. It had nothing to do with her pirate and everything to do with the right mess I'd made.

And still I craved her presence. I wanted my best friend back.

I glanced up to find Eny staring at me. "Are you all right?" he asked.

"I miss her," I blurted.

"Tanwen, the storyteller."

"Aye. She's my best friend."

Was my best friend. But I couldn't bring myself to say it aloud.

Instead, I said, "If I could have one thing right now, do you know what it would be?" I didn't wait for an answer. "I would go home. I'd like to apologize to Tannie somehow, of course, but if I could have just one thing, it would be that. Home."

Eny nodded. "I can understand that."

"Some things can't be undone, can they?"

"No, indeed, my lord." He caught himself. "Brac."

I heaved a sigh. "Maybe this would all look different after a mug of ale."

Eny's eyebrows rose.

"What? You don't know that everything looks better after a mug of ale?" I shook my head. "You gotta get out from behind the desk every once in a while, my friend. But be careful with this here novel information. Some things you ought to stay away from look better at the bottom of a mug, too, and you can get yourself in a right bit of trouble."

His eyebrows rose higher.

I grinned and stood. "I'll pop down to the kitchens and get us both a pint."

"I can send someone."

"Aye, but I'm sick of being waited on." I paused at the door and shook my head. "Sakes. Never thought I'd hear myself say that. Be back in a minute."

I didn't hurry down the hall, because all that was waiting for me on the other side of this brief errand was an impossible problem. Might as well enjoy my break while it lasted.

The servants' stairwell to the kitchens lay just ahead. Naith had scolded me repeatedly for using the servants' passageways, but Cethor's tears, were they faster. Made sense, I supposed, as the servants were expected to move through the palace like lightning—silent, invisible lightning, never seen or heard but always available. Royalty, nobility, and important officials were expected to parade around the front rooms and public hallways, the wide, grand staircases and main thoroughfares.

Give me the shortcuts any day.

The low entrance to the winding stairway was just to my right, but I jerked to a halt before reaching it.

Naith's voice carried out of the door to my left.

That door led to his private chambers—that I knew. But he had excused himself shortly after breakfast, saying he wanted to spend some time in the temple and see to the priestly business there. He complained about that constantly these days—missing the priestly work, wanting to be close to the goddesses again.

I'd finally told him to see to whatever he blasted well felt like and stop whining about it.

But now, there was his voice. Low but unmistakable, still here in the palace.

Now, I knew it wasn't right. Whatever else had happened, I really hadn't forgotten the basics of right and wrong, and sneaking into someone's private chambers to eavesdrop on their conversation was wrong.

But my hand still found the knob and twisted it. I slowly leaned on the door until I had space enough to peer in.

Naith was not in the front room. The door to his bedchamber was open, and his voice carried in from there. It was nearly a miracle I'd heard him to begin with, but there was something about his tone—urgent pleading spaced between explosions of frustration.

The high priest was worked into a froth about something.

And then I heard my name.

"Brac is not quite the easy mark we had hoped for. In some ways, yes. We've gotten him this far, after all. But in other ways, the boy gives me more trouble than you can imagine."

"Try me."

My heart stopped its galloping. That voice. I didn't know it, exactly, but I almost felt like I'd heard it before. Once, maybe, a while back. It was a strange voice, not easily forgotten. Muddled, somehow, like I was hearing it through water or the whistling wind.

Was someone else in there with him?

"The boy keeps making ridiculous statements about undoing it all, taking it back, wanting to go home. He has lost his nerve, that's certain. And . . ."

"Continue, Naith." The tone left no room for argument.

Who was this person ordering around the High Priest of Tir?

"He made a comment—in passing, mind you, probably nothing to worry about . . ."

"Speak, Naith!"

I flinched at the yell, and the strange voice wasn't even talking to me. I could imagine Naith cowering.

"Brac said something about wishing to restore Braith to the throne."

The voice laughed. "Is that all? Well, there's no danger of that."

My heart stuttered. Did that mean . . . was the queen dead? After they'd promised me they wouldn't harm her?

But then the voice continued, "She's here with me, after all."

With this mystery person? Here? In the palace? In Naith's room?

What in blazes was going on?

My heart found its proper beat again. A seed of anger grew inside me. It sprouted a runner, and this seedling of fury replaced any fear in my body. I threw caution into the sea and edged closer to Naith's bedchamber to see what was happening.

I peered around the corner of the bedroom door. Naith's back was to me—thank the stars—and he was on his knees before an open window, despite the chill air of the first winter moon. Strands like Tannie's story strands—but almost invisible—curled all around him. I couldn't see them, exactly, but I could see the way they played with the light and air in the room. Like heat waves rising on a blistering day.

And the voice was coming straight from those strands.

I goggled. I knew I was being reckless, standing there like a dolt. If Naith had turned at that moment, I wouldn't have been able to move, no matter how much I wanted to.

But he didn't turn, and I kept trying to understand what I was seeing.

"I will keep a close watch on Braith," the voice said from the strands. "That is my concern and mine alone, no matter what the boy wishes he could do."

"But if his sentiment is such, couldn't he raise support to—"

"Enough."

Naith's head dropped another inch. "Yes, Master."

"I have it well in hand. Braith will not escape. She is literally in chains in the next room. No matter how much support the boy is able to raise, Braith will not be free to reclaim her place on the throne."

"Yes, Master."

Master. His slips a while back came to mind. He'd said that name to me before and tried to scramble out of it.

So this person in the strands was his Master.

But who? How?

"And the others?" the Master asked.

"Unless they have been waylaid, they should have reached the Mynyth by now."

"My spies in Ir-Golyth report possible sightings."

"I sent them straight into your hands," Naith said quickly. "All you need to do is capture them."

"Yes, just that simple task." The words dripped with sarcasm, even though they were spoken through strands—strands apparently coming from the Mynyth Range? That was way up north.

Then it hit me like a side of grazer. These *others* Naith and his Master were talking about were Tannie and her friends. The rebel weavers.

Naith had sent them straight into a trap.

"No, of course, Master. It will not be simple. They have proved the most troublesome creatures I've ever encountered. But we are very close."

"Indeed. So close."

"And then . . ." Naith paused. "What of Braith? And Kharn Bo-Candryd?"

"It will be time to dispose of them. They are still threats, though I have them in chains."

"Begging your pardon, Master . . ."

A sigh. "Yes, Naith?"

"Why not dispose of them now? If they pose a risk, if they are threats, dispatch them at once."

The clear strands twisted around Naith, swirling slowly.

After a moment, the voice spoke again. "Conveniently, Braith serves as the perfect bit of bait for the moment. I'm using her to lure the others. But it goes beyond that. This is a personal matter. I want Braith to watch as I destroy everything that matters to her."

Naith leaned his forehead against the window ledge, as though bowing low before someone—begging, groveling. "Master, have I not earned your trust? Have I not earned some confidence? I have been your most trusted servant for decades. Your most faithful soldier since the beginning. Will you not tell me at last why this matters to you so? If you will put yourself and the operation at risk to fulfill this personal desire, I will support you. Only tell me why."

Another pause, and the strands whirled like they were thinking.

"Yes, Naith. You have earned as much."

And then, something happened to the voice. The garbled, wobbly sound about it lifted. And when it spoke again, I could hear it, smooth as a solid-frozen pond in the dead of winter.

"It is I, Naith," she said, for there was no mistaking it now. The voice was clearly a woman's. "I have personal business with Braith because *I* am the Master."

Naith clutched a hand to his heart. "Your . . . Your Majesty?"

And then it all rushed in on me like a wave crashing against the empty shore it had left behind a minute earlier.

I'd heard the voice in the throne room more than a handful of times while I stood guard at court: Frenhin Ma-Gareth, Queen of the Tirian Empire.

"Yes, it is I. Your true queen."

Naith began to weep. "Oh, Master. How I've longed to know."

My stomach turned over like I might hork up my breakfast.

But I'd heard enough. Enough to know exactly what I needed to do next.

I backed out of Naith's room as he whimpered and praised

the traitor queen—Queen Braith's own mother. I carefully closed the door to its proper spot.

Then I took off at a full run back to my apartments. I burst into the front room, startling Eny.

He looked at me cheerfully. "Oh, there you are. I had a thought about—" He stopped short as he took in my face. "What is it, Brac? Where is the ale?"

I pulled the door closed behind me and leaned against it. "Eny . . ." I swallowed hard. "Can I trust you?"

He set his papers on the desk and crossed the room to me. "With your life."

"I need you to draft some letters for me." I paused to do some mental figuring. "Fourteen of them. We will need eleven of our swiftest carrier birds to take some to the Eastern Peninsula. Three runners to deliver the others in Urian."

Eny nodded. "Yes, my lord. Of course."

"And have the stable master saddle my horse."

CHAPTER TWENTY-NINE
DIGWYN

THOUGHTS OF VENGEANCE COME TO ME EVERY NIGHT.

Not sometimes. Not on the bad days. Not when things are hard.

Every. Single. Night.

What would I do to them if I had the chance? What *wouldn't* I do to them if I had the chance?

How do you pay a man back for a lifetime's worth of pain?

There is no amount of suffering I might inflict upon them that would take mine away. So, then what?

Death.

Death is the only true vengeance—the only way to make right what has been wronged. The only way to fix what's been broken.

And if they could truly understand, they would see it's a mercy. If I were to inflict equal pain, it would be worse. Death is swift, merciful, clean.

And right.

Because that's what they did to me. They murdered me. They killed everything that mattered, everything that made me whole and hopeful, young and innocent.

They murdered me without giving me the peace of permanent sleep.

I will not be so cruel to them.

Abdomen. Armpit. Inner thigh.
Liver. Axillary artery. Femoral artery.
Abdomen. Armpit. Inner thigh.

The words race through my mind, over and over, as they have for two years past. Abdomen, armpit, inner thigh. Liver, axillary artery, femoral artery. Two movements of my body, three swift strikes, death in less than a minute.

I had practiced in my mind, just in case the chance presented itself. I studied whatever books and bits of information Kawan could get for me from the ships docking at Kanac. Warmil was right. I had studied anatomy for exactly this purpose.

In case I ever ran across one of *them*. So I would know what to do, where to strike. So I could end it quickly and bring what they had coming.

Have my revenge.

Redeem what was lost, even if only in some small measure.

And now, the words rumble through my mind, echoing the thundering pulse of my heart.

Abdomen. Armpit. Inner thigh.

Panic chokes me, and my hands begin to shake. Blood, sticky between my fingers. My breath, ragged. The gasps, short.

"Diggy!" I hear Tannie call.

"Diggy!" Mor's voice seems to reach out and find me in the dark.

But they're far away. I can tell, though the cave tries to deceive me.

I duck into a cleft in the wall and freeze. Try to breathe. Try to think.

I did it perfectly. Exactly as I had imagined. Exactly as I had practiced.

He saw my face, remembered me at last, and then he was dead. Exactly as it was supposed to be.

I wait, because surely it will come. Surely the vengeance will begin to soothe my soul. I need only let the rush dissipate, my heart calm, and then some of the ache will subside.

At last.

Four long years, and finally the ache will ease.

But as I sit in the dark, the ache does not ease. The dark pit of my soul only grows.

It takes another moment, huddling in the shadows, wedged in the cleft of the rock, but finally I understand the truth. It dawns like sunrise on the day you know you're going to die.

Revenge will not restore my soul. Vengeance will not soothe the ache. Ending Lasech's life has not evened the score.

And if revenge doesn't help, what will?

I hold my breath as someone passes.

"Diggy?" It's Tannie, and her voice is full of tears. Hopelessness. Despair. "Diggy?"

I don't speak. Don't breathe. I let her light disappear down the passageway.

Better for us both this way. She doesn't need me, and I don't need her.

I sit for a long while. Waiting for the answer. Waiting for a plan.

Revenge doesn't help. If revenge won't fix me, perhaps I'm beyond fixing. Perhaps there is no use trying.

Perhaps this is all there is for me. If what has been broken cannot be put back together, it's best to accept that. Lean into it. Claim the brokenness as my own. Take action and stop wishing for a different reality, a different life.

I slip from the rock and set out to accept my destiny.

I set out to find the Master.

CHAPTER THIRTY
TANWEN

When Mor found me, I was sitting against the cave wall, my knees pulled to my chest, my head buried in my arms, sobs wracking me.

He eased down next to me and didn't speak for a long time. He just let me cry, and I was thankful for it.

My tears dried up after a while, but the sobs kept coming. I looked up at him. "I lost her, Mor. She's nowhere. Just . . . disappeared. We'll never find her in here."

In the glow of his light strand, I saw his throat bob. But he kept staring straight ahead. "Aye."

"Why did . . . what was—" I hiccupped. But there was no way to complete any of my broken thoughts.

"I don't know, Tannie." He dropped his head into his hands. "I failed her. Again. I keep failing and failing, no matter what I do. No matter how hard I try to—"

He didn't finish, and he didn't have to.

I leaned my head on his shoulder, and we both cried for a while. Finally, I found his hand with mine and laced our fingers together. A glittery thread of blue encircled us.

"Mor, I'm sorry. I tried."

"I know you did."

"Should we keep looking? Maybe we could find her still." I tried to sound more hopeful than I felt.

"No. She doesn't want to be found."

He was right, of course. And if she didn't want to be found in here, she never would be.

A dozen worries tumbled through my mind.

Would she find her way out? What if she got lost? What if she ran into other Hunt teams and they hurt her? What if she ran into other Hunt teams and she hurt *them*? What if she couldn't find her way out and starved to death in here?

"Tannie? Mor?" Father's voice. The light from his lantern illuminated his face a moment later. "Thank the Creator. I thought we had lost you." He paused. "You didn't find her."

Mor still didn't look up.

Father closed his eyes, then drew a long breath. "We've smoothed things over with the other crew—the weaver and the digger. Dylun had to pay them off in the end, and we had to surrender the cavern, which means they have that strand. But they shouldn't bother us now. They said they would see to the body of their comrade. Hopefully Digwyn will not run into them, because I don't think they will forgive her so easily."

I tried to get a better look at Mor's face. It was stony. But I noticed blood seeping from one of his stitched-up wounds.

"Mor, you're bleeding."

"Huh?" He glanced down at his shoulder. "Oh. That."

Father offered his hand and helped me up. Then he reached out to Mor. "Let's get back to Karlith. She'll have something to help that bleeding."

Mor ignored him. Father glanced at me, and I shook my head.

Father crouched down to look Mor in the eyes. "Son, we won't forget about her. We'll keep searching as we carry on our mission."

"I . . . I know." Mor shook his head. "She's just so . . . broken. I don't know that there will ever be something better for her. You saw it. We all watched her kill a man like it was nothing."

Compassion was etched in every line of Father's face. "Digwyn has had deep injustices committed against her. Perhaps she just needs more time. Her mind is fragile, but her body is not. She is strong and able to care for herself while she takes the time she needs. She will survive, and we will find her."

Mor looked up.

"I promise you." Father continued to look him straight in the eyes. "And I never break my promises. Do you believe me?"

Mor nodded.

Father rose and offered his hand to Mor again. This time, Mor took it.

"Good," Father said. "Let's go find the queen."

CHAPTER THIRTY-ONE

TANWEN

KARLITH LEANED AGAINST THE WALL AND WAVED WARMIL away. "All is well," she insisted for the tenth time.

"General." Warmil turned to Father, concern creasing his brow. "Perhaps we should rest again. Karlith tires."

"Warmil Bo-Awirth." Karlith shot an annoyed glance his direction. "I said I'm fine. And I'm not an old lady. Stop treating me like one."

He and Father shared a glance.

"What is it, Karlith?" Father asked. "I've seen you travel great distances on foot, carrying a heavy pack, and you've never needed to rest so much."

She sighed. "It's the evil in this place. It . . . presses." She put her hand over her chest. "Here. I feel it in my spirit all the time now, like it's growing stronger."

Aeron frowned. "Do you think we're getting closer to the Master? Or is it something else?"

We all turned toward Dray. He was the one who was supposed to be keeping us on course to find this Master.

Dray shrugged. "I told you I'd lead you to her. What did you expect?"

Though he played it off, I could see something else in his expression—he was impressed.

He considered Karlith. "Can you really feel it—the Master's presence?"

"I feel something." Karlith shook her head. "Something bad. Couldn't tell you what or who it is. I guess you'd know better than I."

He nodded, definitely impressed. "Interesting. Strange bit of magic, that."

"It's not magic." I glared at him. "Feeling things that aren't part of the physical world is just . . . well, you have to have a soul to manage it."

"Ouch." Dray put his hand on his abdomen, right where Diggy had stabbed Bo-Camdrine. "That hurts, Tanwen."

I glared twice as hard at his hand. He'd put it in that spot on purpose, of course. And it had been *his* words that had made Diggy run off three days past. All of my anger, hurt, weariness, and frustration needed a target, and he was the best one around. "Well, when you trade your soul away, you're bound to miss it occasionally."

He smirked. "You're vicious when you want to be." He held up his hands. "No, no. Don't apologize. I rather like it."

Just having a conversation with this man left me feeling like I needed a bath.

Karlith straightened and took a deep breath. "Another strand is close." She nodded up ahead. "That way, I think."

"Will you be all right?" Warmil took her elbow to help her step over some uneven ground.

"Aye. I'm always all right." She smiled—a little forced.

And then we were on the move again.

"I wish I could sense the strands," I said quietly to Mor. "To take some of the burden off Karlith." The humming in my spirit was faint until we were nearly on top of a strand—not very useful to guide us. "They're supposed to be storyteller strands. Shouldn't we be able to feel them?"

"I can."

I swiveled to face him. "You can?"

"Aye." He shrugged. "Karlith perceives them much more

strongly than I do, so she's leading the way. Zel can't feel them at all."

"But why? How does a colormaster feel these strands stronger than three storytellers?"

"Dylun says Karlith is connected to them—not because of the weavers who made them but because of the Source of their power."

"And the weavers on the other teams? Don't tell me they're all worshipers of the Creator like Karlith."

Mor flashed a half smile. "Not likely. But they're older. More experienced storytellers. They had years to hone their craft before Gareth came into power and the suppression began. It's only because my parents were free to raise me as they wished at sea that my craft developed as it did. You've only had a few moons to truly begin to discover your gift. Dylun thinks that's why I'm more aware of the ancient strands than you are."

"So in another five or ten years, maybe I'll be useful?"

The half smile grew. "Maybe." Then his expression dimmed. "Zel was taught to fear his gift. That fear still grips him, and I don't know that he'll ever break free of it." His gaze caught on his best friend leading at the front of the group with a strand of light. "I'm going to go help him."

I watched him speed his pace, leaving me behind. Then I fell into step with Father at the rear of the pack. Dray was on Father's other side, Warmil and Karlith just ahead of us.

Father's voice, colder than usual, startled me. "What exactly is your objective, Dray?"

"Objective?" Dray asked, as though the concept were foreign. "Whatever do you mean?"

"Enough." Father's tone was sharp. "Don't trifle with me. Why are you here with us? What's in it for you?"

"You're asking this now?"

"It served our purposes well enough to have you here, and it still does. But as we draw closer to your . . . Master, I want to know the truth. Why are you really here?"

"I have my reasons." Dray faced my father. "It was not part of the agreement that I share them with you."

In a moment, Father's sword was drawn and pointed at Dray's chest. "Nor was keeping you alive any longer than I wished."

Dray stayed very still—wisely. But his gaze traveled down to the blade, a hairsbreadth from his heart, and he smiled. "I see where your daughter gets her vicious streak."

The tip of the sword touched the fabric of Dray's shirt.

Dray held his hands up. "I have already told you the truth. I'm here for Braith."

"General," Karlith said gently. "No more violence just now. Please."

Father didn't make any indication he'd heard at first. But after a hesitation, he pulled his sword back and sheathed it.

Dray drew a full breath. "Stars. You people are the most unpleasant traveling company." He folded his arms and smirked, bolder now that Father's sword was stowed. "You know, Queen Braith believed in redemption. I'm surprised you don't."

Father glared. "Can a mountainbeast turn into a hedge-nibbler?"

He spat the words like arrows, and I flinched. His anger frightened me. I didn't like to see him so bitter. Even if I agreed with him, there was something comforting in imagining my father to be above such unpleasant, unpredictable emotions—something comforting in imagining he would never do anything rash or unwise because of passion.

Turned out Yestin Bo-Arthio was human.

"Hearts can change," Karlith said. "People can change."

"Can, yes." Father continued to regard Dray. "It doesn't mean they have."

Karlith sighed. "That's true enough."

"Look," Dray said, his voice serious and not filled with mockery for once. "Braith believed in me. She thought I could change—that I *had* changed. Did it ever occur to you that perhaps I want to prove her right? The only way to do that is to save her. And you'll have to take my word on that."

He didn't wait for a reply. He hurried ahead and joined Mor and the others at the front of the pack.

I lowered my voice so only Father would hear. "He might be telling the truth."

Father grunted.

"It's . . . possible," I said slowly. "His argument makes sense, anyway."

"Careful, Tannie," Father warned. "His argument might make sense, but it doesn't mean it's true. He is a politician, after all."

CHAPTER THIRTY-TWO
TANWEN

WE CAMPED OUT IN AN ALCOVE A BIT TOO SMALL FOR OUR entire crew that night. I slept with Father's arm draped over me, my face in Karlith's back, and someone's elbow pressing against my calf. I woke to thoughts of Diggy and where she might have slept. Same as I'd wondered every night since her disappearance.

"Is it morning?" I asked the others rousing around me.

"Could be," Dylun remarked. "It's impossible to tell in here, but we have slept a night's worth. Or as close to it as we'll get."

I rubbed the sore spot on my calf where the elbow—Mor's, I now realized—had been pressing all night. He pulled himself to a sitting position, wincing as he rolled his injured shoulder. Then he massaged his elbow. "Ouch."

"Oh, I'm sorry." I rubbed my calf harder and scowled at him. "Did my leg flesh hurt your arm bone?"

He grinned. "Sorry."

Zel had managed to create a pocket of flame—just enough to heat some water for tea. We sipped brisk-leaf and nibbled on provisions from our packs.

Not the most delicious breakfast, to be sure. But I'd heaved enough roasted fish over the side of the *Cethorelle* to know it wasn't the worst either.

"We're close." Karlith finished off the last of her tea. "If we weren't so spent last night, I would have suggested we press on. But I don't suppose we would've had the strength to pull up the strand." She stretched. "Everything looks better after a good night's sleep." She glanced warmly at Mor, and he didn't shy away from it.

That was an improvement over the days before.

I searched in my pack a moment and pulled out my briskleaf paste and tooth-cleaning cloth.

Aeron grinned at me. "Wonder why you're worried about your breath."

I tried to glare at her. "Because I wasn't raised in a barn." I paused. "Actually, that's not true."

I had spent a solid six moons living in Farmer Bradwir's barn while fixing up my family's cottage once.

She didn't poke at me further, but her knowing grin seemed to light up the cave.

After my teeth were fresh and everyone had stretched, we plodded onward. I soon learned that, to Karlith, *close* was a relative term.

"I feel like we've been walking for hours," I grumbled to Mor. I wiggled my fingers to get some blood back into them, and the light strand pouring from my hand wavered a bit.

"It's barely been an hour, if I judge right." He raised an eyebrow at me. "You're just bored."

I fought the urge to pout. He wasn't wrong. Our first few days in the caverns had been quite eventful—and much of it I could have done without. But in some ways, it beat stumbling through the semidarkness, searching for an ancient strand only Karlith could sense at a distance, unknown danger lurking around every bend.

"I just want to feel like we're doing something." I passed my hands over each other and switched the strand to my other palm. "Like we're making progress."

"We are." He reached for my free hand, now closest to him. "Even when it doesn't feel like it."

I brushed my fingers over the silkiness of his grazer-hide gloves. "No rainbows?"

"Not today."

I smiled inside. He seemed a bit like his old self finally—not pinched, sad, grieving Mor. *He must feel more hopeful about finding Diggy.*

"Stop," Karlith said suddenly.

I turned, expecting to be greeted by her wide smile and sleepy eyes. Surely we were there, at last.

Instead, her face was sharp with fear. She pointed to a small passageway. "Down there. Someone is already trying to pull it up."

Blast. Not again.

Already one of the eleven strands was in the hands of a different team. One that we knew of. How many others had been found already? Did the Master already possess the three she sought?

I tried to still the tumbling of my wild thoughts.

Right now, we had to rescue *this* strand.

Creator help us.

"I'll go ahead," Father began, but it was too late.

Mor was already marching toward the tunnel.

My spirits sank—crashed, really. He wasn't better today. He was more desperate. Reckless. Wild and unpredictable.

I saw a spark of Diggy in him, and I wished I could will it out of them both.

"Mor!" I hissed, but he didn't turn around.

So I hurried after him.

"This is your job," a man's voice said up ahead. "This is what we pay you for, so get to it."

"Aye, that's right," a woman's voice answered. "Me and the girl are the only ones among us who can see to it, and she's far from capable yet. So I suggest you back away and give me room. Now."

The voice of the unseen woman caused me to freeze so abruptly, Aeron slammed into me. "Tannie?" she whispered. "What is it?"

Words wouldn't come together. My mouth didn't work.

Because that voice was deeply familiar in the most unpleasant way.

I didn't answer Aeron, but I forced my legs to work and sprinted to catch up with Mor just as he entered the cavern where the other party had stopped. Six heads turned toward us, illuminated by the flickering light of torches—four men, an older woman, and a wide-eyed lass of perhaps fourteen.

"Hey!" one of the men shouted.

The older woman shot a strand at us—poison-green satin, aimed straight for our heads.

But I responded easily, imagining a glittering strand of clearest glass. My strand and hers collided in midair. My glassy strand swallowed hers, and the whole mess popped into a crystallized sculpture—a bottle of poison with green smoke wafting from the top. The crystal hung suspended in the air for a moment, then plummeted to the ground and shattered against the stone.

It had been instinct. I understood exactly what to create, just how to respond, because I knew the green strand so well.

She had taught me how to make it, after all.

She leaned forward, squinting, her wiry gray hair fraying from its bun, just like it always did. "Tanwen?"

"Ho, Riwor."

CHAPTER THIRTY-THREE
TANWEN

I BLINKED AT MY FORMER MENTOR. "HOW . . . HOW ARE YOU?" The awkward words felt strange and thick in my mouth.

Mor swiveled around to stare at me incredulously. Then recognition ignited in his eyes—he knew Riwor now. Of course he did. He had followed us around for a while before he and I met officially. When the Corsyth weavers had heard about a story peddler traveling around the peninsula, slowly losing control, they sent out a team to keep an eye on me.

A team made up of Mor, Zel, and Gryfelle.

I pushed back the grief that wanted to press in on me at that remembrance. Not now. Not while Riwor was inching closer to me, an unreadable expression in her eyes.

She peered at me. "Is it really you, Tanwen?"

"Aye. I guess you thought I was dead." It came out a little harsher than I intended.

But it seemed a statement of fact—she'd left me with the guard on my tail. She must have known they would catch up to me eventually and I would be arrested. And then Gareth would—what? Show mercy? Overlook so-called treason out of the goodness of his heart?

The simple fact was she had left me for dead.

I glanced over at the young lass with blonde hair and wide eyes. Riwor had left me for dead and found a new apprentice.

"Oh, no," Riwor said, "I knew you had survived." Her

expression changed, but still I couldn't read it. "Do you not know?" She nodded to the rest of our crew. "You lot are famous."

And then I placed that expression on her face. Her mouth was twisted and her face pinched, but the old, familiar spark flared in her eyes—the one I saw often when we were practicing or she was teaching me something new, and I tried so hard to perform it perfectly for her. The same look she got when my stories netted sums twice the amount hers did. When people praised my crystallized sculptures and commented on the clarity and sparkle.

Envy.

I was worldly enough now—less naïve and wiser to the ways of folks—to recognize it. Riwor had been jealous before, and she was jealous now because we were supposedly famous.

As if she had any idea what we had been through and all we had lost. Famous, infamous—whatever she wanted to call it—we hadn't sought it, and we'd paid dearly for it.

"That must have been terrible for you," I said aloud as my mind churned over this new idea about Riwor.

"Eh? What must have been terrible?"

"To so badly want the money I was earning for us while being filled with bitterness at my ability to earn it."

Her face flushed, then turned purple. "Insolent—"

"I don't mean any offense." And truly, I didn't. "It's just that must have been quite a war inside you." Greed and vanity. "No wonder you beat me so often."

True to form, true to the Tannie she knew and the Tannie I would probably always be, I realized a moment late I had spoken too quickly and freely.

Riwor stepped toward me.

Mor moved to my side, and I felt the presence of several others at my back.

Riwor's eyes flitted upward, and she looked ready to spit as she stared at someone over my head. "Ah yes. The long-lost father, I presume?"

"Tanwen," he said, his voice controlled and quiet behind me. "Who is this person?"

"My story-peddling mentor. She taught me how to tell the crowned stories and perform them for people."

Warmil's hand settled on the hilt of his sword. "She's the reason you were cursed."

I hadn't really thought of it like that before. Was it true?

No, I decided. Even if I had never met Riwor, I would have searched out the accepted way to peddle stories on my own. I had wanted to work my way to Urian and become Royal Storyteller. I would have figured out how to do that, with or without Riwor. My ambition would have brought the curse upon me, no matter who helped me along the way.

But a new thought sparked in me.

"Why didn't you get the curse?" I asked Riwor curiously. "You were so strict about the crowned stories. Surely you had to suppress your gift a lot, and for many years."

"Unless she doesn't have much creativity to suppress." Mor's voice was hard as stone, and I knew he wasn't likely to forgive Riwor for smacking me around the way she had.

Riwor remained silent, glaring at us.

"No." I studied her face and spoke slowly, trying to remember exactly what it had been like in those days that felt so long past. "She could create beautiful strands and tell lovely stories when she wanted to."

And then it hit me. As if the whole cave had crashed in on my head.

"You created in secret, didn't you? You made sure to allow your gift to breathe so you wouldn't get sick, but . . . you forbade me to do the same." Tears pricked my eyes. I shouldn't have expected anything else from her. I shouldn't have thought better of her.

Still, it hurt.

"Why? Why would you let me . . ." I shook my head to clear it. I looked at the blonde lass again and back at Riwor. "What was your plan? To use me as long as possible, and when I became ill, you'd find someone new? Someone else to earn a living for you?"

Her face tightened, and I could see yet another layer to her complicated feelings—shame flickered in her defiant eyes.

"I don't have to explain myself to you." She turned to her team. "If you want me to pull up that strand, you better get rid of this lot. They're all weavers, and they'll have the strand up and out of here before you can blink."

Well, that did it. Swords reflected light all around the cavern, and Dylun already held an orb of fire.

"Don't—" But before I could finish my thought, one of Riwor's partners charged my father.

Father disarmed the foolish attacker and pressed a blade to his throat in a flash. But Riwor was already creating more strands of green poison, and the rest of her team hadn't lowered their weapons.

The room exploded into chaos—streams of fire, ribbons of smoldering green fumes, and the clash of metal on metal as our fighters crossed blades with theirs.

"Wait, stop!" I shouted.

Mor cast another incredulous glance my way. And I didn't really know how to explain myself, except I didn't want any more violence. My soul sagged beneath the weight of fighting and bloodshed and strife.

Couldn't we talk things through with Riwor and her crew? Come to some agreement?

"Fight, foolish girl!" Riwor's growl carried above the cacophony in the cavern, and for a moment, I thought she was yelling at me.

She had shouted commands at me so often before, it felt as natural as storm clouds that she'd be shouting them now.

But she was looking at the blonde lass.

"Dithwyr!" Riwor yelled. "Do something, you lazy, useless lump!"

Dithwyr's eyes grew wider by the second as she stumbled backward, away from the fighting. Warmil blocked a sword strike inches from Dithwyr's head. She flinched, then gasped and ducked, cowering near the floor.

"Foolish girl!" Riwor closed the distance between them in one long stride. She gripped Dithwyr's blouse in one hand, yanked the girl to her feet, and then reared back and slapped her across the ear.

Dithwyr cried out—a tiny sound amid the chorus of battle, but it cut clear and sharp into my mind. Something inside me snapped.

So much about the world had changed over the past year. So much about *me* had changed.

But Riwor was the same. It was Dithwyr instead of Tanwen now, but the story was identical. Surely I had not been her first apprentice to be slapped around and used cruelly, but by the stars, I would be the last.

I pushed every ounce of my twisted-up emotions into my hands. I didn't have to think the exact words. My gift had become so deeply connected to my thoughts and feelings that, with just a focused intention, the right things came out.

And I certainly had intention.

I thrust my hands forward, and ten lengths of rope shot from my fingertips. The ropes sailed all over the room. Four swords clattered to the stone floor as their bearers each became entangled in a rope. In seconds, the men's arms were pinned by their sides, and they stood helplessly, striving to maintain balance and not topple like felled trees.

One rope—a thin string that had come from one of my

pinkies—headed toward Dithwyr. It wrapped itself gently around her wrist and drew her toward me.

The other five ropes were for Riwor.

The first around her legs, another restraining her arms to her sides, two more that stuck to the stone wall like night-trapper webs, ensnaring her beneath their sticky cords.

The last wrapped itself around her mouth. It was my turn to talk.

Everyone was suddenly very still.

Warmil's eyebrows rose. "Well, if Tanwen could always do that . . ." He shrugged and sheathed his sword.

I shot a glance at him as Karlith, Dylun, and Zel worked on collecting the ancient strand from the corner of the room. "Aye, if I could always. But remember the mountainbeast and the rainbows?"

"Right."

I needed a particular intention for it to work this way, but I guessed if anything could make my focus sharp as a blade, it was Riwor and her backhand.

Father loomed beside me, but I laid a hand on his arm. He looked at me with understanding as he stepped away and allowed me room.

I stood within inches of Riwor now. Hatred seethed in her eyes, her words muffled by the rope.

"No," I said. "You be quiet. It didn't have to be like this, Riwor. None of it did. I looked up to you. I wanted to please you. We could have been . . ." I cleared my throat. "We could have been like family."

I looked around the cave—at her bound and struggling fellows, plus Dithwyr, who still looked like a frightened light-foot.

An ugly red mark spread over Dithwyr's ear onto her cheek.

I turned back to Riwor, fighting to keep my voice steady. "You will let this girl alone. Do you understand me? You will let her and every other storyteller across Tir alone. You will never take another apprentice. Sell your own stories. Or don't. Find something else to do with your life. Retire. Take up brickmaking or basketry. It makes no difference to me. But if you ever strike another person, I will find you."

I edged closer to her and made sure she could see the truth in my eyes and know I meant every word. "I will find you, and I will make sure you regret it. I will make sure you pay for your cruelty. You know what my strands can do."

I held her gaze, then turned and went back to Dithwyr. With a wave of my hand, the rope strand around her wrist disappeared.

"I . . ." She glanced at Riwor, then back to me. "Thank you."

I nodded. "Dithwyr, do you think you can find your way out of here?"

"Aye. I think so. We marked the path."

"Good. Find your way out and tell the huntmaster there's a bunch of tied-up . . ." I searched for the right word. "Er . . . tell him there are some hunters tied up in here who need rescuing. And please"—I took her hand and forced her to meet my eyes—"know you are worth more than this. Don't let anyone treat you like Riwor has ever again."

She nodded and swallowed hard. "But . . . what will I do? Where will I go?"

A little laugh bubbled up inside me. I looked around at my little crew of rebel weavers—my dear father who I'd believed to be dead, my friends who had become like family, the people who had helped me discover who I really was.

"Dithwyr," I said at last, "if we can figure out how to save the world, you will go and do and be whatever you want."

Hope lit her eyes, and I could almost see her imagining a future filled with stories and friends and wild, beautiful strands of ideas.

She nodded, then grabbed a lantern and slipped from the room without sparing Riwor another glance.

Time for me to do the same.

I strode from the cavern, ignoring the muffled shouts of my one-time mentor and allowing the others to deal with the strand collection for now.

The darkness swallowed me as I stepped into the tunnel. I stopped and drew a shaky breath and closed my eyes. I guessed I would have to make my strands disappear and set Riwor and her team free before too long. They could die for lack of water before the huntmaster was able to get to them here.

But I didn't have to tell them so.

"Tannie?" Mor's voice, close in the dark.

"I'm here."

"Are you all right?"

"I'm not sure." I turned toward the sound of his voice, even though I couldn't see him. "That was . . ."

"Not the way you hoped it would turn out?"

"Aye."

"What will you do to Riwor if you hear about her mistreating someone?" I could almost hear the smile in his voice.

"Oh, I don't know. I could think of some way to punish her. Force her to watch superior storytellers get all the attention for the rest of her life."

Mor chuckled. "Such brutality."

I imagined a strand of glittering gold and silky black—something that brought to mind my heart during my days with Riwor. A strand filled with goals and ambition and dreams of the palace and the capital. Not bad things, necessarily, but when they ruled a person's heart, dictated her every move? No. That wasn't my path. I lived for something else now—something greater.

I imagined a little chest, like a tiny lockbox. The black-and-gold strand floated into the box, and I mentally closed the lid and turned the key.

"Tannie?"

"Aye. I'm fine. Just . . . putting the past away where it belongs."

"And what now?"

"Now?" I found his gloved hand in the dark. "We go save the world so Dithwyr can have a future."

CHAPTER THIRTY-FOUR
BRAC

ENY FROWNED AT ME—ONE OF HIS FAVORITE PASTIMES.

But I'd long since learned it didn't mean disapproval the way it did when my mam frowned at me, and it didn't mean he had a restless, unpleasant thought he wanted to share but couldn't, the way it did when Tannie frowned at me.

It just meant he was concerned. Worried. Wondering if I was being wise.

Truth be told, I was wondering the same thing myself at the moment.

We sat at a table in a pub on the outskirts of Urian. My cloak was rough and reminded me of home. Eny had borrowed it from a servant in the stables. He wore one nearly identical, the same homespun wool, soiled by work and poverty. We had both pulled the hoods low over our faces on our walk to the pub. Mine was over my head still, but somehow his frown managed to find me anyway.

Fourteen empty stools were crammed against a table too small to seat half as many. Eny's ink-darkened fingers wrapped around a mug of ale he'd barely sipped. My calloused fingers gripped my nearly empty mug, but still my hands shook.

At last, the pub door opened.

And I knew who was approaching our shadow-draped corner before he pulled back the hood of his cloak.

Hayfal, whose farm was half a league northwest from the

boundary of my father's land. I recognized the scar that slashed the back of one finger and ran up his hand.

Hayfal sat, giving Eny a suspicious glance and me a quick nod.

Next came Hywon and Helgan. Brothers just a bit older than me and Tannie. We'd worked the fields together as children and enjoyed the occasional dip in the summertime sea.

Then my cousin on Dad's side—Breseth Bo-Braden. His hood wasn't low enough, and it looked like half his hair had escaped its tail. Blond clumps of it tumbled over his shoulders.

At least he'd come.

Farlis, Wenth, and Gwlan arrived together. Three of Dad's most trusted friends who were still young enough to wield swords.

Then Hyde, who stopped at the bar first to order a drink. Typical.

And next Rawn, my uncle on Mam's side—her youngest brother.

I would have thought it foolish for the next three to enter together as they did, except they were so well disguised, I almost didn't recognize them until they were close to the table. Guardsman Bo-Yemlath, Guardsman Bo-Droth, and Guardsman Bo-Saeth.

The guardsmen eyed the ragtag clump of farmers, then shared glances among themselves.

"Please," I said, motioning to three of the empty stools.

The soldiers sat, and I got to feel the heat of nine farmers' glares on me.

Truly, I didn't know if I could trust these guardsmen. They had been my friends once. And loyal to Braith—at least I believed. Hoped and prayed.

When your life's on the line for declaring your opinions, how can a man possibly tell where someone's true loyalties lie?

But we had sat many watches together, trained at each

other's backs, defended the realm side by side. If I could trust anyone in Urian, it would be these three. And we definitely needed allies in Urian.

Tafarn entered next, limping a little. That was new. Had he been hurt on the journey? Or perhaps in a skirmish? Had he been one of the many who had helped me take the capital? Or had he resisted?

My stomach flopped over at the thought.

Tafarn eased onto a stool, one eyebrow raised. "Blodwyn sends her regards."

Blodwyn, his wife, ran my favorite tavern in Pembrone.

Tafarn's lip twisted in a wry half smile. "Says you owe her a few coppers."

I laughed, and it sounded more like a sigh of relief. "She's not wrong, I'm sure."

Eny pointed his frown at me again. "We are still missing one."

I glanced at the familiar faces around the table. "Where's Farmer Rhys?"

"Dead," a woman's voice answered. She strode from the door—must have slipped in quietly beyond my notice—her hood pulled too low for me to see her face.

She reached the table and pulled a letter from her cloak—the one I had sent to Rhys. "But I came in his stead."

Then she pushed back her hood, and curls the color of spun flax tumbled out.

"Celyn!" I jumped to my feet.

A chorus of snickers around the table set my face ablaze.

But Celyn En-Rhys didn't flinch, and she didn't laugh at me. She held my gaze and stepped closer. "Tell me what you need, Brac."

And that was a question that weighed on me heavier than if every stone in Urian was tied to my back.

The weight of what I was about to ask of these folk, some of the most trusted people in my life.

"I..."

Eny cleared his throat. "Perhaps you should sit, my lord?"

Oh. Right.

I plunked back onto my stool, a little too heavily. I stared into my ale because I couldn't bring myself to meet their eyes again. Just needed a moment before I came clean.

Finally, I looked up. "I've made a mistake."

Farmer Wenth cast a glance around the pub. "Is this place safe?"

"We won't be disturbed." I nodded to the barkeep. "He's got people watching the street. Directing folks elsewhere. And he's paid well to lose his hearing when I need him to. Isn't that right, Barkeep Crawr?"

"Eh?" Crawr lined up mugs of ale along the counter. "Didn't catch that, my lord."

"See? We're safe here for the moment. I was more worried about you folk being seen traveling here together."

Wenth looked unconvinced. Who could blame him?

"Brac, how? An empty pub. The guarded street. The silent barkeep..." Celyn held up a hand to refuse the ale Crawr was offering to her. "How have you managed it?"

"Being steward has some upsides, I guess." My smile fell. "But that's just the thing..."

And I told them all of it. How I had been fooled and used, but also how I had been weak and blind. So consumed with my own feelings and assumptions that I had been the dumbest pile of rocks ever to sit on a farm hill.

"I trusted people I shouldn't have." I stared into my mug of ale again. "I did things I knew was wrong, even as I did them. I just tried to convince myself..." I let the words die. There was no excuse. No explaining it.

Uncle Rawn spoke up. "All right, Brac. You made a mistake. Now what? What do you need from us?"

I forced myself to look at him and then around the table.

"It's too much to ask. I know it is. But if we don't do something, they're going to kill Queen Braith. And—" A lump in my throat choked off my words. But I had to keep going. "And they'll kill Tannie. She and her friends are walking right into a trap. This wouldn't be happening if not for me, so if she and the queen die, it's . . . it's my fault."

"Brac," Farmer Farlis said slowly. "Lad, forgive me, but what you're sayin' . . ." He shook his head.

"It sounds mad. I know it does. Queen Frenhin betraying her own daughter. I wouldn't have believed it myself if I hadn't heard it with my own two ears. But I did. I heard it. Saw the . . . strands, whatever they were."

Farlis hesitated, and I knew it cost him to say what was on his mind. "Brac, how can we believe you?"

I thought about how to answer. It was a fair question that cut sharp as a blade.

At last, I said, "You'll have to think about what you know of me. I ain't never claimed to be the brightest or the best at anything. But I once was known as an honest lad. A good person, if a bit simple. Think about the Brac you used to know. Would he lie? Would he spin tales about something like this?"

Guardsman Bo-Droth rubbed his temples. "I understand your desire here, Bo-Bradwir. Really, I do. But"—he gestured around the table—"what's your plan? To storm some unknown fortress of Queen Frenhin's? With fourteen swords?"

"Fifteen," Celyn put in. "I'm going too."

Bo-Droth raised an eyebrow, and I had to set aside the argument that looked to sprout up.

"Even with fifteen," Bo-Droth said. "Four trained soldiers, ten farmers, and one lass. How can this be possible?"

"If we can get there in time, Tannie and her friends will help us. We just have to find them first so we can warn them." Even to my own ears, it sounded weak and impossible.

A fool's errand.

But what choice did we have?

Farmer Hyde drained his third tankard of ale, then wiped his mouth. "Course we'll go, lad."

A couple heads swiveled to stare at him, but he didn't pay them any mind. "I was a guardsman once, you know."

I hadn't known.

"When the mission is right," Hyde continued, "when you're fighting for good, that weighs out against the odds. Right wins. Leastways, it should." He signaled Crawr to bring him another drink.

My resolve deepened. "If anyone doesn't want to join, that's fine. There'll be no hard feelings from me. I'm asking too much of you, and I know that. But for those of you who believe that right wins out against the odds . . . will you join me?"

Hyde thrust his fist over the center of the table. Uncle Rawn followed immediately after, touching his knuckles against Hyde's. Then my cousin Breseth, who looked right excited about the prospect.

Fool lad. So like me. I supposed life would break him soon enough.

Celyn's delicate hand joined the circle, and soon she was met by Bo-Yemlath and Bo-Saeth, then Hywon and Helgan. And one by one, everyone's fists met in a ring over the table.

"Blodwyn'll kill me, even if Frenhin don't." Tafarn cast his lot with us.

I was last.

Uncle Rawn gripped my forearm and forced me to look at him dead-on. "We're with you. For the queen."

"And for Tannie." Farmer Hywon nodded.

A wave swelled in my chest, and I couldn't speak. Could only nod as the circle of fists broke apart.

"Very good." Eny pulled several pieces of parchment from his cloak. "Now that this has been settled, I can tell you this fortress of Frenhin's is not unknown to us." He opened one of the pieces of parchment and revealed a finely drawn map of northeastern Tir.

"Look, there's Pembrone!" Breseth grinned. "Never seen what the peninsula looks like on a proper map afore."

Eny nodded politely. "Yes. And Brac and I have been busy while we awaited your arrival in Urian."

I glared at the map. "Spying on that hay-rat, Naith, mostly."

The seedling of fury in my chest had grown into a full-fledged vine. It was all I could do to keep my calm while in Naith's presence. Especially when he *humbly* requested a leave of absence so he might take a pilgrimage to the west. He fed me some lie about worshiping the goddesses at a sacred site in the Wildlands.

But I knew what he was really after. He'd go north to rejoin the murderous traitor Frenhin. And who knew what evil they would scheme up once they were back together?

I'd delayed him as long as I could, but finally Eny said I needed to release him to his journey, else he become suspicious.

No matter. We would catch up soon enough.

"We have a course charted," Eny told the others. "And a precise location for the entrance of Frenhin's mountain fortress. At least the one the strand hunters are supposed to use. This Hunt will be Frenhin's fatal mistake. If not for that, we might never have found her." He smiled mildly. "Our gain."

"Our?" I eyed him. "Will you travel with us?"

"You need someone to look after you, my lord. I'm afraid a sword in my hands will do little good, but I can be useful in other ways. If you wish to have me along."

I didn't bother restraining my grin. "Of course."

"Very well."

"Then it's settled," I said. "We ride for the Mynyth at dawn. And . . ." That blasted wave rose in my chest again. "Thank you, my friends."

Most of the men were solemn. Several found their way over

to the bar to order another round from Crawr. I stared straight ahead, planning. Thinking through every step that would need to be carried out the next morning. The guardsmen would be my official escort through Urian, so as not to draw suspicion. I would ask them for a few extra uniforms. We could pass off several of the farmers as soldiers too.

Not Breseth, though. I'd have to dress him up as my groom, or something.

Eny had handled all the details of our cover story, and with Naith gone from the city, there really wasn't anyone to question the fib that we were traveling north to pay a call to the Governor of the Southern Highlands.

"Brac?"

I started at Celyn's voice. "Ho, Celyn."

"Can we speak?" She nodded to the fireplace nearby. "Alone."

My stomach backflipped. She'd had that effect on me before. I smiled, aware all at once of the lopsidedness of my grin. "Aye. Course."

I followed her to the fireplace and picked up the iron poker leaning against the hearth. The fire flared as I stoked it back to life.

Why did my hands suddenly feel too large? At least twice as large as they should be. Like mountainbeast paws had been attached where human hands ought to be.

The poker fumbled between my oversized fingers.

"Brac."

I couldn't avoid looking at her any longer. I set the poker back in its spot and met her gaze.

Hazel eyes—always earnest, always honest. They were fixed on me now, and there was no escaping. "I know you don't want me to go," she said simply.

"Just don't want you to get hurt, Celyn. I've put enough people in danger."

"You ever considered it's my risk to take?"

I scratched my head but didn't respond. Not just yet. I'd learned the wisdom of biting my tongue.

Least for a minute.

"I'm sorry about your father," I said finally.

"Thanks." She smiled a little.

"What happened?"

"Heart gave out while he was working in the fields." Pain flashed behind her eyes, but her hearty farm-girl upbringing tamped down the tears. "Wasn't nothin' to be done. It was just his time. He hadn't been the same since Mam died."

Two years past, that had happened.

"Are you managing the farm on your own?" Celyn's sisters were older and married already, tending to their own packs of wee ones.

"I've hired some help, but I manage."

"What if something happens to you?" I stepped closer, pushing aside thoughts of my lopsided smile and too-big hands. I put one of those mountainbeast paws on her shoulder. "Celyn, what's to happen to your father's farm if I lead you to your death on this fool mission?"

She didn't flinch. "Do you want to know why you lost Tannie, Brac?"

She didn't flinch, but I sure did.

"Tannie wouldn't have you because you didn't let her make her own choices. You tried to cage her, and boy, did you pick the wrong lass for that. But if you want to know the honest truth, none of us like cages overmuch."

A thick silence hung about us for a minute.

I finally broke it. "Isn't it . . . supposed to be like you and your mate are a team, though?" I clawed at some sort of reason, some explanation for why I had acted as I did, other than me being wrong as a blossom in winter.

Celyn's eyebrows lifted, and a wry smile twisted her lips.

"And is that what you think you were with Tannie? You think you two were a team?"

No. We hadn't been, I knew. I'd tried to bend her to my will. She had tried to tell me so many times—tried to tell me what she needed, what she wanted, and I never heard any of it.

"You're right," I said. "We was always talking past each other—chasing different things."

Celyn turned her big hazel eyes up at me. "Let me be on your team."

My stomach lurched, did a somersault, crashed into my boots, and vaulted back into place. "I—what?"

She seemed to be trying to hold on to a laugh. "I mean this team." She gestured around the pub to the others. "Let me make my own choice here."

"I . . . I don't understand why you would want to."

She watched the farmers gathered at the bar. "For my father." Then she turned my way again. "And for you."

"For me?"

"Dad and I came to hear you, you know. One of your rallies."

We had only done one rally on the peninsula. Not too close to Pembrone. Naith had said it was because we couldn't spare the time to travel so far. Now I wondered if he wasn't making sure to keep me far away as possible from home, family, and the people who loved me most. So that no one could talk some sense into me.

Celyn and Rhys must have traveled to see me anyway.

"I didn't know," I told her.

"You didn't see us. There were so many people." She looked into the fire, the glow lighting her suntanned face. "So many people cheering for you, pledging their loyalty to you. My father . . ." She didn't seem able to meet my eyes. "My father said you'd changed. He knew an ill wind blew and you were caught up in it. He grieved that. Grieved the loss of a son of Pembrone."

Guilt swelled in my rib cage. "He knew I was making a mess. And now you want to help me undo it."

She looked up at me. "Aye."

I took her hand. "All right, then. Stars know I've made a mess of everything well enough. Let's see what we can manage on the other side of the fence."

CHAPTER THIRTY-FIVE

DIGWYN

Who am I?

Daughter of Lidere. Daughter of Sinau. Sister of Mor.

But what else?

How do we become who we are? Is it written in the stars, carved into the foundation of the earth itself, woven into the fabric of time?

Or are we molded, shaped, hewn by our experiences? Do we all start as the same blank slab of marble, chiseled away over time by a moment here and another there—this flash of pain, that heartache? Then polished smooth by seasons of love and tenderness, happiness and warmth.

If such things exist.

Or perhaps . . . perhaps we decide who we are. Perhaps I get to say, "This is Digwyn En-Lidere. She is who I say she is."

I wish it were so.

It seems truer that we are merely buffeted about on the sea by life, circumstances, the choices of others.

Or else . . . or else who we are is written deeply within our blood.

So, who am I?

His lantern light fades, and I slip from my hiding spot.

Again.

Always.

I have been following him a long time.

A lucky happenstance, running across him in the first place. Or fate, perhaps.

Either way, I follow. I duck in and out of the shadows as he patrols.

A soldier.

Not one dressed in black, the way they used to at the palace. And not the red and drab green of the steward's men.

This one's uniform is darkest gray. And the way he walks—it's clear he's comfortable here. Familiar. This is his home.

One of the Master's soldiers.

I watch as he stops again. Stretches. It seems I have been following him for hours. I'm tired too.

He draws a deep breath, and I see my chance.

Just as his eyes drift closed on his exhale, I spring from the shadows.

I have his back and my dagger is out, blade at his throat, before he has time to cry out.

He gasps.

"Quiet," I breathe in his ear.

He swallows. Nicks his throat on my blade. "What do you want?"

"Very little." I give a slight laugh, and I feel him tense up even more. "Small favor."

"What?" he manages.

"I want to visit your Master."

CHAPTER THIRTY-SIX
BRAITH

THE DOORS TO THE CAVERNOUS ROOM OPENED, AND BRAITH started awake. A stream of fire sailed through the air and lit one of the torches resting in a wall bracket.

It was the way the former queen announced her arrival each day.

"Good morning, my darlings." Frenhin strode into the room, firelight twinkling off her gown. "Hungry, are we? Breakfast is on the way. I hope porridge and water suits. Does it? Excellent!"

Braith glanced across the room at Kharn. He was awake, but his mouth was clamped shut. They had learned many days ago that it was best to just let Frenhin talk as much as she liked. She would eventually tire and leave them to themselves.

Unless she was in the mood to have Kharn beaten.

"Dears, today is a special day," Frenhin said as she settled onto her chair.

Oh no.

A *special* day in Frenhin's opinion might be a *final* day for Braith and Kharn.

"Shall I keep you in suspense?" Frenhin snapped her fingers, and an attendant brought her a goblet of wine. She watched Braith for half a moment, then glanced at Kharn. "No? Oh, you two have lost your humor. How unfortunate. Very well, then." She beamed. "We have a guest."

Braith dreaded the revelation of who was about to join them.

"Braith, darling, I thought you would particularly enjoy this guest."

Yestin? Cameria? Tanwen? Did her mother wish to beat the poor old scholar, Master Insegno, again? Her stomach pinched. Was it Dray?

She didn't have to wonder long. Frenhin nodded to the guards by the door. They ushered in a man bent in half as he sought to bow before Frenhin and walk at the same time.

But it didn't matter that Braith couldn't see his face. She knew his clean-shaven head and embroidered robes by heart.

"Naith Bo-Offriad," she said aloud.

Her mother's ally. That she knew. But even as he stood before her, her perception of him clear for the very first time, Braith couldn't seem to muster any anger.

Only pity.

"Master." Naith dropped to his knees and pressed his face into the floor before Frenhin. "Master, it is such an honor to see you unmasked at last."

Interesting.

And indeed, now that Braith looked, it was clear Frenhin had taken special care with her appearance.

Her pale hair, blonde streaked with gray, hung in perfect waves all the way to her waist. So like Braith's. But Frenhin had always been prettier—at least Braith thought so. Frenhin's age showed in tiny lines around her eyes, but she knew how to care for herself. How to apply makeup to highlight her best features. How to dress to accentuate her still-lovely figure.

In her royal-blue satin gown with a beaded corset, she cut a striking, if strange, figure in the cave-like hideout.

"Rise, Naith."

The high priest obeyed.

Frenhin looked pleased. Truly pleased. "It is good to be unmasked before you, Naith."

Naith wiped tears from his cheeks. "It does me so well to see you in such spirits, Master. So well, indeed."

"What's not to be pleased about, Naith?" Frenhin nodded to where Braith and Kharn sat in chains.

Naith turned and staggered back, as if noticing them for the first time. "Cethor's tears."

Frenhin waved a hand. "Happier news, Naith. Tell me of Urian. How fares the steward?"

"Ah yes. That. The steward, Brac Bo-Bradwir, is still . . . besieged, as it were."

Frenhin's good humor drained in an instant. "Besieged?"

"I spoke of it to you. You remember."

"Yes," Frenhin snapped. "I remember. I also remember you telling me you had him well in hand."

Naith fell to his knees again. "I needed to see you," he whined, reaching for the hem of Frenhin's gown. "I needed to be in your presence. I needed to get away from there for a while. I thought . . . well, I thought he would remain steadfast, at least until my return."

"But?"

"But last night, as I reached Ir-Golyth just before sundown, I received word via carrier bird. One of our swiftest fliers brought a letter from an ally in the palace informing me the steward had left Urian."

"Left?" Frenhin's eyes blazed. "Left and went where?"

"The story is the boy rides to meet the Governor of the Southern Highlands."

Frenhin's lips pressed together until they whitened. "But that isn't true, is it?"

"He would have no reason—nor inclination, for that matter—to meet with any of the governors or territory stewards or lords."

"And that means?"

"I believe . . ." Naith hesitated. "I believe it's possible he has abandoned his post and fled."

Hope flared in Braith's chest.

"Rise, Naith."

Naith obeyed. Frenhin backhanded him across the face, and the high priest cried out.

"Fool! We need him! We've spent moons crafting him into the figurehead the people want!"

"I'm sorry, Master!" Naith cried, clutching his cheek. "But perhaps the timing is fortuitous. Is it not time for you to emerge as the true ruler of Tir? Openly once again, and this time, without Gareth to take credit for your work?"

Frenhin pursed her lips and combed her fingers through the ends of her pale locks. "Yes," she mused. "It is true that—"

A shout from outside the cavernous room interrupted Frenhin's words.

"I swear by the stars," a small, sharp voice shouted, "I'll kill him if you don't let me pass!"

The guards just inside the door drew their swords, and Frenhin craned her neck. "What in blazes—"

"Move!" The small voice again—a woman's.

"Goddesses' sake, do what she says!" A man.

A moment later, two people shoved into the room past the guards.

A small woman—perhaps just a girl?—had one of Frenhin's soldiers around the neck with a blade at his throat. A trickle of blood ran down his skin and disappeared into the gray of his tunic. She used his body to block potential strikes from the guardsmen, and they all seemed wary of putting their fellow in harm's way.

"What is the meaning of this?" Frenhin demanded. "How dare you assault one of my soldiers? State your purpose."

The young woman hissed in the soldier's ear. "Tell her why I'm here."

He remained stiff, moving only his mouth. "She says she wants to see you, Master."

Frenhin narrowed her eyes. "Why? Who are you?"

"Digwyn En-Lidere."

Lidere. The name struck like flint on stone, and Braith's memory flared. "En-Lidere?" The same blue eyes, dark hair, and olive skin.

This was Mor Bo-Lidere's sister.

Frenhin's eyes lit—wild, excited.

Hungry.

"We meet up close at last," Frenhin said. "I have only watched you from a distance, my dear—from the deck of an ill-fated ship, I'm afraid. I couldn't see *you*, exactly, but I saw what I believe was your handiwork. Impressive, unusual things happening to the strands of those rebel weavers." She smiled. "But why, pray tell, would the daughter of Lidere want an audience with me?"

"I'm here to pledge my loyalty to you." The girl lowered her head slightly while maintaining her grip on the man. "Master."

No. Mor's sister? How could she?

Frenhin laughed. Then she narrowed her eyes at Digwyn. "Prove it."

The girl frowned. "How?"

Frenhin lifted a hand to hold back her other guards awaiting her command. She kept her focus on Digwyn. "Dispose of that man."

The girl didn't pause. Didn't hesitate. Didn't think.

She dragged her blade across the throat of the soldier—deep and decisive. The guards at the door started forward on instinct.

"Do not come closer," Frenhin ordered.

The girl pulled a rag from a pocket in her shorts and began wiping the blood from her dagger.

The soldier slumped to the floor at Digwyn's feet, his hands clutching the wound in his throat.

Braith let out a dry sob and turned away toward Kharn, whose face was a mask of dismay.

"Well, this is unexpected, indeed." Frenhin beckoned Digwyn forward. "Come here, child."

Digwyn hesitated for the first time since she had entered the room. She stepped over the body of the downed soldier and took another step toward Frenhin, then stopped.

"Say your name again, my dear. I want to hear it."

"Digwyn En-Lidere."

"Is it true, then? You are the one?"

The one who what?

But Frenhin thrust her hands forward. Two streams of fire shot out, one from each palm. Straight toward Digwyn.

Braith cried out, but Digwyn reached up and snatched one stream from the air, then spun and grabbed the other. Plumes of fire, gripped in her bare hands. She spun again and jolted her fists. The ribbons of fire turned solid—two daggers with flames licking across the blades.

Frenhin cackled. She tossed her palm up toward the ceiling, and a swathe of fabric like a delicate scarf waved into the air.

Digwyn didn't pause. She adjusted her grip on one of the flaming daggers, then threw it, end over end. It pierced the fabric in midair. The guards by the door scattered just in time to avoid the blade as it *thunked* into the wooden door, the scarf pinned there like a banquet decoration.

"It *is* you." Frenhin's voice sparkled with delight. "The one from the island."

"Aye."

"And why have you come to me, child?"

"I tried," the girl said. "I tried to be what my brother wanted me to be. But . . . I think I'm broken. I came to you because . . . if I can't be fixed, I want to be strong. Strong enough that no one will ever hurt me again."

Oh stars above.

"Digwyn, please," Braith begged. "I know your brother. And this . . . this will kill him. Please don't do it. I beg you. Do not help this woman."

"Quiet!" commanded Frenhin.

Digwyn glanced halfway over her shoulder but did not meet Braith's gaze. "I'm sorry, my lady. They spoke well of you."

"The rebel weavers?" Frenhin leaned forward. "Tell me what you know."

But Digwyn was still speaking to Braith. "My brother's battle is his own. We no longer travel the same path." She turned back to Frenhin. "They had already found one strand by the time I left, some days past."

"Excellent." Frenhin nudged Naith beside her. "Maybe you aren't as useless as I feared."

Naith frowned. He did not look at all pleased by this new arrival.

Frenhin was practically beaming at Digwyn. "Perhaps the weavers will show soon, and I can put you to good use, my dear."

"I will prove myself to you, Master." She balled her empty fist and gripped her flaming dagger in the other. "No one will ever hurt me again. Including my brother."

"Most excellent."

Digwyn blew along the length of the dagger until the magical flames were extinguished. Then she placed it in an empty sheath at her hip. "Tell me what you want me to do."

Braith slumped back against the stones, defeated.

Because this girl—this broken, terrifying creature—seemed to be Frenhin's soul mate. Her most dangerous tool, her deadliest weapon.

The daughter she'd never had.

CHAPTER THIRTY-SEVEN
TANWEN

Karlith rested her head against the stone wall of the cave.

"Karlith?" I said gently. "Can I get you something? Briskleaf tea, maybe?"

She tried to smile. "I sense another strand nearby here, but we must be growing closer to this Master. My soul is so heavy, Tannie."

I looked at Father, the question in my eyes. What could we do for her? He shook his head and spread out his hands helplessly.

"I'll be all right," she said, clearly trying to force some strength into her voice. She wasn't very successful. "Just to the left up here. I think."

I found myself beside Warmil in the dark as we all followed Karlith.

"She's not well, War," I murmured.

"Aye. I know. She's exhausted. So is Aeron."

"Could we spare a few days of rest?" But I already knew we couldn't. Rations were low enough as it was. And who knew if another team had already collected three strands and delivered them to the Master?

No, we had to keep pressing on, and Warmil and I both knew it.

I lowered my voice even more. "Aeron shouldn't have come."

He snorted. "You try telling her."

"But if she could go back and make a different choice—"

"She'd still come with us, Tannie. She's a soldier. She doesn't know when to quit, unless the mission is complete."

I gave a little smile. "But I guess that's why we love her."

"One reason."

How far we had come since that one awkward conversation by the river where I'd clued him in that Aeron was in love with him. And even since the moment in the Daflin pub where he'd thought he'd missed his chance.

But as I opened my mouth to tease him, the captain let out a sharp cry, then disappeared from my side. Simply vanished. I screamed, and it echoed strangely about the cave.

My mind hiccupped—what in Tir had just happened? The rocks shifted beneath my feet, and I heard him shout from . . . below me? "Tannie!"

"Mor, Father!" I fell to my knees and felt blindly before me. "Warmil's gone! Something collapsed!" More rocks tumbled beneath my fingers, and a gap became visible for a moment, revealing the space into which rocks were tumbling—the space into which Warmil had fallen.

Mor and Zel skidded to the ground beside me and reached into the void.

"Be careful!" I yelled. "It's still falling!"

"War!" Mor called. "Can you hear me?"

His voice came back faint. "I'm here."

An awful realization struck me. Warmil was being buried in rocks from the cave-in.

"He's being bur—" Before I could finish, Aeron dove headfirst into the gap. "Aeron!"

Mor and Zel followed her somewhat more cautiously. One minute they were there, and the next, they had slid out of sight.

Father stopped Dylun from following. "No. We could cause more ground to collapse."

Sakes.

I held my breath for what seemed ages. When I couldn't stand it any longer, I called into the blackness. "Mor?"

"We're here. We're all here, Tannie. But . . ."

Oh, Creator. What didn't he want to say?

"We're here, but we're standing on a bit of a ledge. There's some underground river here, and we just about fell into it."

A small whimper escaped me. "Tell me what we can do, Mor."

"Here," said an unexpected voice from beside me.

I almost keeled over in shock to see Dray next to me, pulling rope from one of the packs. "Dray?"

"Don't sound surprised. That's very rude." He handed me a length of rope. "Do you know how to tie this? I'm afraid I don't."

"Aye." I took the rope and ignored the pang in my heart when I recalled practicing with Wylie. He would have whipped it into a perfect lasso in a heartbeat.

My ugly but functional knot would have to do. "Here. That's the best I'm able right now."

"Good enough." Dray lowered the rope into the dark hole left by the cave-in. "Bo-Lidere, wrap this around the lass's waist." In response to my raised eyebrow, he huffed. "She's missing a leg, you know. She acts like she forgets sometimes."

Mor's irritated voice carried up from the pit. "Put it on, Aeron!"

"We're working on more," I called down, in case that would help. She probably wanted the first rope to go to Warmil.

I prayed he wasn't terribly injured.

We tossed down a second rope, then two others. Dray, Dylun, and Father each anchored a rope from above, and Karlith and I held one together.

"You should tie it around me, Tannie," Karlith suggested. "I'm afraid we wouldn't be able to hold fast if someone tugged on it suddenly."

It didn't seem safe. If someone fell hard and fast, wouldn't they pull Karlith down with them?

Though none of this was particularly safe, if we wanted to sort sniffler fur . . .

I was still trying to decide whether or not this was a terrible idea when Karlith let out a soft moan. "Oh no."

"What is it, Karlith? Are you hurt?"

"No, dear." She turned to me and flashed a pained smile. "The strand."

"Aye?"

"I think it's down there." She nodded to the abyss below.

Brilliant.

I wasn't sure what to do. "Father?"

"I heard."

Of course he did.

"Mor?" he called down.

"We have Warmil uncovered," Mor shouted back. "Getting ready to climb."

"Hold that thought." Father's face was tense. "We're coming down instead."

"General?"

"Karlith thinks the strand is down there."

Mor's reply was hesitant. "All right. The ledge is . . . narrow. We can help you down. I think."

"I swear to the goddesses," Dray said, already testing footholds, "if we actually make it to the Master, it'll be a miracle."

Karlith clucked her tongue. "If you want to see miracles, maybe you should stop swearing to the goddesses."

"Maybe we could argue this later?" Dray held out a hand to me. "Well, story girl, are you coming?"

I glanced at Father. He pulled his rope taut. "Use this as you climb down."

Between Father's rope and Dray supporting some of my

weight, I was able to slip into the gap and down the rocks without tumbling off the ledge. Mor caught me as my feet hit solid rock.

Solid for the moment, anyway.

Karlith and Dray came down next—together, mostly, with Dray helping support Karlith's unsteady steps. The others scooted forward to make room on the ledge, then Father and Dylun shinnied down.

The rocks began to shift.

"General, move!"

"Dylun!"

A cascade of rocks and dust flowed from the gap above, splitting our party in two—Aeron, Zel, Warmil, and Karlith ahead on the ledge, and me, Mor, and Dray on the other side of the tumbling debris.

And Father and Dylun were . . . where?

Mor, Dray, and I were all gripping the same rope, and I could have burst into tears of relief when I realized my father was on the other end, bracing himself against the wall as the rocks slid.

"Dylun! Where's Dylun?" I shouted. "Dylun?"

"He's here." Zel's voice, on the far side of the stream of rocks.

Finally, the rocks stopped falling. The dust began to settle. The others came into view. All of them were there, hugging the wall, just like us. A gash bled on Warmil's cheek.

A long moment of silence passed. I fought to reclaim my breath, to soothe my heartbeat.

Karlith nodded ahead. "This way."

I gave Dray one last curious glance before scooting along the ledge after Mor and into the darkness ahead.

Chapter Thirty-Eight
TANWEN

THE STRAND LOOKED ABOUT HOW WE FELT. BATTERED. Bruised. Exhausted.

Several inches of it slithered out from the rock, then lay limp and listless. Did the strand feel defeated? Or was it merely reflecting the weaver trying to pull it out? I redoubled my effort.

With a sigh I could almost hear, it slipped from the rock wall and tumbled into a pile on the floor. Dylun lay his open jar on the ground, and the strand slowly snaked toward the glass.

The white lightning within the strand crackled, fizzed, then faded. I frowned. Perhaps another crew had tried to pull it up and damaged it somehow.

Or else we were the damaged ones, and this was all the poor strand could muster in our presence.

I tried to help it along by directing it into the jar with my hands, but these ancient strands didn't behave the way mine would.

"It looks sad," Zel observed as Dylun placed the lid on the jar.

"Weary," Karlith corrected. "It's nearly time."

"Time for what?" I asked.

"The end." She turned away as though this were a real and complete answer.

I looked up at Mor with wide eyes. "The end of what? The world?"

"Let's hope not."

"Come." Father hoisted his pack. "We best be—"

"Handing over that strand?" a woman's voice cut in. "I quite agree."

Swords flew from scabbards as a figure emerged from the shadows. She wasn't alone. A crew of ten flanked her. They edged toward us, weapons drawn.

It wasn't until my palms were burning hot with barely contained strands that I realized I knew this group. The leader with her twisty smirk and blonde-and-purple hair. The big sandy-haired one, and the even bigger one who looked like he was carved out of a block of muscle. The beautiful Meridioni woman who had flirted with my father, an older Minasimetese man, and several others.

It was Mor's old crew.

"Venewth?" Mor squinted in the unsteady lantern light. "What are you doing here?"

"Same as you." Captain Venewth En-Gorgyn didn't sheathe her sword. "Hunting strands."

I scanned their crew. All armed. No one was lowering their weapons.

Venewth tilted her head. "The strand, please. In fact, why don't I take that whole jar."

"You don't have a weaver on this team." Mor looked around. "How did you even enter the Hunt?"

"Lied, of course." She shrugged. "I knew you would come, if you were still alive. You wouldn't be able to resist this particular adventure. So we wouldn't need a weaver. We have you." Venewth held out her hand. "Strands, please."

"Your plan was to follow us and rob us." Warmil glared at them.

Venewth grinned and offered half a bow. "Pirates."

"Mmm." Dray flashed his smarmy smile. "Care to grab a drink later, my lady?"

If glares could incinerate, Dray would be a pile of ash on the floor, the way the rest of us looked at him.

The big one—Mor's former first mate, Gyth—offered Mor a sheepish smile. "Sorry, mate. Nasty business, this. But you remember the life. Gotta take what we can, when we can."

"Listen." Mor lowered his sword but didn't sheathe it. "There's more going on here than you realize. This is bigger than a strand hunt. Much bigger."

"Ah yes. Another quest to save the world, I'm sure." Venewth moved forward, her sword inches from Mor's chest. "We'll not delay you. Just hand over the strands, and you're free to save all the worlds you like, Bo-Lidere."

"Ven. Please." Mor took a step back and sheathed his sword. But his fingertips ignited with blue light. "This is not how this has to go. This isn't who we were. This isn't you."

"Ah, correction. This isn't *you*, and it's not who we were when you were captain." She advanced again. "I'm the captain now, Mor."

The sandy-haired one—Croy, as I recalled—nodded to Mor's hands. "Can't fight like a man anymore? Need to resort to those magic strands?"

"It's for your protection, sailor." Father's voice was like winter rain. "Bo-Lidere doesn't want to shed blood. None of us do."

"Who said anything about blood?" Venewth held out her hand and wiggled her fingers. "Jar?"

"I'm sorry, Ven." Mor shook his head. "It's not happening. If you would just listen to—"

But Venewth and her crew didn't give Mor a chance to finish. She gave the signal, and the pirates charged.

Warmil blocked the first strike from a Meridioni man, but I saw him wince. He had hurt his shoulder in that cave-in. That did not bode well.

Aeron, Zel, and Father crossed blades with some of the

others. A wall of water sprang up in one corner of the cavern, and I realized Karlith and Dylun were behind it, protecting the jar of strands. If the pirates were able to fight their way past our defenses and steal the jar, all would be lost.

Mor's fingertips still shone blue, but he stood transfixed in the middle of the cave.

Who could blame him? How was he supposed to fight his former crew?

Maybe he couldn't, but I could.

I shot a beam of hot light at Venewth's face as she charged at Mor. She flinched, stumbled, then whirled toward me.

"Ah, your new lass, Mor?" She bared her teeth. "And here I thought I was the only one for you."

That seemed to shake Mor out of his trance. "Not funny, Ven."

Venewth's sneer melted into her twisty smirk. "Just jesting, lass. You going to strangle me with those strands now?"

I glanced at Mor. He wouldn't want me to hurt her, and yet these pirates were not playing around. They wanted those strands, and it seemed like they were prepared to kill us to get them.

As I stood there, unsure if I should attack, Venewth charged again.

This time at me.

Mor's blade blocked her strike just in time. He fought his former crewmate like she was any one of the enemies who had attacked us over the past year. She spun to parry his blow, then danced away, slipping beneath another of Mor's swings. When she lunged forward to strike, her blade just missed the stitches along Mor's neck and shoulder.

She was a swordswoman nearly to match Aeron.

I shot whatever strands I could think of that would hinder the pirates without hurting them much—hot air, beams of light, something to tangle their bodies or weapons in.

I'd just bound Gyth's sword arm in a length of rope when

I heard Venewth cry out. I whipped around to find her holding her side. Blood stained Mor's blade.

"Go, Ven," he commanded. "Leave, now! I don't want to hurt you again."

Her eyes blazed, but she bent over the wound in her side. Red blood seeped through her fingers. She drew ragged breaths through gritted teeth.

A hint of a smile ghosted her lips. "So. You're still a pirate."

Mor shook his head. "No. But this is bigger than you or me." He gestured toward the tunnel. "Go on. Get out of here."

Venewth paused for one long moment, but then she whistled softly. At her signal, her crew sheathed their swords.

Schiva, the Meridioni woman, winked at my father. "I hope to cross blades with you again someday, General." Then she turned and glided toward the exit.

From the expression on Father's face, I didn't know whether to shoot fire at her back or laugh.

"I could have stitched her up." Warmil lowered himself gingerly onto a rocky ledge, rolling his shoulder. "Venewth, I mean. Was the wound deep?"

"I don't think so." Mor wiped blood from his sword and sheathed it wearily. "She wouldn't have let you. Anyway, Seni Kaizu has some skill with a needle and thread. He'll put her back together."

We took a few moments to survey the damage. A few scrapes, bruises, and cuts, but nothing serious.

Dray's scandalized cry startled me. "He took my waistcoat! The blasted pirate stole it! Forced me to give it to him."

And, indeed, the fine leather garment was gone, and Dray had only his linen shirt to keep him company.

"Look on the bright side, Bo-Anffir." Father patted him on the shoulder. "At least he let you keep those expensive leather trousers."

Aeron raised her eyebrow. "A mercy for us all."

Mor sat on the ground, his head lowered onto his clasped hands.

I sank down next to him. "Are you all right?"

He shook his head and didn't look up.

"I'm so sorry. I'm sorry that all happened."

"They were like my family once."

"I know." And truly, I did. I could imagine how I would feel if I had to fight the Corsyth weavers.

"Was I ever like that, Tannie?" he asked. "So mercenary?"

"Not as long as I've known you." I placed my hand on his back. "And I don't think before that either. From what Venewth said, seems like you always had standards. Fought for good causes, and such."

"I guess."

And then I realized he wasn't just thinking about himself. He was also thinking about Diggy—his actual family. His baby sister, who he'd watched kill a man. Maybe wondering if the same vicious streak ran through them both. If he could even save her from herself.

"We're going to find her," I promised him. "We're going to find her, rescue Braith, save everyone, and then we'll help her. Diggy, I mean. We'll help her put all her pieces back together."

He turned to me, a small smile on his lips. "You're awfully optimistic, you know."

"My sunshiny personality is why you love me." I froze. "I mean . . . not that you *love* me. I just meant that's—I mean . . ."

He grinned, then leaned forward and kissed my forehead.

Hopefully he wouldn't burn his lips on my mortification.

Karlith interrupted, "Mor, how is your wound?"

"Sore." He pulled back his shirt so she could see his stitched-up mountainbeast scratches.

She tsked and began to apply salve.

"If you're all quite rested now," Dray drawled, "I believe it's time for me to do my part."

Zel raised an eyebrow. "Oh?"

"We have three strands now. You wanted eleven, but we know at least one is already claimed by another team. Best to get these three to the Master, don't you think?"

"He's right," Father said, though it seemed to pain him to agree with Dray. "We want to make sure we get to the Master before anyone else delivers any strands to her." He leveled a sharp gaze at Dray. "You know the way?"

"I haven't lost track of the markings." He motioned to the ceiling. "I think we're close."

They were right. There was no time to lick our wounds and rest our weary spirits.

It was time to rescue Queen Braith.

CHAPTER THIRTY-NINE

BRAC

My foot caught on some unseen crevice in the tunnel floor, and I lurched forward. "Oof!"

Celyn caught my arm before I fell completely. "Honestly. Do you want to hold the lantern? Would it even matter? I don't recall you being so clumsy."

I allowed her to help me get my legs beneath me. "Don't be unkind," I grouched.

She smiled in the lantern light. "Just being honest."

"Ain't that the same thing half the time?"

She chuckled, then hushed me. "I'm going to lose count."

"Count of what?"

"We're supposed to meet the others in another ten minutes. I've been trying to keep count of the time passing in my head."

Sakes. We'd been at this for almost an hour. Stumbling through pitch-black tunnels and poking our heads into caverns. How Celyn managed to count anything while doing that was beyond me. But I was glad of it and glad to have her along.

We had split up into pairs to search the caves, but we were careful to meet back often so no one got lost. Then we'd all push forward together and search a new section. Seemed we'd been at it for moons, but it had only been one full day and half of another by my reckoning.

There'd been no sign of Tannie. We had run across a

mountainbeast carcass, but I didn't think Tannie had a hand in that.

And if she had, I didn't know the lass anymore. Which was possible, I realized. She had been adventuring and fighting and doing all kinds of things I knew nothing about for moons now. And I'd certainly been on some kind of path myself, one I'd likely never be able to fully explain to her. We didn't know each other anymore.

But that didn't matter. My mission was the same, either way.

"What are you thinking of, Brac?" Celyn's question startled me.

"Hey, you just shushed me so I wouldn't distract you."

She laughed.

"Just thinking about that mountainbeast."

"It sure was something else, wasn't it?" Celyn shook her head. "Never seen anything so big in my life."

"I saw a marsh-grazer once. At the time, I thought that had to be the biggest animal to breathe. It was nothing compared to that mountainbeast."

"That was three summers ago, wasn't it?"

"Aye, I think."

"Brac?" She slowed and looked at me, serious hazel eyes fixed on my face again in that way she had that made me feel bumbly and like my insides weren't quite in the right places.

"Aye, Celyn?"

"Do you remember what else happened three summers ago?"

I did. Of course I did.

But it seemed I'd swallowed my tongue. "I . . ."

"You kissed me behind my father's barn at the summer-harvest celebration."

Aye, I had. Tannie had never let me forget it either. "I . . ."

"I know we might not make it out of this alive." She put a hand on my arm to silence me before I could say anything.

"I knew that going in. My risk, remember? But I didn't want things to end like that without ever telling you."

"Te-telling me what?"

She smiled. "I didn't hate that kiss." She began walking again, her head lowered. "We've got two more minutes."

Aye, brilliant. Is two minutes enough time for a person's insides to turn solid again?

"We should go back," she said.

"Oh, aye. Right."

Just as we turned, a noise sounded further down the tunnel. Maybe it was just my ears playing tricks on me in the blasted caves again. But I was almost sure . . .

I grabbed Celyn's arm, and we stood, listening. After a moment, I turned back and peered into the darkness. "Ho, there?"

Movement flashed, and before I had a chance to speak another word, a lass sprang out of nowhere, pulled two daggers from her hips, and held them out—one at my throat, one at Celyn's.

I heard Celyn gasp.

"No!" The word felt so feeble, but what else could I do? "Don't hurt her, please!"

The lass snarled like an animal, but then her eyes lit in surprise. "You!"

And then my mind caught up. Because, of course, I knew her and her wild dark hair and the crazy markings all over her arms. She'd stood beside Tannie in the throne room at the palace.

The pirate's sister.

She didn't take her daggers away from our throats. She pressed in closer and hissed, "What are you doing here?"

"We're here for Tannie and Braith." I leaned away from her blade so I wouldn't accidentally get a shave I didn't want. "I swear it."

She glanced over our shoulders, then back to me. "Aye? No green-suited thugs with you, steward?"

"I'm not the steward anymore. I left and came here. To help. Please, where's Tannie?"

Her only reply was a snort.

I tried again. "Please. I need to know where to find them. I have to warn them. It's the former queen. The Master is the former queen." I wasn't making much sense. I had no idea what Tannie and her friends knew. "Not Braith. I mean Frenhin."

"What's all this?" the voice of Uncle Rawn cut in from behind us.

Oh difflesnouts.

"Hey!" That was Farmer Wenth.

"Stay where you are," the lass said. "I have blades enough for you all, I promise." She studied me. "You're telling the truth, aren't you?"

"Aye."

"You truly no longer serve the high priest?"

"Aye."

"Master Frenhin will want to speak with you." She squeezed her blades tighter to our throats.

"Ma . . . what?" Had she said *Master* Frenhin?

The lass's gaze slid between each of us. One side of her mouth curled upward. "Are you ready to die today?"

CHAPTER FORTY
TANWEN

DRAY PRESSED HIMSELF AGAINST THE TUNNEL WALL AND peered around the corner. We didn't need a lantern now. Torches in brackets had dotted the walls for the past half hour of our journey. We were within the bounds of the Master's lair.

And when Dray turned back around, I knew we'd found it at last.

He pointed to a marking on the ceiling. "That's the one. See the flame there? It points this direction because her chambers are this way."

"What's the plan?" Warmil scowled. "I don't like these conditions one bit. She'll have complete advantage no matter how we approach."

"Perhaps," Father conceded. "But if we can maintain the element of—"

"Halt!" A soldier dressed in a dark-gray uniform appeared before us, drawing his sword.

"—surprise," Father finished dryly. "Ah well." He held up his hands. "We're a Hunt team. We're here to see your Master."

The soldier paused and sized up the situation. Nine of us—several of us armed and at least one of us able to shoot strands out of our hands.

He lowered his sword slightly. "All right, then." He craned his neck to look down the corridor. "Oi! A little help here, please."

Another gray-uniformed soldier appeared from down the hallway, then reared back at the sight of us. "What's this?"

"Hunters here to see the Master."

"They ain't supposed to be here, I thought." The second soldier surveyed us.

"Aye, but they are now."

After a pause, the second soldier said, "They shouldn't have found their way here. Master will want to talk to them, I wager."

He drew his weapon and pushed past our little party to guard us from behind. The first soldier led us down the hall.

At long last, we were walking into the Master's lair.

My stomach lurched.

Two more soldiers guarded an archway unlike the rough-hewn, natural openings that led to tunnels all throughout the caverns. This one had been shaped, polished smooth into a beautiful curve. A wooden door with iron fittings had been installed at some point, and I could see that a few other doors lay further down the corridor.

"Wait here," the first soldier said, and he disappeared through the door.

So this was it. This was where she lived and plotted and held the true queen captive.

My mind somersaulted over itself. How would we rescue Braith without also surrendering the strands? Perhaps we would surrender them at first, then fight to get them back. But what if the strands weren't enough? What if she would only trade Braith for me, Mor, and Zel?

That's what she wanted—the three of us. I knew it was. She had been after us for moons now, first on the *Cethorelle*, then on Kanac, and now with the Strand Hunt in progress.

Three strands. Three storytellers.

I drew a full breath and steeled my nerves. If that's what it took, that's what we would do. We would do whatever was necessary to rescue the queen. And we would figure the rest out later.

That seemed to be our custom.

I almost smiled. Especially when I felt a leather-clad hand lace its fingers with mine. I looked up at Mor.

"Together?" he whispered.

"Always."

The soldier returned. "She will see you now."

And we followed him through the doors, probably to our doom.

MY EYES WERE NOT READY FOR THE LIGHT. AFTER SO MANY days spent in darkness with the barest lantern light or Diggy's star speckles cast upon the cave walls or the sporadic torches dotting the lair, the blaze of many torches illuminating the cavernous room felt like an assault on my senses.

I blinked. Squinted. Shielded myself from the attack.

"Well, this is a surprise." Dray ground to a halt, his eyebrows raised, true astonishment marking his features.

He was staring at the other side of the room where a woman in a fine gown stood.

My mind crashed.

Surely my eyes were lying to me. It couldn't possibly . . . I had to be mistaken. I couldn't actually be seeing . . .

"Frenhin Ma-Gareth," Father said, his voice numb, tone flat.

The pale lady approached. Smiled. Stretched her arms wide. "You have found me at last." She moved closer to Father—but not within range of his sword. It was in its scabbard at his hip, in any case.

"Oh, Yestin," she said, and fry me if her eyes didn't fill with tears. "It has been many years, old adversary."

"I . . ." Father's voice faltered. "I had not realized we were enemies."

"You never suspected?" Her eyes crinkled at the corners as though she were genuinely delighted. "Am I the first person to fool Yestin Bo-Arthio?"

"I never suspected until you called for the Hunt."

"Ah yes. It was a risk. A bold one, though, don't you think? Bold and timely. After all, it is almost time to reveal myself to the people of Tir as their ruler again."

"It is almost the end," Karlith said softly, her head bowed.

And it was then that I heard a quiet sob behind me. I turned and gasped.

"Braith!" I ran for her—my queen, chained against the darkest stretch of wall like an animal.

A guard caught my arm before I could reach her. I repelled him with a burst of light from my palms. He stumbled backward and fell on his rear.

"Queen Braith!" I dropped to my knees beside her. "You're alive!"

Raw sores ringed her wrists where the irons had bitten into her. She looked like she hadn't eaten a proper meal or had a real bath since she had been taken.

And the man chained to the same wall but shoved in the far corner hadn't fared better. It had to be Kharn Bo-Candryd. He seemed to have suffered a beating or two.

Or twenty.

"Oh, Tanwen." Braith's bony frame shook. "Why have you come here, my friend?"

"It's going to be all right," I told her, although I knew I didn't have any such assurance. "We're here now, and we're going to get you out."

"My, what big promises you make," Frenhin said lightly.

I tried my hardest to glare holes into her. "You will release Braith and Kharn to us. We have what you want."

"Ah, small correction." Dray stepped away from the rest of the group.

A guard shadowed him.

"Yes, please do." Dray ushered the guard between himself and the weavers. "I should like the extra protection, if you don't mind." Then he turned to me. "*You* do not have what Frenhin wants. I do." He held up the jar with the three strands of white lightning inside.

Dylun made an unintelligible sound and yanked his pack off his shoulders.

"Bo-Ino, you got careless." Dray shook his head. "Comfortable. It was as simple as could be, really."

Dylun's face filled with anguish as he pushed his arm through a hole that had been cut in the side of his pack. Must have happened as we all pressed together in the hallway outside.

Simple as could be. Just as Dray said. He had sliced the pack and pulled out the jar.

"This has been your plan all along?" Anger radiated from Mor.

"Plans are a fluid concept, lad. I adjust as needed to suit the current circumstances." Dray smirked. "A bit of a pirate myself, I suppose."

Frenhin laughed. "This gets better and better." She held out her hand. "Here now, Dray, dear. Hand it over."

"Not so fast." He pulled the jar to his chest, out of her reach. "I have some demands."

"Of course you do." Frenhin's smile slipped as she eyed the jar of strands that squirmed beneath her stare. Lust flared in her gaze. "What do you want?"

"Braith's hand in marriage, naturally."

"My, my." Frenhin held a hand to her heart. "So he wants the lady, not just her throne. Braith, I had no idea you netted so many suitors. I rather thought it would be like courting a cold fish, but to each his own."

Dray flashed an icy smile. "You can keep your insults to yourself, Frenhin. Release Braith to my care, and you may have the strands. Those are my terms."

"No." Braith's voice was strangled. Choked and full of despair. "I will never go with you."

"Darling, really." Dray rolled his eyes. "Saving your life here."

"I don't know, Dray." Frenhin examined her nails. "Three little strands for one whole pretender queen? That doesn't seem a fair trade. What else have you to offer?"

Dray gestured to the remaining eight members of our team. "Them."

Father growled low in his throat. "You might have at least pretended you had to think about it."

Dray shrugged. "I thought we might dispense with any charade." He swung back to Frenhin. "You give Braith to me, and we will disappear from your life forever. I swear it. You can have the strands and these rebels, and I'll leave you to it. They will prove most useful to you, I'm sure. And your daughter will never darken your doorstep again."

Frenhin tapped a finger to her chin. "Now that . . . that idea has merit. Three strands, plus a band of traitorous rebels, including three weavers to wield my new strands. And best of all, Yestin Bo-Arthio, to use as I might." She closed her eyes and took a deep breath. "Oh, how I have longed for this moment." Her eyes snapped open and fixed on my father. "I have big plans for you."

"Then we have an accord?" Dray held out the jar of strands.

"We have an accord."

"No!" Braith thrashed against her bonds. "Dray, no! Don't!"

I tried to help. Searched for some kind of weakness in the metal, some way to free her and keep her away from that snake. I willed fire to pour from my hands, but it refused to come.

There was nothing.

Braith let out a wail. She turned to Kharn.

He wrestled against his shackles, but utter despair had already begun to fill his eyes. "Braith, my love. I'm so sorry."

Frenhin snapped her fingers. "Guard, seize the story peddler."

Next thing I knew, two strong hands gripped me under my arms and I was pulled from Braith's side. "No!" I kicked and struggled. "Stop!"

"You stay." Frenhin held up both hands, and a sheet of clear strands pulsed through the room toward us.

My father, Mor, and the rest of my weaver family were pressed against the wall by the nearly invisible web of strands. Frenhin had even pinned some of her guards along with us. I could only watch yet another guard unlock Braith's irons and yank her up from the floor.

"Easy, there." Dray shoved the guard away and hugged Braith to his side. "Come, Braith. I'll bring you to safety. I'm here. It's all over now."

Braith's cry rent the air. Kharn's every muscle strained, his teeth gritted, his cry of frustration enough to pull the stars from the sky.

Braith fought and screamed and pulled away, but it was no use. She was too weak, the rest of us too helpless, and Dray too determined.

"Quiet, Braith. We'll be together at last and put this all behind us."

I closed my eyes because I couldn't watch anymore. But I couldn't close my ears to Braith's screams.

They echoed through the cavern, out the door, and down the hall as Dray dragged her away.

CHAPTER FORTY-ONE
BRAITH

Dray pushed Braith into a room. Her throat felt raw from screaming.

"Enough already." He turned and slipped a coin to the guard standing out in the hallway. "Guard it well, and there will be more where that came from."

Braith shrank away until she hit a—bed? Where were they?

Dray also seemed to be sizing up the situation. "Well, well. Your mother's sleeping quarters?"

"I wouldn't know. I've been chained to the wall for days. I never got a tour."

But she looked around and saw the embroidered bedclothes, the silver-framed looking glass on the night table, the wardrobe in the corner, doubtless full of expensive gowns. The space was illuminated by torches in brackets all along the wall, unlit oil lamps on tables waiting to add their glow to the mix. Yes, this had to be Frenhin's bedchamber.

"Ah, dearest. I am sorry," Dray said. "That's all over now."

A thousand replies—some of them very unladylike—rolled through Braith's mind. But she remained silent.

"I know this was not ideal," he continued. "This has all been quite the fiasco." And to Braith's horror, he pulled off his shirt and began rifling through the wardrobe. "Don't suppose she would have any men's clothes in here. I'd kill for something fresh."

"Replace your shirt immediately, Dray."

"I'm trying." Then he pulled his head out of the wardrobe to look at her. He snorted. "Really, Braith? Still so demure?"

Braith eyed the door. Could she run for it? The guard outside would stop her, surely. But perhaps she should try . . .

"Braith."

She started and looked up to where Dray now loomed over her.

"Please don't misbehave, dearest. You don't understand everything that has happened."

Braith pulled herself up using her mother's bed for support. "Then why don't you tell me what has happened."

"Well, I helped those rebel weavers, for starters. They are your friends, are they not?"

"Yes. They are my friends."

"I helped them escape from Urian. I led them north. Brought them here, to Frenhin's hideout, just as they desired. They would not have found it without me. I even held my nose and allied with Yestin Bo-Arthio." He laughed briefly. "That has to count for something."

"You did all these things so you could kidnap me, not out of the kindness of your heart."

"Don't be so dramatic, Braith. It's not attractive."

Had he completely taken leave of his senses? How could he see this as anything other than what it was? He had traded her for the friends he'd claimed to help.

She forced her voice to sound as calm as possible. "You don't call this kidnapping? I am held here against my will."

"Only because you're confused." Dray sat on the bed and took her wrist in his hand.

She strained against his grip, but she was too weak to resist much after days on scant rations. One swift tug and Dray had pulled her to the bed beside him.

He wrapped his arm around her shoulders. "I know this has been difficult. Painful. I can only imagine how that must have been, discovering your mother was behind all of . . . this. I did not even know that piece myself until today. But I keep trying to tell you that you're safe now. I'm here."

"I do not need you to save me, Dray. I don't want you to. I want you to let me go."

Dray put his hand on her cheek. "Remember when you visited me in the dungeon?"

Braith did not answer.

"Remember—we spoke of my changed heart?"

She had been a fool.

"I have done so much good, Braith. Does it not count?" He brushed her tangled hair from her forehead and took a deep breath. "I'm going to kiss you now."

Braith pulled back, but before she could scramble to her feet, his lips pressed against hers.

She jerked herself away and jumped up. "No!"

His brows lifted in surprise.

She moved from the bed, fear and anger surging through her veins. "I understand you now, Dray. So much better than I did that moment in the dungeon. I thought you had changed, yes. I wanted to believe that was true, and perhaps it was for a time. When you had no angle to play, no advantage to gain, perhaps you had begun to change. But I misplaced my faith. I know now you will never understand how to live without taking what you want, even if it hurts others. And because of this, I could never, ever align myself with you."

Dray's face hardened. "Not *align with,* Braith. *Marry.* Those were my terms."

Braith's stomach roiled. "I refuse. I will always refuse."

He paused a moment, sighed, then rose and strode past her to the door. At first, Braith thought he might leave. Concede defeat and let her be free.

But at the door, he stopped and turned. "Is it him?"

"What?"

"The blood heir. Kharn." He spoke Kharn's name like a curse. "Is that why you will not have me?"

"I wouldn't have you anyway, but I do love him." Braith's anger surged over her fear.

"And what does he have that I don't?"

"Integrity. Kindness. Compassion. Goodness." Braith lifted her chin. "A heart."

Dray stood still so long he might have turned to stone. But finally, he flashed a humorless smile. "You always were so proud. But you know what?"

He pivoted and lowered the heavy bolt across the door, barring it from the inside.

Then he spun and faced her again. "I grow weary of being refused, Your Majesty."

CHAPTER FORTY-TWO
TANWEN

"Well"—Frenhin lowered her hands, and the invisible web vanished—"my apologies for that unpleasantness."

Naith was clutching the jar of ancient white strands. I stared at it. I had seen what Frenhin was able to do with one such strand. Now she had three more. Anything we tried, any move we made, and she would swallow us whole in a cloud of darkness like the one that took Gryfelle's life. Or she would fill the room with molten-metal strands like the one that killed Wylie.

As long as she had those strands, we were helpless.

Despair edged in on me like black fog at the corners of my vision. I tried to fight it, tried to grasp at some shred of creativity, some wild idea that just might save our lives.

But there was nothing.

Plans are a fluid concept, Dray had said. And I guess at some point, that well finally ran dry.

I glanced up to find Frenhin standing before me. "Hello, Tanwen."

I grimaced and leaned away from her, into the soldier holding me from behind. I couldn't help it. I felt repelled by her—like a drop of oil in water.

"Surely I'm not as bad as all that." She smiled. How could she look so like Braith and yet not? "In time, you will learn to love me, dear."

"I'm trying to keep my breakfast down, if you don't mind."

She didn't pause to consider the insult. She slapped me across the face, and my head snapped to the right. I briefly wondered if she might be part mountainbeast for the strength of her strike.

Several of the weavers shifted as if they might move to defend me. I shook my head, tasting the blood on my lip. Then I turned back to Frenhin and met her gaze. Wouldn't let her see me wither.

"You will learn respect, Tanwen. And, with time, you will love me because of the power I will give you. I will teach you things beyond your imagining."

"Oh, I don't know. I have a pretty vivid imagination."

"Believe me, the power I offer to you is something you have never conceived of."

"It's not yours to offer."

She lifted her hand again, then lowered it. "No. Not yet. Don't want to bruise your pretty face just now."

I tasted my swollen, split lip. "Aye, wouldn't want that."

"You will be my right hand, Tanwen. Together we will subdue Tir, once and for all."

Behind Frenhin, Naith recoiled as if he had been the one slapped. "Your Majesty," he whined.

She glanced over her shoulder. "What is it?"

"Where . . . where do I fit into this plan?"

"Stars' sake, Naith, is that all you can think about at this crucial juncture? On this, the most exciting, successful day of our entire journey, you wonder what sort of titles and accolades you might receive." She spoke as if addressing a small child. "You may be my royal tea fetcher. How is that?"

He shrank away from her sharp words, and the smallest part of me almost pitied him. Such a pathetic creature he was.

A new guard arrived and cleared his throat. "Master?"

"Yes?"

"There's . . . ah . . ."

"Master!" a voice called from just outside the door. "Master!"

My heart stuttered in shock. *It can't be.*

Frenhin's face twisted as she stared at the guard before her. "Let her in, you dolt!"

The guard nodded. "Yes, of course, it's just she's not alone."

"Master," the voice sang, "I brought you presents."

I braced myself for her entrance. Tried to prepare to see her in the flesh. But I couldn't have ever succeeded. Not if I'd had an hour, not if I'd had a year.

Diggy breezed in, calling this evil, twisted shell of a person *Master*. Only one word thrummed through my mind, pulsing with every beat of my heart.

Lost. Lost. Lost.

I truly had lost her.

"Diggy?" Mor choked out.

I fought for words. "Diggy, wha—" But then I froze. Because the "presents" she had brought were following her into the room.

She held daggers at the throats of two of her hostages.

And one of those hostages was Brac.

His gaze found me, and I could practically feel his sigh of relief, even from this distance. "Tannie, you're alive."

"Brac . . ." I tried to understand what I was seeing, but it was too much. I looked at Diggy's other hostage, and things only got stranger. "Celyn?"

Celyn En-Rhys, one of my neighbors from Pembrone, offered a sad smile. "Ho, Tannie."

And then, as if matters couldn't stump me more, I realized half the farmer's guild from Pembrone stood behind them, flanked by guards with drawn swords.

My knees gave out, and I sagged against the guard holding me.

Nearly everyone in the room seemed stunned.

Naith finally broke the silence. "So," he scoffed, "you truly defected, did you, Brac? I should have known better than to trust you."

"Trust me?" In spite of the blade at his throat, Brac spat at the floor. "You never trusted me. You used me. Lied to me." He swept his gaze to Frenhin. "And don't even get me started on you."

Something in my heart unpinched, and I fought a small wave of tears. There was just something in his tone—something of the boy I knew once.

It was a nice moment to have before we all died.

For I knew I would die. Whatever escape Frenhin tried to offer me, I would never serve her.

"You said you had him well in hand, Naith," Frenhin growled. "Your incompetence could have cost us everything. Everything!"

Naith flinched. "But he's here and subdued, Master. He will not be our undoing."

"No thanks to you." She snatched the jar of strands away from him and set it on a small table near a padded chair at the back of the cavernous room. "Go stand in the corner."

Naith looked at her with wide eyes as though he were unable to believe she would humiliate him like this.

Pitiful fool. He didn't realize he was the pup she kicked whenever she was angry. And little more. He swallowed hard and then obeyed, disappearing into the shadowed corner and his cloud of shame.

"Diggy." Mor's voice was gentle, yet it carried through the whole room and punched me in every hollow, empty spot in my heart. "Diggy, I'm so sorry I failed you."

Diggy studied Mor, then looked away. "You should have come for me."

"Yes. I know." Mor's shoulders and head drooped as he closed his eyes.

Was he going to give up? Not even fight?

"Mor?" My voice came out strangled with tears.

He opened his eyes and looked at me. Smiled sadly. "Tannie, I'm so tired."

And now my heart pulsed with a different word.

Surrender.

But we couldn't. Not yet.

"Diggy." I looked straight at her, trying to keep steady and calm. Maybe there was still hope. "Diggy, please don't do this."

She nodded to a guard, then shoved Celyn his direction. She spun one dagger around and sheathed it on her hip. "Too late, Tannie. It's already done."

"You see, Tanwen?" Frenhin was smiling again, and what I wouldn't have given to knock her teeth out one by one. "Digwyn has come around. Do you not understand what we will be able to do together—you, me, Digwyn, and that one?" She nodded toward Zel.

Even Zel seemed surprised. "Me? You're daft."

Of course. She had been after me, Mor, and Zel at first because we were storytellers. And now she knew all about Diggy's gift and had traded out Mor for Diggy.

"You need all of us," I said quickly. "Mor and I are the ones who share the link."

"Yes, dear, that was the plan. But, as my colleague aptly pointed out, plans are fluid." She indicated Diggy. "I don't think we could rest easy with this prize and the sea captain under the same roof, do you? Family is a messy affair. Too much history. So much angst. I tire of it. So I shall settle for one of the children of Lidere. Digwyn's gift is much more powerful than the link you share with Bo-Lidere."

I cast another desperate glance at Mor.

"No." I scoured my mind—there had to be something I could say to get her to change her mind. "No, you can't." I had nothing.

Everyone I loved was slipping through my fingers.

I turned to Diggy once more, a final plea in my eyes.

She edged backward with Brac, slowly drifting away from us toward Frenhin.

No . . . not toward. Behind.

And suddenly, her eyes were clear—not panicked and shifting and wild. She met my gaze and held one finger to her lips.

Shh.

And then the tiniest smile.

CHAPTER FORTY-THREE
DIGWYN

We can't control the things that happen to us.

We can't even decide how those things will shape us. In some ways, we *are* like ships without sails, tossed about on the waves of life, beholden to the currents and storms that carry us off our charted courses.

I can't control what was done to me yesterday or last year or four years ago.

But I can decide who I want to be tomorrow.

I am not a result of the things that have happened to me. I am not defined by the ways others have harmed me, used me, broken me. They don't get to win anymore.

I decide how to move forward. Tomorrow belongs to me.

My name is Digwyn En-Lidere, and I choose to die fighting for the people I love.

I hope Tannie sees me, knows what I'm attempting, understands I'm doing the best thing I can with my final act.

I won't make it out alive. For this to work, I'll have to throw all caution overboard and be as reckless as I like. But it doesn't matter. I will give the others a fighting chance. Turn the tables. Shift the balance of power. Throw our enemy off course just long enough for the others to make a difference.

That's who I want to be. The one who helped them overcome evil.

Because it all has to be worth something.

I press my free hand against the farmer's back, giving him the signal. Almost imperceptibly, he nods.

He has understood. I see his fingers flick, sharing the signal with the others.

I pause for one long moment to gauge my distance. I will have a single chance to do this right.

Yes. It's time.

"Now!" I shout.

Brac grabs my dagger and bolts for the corner toward the priest. The farmers and guardsmen on Brac's crew draw hidden weapons and turn on Frenhin's guards. I dive and snatch the jar of strands off Frenhin's table.

For ten ticks, it's like the world is moving underwater. A farmer buries his sword in a guard's gut. The general jerks away from his captor and draws a weapon before anyone can blink. Mor has not moved except to widen his eyes at me.

Frenhin's face twists into an expression like she's made of candle wax and someone has held her to a flame.

I tighten my grip on the jar.

"Seize her!" she screams.

I can't help my smirk. "Good luck with that."

And before anyone can touch me, I tuck the jar into the loosened belt about my hips, scale the easy stone handholds on the walls, and disappear into the darkness of the cavern's upper reaches.

CHAPTER FORTY-FOUR
TANWEN

I MIGHT HAVE BEEN FLYING.

Something inside me sure felt like it was sailing high above all the danger as I watched Diggy snatch the jar of strands and skitter away with them.

Out of Frenhin's reach—for now.

I had no idea how it was possible. No idea how Brac was there or how he had brought half of Pembrone with him.

But my heart was light. Because I had not lost Diggy, and through some miracle, Brac had come back to me too. He wasn't lost forever either. He was trying to do the right thing.

My exhaustion of mind and body floated off, up, away. Hope flared in my veins.

We had a chance.

"Move, Tannie!" Father shouted. He was already crossing blades with two guards.

Oops. I wouldn't have much chance if I kept standing here like a bull's-eye nailed to a wooden pole.

I glanced at Mor. He was already pulling off his gloves.

Brac's voice came from nearby. "Tannie." He blocked a strike with his sword. "I'm sorry."

A beam of purple light shot from my hand and smacked Brac's opponent in the face. "Do we have to talk about this now?"

"Now might be all we've got." He ducked under the punch of a guard. "I was so foolish, Tannie."

"I know you were." I spared half a smile over my shoulder so he would know I was jesting, at least a little bit. "I made mistakes too. We were both fool—get down!"

He hesitated and almost got a blast of strands in his face. But he dropped to the ground just in time, and my blinding strand of sunshine hit the man charging at us instead. Brac took the moment, sweeping the guard's legs and toppling him.

"Tannie?"

I created a column of wind and directed it toward a cloud of Frenhin's smoke encircling Dylun. "Aye, Brac?"

"We make it out of here, and all I ever want to do for the rest of my life is plow fields."

A laugh, shaky through my sudden tears, bubbled up like a spring. "Sounds nice, Brac."

But I wondered . . .

Would Brac ever be able to have that now? The farm and the small town and the wife and children? He had committed high treason. He was sorry for it, it seemed, but would that matter?

And did he realize any of this? Brac never did understand much about the way the world worked. Maybe he thought he could just undo it all with a snap of his fingers.

I turned to find him looking at me, a strange expression on his face—a sad, understanding smile. "I know, Tannie. I know it."

He could see what I was thinking, see the worry and pain and wondering on my face.

"You've changed," I said around the lump rising in my throat.

"Aye?"

I couldn't give voice to it in that moment, but he truly had. He had considered the personal cost of this mission and done the right thing anyway. He understood the consequences and made the hard, right choice. And there was something about him . . . older and wiser by years, not moons.

"Aye, Brac. You have."

"For the better, I hope." He shoved a guard away with his boot.

"Aye, for the better."

"Tannie, about our betrothal . . ."

Oh stars. Maybe he *hadn't* changed.

"It was foolish," he added quickly. "I knew you didn't want to, and I practically forced you."

A few tears broke free. "You didn't force me. I just never thought—"

"That I would live long enough to go through with it. I know. And I knew it then, deep down, but I wanted us to be together so bad. I couldn't see straight. But I've sorted my snifflers now. I think I understand what you've been saying all this time."

I didn't fail to notice the glance he snuck at Celyn En-Rhys, who was helping Farmer Hayfal take down a guard. Holding her own with a wooden pole as her weapon.

A grin spread across my face as I sent a stream of icy water toward a strand of fire. "Well now, Brac Bo-Bradwir."

"What?" He started. "That's not . . . she just . . . that is . . ." He reacted just in time to block the strike of a guard.

"I'm happy for you, Brac. Whether it's Celyn or someone else. You deserve to be happy and have the things you want most in life."

His face reddened so badly I could see it even in the warm firelight of the cavern. "Ah, Tannie. Why'd you have to bring it up?"

I laughed. Right then, he was so much the old Brac. The real Brac.

He narrowed his eyes. "I ain't never going to be able to say that pirate deserves you."

"I know it." I wrapped my opponent in a cocoon of rope strands.

"But I want you to be happy," he said.

We stopped fighting for a moment and exchanged a look—a look full of our shared lives, a look full of friendship and understanding and a common bond.

"I love you, Tannie."

"I love you, too, Brac."

He flashed a lopsided grin that felt like grain fields and sunburned noses.

But then his eyes went wide, and his smile faded. He looked down. A strand had pierced him from behind, running all the way through so I could see it as I stood in front of him.

My mind bolted back to the *Cethorelle*. I was standing on the stern watching a strand of molten metal slice Wylie through the chest, steal his life, pull him to his grave at the bottom of the sea.

Screaming rang in my ears, and I knew it was mine. But it sounded like it was from somewhere else. Back in time, back to that moment of horror, but now it was Brac's face on the pierced body, and we were surrounded by rolling waves of black cave rock, not the Menfor Sea.

Brac's stifled cry brought me back to myself.

I tried to make my mind catch up. Because now I saw that Frenhin's strand of molten metal had not pierced Brac through the chest as it had done to Wylie. It skewered Brac through the back of his shoulder and barely protruded out the front. He was alive.

He's alive. He's alive.

I had to repeat it over and over, because my memories wanted to intrude, wanted to overlay Wylie's face with Brac's, threatening to convince me I had lost them both.

"You're alive," I cried aloud, just to make it more real. I pulled him toward me, away from the strand, then sent ice and rage at that strand to cool it off and douse the monster who had created it.

"Aye, I'm alive." Brac grimaced. "But that smarted."

He moved his shoulder. Left one, not his sword arm. And it wasn't bleeding, because the heat had cauterized it. That was something. But he would need to treat the burn.

"Karlith!" I had no idea where she was, but if she could hear me, she would come. "Brac, Karlith will help you. I need to go. It's going to have to be weavers to stop Frenhin."

"Aye." Then as Karlith approached, he added, "I didn't get Naith."

"What?"

"I charged him and took a bite out of him with that dagger, but then Frenhin's strands protected him. I don't know where he went."

Brilliant. Stop Frenhin, find her minion. No problem.

"I have to go, Brac."

"Aye. Go." He gave his lopsided smile, looking a little pained as Karlith slathered something over his burn. "Save the day, Tannie."

I grinned. "That's the plan."

Then I spun, searching the room for Mor.

There, in the corner, directing fire strands toward the chains binding Kharn. The metal glowed red-hot now, and Kharn held the chains taut against the wall while Warmil took a swift swing with his sword. A few more strikes and the heated metal relented.

Kharn was free, and I saw his attention dart toward the door, registering the many guards and blades and skirmishes between him and his exit—his path toward Braith.

Right—stop Frenhin, find her minion, save the queen.

"Mor!" I called as I ran toward them.

His face revealed his relief. "Tannie. You're safe."

"We need to get Kharn out of here so he can find Braith."

"Aye, but we also need to take care of this"—he gestured toward the fighting all around us—"or else Frenhin will just follow us."

We both looked over to the other side of the cavern where Frenhin launched strand after furious strand toward the ceiling. Almost out of view, I could see a glowing jar of lightning flitting from point to point.

How long could anyone, even Diggy, keep that up?

Stop Frenhin, find her minion, save the queen, rescue Diggy, keep the strands safe.

"Blast." I pressed my palms to my temples. Too many things were happening at once. That always seemed to be the case at the worst possible moments.

Mor crossed blades with a guard who appeared beside me. After a few exchanges, Mor managed to disarm him. He cast a web of sticky strands and trapped the man against the stone floor. "Tannie." He sheathed his sword. "I need to help Diggy." His gaze traveled up to the ceiling and the little point of light flittering to and fro like a glowbug.

"But what about Braith?"

"Split up, then?" He frowned, and I could tell he didn't much care for the idea.

Nor did I. "No." I held out my hand. "Stronger together."

A smile warmed his expression. "Aye. Stronger together."

His fingers grazed my palm, and our gifts found each other—linked, grabbed on, and sealed our hands together. I took a deep breath as the energy coursed through me.

Mor seemed to be feeling the same power. "Kharn first?"

I nodded. "We just need to clear a path, then he can go after Braith."

"That can be arranged."

I wasn't sure what he had in mind, but we thrust our hands forward together. Streams of wind flowed from both of us. Lots of wind. The kind we had used to fill the sails of the *Cethorelle*. But even more than that—a windstorm was arising inside this mountain hideout.

We hadn't had a way to warn them, so some of the

weavers—Warmil, Dylun, and Zel—and several farmers were caught into the air alongside Frenhin's guards. But, whether by luck or because my suspicions were true and Father really could read minds, he had pulled Kharn back against the wall, out of the middle of the gale.

My muscles screamed, and Mor's tendons looked like they'd break through his skin with the strain of holding a couple dozen people in the air by strands.

"Kharn, go!" I shouted. Whether he could hear me over the roar, who could say?

Kharn tried to run for the door, but the wind pushed him back and threw him against the wall beside Father. Father ducked and, with effort, pulled Kharn to the ground. Together they crawled for the door.

The suspended guards fought to get their legs beneath them and touch back on solid ground. Mor was squeezing my hand so hard I was pretty sure both our fingers would break soon.

Kharn lunged for the door and grabbed hold of the heavy iron handle.

He was so gaunt and battered I worried his arms might break off if the wind became much stronger.

But he and Father muscled the door open, and Kharn managed to get through. Just in time, for a guard who had overcome our strandstorm got his feet beneath him and charged at them.

Father drew his sword and met his attacker's blade before I could blink, but it didn't matter.

Kharn was gone and on his way to rescue Braith.

Unless Dray had escaped with her already.

Or worse.

CHAPTER FORTY-FIVE

BRAITH

BRAITH DIDN'T HAVE TIME TO MOVE. DRAY SLAMMED INTO HER so hard her knees buckled. But she didn't fall. He held her around the waist, keeping her on her feet, and pressed his mouth to hers.

She pulled away and screamed. Twisted her neck so he couldn't reach her. But he pushed both his hands on her face and forced her toward him.

"Don't turn away from me."

She struggled against his grip. "Get off!" Furious tears coursed down her cheeks. "Leave me alone!" She strained away with every bit of power she could muster.

"Enough." He shoved her onto Frenhin's bed.

The impact knocked the wind from Braith's body. She tried to gasp. But before she could catch her breath, he was upon her.

She clawed at his face. Screamed again. Shoved against his chest. But he was heavy—so heavy.

"Quiet, Braith. Goddesses' sake, will you be quiet for once?"

She screamed again.

But then his fingers wrapped around her throat. She gasped. Reached for his hands. Then he began to squeeze.

She couldn't move. Couldn't breathe.

Oh, Creator, help me.

Her eyes widened, and she met Dray's stare, his face inches from hers.

"I just wanted to love you, Braith. And now, look. Do you see what you've done? You've turned me into what you always accused me of being." He lessened his grip on her throat, just enough that she could pull half a breath, enough to keep conscious and alive. Alive and awake and aware of what he planned to do next.

"Whatever you do to me, Dray," she whispered, "I will never be yours."

His grip tightened again, and he pressed his mouth to hers. Then his lips found her neck. "I wouldn't be so sure of that, Braith. We were always meant to be together." He kept one hand wrapped around her throat and began to tug at the shoulder of her dress with the other. "This was written in the stars. Can't you see that?"

Braith fought the desire to close her eyes—to give up and stop resisting.

"You are my soul mate."

She reached out and felt for the bedside table—for anything she might grab hold of to try to pull herself away. To give her leverage against Dray's greater strength and ill intent.

Instead, she found her mother's looking glass.

She gripped it as tightly as she could, then picked it up and smashed it against the bedside table. The frame broke, and the glass splintered with a crash. Dray released her throat in surprise. But before he could realize what she had done, she jammed the jagged edge of the broken looking glass into his abdomen as hard as she could.

His eyes widened—whether in shock or pain, Braith couldn't tell—and then he fell forward, his weight pressing down on Braith and pushing against the broken shard in her hand.

Braith felt the edges of the fragment slice into her palms and fingers as Dray slowly crumpled onto the weapon in his gut.

And finally, after several long moments, he pressed himself up and stumbled to his feet. He faltered a few steps backward, away from the bed, blood seeping from his wound. He collapsed to his knees and then dropped all the way to the floor, the shard protruding cruelly from his belly.

Braith sat up, every inch of her body shaking.

Dray turned his head toward her. Confused. "Braith?"

And then his eyes blanked. His chest stilled. His lips turned ashen.

Braith slid to the floor and leaned against the bed, her breath coming in panicked gasps. Her gaze traveled down to the gashes on her hands, her blood mingled with Dray's.

Oh, Creator.

CHAPTER FORTY-SIX
TANWEN

Stop Frenhin, find her minion, rescue Diggy, keep the strands safe.

At least Kharn was looking for Braith now. The list had shrunk.

Brac's crew and our best fighters had fared well up to this point, but we were still outnumbered by Frenhin's guards.

Aeron caught my attention nearby, and my heart clenched a little as I watched her struggle without the mobility she once had in her legs. She'd told me that good swordplay was as much about footwork as it was fancy blade strikes.

But Warmil stood at her back, same as he always had done, and together they took on three guards at once.

When I saw Dylun, I couldn't help but smile a little. On our various quests, he had been the one carefully guarding the important treasures, putting himself between our enemies and the strands he considered more valuable than his own life.

But now, with the ancient strands as safe as they could be in Diggy's care, Dylun the colormaster was back. He stood in front of Karlith as she tended a stab wound on the midsection of Farmer Wenth.

Dylun lifted his hands, and streams of colormastery fire poured from them. Gone was the reserved scholar and his protective reticence. Instead, here was all the passion of the artist whose temper had once exploded when he saw how influenced I was by Gareth's oppressive policies toward weavers.

He waved his palms in circles until his strands spun into a tornado of fiery art. Then he thrust his hands forward. Four guards toppled over as the strands hit them—two unconscious, the other two dropping their weapons on impact.

I glanced toward the front of the cave and saw Frenhin still shooting strands toward the ceiling. But Diggy's glowbug light was no longer visible up there. Had she found a place to hide? Or at least a place to stash the strands? I prayed both she and the strands were safe.

I almost missed him in the unreliable light of the cave, but there he was.

Naith.

He was ducking into Frenhin's shadow. I could imagine his pathetic whining and wheedling.

"Tannie!"

I saw Mor's face a second before he tackled me to the ground. One sword and then another sliced the air above us.

Both Father's. He'd collected another weapon at some point, and I couldn't say I was surprised. The guard who had been about to attack me from behind was the unfortunate recipient of both strikes.

Father acknowledged us, then moved on.

Mor's eyes burned. "You have *got* to stop standing still in the middle of battles, Tannie."

"Sorry." I looked around. "Where's Zel?"

Mor climbed to his feet and pulled me up after him. "I don't—oh. There."

Zel had fought his way through Frenhin's line of guards. And now he was striding with purpose toward the woman behind it all.

The one who was responsible for Ifmere's death.

My heart turned to ice. "Mor."

"Aye." He grabbed my hand, and we took off after Zel.

He was going to get himself killed if he tried to take on Frenhin alone.

"Zel, wait!" My voice was swallowed by the clash of blades and the shouts of men fighting.

Mor released my hand and drew his sword as we met three guards intent on protecting their Master.

"Zel!"

He either didn't hear, or he ignored us. His hands lit up with an orange glow.

"Zelyth!" Mor ran a guard through, then shoved him away with a kick. "Zel!"

Zel thrust his right hand forward, and a wave of wild orange hair poured from it. The strands sailed toward Frenhin, who was still focused on the ceiling and the stolen jar.

Some of the orange strands wrapped around Frenhin's hand and yanked it down toward the ground just as she tried to send fire into the darkness in search of Diggy. The fire strand fizzled harmlessly against the stone floor.

Frenhin whipped around to face Zel, her eyes filled with rage. She flexed her arm muscles, and her whole hand smoldered. The heat traveled from her fingertips, across her palm, and to her wrist. She shook with the exertion, but Zel's strand made of hair like his wife's began to sizzle, then fell off and pooled in a useless puddle at Frenhin's feet.

"Have you come to challenge me?" Frenhin sneered. "All alone? This will not end well for you, storyteller."

Zel didn't respond. He just fired off two more strands.

I had to look away because two threats were closing in on Mor and me. He was right. I had to stop standing there trying to make sure everyone else was alive if I expected to make it out of the cave, myself.

Which I sort of didn't.

But I'd be fried if some nameless minion of Frenhin's would be the one to do the deed.

I grabbed Mor's left hand, and the sword in his right fist crackled with lightning. He paused a moment, eyebrows raised, then moved. This was a new trick, but we would take it.

He fought the two guards nearby, catching the first unaware and sinking his sword into the guard's gut. I looked away. Still wasn't used to it and didn't want to be.

Mor crossed blades with the next, and at that contact, the guard jolted. Shook, then froze, his wild eyes staring straight ahead. He had been struck by lightning—through Mor's sword. The guard fell to the ground and lay still.

Mor turned to me. "Well, that's . . ."

"Terrifying."

He nodded in agreement, but we didn't have the time to consider it. We spun back toward the front of the cave where Frenhin and Zel were trading strand for strand, Zel's grief for Frenhin's rage. Ifmere's memory for Frenhin's insanity.

Hair and fire swirled everywhere, and I recalled that moment in the battle when Gareth fell. When Zel's strands exploded and knocked people senseless. Even knocked some people dead.

Would he do it again? And would he accidentally kill Diggy and himself in the process?

Just when I didn't think the situation could get any pricklier, someone new ran into the fray.

Brac.

His sword was drawn, and he charged straight for Naith Bo-Offriad. The priest was gripping a dagger in one hand and creeping toward Zel.

Zel hesitated. It was just a second. One moment. A short breath as he considered this new threat edging toward him.

It didn't matter. Frenhin saw her chance and took it.

A molten-metal strand poured from her hand. In a blink, it

solidified. Almost like it had crystallized, except she had turned it into a blade.

She ran it through Zelyth.

"No!"

We were there now, and Mor was shouting. A rope shot from one of my hands, aimed for Naith's legs as Brac engaged with him. But he dodged my strand.

I hurled another strand, this one like a ribbon of ice, toward Frenhin. It hit her in the arm, and she hissed. She pulled back, yanking her blade out of Zel. He collapsed into Mor's arms. Zel's strands fell from the air, pooled on the ground, and disappeared.

Creator, protect Brac in his battle with Naith. I couldn't help him just now. Frenhin turned toward Mor and Zel, murderous intent flashing in her eyes as she targeted the two lads on the floor.

I shot two more strands of ice at the traitor queen. One sailed just over her shoulder, and I bit back a curse. But the other found its mark and smacked her right in the face.

She cried out and stumbled back. But for how long?

I wished I could create the halo-head story I'd managed in Gareth's throne room. That creature had taken vengeance for me, taken the violence out of my hands.

But I hadn't created it on purpose. It had just happened. The concentration I would need to recreate it would be great, and I didn't have the time or the space. Frenhin was already recovering her wits.

And Mor was cradling his best friend while Zel's lifeblood spilled out onto the ground.

My efforts were too feeble. I would never be able to defeat Frenhin—only defend against her attacks—but it was all I could do at the moment.

I cast a beam of turquoise light at her.

Maybe if I used the reprieve to create something bigger, stronger, more aggressive, I could give the others a chance.

But as the strand of light sailed through the air, a figure emerged from the shadows—as though she'd been crouched against the wall, waiting. Timing it perfectly.

And she had.

Diggy sprang toward us, reaching up and touching my strand of turquoise light as she crossed under it. In a blink, it was solid, like a spear of flashing aqua, suspended in the air. She completed her dive, tucking into a somersault, and popped up to her feet. She grabbed the spear and whirled around, her movements so fluid it was like she was dancing.

Frenhin's shock seemed to hold her frozen in place. The whole sequence had taken ten ticks, and now there was a new opponent with a formidable weapon spinning into her space.

She recovered herself just in time to dodge—but not quite enough. She took the spear in her side. Swift as a fluff-hopper, Diggy pulled the spear back and darted out of Frenhin's reach.

"Master!" Naith cried.

She shoved him away. "Get off, you fool! Fight back for once instead of cowering in my shadow!"

Naith recoiled.

I glanced to my left and saw Brac and Mor carrying Zel toward the wall, away from the melee. I couldn't tell if he was alive or dead.

"So"—Frenhin stared down Diggy, one hand over the wound in her side, the other crawling with flames, ready to strike—"this is your choice?"

Diggy didn't speak. Just held her spear in a blocking position, waiting.

Frenhin pulled her hand away and examined her blood-darkened fingers. Then she smiled and tasted the blood. She breathed deep, like the wound fed her blackened soul.

"You've hurt so many people," I said, my voice somehow carrying above the din of battle.

Frenhin regarded me in silence, smelling the blood on her fingertips.

"You betrayed your own daughter—your king, your husband, your people. How could you?"

She flashed a cold smile. "What they took from me could not be returned, but I had my revenge."

I didn't know what they had done to her or why she needed revenge. Or even who *they* were. It didn't matter. Could anything justify what Frenhin had done? She had chosen the way of darkness.

"Revenge didn't fix it, though." Diggy didn't say this like a question, and I knew why. She knew how revenge sat on a person's soul. "You got back at them all, and now what? What do you have, *Master*?" Her voice was as sharp as her daggers. "How is this better?"

"They had to pay."

"You can stop this," I said to Frenhin, gesturing to the battle raging behind us. "You don't have to keep making this choice. You can turn away and find some peace. True peace, at last."

I realized as I said it aloud that I believed it completely. Even someone like Frenhin or Dray, who had spent lifetimes living for themselves and doing evil, *could* turn away, like Karlith had said. Brac had changed course. Diggy had stepped away from darkness. Maybe Karlith was right, too, that we needed help from the Creator, someone greater and better than ourselves, to do this. But it *was* possible.

"Frenhin." I held my hands up, no strands tingling in my fingers. A sign of peace. "You can live for something better than vengeance."

She considered me. Her eyes narrowed. Then she leaned forward, thirty years of pain, rage, and bitterness etched on her face. "I have the power now. They had to pay, and all of them did." Then her lips formed a cruel smirk. "Except one."

My stomach felt like it had crystallized. Turned to stone. Filled with ice.

I drew back.

"I have not yet had my revenge on Yestin Bo-Arthio," she said. "But that's about to change."

CHAPTER FORTY-SEVEN
BRAITH

BRAITH HEARD THE POUNDING IN THE ROOM NEXT DOOR. BUT she couldn't move.

She stood a little way from Dray's body. She had covered his bare chest, closed his eyelids, and thought about removing the shard of glass, but she couldn't bear it.

The knocking next door stopped. There was a muffled sound, then the pounding began again on the door to her mother's bedchamber. Were the guards after her again?

Even this new fear couldn't overcome the numbness that drenched every fiber of her being. She couldn't move.

And then, like a ray of sunlight, his voice broke through the fog in her mind.

"Braith?" Kharn, banging at the door. "Braith, are you in there?"

She broke into a sob. "Kharn?"

He uttered something between an oath and an exclamation of relief. "Braith, can you open the door?"

She couldn't speak.

"Braith, are you hurt?"

She looked down at her sliced hands. "Yes," she whispered.

"Braith?"

The pounding became more insistent and intense, and Braith realized Kharn was kicking the wood. The hinges began to pull from the doorframe. Remembering how weak Kharn was from lack of food, Braith worried his strength couldn't hold out. She had to get to the door.

She used the wall for support, made her way to the door, and lifted the heavy latch. She grimaced as the wood and metal bit into her cuts.

Kharn nearly crashed into her as he pushed into the room, his eyes wild. "Braith!"

"I'm here," she choked.

He held her shoulders, looking her over carefully. His eyes widened as he saw Dray on the floor. He looked back at her.

She extended her hands.

Kharn took her into his arms. "Braith," he whispered. He embraced her a moment, then gently pulled back and looked into her eyes. "Braith, did he hurt you?"

Braith's mind felt like it was working through water. "I killed him."

"Yes, I know, my love."

"He . . ." She began to shake. "He attacked me."

Kharn pulled her to himself, and she wept into his chest. She could hear the fury of his heartbeat.

But his voice was surprisingly calm. "You're safe now, Braith. It's over. He's gone."

She clung to him. "I took his life." Her sobbing intensified. "Oh, Creator, forgive me. I took a life. I killed him, Kharn. What have I done?"

Kharn took her face in his hands. Braith could see him blinking back tears. "This is not your fault. You defended yourself. Do you hear me? This is *not* your fault." He held her close again.

Eventually her sobs quieted as she rested her head on his shoulder. Then awareness of the last few weeks tumbled back to her all at once.

She stopped. "Kharn, how are you here? Where is everyone? My mother—is she . . . ?"

"No. I mean . . . I don't know. The others are still in there, I think. They got me out so I could come find you before . . ."

Braith could tell he was trying carefully to speak around his rage.

"So I could get to you before Dray stole away with you."

"We have to help them," Braith said. What help they could offer, she had no idea. But if they had anything to lend, they must do so.

And quickly.

"Braith . . ." Kharn's tone was awkward, but his face showed compassion. "We need to find something else for you to wear."

She looked down. Her dress—the simple gray shift provided to her by Frenhin's servants on her first day here—was covered in blood and torn at the top where Dray had clawed at it.

"I'm so sorry he hurt you."

Braith closed her eyes. "It . . . could have been worse. Oh, Kharn. I thought he could change and truly be a better person."

"I know you did."

"He could have been. But . . ." She covered her face. "He just couldn't stop trying to take." The tears came again.

Kharn hugged her and stroked her hair until she moved to wipe her face. She took a breath and held up her head. "Come. Let us see what my mother has in her wardrobe. Then we will go help our friends, if they live still."

A FEW MINUTES LATER, IN A FRESH DRESS, THE BLOOD WASHED from her hands, and her wounds wrapped in strips of clean linen, Braith emerged behind Kharn into the hallway of the Craigyl.

It was empty. No guards lined the passage as they had when Dray dragged her through it—an hour ago? More? Braith had lost all concept of time.

"Where is everyone?" she asked Kharn.

"In that room. Whatever it is. Frenhin's court? Her dungeon?

Battlefield? I guess it's sort of a multi-purpose meeting space, isn't it?"

Braith allowed a tiny smile. It was the first bit of humor from Kharn since he had found her in that dreaded room. It felt warm and familiar.

Kharn peered up ahead. "I'm not sure what we should—"

"Your Majesty?"

Kharn whirled around and pushed Braith behind him. "Who goes there?"

A thin, pale man stepped into the torchlight, his hands held up. "Apologies, my lord. I am unarmed."

Braith gasped. This thin man supported an older man tottering behind him. "Master Insegno!" she cried. She had wondered if the Meridioni scholar was still alive.

Insegno smiled, but he looked spent. "Hello, Your Majesty. I confess I am pleased, though surprised, to find you alive."

"Likewise." Braith resisted the urge to embrace him—it was not the Meridioni custom. Instead, she stepped out from behind Kharn and kissed both Insegno's cheeks, then turned to the pale man. "And who is your rescuer?"

"Hysgrifenyddion Bo-Fergel. Er . . ." He flushed and looked down at the floor. "Scribe and advisor to the steward, I'm afraid."

Kharn put a protective arm around Braith's waist. "You had best state your business quickly. Before we have reason to conclude you are our enemy."

"Yes. Forgive me."

"Your given name is Old Tirian," Braith said. "That is an interesting choice, but I am not surprised. I knew Fergel." The memory sharpened into focus. "He tended the palace libraries, did he not? I can recall his help—when my tutor would send me to the library with a list, Fergel made sure I found every book so I would not have my knuckles rapped."

Bo-Fergel gave a slight smile. "Yes, that is my father."

"Is he well?"

"He is retired, Your Majesty. He retired and left Urian shortly after your father's reign began."

Braith understood the unspoken implication. The family of Fergel had not been loyal supporters of Gareth. But how had this son of Fergel become involved with the Steward of Tir and the Master's machinations?

Bo-Fergel shifted his weight. "I do not wish to make excuses, Your Majesty. I worked in Gareth's treasury, then yours. After they stormed the palace, they rounded up those still living and gave us the choice to help or die. I could have refused. But Brac—that is, the steward—he seemed so lost and alone. I thought I might help him." He bowed low. "Forgive me."

"Rise, sir," Braith said. When Bo-Fergel's startled eyes met hers, she continued, "It is not wrong to try to help someone in need."

"I do not know if I made the right choice, Majesty. But had I made a different one, I would not have been able to help Brac carry out his plans. He is here, Majesty. Here to help rescue you and the weavers. He wants to undo what has been wrought."

Kharn let out a slow breath. "Tall order, that."

"He knows this, my lord. But it was as if a spell over him finally broke. Suddenly he could see the wrong that had been done, and he has thought of nothing except righting it since."

"Bo-Fergel," Braith said kindly, "it is exactly like there was a spell over him. We have not the time for me to tell you all I have learned from my mother, but perhaps I will be able to ease Guardsman Bo-Bradwir's conscience someday soon."

"I do not think he expects to survive this encounter, Your Majesty. But any kind word from you would certainly ease his conscience, I'm sure."

"Then perhaps we should go do what we can to help our friends and ensure such words will pass between us."

Bo-Fergel nodded and flashed another tight, worried smile.

He seemed to feel about as comfortable with the idea of battle as Braith did.

No matter. They would do what they could.

Kharn frowned. "I wish I had a sword, at least."

"Do you know how to use one?" Braith asked.

He raised an eyebrow. "I was properly educated as a nephew of the king, thank you very much."

"But all the intervening years on the farm?"

"Yes. A rake might be a more comfortable weapon."

She smiled and took his arm. "Come. We will all do what we can."

They turned and made their way back down the hall toward Frenhin's Craigyl court. But just as they were about to reach the doors, they came upon a group approaching from the other direction.

The group had their swords drawn and seemed ready for trouble.

Braith's heart stuttered. She took in their appearance from head to toe and realized this lot would always look ready for trouble.

"Pirates," she murmured.

The big one at the head of the pack grinned. "Aye. Gyth, at your service." But then his eyes widened as he took in Braith. "Your . . . Highness?"

"Majesty," Bo-Fergel corrected. "This is *Queen* Braith En-Gareth."

"You was princess last we was in Tir, Majesty. Apologies." Gyth nodded to the group behind him. "Hope you don't mind, but we got some business to attend to just now."

A woman edged her way to the front of the pack. There was blood on her blouse, though it looked like whatever wound spilled it had been bandaged up tightly. Braith's brows rose as she took in the woman's purple-streaked blonde hair knotted together with ribbons and seashells.

"It's you, isn't it?" the woman said, eyeing Braith. She shook her head. "I should've known." She glanced over her shoulder. "Told you all it was something big. Else Mor wouldn't have put up such a fight."

"Bested us, you mean, Ven." Gyth folded his arms across his chest. "You refusing to say it don't make it less true."

The woman glared. "Aye, I get it." She adjusted her stance. "He said it was bigger than him." She glanced back at Braith. "He wasn't jesting."

"Excuse me," Braith interrupted. "But did you say Mor? You know Mor Bo-Lidere?"

Gyth snorted. "He was our captain once."

Heavens. Braith looked at the ragtag bunch again and tried not to be judgmental. She had always known Captain Bo-Lidere had once been disposed to piracy, but it was a tad strange to see the vestiges of it right in front of her.

Kharn pulled Braith tighter to his side and addressed Ven. "Will you tell us your plan? I assume you do not wish harm to your former captain." He shot a skeptical glance at the wound in Ven's abdomen. "Can we take that to mean we share common goals?"

"If Mor's on your side, then aye, we share a common goal. We tracked him here to offer him and his crew our swords. To make up for a previous lapse in judgment, if you will." Ven raised an eyebrow at the foursome before her. "And what, pray tell, is *your* plan, Sir Fancypants?"

A sandy-haired man elbowed her in her uninjured side and muttered, "Can you not get us executed, please, Venewth?"

She shrugged.

But Kharn didn't react. "We're on our way to assist our friends. They are facing a terrible foe in there. We will do whatever we can to help them."

The pirates all seemed to be trying to hold on to their

laughter. A Meridioni woman covered her mouth and looked away. The sandy-haired one clamped down on his lip.

Venewth crossed her arms and smirked. "No offense, but if you really want to help them, you'll stay out of the way. Fancypants here might be useful with a sword—no idea. But the rest of you?" She nodded at Bo-Fergel. "That one would blow over in a strong breeze." Her gaze traveled to Master Insegno. "And *nonno* looks like he might have been alive to witness the dawn of time." She flashed a smile that looked semi-apologetic. "No offense."

Braith tried to force the indignation from her voice. "They have come to rescue me at great personal risk, and if I can—"

"Your Majesty." Venewth's smirk was still twisting her lips, but her eyes had softened. "That's my point. They have risked everything to save you. If you want to honor that, the best thing you can do is hide." She looked at Kharn. "Hide the queen. Make sure she gets out of here alive or else their sacrifice is for nothing." She laughed and shook her head. "I knew it was important when Mor was willing to cross blades with me over it. But the Queen of fire-blazing Tir. That lad always did know how to find trouble."

"But I . . ." Braith couldn't finish the thought. Despite the somewhat-rude delivery, this pirate lady was right.

"Queen Braith." Venewth lowered herself to one knee, a bit slowly with her injury. She bowed her head, and the rest of the crew followed her lead. "As captain of this band of barbarians, I swear our fealty to you—for at least the next twenty minutes." She glanced up, eyes twinkling. "Let us serve you in this way."

"For Mor," Gyth added.

"For Mor," Captain Venewth conceded. "Please promise you will stay safe."

It pained Braith to admit it, but she would be a liability and a distraction if she walked into that room. "Yes. I promise."

"Excellent." Captain Venewth rose. "We'll find you after we save the day."

And with a grin wide enough to reveal a few gold teeth, Venewth swept into Frenhin's domain, her crew trailing loyally behind her.

CHAPTER FORTY-EIGHT
DIGWYN

TANNIE HAS TRIED HER HARDEST. DONE HER BEST. SHE REALLY believes it—that people can do and be better.

I guess I do too. Because that's what I'm trying to do, even if it'll be my last act.

It's a good final choice.

But I know Frenhin will not turn back. I see it brewing in her eyes—the kind of hatred and rage that eats a person from the inside out.

That was my future, so I know it well.

Tannie waits. Listens to this wicked woman threaten the general, threaten her, threaten everything.

But I am not holding my breath in anticipation of what Frenhin will say next. Because I already know. Instead, I'm ready. Ready to strike.

I adjust the spear in my hands, thankful for my training from Kawan some years ago.

Not my favorite weapon. I prefer my daggers. But spears are better than swords, at least. Longer range, lighter weight.

"You don't have to do this," Tannie says again.

Frenhin leans forward, her smile glinting. "But really, I do."

And I take that moment. Fast, like lightning. Like the strike of a snake. Like Kawan taught me.

I sink the spear into her right shoulder—opposite side from her abdominal wound. I had aimed for the soft, unprotected flesh of her neck, but my reach isn't what I'd wish, the weapon not my most comfortable.

Frenhin's shriek fills the cavern.

For some reason, my gaze drifts up. Up toward the ceiling. Up to where I have hidden the jar of strands. A faint glow emanates from the cleft in the rock. Something about her shriek ignites my instinct to protect those strands—to make sure they don't come anywhere near her hands again.

Frenhin's focus goes toward the jar, and I know I've made a mistake. I don't have a tick to think. I feint with the spear as though I'll strike her again, and she leans away. But before I complete the thrust, I release the strand-spear. It clatters to the ground, and I'm three handholds up the wall again.

"No!" Frenhin screams. We both know she can't chase me.

But her strands can.

A tongue of fire licks my right leg. I cry out. But I regain my rhythm after half a breath.

"Naith!" Frenhin shouts. "Kill them all except the pirate and the story peddler. Bring them to me!"

I keep climbing, but I wonder at this—how can the wheedling, impotent priest kill anything when he has spent the entire battle lurking in the shadows and shrinking behind Frenhin?

But when I glance down, I see that Frenhin is somehow channeling strands of fire and metal and death through her flatterer. Now they have four hands instead of two, two targets instead of one.

I slip most of my body into the cleft of rock where I've tucked the jar. She could still burn me from here, and I can scarcely breathe, so small is the space. But I can catch my wind. Think about what to do next.

And watch.

I see Naith, his borrowed power emboldening him as he charges my brother. Mor is still huddled with his wounded friend—mortally wounded, if you want my opinion, but Mor wouldn't hear that. Even if I could tell him.

"Stop." Karlith steps in front of Mor and Zel, her palms facing the priest. "Naith Bo-Offriad, you will come no further."

Naith freezes. But then a cold smile spreads across his face. "Karlith Ma-Lundir."

"You should not speak his name." Karlith's hands are still raised, her voice calm—but cold as a snowy day. "You should not speak the names of those whose lives you have stolen."

"I am not beholden to you or your code of honor." Naith spits on the ground at her feet.

"Aye, that's true enough." Karlith's fingertips light up. "So be it."

A flood of blue colormastery strands pour from Karlith's hands. Naith meets the water—calm, soothing, and pure, just like Karlith—with Frenhin's fire.

I duck away from the edge just in time to avoid a similar fire strand, this one from Frenhin, directed at me.

I pause for a breath, then peek back over the edge. Tannie and the general are together now, battling Frenhin. She engages them both while firing a strand at me whenever she can.

Without Yestin's help, the battle with the guards on the far side of the room seems to have turned against us.

But it is mostly blocked from my view by the massive whirlpool of water and fire swirling just beneath me.

I've never seen Karlith fight so fiercely, and I realize suddenly the full truth of what she said. Naith killed her husband. Her children too? I'm not certain, but I see the mother in her rise up as her blue strands swell to twice their usual size—then thrice. They swallow up Naith's fire completely. Frenhin falters as her proxy strands are snuffed out. The streams of water throw Naith to the ground.

And then Karlith closes her hands. "Enough."

The water swirls one final round, then crashes down with a splash. The rock is painted in waves, like the sea.

Naith is soaked—shivering and cowering on the stone. He glares up at Karlith. "Go on, then. Take your revenge at last. You have waited a long time. Ten years, is it?"

"Longer," she says. She stares at him for a moment, then closes her eyes. Draws a deep breath. "No. I will not take a life. Not even yours."

Naith gapes. Then his mouth snaps shut. "Not even if I will take yours instead?"

Karlith smiles. "Oh, Naith Bo-Offriad. You understand so little. I am ready to meet my Maker. He dictates my steps. Are *you* ready to meet him?"

He glowers. Stares hatred into her. "Today is not the day we'll find out."

And then I see it. He reaches toward his ankle, and I detect the concealed sheath—the place where he stores his dagger.

"No!" The word rips from my throat as I swing out of my hiding spot, grab a handhold with my right hand, and draw my own dagger from my left hip.

It's not a good position. I don't have the right angle, proper leverage, or anything else I ought to have to throw properly. And I'll be giving up one of my weapons if I make the throw.

I do it anyway, because this is Karlith—the kind woman who sat with me on the *Lysian* as I sipped spike-fruit tea and shook with fear and remembrance, unraveling at my seams. The one who knitted me sweaters and called me *love* and treated me like I was a human being, not an animal.

Naith lunges forward, and my dagger misses its mark. Grazes his back as he thrusts his blade into Karlith's gut.

His was a wild swing. Not one designed to end life quickly or mercifully, or even painfully. Just the rough stab of a cowardly man hoping to save his own skin. And then he pulls back and does it again, then once more.

Karlith contracts over the third strike, and I see where it's buried. He has found her liver by pure happenstance.

And I know Karlith will be dead in a few moments.

I swing down the wall, jump the last ten feet, and come up with a dagger in each hand.

Naith's eyes go wide at the sight of me, and that brings more satisfaction than it ought.

He scrambles away, but I'm too fast. The first dagger sinks into his thigh—because I'm enraged and my aim is off. The second hits his shoulder, just above his heart. But it doesn't go in as deep as I want.

"Diggy, love." Karlith's soft voice behind me. "No more, dearest."

I turn and crouch beside her. This part of the cavern is turning into an infirmary. An infirmary where my friends lie dying.

"Karlith." I examine the wound to make sure I'm not wrong. To make sure there really isn't anything Warmil could do if he were here and not trying to keep those gray guards at bay.

But I'm not wrong. Blood gushes from all three stab wounds—worst from the last, and I'm almost sure he has cut the artery. Her color is already fading, lips ashen, skin blueing.

"It's all right, love." Karlith draws a shallow breath. "It's all right."

"Nothing about this is all right, Karlith." I hate the tears choking my voice. "Nothing."

She smiles a little, but it falls almost immediately. Too much effort. "Diggy, I . . ." Her eyes close, then she forces them halfway open. "I'm proud of you."

I take her hand.

"You will find your way back," she whispers.

I don't tell her I plan to die. To go out in a blaze of heroic sacrifice.

But she tsks at me, almost like she can read my mind. "Life is the harder, better choice." Another faint smile. "Do it."

And then she's gone. She's gone, and I'm ready to tear down the walls of this place at the injustice.

"Well, Bo-Lidere," an unfamiliar voice shakes me from myself.

A woman with purple-streaked blonde hair is standing in front of us, her sword drawn and her eyes darting around the room. "What mess is it this time?" A gleam appears in her expression. "And how can we help?"

CHAPTER FORTY-NINE
TANWEN

My first instinct was to shoot a strand of webbing at Venewth to stick her to the wall and get her away from Mor.

But then I saw they were talking—Mor was gesturing toward Zel, then the Minasimetese pirate Seni Kaizu crouched down and examined the fallen storyteller. And Mor climbed to his feet at last. My gaze drifted to Diggy, and I saw her reach up to close Karlith's eyes.

No.

I swallowed hard—swallowed down all the grief and pain that wanted to rise up and spill over, and tucked it away for later.

Because now was not the time for it. Now was the time to end all this.

Venewth's crew joined the fray with Brac's little army. I turned to Father. "Go. Help them."

"Tannie..."

I placed my hand on his arm and guided his attention to Frenhin. She was leaning against her chair, her chest heaving. Resting. Gathering strength. Naith whimpered and bled at her feet.

"It has to be us, Father. It has to be me and Mor. And Diggy. The moment you get close enough, she'll resort to her magic again. We have to defeat her on her own ground."

He frowned, but then he nodded. "Aye. I know."

I squeezed his arm. "I love you, Daddy."

"I love you, Tannie girl." He kissed my forehead.

And he was gone. Back into the skirmish to do what he did best.

Well . . . if I'm being perfectly honest, he's pretty good at being a father too.

I looked up to find Mor and Diggy striding toward me.

Aye, it was time.

"We're going to have to work together," I said. Frenhin was beginning to draw herself up. "None of us are strong enough to do it alone."

"Link," Diggy said. "Link and I'll help."

Mor and I faced each other. The smallest smile lifted the corner of his mouth. "I'm glad I met you, Tanwen En-Yestin."

"Is that so?" I raised an eyebrow. "Seems I made quite a mess of your life."

He leaned forward and rested his forehead on mine. "Worth it."

I might have kissed him if Diggy hadn't cut in. "This is precious. But shall we?"

I turned to see Frenhin moving toward us, her hands on fire.

Aye, we shall.

Mor took both my hands in his. Our gifts linked.

"What are you thinking about?" I asked him.

"All the tomorrows we could possibly want."

He kept my left hand gripped in his right but released the other.

"Diggy, move," I said, just barely hanging on to the strands that wanted to burst forth. She was right in front of us, and I didn't want to hit her with whatever our link created.

She glanced over her shoulder. "Just trust me." She stayed in front but crouched so we might launch our strands over her head.

Perhaps it was strange after everything that had happened, but I did trust her.

Mor and I released a volley of strands—very like those we had loosed on the Kanaci beach, all hope and light and color.

Goodness, justice, and grace.

A rainbow of light poured into the cavernous room. The torchlight paled, disappeared in the stream of color. The rock walls, the floor, even the top of the ceiling all began to glow.

And then Mor and I leaned forward and directed everything we had toward Frenhin.

Strands of starry night met ours—swallowed some of them, fought to gain control and snuff out the radiance.

I saw her brace herself—put her foot behind her so she might withstand the force of our power. She was stronger in some ways. More experienced. She had been working at this longer and had twisted her gift to make it more potent than it was supposed to be.

But Mor and I had honor on our side. We fought for what was right, and that gave us power Frenhin couldn't touch, didn't understand, would never have. She could offer us whatever she wanted—a place at her right hand, the ability to twist our gifts as she had hers—but it didn't tempt us like she'd thought it would. Because we didn't need to hurt others or warp our strands to get what we wanted.

All we wanted was a life well lived, given over to the service of others.

Our strands coursed with renewed energy. Frenhin grimaced.

But then she redoubled her efforts. With a shout, she shoved her hands forward, and her night ribbons burst into flame. A stream of fire sailed by my head, grazing my shoulder. I bit back a cry.

A night strand punched Mor in his shoulder—and sailed right through his body.

I did scream then, because it seemed he must have been fatally pierced by it.

Even Frenhin, shrieking out an insane cackle, seemed to

believe she had not only stabbed him but had killed him. Then I realized—the strands that looked like night weren't night at all. They were strands of death, and the one that pierced Mor ought to have ended his life.

But it didn't.

The wind was knocked from him, and if not for my grip, he would have released my hand. But I held fast. And then he gasped, drawing the air back into his lungs, and his eyes widened.

He glanced at me. "That was unpleasant."

"Are you—"

A plume of fire sailed right between our faces.

"The link," Frenhin said through clenched teeth as she directed more fire at us.

Of course. The link was protecting us somehow. Maybe his life was inseparably tied to mine while we were bonded.

Whatever it was, I thanked the Creator for that protection and poured every ounce of myself into the kaleidoscope of strands cascading toward Frenhin.

Two small hands appeared in my line of sight. Small hands covered in tattoos.

"Diggy, what are—"

"Trust me," she shouted over the roar filling the cave. She thrust her hands directly into the bands of light flying over her head.

Then she screamed loudly enough to peel the crust from the earth.

"Diggy, stop!" Mor cried. "Move your hands!"

But she wouldn't. She kept them in the stream of light, screaming and flexing every muscle in her body.

Why? Why was she doing this? The strands would kill her, surely. They were powerful, and Mor and I didn't really control what happened when we linked.

She was going to die. And for no reason at all.

Trust me, she had said.

But this?

With a final roar, Diggy's hands clenched. And then I saw. Lightning always seemed to crackle about the strands Diggy pulled from the sky and turned into weapons. But this time, the lightning filled every rainbow strand in the entire room. Everything Mor and I had created crackled and sizzled.

And with a snap, the sparking rainbows vanquished Frenhin's strands.

All of them. Gone.

Frenhin gasped and yanked her hands back. They were blackened and smoking as if the lightning had zapped her. She balled her fists and held them to her chest.

"Diggy?" Mor's voice brought my attention back to the floor where Diggy was hunched over. She was down on one knee, both palms on the stone.

"Diggy!"

Diggy glanced over her shoulder at her brother. "Mor, move. Your big head is blocking me."

We both turned and saw what she was doing. With her hands to the rock, she was coaxing the jar of white-lightning strands toward her.

The jar rolled from a cleft up above. I could see it now that the rocks glowed with colorful light. It slid slowly down the wall, the strands moving it gently toward its destination.

It reached the cave floor and swiveled toward us.

The jar trundled to Diggy's boot and stopped. She picked it up, eyed it a moment, and smashed it against the floor.

I gasped. And silently prayed Dylun hadn't seen her do that.

But the white-light strands didn't seem to mind Diggy's jagged edges, nor the jagged edges of the broken glass. They swirled into the air. Diggy wasn't commanding them, exactly. It was like she asked them—silently requested their help, and they responded to her intentions.

Diggy's head snapped toward Frenhin, and the strands followed.

The traitor queen screamed again, and this time, I didn't blame her. Two of the strands wrapped her wrists, then pinned her to the rock wall opposite from where she had chained Kharn and Braith. The third strand clamped around her waist and threaded its ends into the rock.

She was completely trapped.

"It burns!" Her eyes were wide and wild. "The strands burn me!"

"Pity, that." Diggy took a deep breath, then stood.

She swayed on her feet, and I let go of Mor's hand to catch her. She steadied herself on my shoulder. "I'm fine."

The three of us turned to find a quiet battlefield behind us. With the room lit up, it was plain to see the toll the fight had taken. Frenhin's entire guard was either dead on the ground or had fled. And we weren't without casualties either.

Diggy surveyed the scene. "This first." And she made her way toward Frenhin.

Pulled out two of her daggers as she drew near.

She stopped in front of the writhing Master. "Now. What shall we do with you?"

CHAPTER FIFTY

TANWEN

WE WERE BESIDE DIGGY IN A HEARTBEAT.

"Diggy." Mor placed a hand on his sister's shoulder.

She shrugged him off, her eyes fixed on Frenhin. "What would be fitting for someone who has brought so much pain to the world?" She cocked her head to the side and spun her daggers in her fingers.

I took hold of Mor's arm and lowered my voice. "Trust her."

Diggy continued to stare at Frenhin.

"Do it," Frenhin hissed. "Go on. Do your worst."

"That is a very dangerous thing to say to me. But if you insist." Diggy shrugged, then sheathed her daggers.

Frenhin's face screwed up in confusion.

"Now, sit there and think about what you've done."

Mor released his breath in a stream of relief.

Diggy turned to him. "You're going to have to learn to have a little faith, broth—"

He scooped her into a hug before she could finish. And, fry me, she let him.

But next I knew, the moment was shattered and Mor had his hand out, ready to release a strand. I spun about.

Naith was slithering from the shadows toward Frenhin. He was bleeding still but not fatally, it seemed.

"Master!" he cried out.

"Naith! Get me down from here!"

"I do not know how."

Frenhin writhed, then screamed. "Useless!"

Naith flinched. "I am not useless. I have served you faithfully, Master, for so many years."

"You have *always* been useless. A foolish, stupid man I only used because you had the right title." She squirmed against the burning strands. "I needed a priest, and you were more than willing to abandon worship of the goddesses to serve me instead."

Those painful bands were causing Frenhin to become reckless. Control was slipping away from her.

"Prove me wrong!" she shouted. "Get me down from here!"

Naith moved closer to her. He seemed to register for the first time just how powerless Frenhin was. "Why do you not create strands, Master?"

"I cannot." Frenhin strained against her bonds, her eyes filling with angry tears. "These strands have stolen my gift. I can't create anything."

I felt a gentle hand on my back and turned to see Father beside me, watching what was unfolding. And there was Brac with two of his men, closer to Naith and Frenhin. Brac was bleeding from his side, but he was on his feet, sword in hand.

"I loved you." Naith stared at Frenhin. "I trusted you—believed in you. I did all you asked of me. But you never cared for me." His voice rose. "You used me, just like you used everyone else."

Frenhin's face twisted into an ugly sneer, and she opened her mouth to retort.

But she never got the chance.

Naith thrust his dagger into her chest. Surely he was aiming for her heart, but it was a difficult strike to land properly. She gasped and cried out, and Naith tried again. And then once more. Then a fourth, this time leaving the dagger buried there.

Frenhin let out a small whimper, then slumped over. Almost

immediately, the white strands released her. Frenhin's body crumpled to the floor, and she lay still. A flaming white strand snaked from beneath one of her sleeves and joined its fellows on the floor—Frenhin's original strand, free after so many years held captive.

Naith stood looking at his Master a moment, then he began to turn to us. But before he got the chance, he met Brac face-to-face.

Brac placed his hand on Naith's shoulder. "Likewise, Your Holiness." Then, with the sword in his other hand, he ran his one-time mentor through the gut.

I covered my mouth with my hands.

I'm not sure what I had expected, but it hadn't been that.

Brac yanked his sword back, and Naith collapsed to the ground beside Frenhin. Brac caught me looking at him and lowered his eyes.

I didn't blame him for doing it. And I couldn't bring myself to be sorry Naith and Frenhin were dead.

Yet something else had died too. This was the other side of the coin. Brac *was* worldlier and wiser than a year ago because of betrayal and tragedy.

The Brac of my childhood was gone. He was hardened now, and that opened up an achy spot of grief in my chest.

With the help of the two men beside him, Brac made his way over to us. The blood darkening his shirt was significant.

"Brac, you're hurt."

"Aye," he mumbled.

Warmil's voice startled me. "Already patched you up in this spot once, lad. Be nice if you could stay in one piece for a bit."

Brac nodded over our heads. "There's more pressing injuries just now. Them first."

He meant Zel. Mor was already back at Zel's side, and I hurried over to them. I hadn't thought it possible Zel was still alive, but apparently he was. Maybe there was still a chance . . .

But as I dropped to the ground beside Mor, I could see it was no use. It was a miracle Zel had held on this long, and I suspected it was only because Seni Kaizu had provided some aid.

Mor clasped Zel's hand. "Anything, mate. Ask and it's yours."

Zel swallowed, his gray lips working with the effort. "Make sure Dafyth is taken care of."

Warmil loomed over us, and I glanced up at him, aware of the foolish hope on my face. He shook his head, lowered himself to the ground, and placed his hand on Zel's sweaty forehead. "It's all right, lad. You can let go. Be with Ifmere."

Zel took another shaky breath, and his chest stilled.

Seni Kaizu immediately began to pull strips of fabric from a bag at his hip and wrap them around Zel's feet. I saw now he had done the same with Karlith—she was swaddled in a cocoon of fabric from head to toe. I supposed it was a Minasimatese custom. When he got to Zel's hands, he removed Zel's wedding ring and handed it silently to Mor. Then he pulled another ring from his own pinky finger and handed that to Mor too.

Karlith's.

"Come, Mor," I said, my throat choked with tears. "Let's not watch."

He didn't move for a moment, but then he slowly stood. We made our way over to my father. "Who else?" Mor asked simply.

"Two of Brac's men—Farmer Hywon and Guardsman Bo-Droth. He was saving the Breseth boy."

Breseth, Brac's cousin.

Mor drew in a breath. "Anyone else?"

"Your man, Gyth."

Mor's former first mate.

"Not Mor's man." Venewth was checking her bandages. "My man."

She bit out the words. But I saw her eyes glisten.

"I'm sorry, Ven," Mor said to her. "This is all because of me."

Venewth sighed and straightened. "You always did think the world turned on your word." She took his head in both her hands and touched their foreheads together. "Don't carry this one around, too, Mor."

And I had to agree with her there.

"Well," she said, forcing brightness into her voice. "Surely we have some ports to raid somewhere, a bit of pillaging to get to."

But before she could make her flouncy pirate exit, the floor rumbled beneath our feet. It stopped for a heartbeat and then rumbled again, stronger this time. I almost lost my footing.

My gaze shot to the back of the room where Dylun stood examining the ancient strands.

He looked over at us. "They are returning home." Just as he spoke, the cave rumbled, and the four white strands snaked into the glowing, multicolored stone, disappearing from our view.

Father gripped my arm. "We need to go. Now." How many times had I heard him say those words over these past days and weeks?

"Braith," I remembered aloud. "We have to find her and Kharn. How will we ever get out of here?"

"I marked the path out," Father told me. "I think I can follow it and bypass all the detours we took to collect strands."

"Sounds easy."

He didn't bother to reply, only raised his voice to the room. "Everyone, we need to get out of here! Immediately."

As if in response, the cave rumbled again. This time, I had to grab Mor to stay on my feet.

Father motioned to the door. "You two, go. Find the queen."

We didn't delay. Mor and I darted for the door so that our whole quest to save Braith would not be in vain.

CHAPTER FIFTY-ONE
TANWEN

"We could split up, but if we meet Dray I don't want to—oof!" Mor's sentence was cut short as we crashed bodily into a man coming from the other direction.

Another shake from the mountain and we all stumbled. But as soon as my feet were beneath me again, I saw his face. "Kharn!"

"The mountain is collapsing," he said simply.

Mor raised an eyebrow. "Aye, thanks for the bulletin."

"It is the strands," a familiar voice said from behind Kharn. Master Insegno's face peered around the larger man. "Hello, ragizzi. I see you are healed."

"Master Insegno?"

"The strands have done their work and are returned to the mountain. But this has been very disruptive. Very disruptive, indeed. They are bringing an end to this place of evil."

"Then let's get out of here." Mor frowned as a third man stepped forward. "Who are you? Where's Dray?"

"Dray is dead," Kharn said, "and this is Bo-Fergel. But there's no time to tell you his given name, let alone explain any of this right now."

Dead. The word struck like a hammer. *So many dead.*

"Is it safe?" Kharn asked, urgency in his voice.

Mor's frown deepened. "Sounds like the mountain is about to crumble down on top of us, so I'm going to go with *no.*"

"I meant Frenhin. Is she . . ."

"He wants to know if it's safe for me to show myself." Braith stepped from one of the doorways carved into the rock.

Tears of relief sprang to my eyes. "Braith!" I threw my arms around her, then thought better of it and stepped back. "I mean, Your Majesty."

She gave me a weary, sad smile. "It is good to see you, Tanwen."

"All here?" Mor waited for acknowledgment from the others. "All right, then. Let's get out of here, for stars' sake."

WHATEVER MOR, DIGGY, AND I HAD DONE TO THE ROCK WITH our strands, it seemed to have carried throughout the entire cavern. The rocks pulsed with multicolored light, and I was almost sorry to see it all crumbling, so dazzling it was.

All at once, I was glad I'd dissolved my strands and released Riwor and the others within a day of when we'd captured them. Otherwise they might still have been trapped in that cavern, rainbow walls about to crumble upon them.

I couldn't wish that end on anyone, not even Riwor.

By the time we found the slash of daylight cutting into the rainbow glow from the cave's low entrance, the ground roiled so badly we were crawling on all fours alongside everyone else who had survived the fight in Frenhin's lair.

Father braced himself by the small cave mouth and helped assist the others through it, although the opening was like a moving target the way the ground churned. He grabbed Diggy's hand and pulled her toward him, then pushed her into the daylight. She disappeared, to safety, I hoped.

The ground kicked up in front of me, and Mor was pitched forward, toward the cave mouth and out of sight.

"Tannie!" His shout was muffled.

Father reached for me.

I grabbed hold, and he swung me toward the opening. Mor's hand appeared, and I took it. He dragged me free of the rollicking sea of rock onto winter-laced ground.

For a moment, I didn't think Father was going to escape. It seemed he had waited to help everyone out and now couldn't get out himself.

"General!" Mor shouted.

But then my father reached out from the cave and clasped Mor's forearm. With one final tug, he was free, tumbling out into winter daylight so bright I thought my eyes were on fire.

"Go!" Father yelled.

And everyone stumbled away from the rolling mountain.

Not a tick too soon. Whether the strands had been waiting for us to get clear or we were just lucky for once, the ground gave one final heave and the mountain collapsed.

The intricately carved hideaway of Frenhin Ma-Gareth was now a pile of rubble.

We lay there, all of us, as a cloud of dust billowed into the air above the toppled mountain. I counted twelve long breaths before anyone spoke or moved.

"The strands are safe now," Master Insegno murmured. "As is right."

And then suddenly, everyone was moving. Crawling to their feet, checking over wounds, examining their comrades.

Dylun was kissing both Insegno's cheeks. "Master Insegno, *what* are you doing here?"

I left them to their conversation—Dylun would tell me the story later—and turned to Mor. He was still on his back in the snow, breathing heavily. "Mor, are you all right?"

He nodded. "Just . . . need to rest a minute."

I touched his shoulder, then noticed Diggy nearby, sitting in the snow with her knees pulled into her chest, rocking back and forth.

"Diggy?"

She looked up at me. "Ho, Tannie."

"Are you hurt?"

"Probably."

I waited, knowing she had more to say.

"I . . . was planning to . . ."

"Die in the battle?" I had gathered as much.

"I didn't think there was any way I would survive. She was so powerful."

"But so twisted. She made a lot of mistakes. She had a lot of weaknesses."

Diggy paused. Rocked a little more. "I don't know what to do now. I was going to do something good and then—"

"Never have to do anything else again?"

"Karlith said living is the harder, better choice."

"She wasn't wrong."

Diggy chewed her lip. "I'm not sure I can be better."

I stooped beside her and waited until she met my gaze. "We can work on it together."

She smiled a little—just a tiny bit. "Thanks for not giving up on me."

"When the stars fall from the sky, the sun fails to rise, and the ocean dries up, maybe then I'll give up." I nudged her.

Her smile grew another fraction. "Maybe then."

I rose and left her to her thoughts. I scanned the bedraggled group of farmers, pirates, soldiers, and weavers, looking for Brac. Warmil was working on him, Aeron at his side.

I approached and smiled at Aeron, tears brimming in my eyes. I wasn't even sure why. "How is your leg, Aeron?"

"Sore." She grinned, but it looked more like a wince. "I should like to get home and rest for a while."

And then it hit me. Usually it would be Karlith by Warmil's side, supporting their patient with her tinctures and herbs while he put in stitches.

The Corsyth had lost three weavers since I met them.

I bent and put an arm around Aeron's shoulder. "I'm glad you're here, Aeron."

"Me too, Tannie."

While Warmil stitched up Brac's side—again—I weaved my way through the Pembroni farmers, greeting the familiar faces. "Farmer Hyde. Uncle Rawn. Well, call me a fluff-hopper—is that Tafarn I see? Blodwyn will kill you for coming, you know."

He grinned. "Not when she hears I helped save the queen. And you, Tannie."

I returned his grin.

"Awfully proud of you, Tannie," Farmer Wenth said.

I raised an eyebrow at his freckled face. "Prouder than when you beat me and Brac in that three-legged race when I was ten?"

"Twice as proud, at least."

I hugged first him, then Farmer Gwlan beside him. Maybe I was imagining it, but they smelled of Pembrone—fresh-turned earth and green leaves and the salty spray of the Menfor below the cliffs.

And then I came to Celyn. A bruise purpled her jawline. I looked at her with concern. "You take a punch, Celyn?"

She worked her jaw. "Aye."

"I'm still not sure how all this happened. I suppose Brac will fill me in at some point. But whatever got you here, thank you for coming."

She nodded and flashed a tight-lipped smile. She seemed unable to meet my gaze.

"Celyn."

She finally looked at me.

"I know you didn't do it for me. But thank you anyway."

Her face blanched. "Oh, Tannie. I didn't *not* do it for you. I just . . ."

"Fancy Brac."

"I—"

"He's always fancied you too."

"Tannie, I didn't mean for it to be like—"

"Celyn." I placed my hands on her shoulders. "Please. Make him happy, and let him make you happy."

She laughed, and we both relaxed as the tension faded. "All right, then."

But a dark cloud of truth suddenly eclipsed our lightheartedness. Did Brac even have a future to give to Celyn? Was it possible he would be traveling back to Urian in irons?

I turned back to where Warmil had just finished stitching Brac's wound. Queen Braith, Sir Kharn, and Master Insegno were gathered around him, and they seemed to be having a very serious conversation.

I glanced at Celyn. She looked as worried as I felt.

After a few moments of agony, we watched in confusion as Warmil helped Brac lower himself to one knee before Braith. She placed her hand on his head.

Celyn and I looked at each other. What in the world of hairy hedge-nibblers . . .

Warmil wrapped an arm around Brac and helped him stand and hobble over to us. Brac's face didn't give us any clues to what had happened—unless *stunned* was a clue.

"The queen . . ." he began, then paused.

"Yes?" I prodded.

"The queen just gave me a full pardon."

Celyn let out a cry and threw her arms around his neck.

Brac winced.

Warmil cleared his throat. "Careful, if you don't mind."

Celyn's cheeks flushed. "Oh, I'm sorry." She stepped back a little, her eyes fixed on Brac. "How? What happened?"

"She said her mother admitted to using strands on me somehow. I don't understand it. I don't know quite what she means by, uh, *manipulate sentiment*."

"Control your feelings." I started to move toward him, then caught myself and kept my distance. I was going to have to get used to giving Brac and Celyn space. "That was how they got you to do all those things, Brac. She was using her strands on you."

"Aye, I guess." He scratched his head. "Thing is, I didn't feel like they was forcing me at the time."

And maybe *forcing* was too strong a word. They'd played on Brac's weaknesses that already existed—selfish desires and jealousies that did truly belong to him. But Frenhin used those wicked strands to overpower whatever good sense Brac had—and his Pembroni-bred values.

"And what did you tell the queen?" Celyn asked anxiously.

"I told her I had made the wrong choices myself and should pay the consequences."

"Brac!" I knew I shouldn't scold him. He was trying to be noble. "Did Frenhin accidentally give you more honor than you started with in the first place?"

He made a face at me. "Ha ha."

"And what did the queen say to that?" Celyn pressed.

"She said I had certainly made some bad choices, but in light of my efforts here on this mission, she was pardoning me anyway."

Celyn burst into a teary laugh.

Brac looked at her, the shock finally melting away. "I get to go home."

"Aye." She laughed again and gripped his hand.

Despite his wounds, he scooped her into his arms, and my heart just about burst.

It was just what I'd always wanted for him.

He squeezed Celyn, then released her. "Just give me a minute, Cel."

He motioned to me, and we stepped away from the group. "Tannie, I'm sorry about all that's happened. I know I said it before, but I need to say it again. I hope you'll forgive me."

"Already done. And I hope you'll forgive me. If we could

start everything all over again, I think . . . I think we would hurt each other less. Love a little better."

"Aye."

I glanced over his shoulder at Celyn. "Brac?"

"Aye?"

"Marry that girl," I whispered.

His ears flamed red. "Aw, Tannie."

"She's way too good for you, but for some reason, she's willing to put up with your sunbaked self." I poked him. "Marry her, before she changes her mind."

He laughed. Then he scooped me into a hug that felt like the summer sun and warm hay and a floppy farmer's hat.

Tears trickled down my cheeks. "Go remember how to be Brac, all right?"

"Aye, I will." He hesitated. "Tannie?"

"Hmm?"

"Your pirate looks lonely."

I pulled away and turned. Mor was leaning against a tree on the other side of the group, all by himself.

I smiled at Brac, then took my leave.

Mor's arms were folded across his chest, his head drooping. If he had been smirking at me, I would have thought we were back in the Corsyth during that spring moon when I'd first met him.

But he wasn't smirking. He was staring, and I knew it would take time for the wound of Zel's loss—all the losses—to heal.

He noticed me finally, and a genuine smile warmed his face. "Tannie."

I just about collapsed into his arms. I nestled in against his chest, pretty sure I could have stayed there for the rest of my life.

"Mor?"

"Aye?"

"I have no idea where home is, but can we please go there?"

He took my face in his hands. "Tannie, my home is wherever you are." He grinned. "Farm girl."

It didn't matter that my father was somewhere nearby and that anyone who happened to look over could see us. Mor leaned down and kissed me—properly, this time, so that my knees buckled and painted-wings flitted in my stomach.

Strands of happiness and hope for the future poured out from us and swirled into the air. They lifted my hair and rattled the bare branches of the trees above us.

We might have stayed there another hour except the strands had definitely drawn some attention. Whoops and whistles sounded. Even a smattering of polite applause.

Mor and I finally broke apart with a laugh. And then a voice sounded from the trees above, and we looked up to find Diggy staring down at us from her perch.

She shook her head. "*Akē*."

CHAPTER FIFTY-TWO

TANWEN

I stood on the cobblestones of Pembrone's main thoroughfare.

Pembrone—dusty, poky, ordinary, and beautiful.

It was the middle of winter, and the wind was snappish. Or else we might have had a welcoming party to greet us, since so many Pembronis were returning home. Father had sent word to Cameria from Ir-Golyth, so we were expected.

We had left Dylun, Aeron, and Warmil in Bowyd so that Aeron might rest at a proper inn with a real bed, but they would be close enough to the Corsyth to check in there. The guardsmen, Kharn, Brac's aide Eny, Master Insegno, and, of course, Queen Braith had headed back to Urian.

And Venewth's crew had slipped away before anyone had a chance to say good-bye—except for Mor. They had made amends properly, at least, and Mor said he knew how to reach them when he wanted.

I guessed pirate crews didn't fancy hanging around government officials and royalty.

The rest of us had traveled back to the peninsula. Back to Pembrone. Back home.

Cameria met us in the front courtyard of our cottage. She burst into a wide smile. "Well, well." Then she laughed and threw her arms around my father. "Welcome home, my lord."

He grinned in return. "Will you never stop calling me that?"

"No, I will not." She kissed both his cheeks. "Tanwen!" She embraced me, then nodded to Diggy.

Diggy offered an awkward wave, then slipped behind Mor.

"Come inside," Cameria said. "I have cider ready."

We followed her into the cottage, and my jaw dropped. Last I saw this place, it had been tossed by Gareth's soldiers who'd been sent to capture me. It had been a disaster—everything strewn about, most of the furniture broken.

I remembered well the devastation of seeing everything in the world that mattered to me scattered about and ruined.

How small my world was back then.

But Cameria had righted everything.

Broken furniture was repaired. That which was beyond repairing had been replaced. Everything sparkled, totally spotless, and she had even added new curtains and decorated with evergreen branches. Soft, woven blankets took the place of threadbare ones, and a pot of spiced cider simmered over the fire.

Father looked stunned too. He turned to Cameria. "Everywhere you go is better for you having been there."

Her cheeks flushed crimson. "Oh, do stop that." She called out, "Arystia! They're here!"

The nurse we'd met in Urian emerged from the hallway, holding an orange-haired infant on her hip—little Dafyth.

We all stood for a long moment. Grief rose in my chest, and I could almost feel it in Mor too. I knew Father had told Cameria about Zel in his letter.

But Diggy's eyes lit up. "There you are, little one!" She rushed to Arystia's side. "May I?"

Arystia nodded and handed off the baby.

Father turned toward Cameria. "And the other refugees?"

"Safe. We all came here first, but eventually, we got everyone placed in towns across the peninsula. Some in Pembrone—you were right, Tanwen, the people here are generous. Many opened their homes and have been willing to share what they have, even when it's not much."

It hadn't even been a question for me. Of course they had.

"Commander Jule has been staying in Physgot," Cameria added. "I sent word when I received your letter, so I expect he'll pay a call in the next day or two."

I let the sounds of Father and Cameria discussing all that had happened in our weeks apart drift away. After grabbing a cloak hanging on a peg by the back door, I went out into the garden.

Cameria had done work out here too. She had weeded and prepared it for the spring planting that would occur in a few moons once the threat of frost was past. Though the ground was cold, something felt comfortable about it, and I plunked down cross-legged in the dirt by the far wall.

The Menfor Sea beat its steady rhythm against the cliffs below, just as it always had and as it always would. I longed to return to it someday. To sail and adventure, maybe without the threat of death hanging over our heads. Then we could return home—here to Pembrone. Visit Queen Braith in Urian.

I was ready to *live* instead of simply escaping death all the time.

And at the thought of escaping death, strands swirled out of my hands.

The story didn't need my voice, because it wasn't really a story at all. Just memories. Memories of a kind lad from a farm—the one who had felt so familiar to me when I first met the Corsyth weavers. The one who had made me feel like I wasn't alone among a group of people so much worldlier than I.

And his beloved wife with her beautiful hair, sweet smile, and daring final sacrifice.

A feathery, light-green strand and a rich, orange ribbon swirled together, then popped into a crystallized story—a sparkling sweet-root. It dropped into my hand, and I placed it up on the rock wall.

More memories poured from my hands—memories of kindness that warmed the aching hole in my heart and eased my longing for family. No, not just for family. For a mother. And she had cared for me like a mother. She had cared for all of us that way—healing, guiding, and sharing the light that filled her soul.

A rainbow of story threads danced together, then popped into a sparkling ball of crystallized yarn.

I placed Karlith's story on the wall alongside Zel and Ifmere's.

If I could have sung the next recollections, I would have, because it would have been fitting. Her voice was so hauntingly beautiful it was like it didn't belong in this world. I closed my eyes. I could almost hear her music, feel the way it lifted my heart. And when I allowed the memory of her final moments in this life to come to me, her death was no longer the horrifying, traumatic event it had been at the time. I could see it now the way Karlith had.

Sparkling pale-green strands crystallized into a formal dancing shoe—the kind the ladies at the palace wore for special occasions.

I placed my story of Gryfelle next to Karlith's.

And then came the memory I still struggled to make sense of. The one that smarted the worst, somehow, though I had known the others longer. Maybe it was because he was the first to go. Maybe it was because I was inches away from him when his final seconds ran out—right there yet unable to do a thing about it.

Whatever the reason, I couldn't put it away or make it beautiful. His death was ugly and cruel. Useless. There was no message behind it, no lesson to be learned except that sometimes the world is like that—senseless and wicked. And, sometimes, people we love are casualties of that wickedness.

"I'm sorry, Wylie," I whispered.

With a soft *plink*, the strand crystallized into a knotted rope and dropped into my hand. I placed it next to Gryfelle's.

I felt the presence of someone behind me. The footfalls were so soft that I knew who it was.

He spoke first for once. "Tannie girl."

I wiped my face and stood up. "Aye, Father?"

"Are you well?"

"Sort of." I laughed—a bit muddled with tears. "Aye, I'm all right. Grateful to be alive. And missing the ones who aren't."

Father eyed the crystallized stories along the wall. "You have lost a lot of friends on this journey."

"Aye. It hurts."

He nodded.

But before he could say anything, I added, "I know, I know. It's supposed to hurt."

He feigned surprise. "So you *do* listen to me."

I gave a shaky laugh, and he wrapped his arm around me.

"Father?"

"Aye?"

"Karlith believed this life wasn't the end—that she would see her husband and her wee ones and Gryfelle again. Do you think that's true?"

He smiled and pulled me in close. "Tannie girl, this life we live, this world that has been given to us, it's a wonderful thing. But believe me when I say this is just the beginning."

CHAPTER FIFTY-THREE
BRAITH

BRAITH STOOD IN THE PALACE GARDEN WHERE THE NIGHTMARE had begun. Snow drifted through the air, a few flakes finding her bare arms and sticking there. She closed her eyes and allowed herself to feel each sting.

"Braith?"

She turned. Kharn ducked under a trellis covered with winding branches—bare twigs devoid of a single sign of life.

He scrutinized her dress—black, again. Braith dressed for perpetual mourning now.

But he didn't mention it. "Where is your cloak?"

"I left it inside."

"It's freezing out here."

"I know."

He looked at her with concern. "You'll catch your death."

"I wanted to feel the snow."

"Here? In this exact garden?"

"I just . . . wanted to feel the snow."

He held out his hand. "Braith. Will you come inside with me?"

The barest of smiles touched her lips. "Yes."

He wrapped her hand in both of his. "You're freezing." He led her under the trellis and stopped.

Braith glanced up, then shifted to face him. The unspoken question hung between them.

"It looks dead," Kharn said softly. "But it's not." He touched the barren twigs. "Come springtime, these same vines will be in full bloom. Velvet-petals, are they not?"

"Red ones."

"Red ones." Kharn's eyes were so tender it was almost painful. "Winter will not last forever, my love."

Braith's lashes fluttered closed as the thoughts rushed in—thoughts of her parents, Dray, those who had been lost in the attack on the palace, the broken pieces they had only just begun to put back together. "I feel . . . damaged. And alone."

Warmth encircled Braith's shoulders, and she opened her eyes to find Kharn clasping his fur-lined cloak around her. "You are neither of these things, Your Majesty."

Braith's smile broke through her gloom. "I believe that may be the first time you have called me that."

"Is it? I must have forgotten myself." He grinned a moment, then turned serious again. "There has been so much loss. Death and pain, heartbreak and brokenness. Can we not have something glad?"

"I would very much like something glad."

"Good."

He reached into the pocket of his waistcoat and pulled out a beautiful strip of black grazer hide. He twisted it this way and that, and the silver sparkle within the band caught the wan afternoon light.

"The weavers." His eyes twinkled. "Tanwen said you needed silver. It is a wonder the way they make things."

Braith could only nod. "Do you—" The question was choked by the lump rising in her throat. "Do you still wish to ask this question, Kharn? After everything that has happened? I would not fault you if . . ." She couldn't bring herself to finish.

"Braith, I wished for many things when you and I were chained to the walls of Frenhin's cave. I wished to rescue the Tirian people from her clutches. I wished that we would make it out safely. I wished for brisk-leaf paste."

Braith laughed, in spite of herself.

"And I wanted to be unselfish. I wanted to be like you, always putting your people before your own desires. But do you want to know what I wished for most often?"

Braith raised her eyes.

"I wished for the chance to do this properly. To ask you the way I ought to have before our world turned upside down."

He lowered himself to one knee and held up the glittering leather engagement band. "Braith, if you will have me, I'll see to it that you are never alone. If you will let me, I will spend every day of the rest of our lives helping you see yourself the way I see you—not broken or damaged but strong and beautiful. Capable. Kind. The best person I have ever known.

"Braith En-Gareth, will you marry me?"

The queen brushed the tears from her cheeks, then held out her wrist—still marked by not-quite-healed sores from the irons. "Yes, Kharn Bo-Candryd. I will marry you."

He broke into a smile and tied the band around her wrist. Then he rose.

Braith pushed back one of his sleeves and ran her fingers over his mostly healed abrasions. Then she pushed back his other sleeve—and found he already wore a deep-brown engagement band that shimmered slightly with gold.

She looked up, an incredulous eyebrow raised. "I thought I was supposed to put this on for you. *After* I accepted."

He grinned and shrugged, not looking nearly as sheepish as he ought to. "I knew."

Braith reached up and brushed his hair from his forehead. He caught her hand and held it to his face. Then he drew her close and brought his lips to hers—gently, with the promise of so many more kisses to come.

After a moment, Braith stepped back and smiled up at him. "Winter will not last forever."

CHAPTER FIFTY-FOUR
TANWEN

WHEN FATHER AND I WENT BACK INSIDE THE COTTAGE, DIGGY was sitting on a soft blanket before the hearth with Dafyth. Mor leaned against the wall next to the fireplace, watching them.

Diggy covered her face, then popped out from behind her hands. "Boo!"

Dafyth's tiny giggles pulled smiles from everyone. But Mor's eyes were sad. He crossed to the blanket, then reached down and picked up the little lad.

Dafyth squealed and clumsily clapped his hands together.

"He likes you," Diggy said as she stood and brushed the dust off her trousers.

Mor raised an eyebrow. "He likes everyone."

"Lucky that includes you."

Mor tilted his face down to look at the baby. Grief washed over him again. "Your parents loved you so much, little one." He ran a hand over Dafyth's feathery orange hair and held him a moment more.

Then he sighed and handed the child back to Diggy. "We'll have to find a safe place for him."

Diggy's frown moved in like a storm cloud. "What do you mean?"

"It shouldn't be with Zel's family," Mor went on. "They disowned him because of his storytelling gift. I don't think Ifmere had any family to speak of. Else she would have stayed with them when Zel was cast out. But we will find someone—maybe in Zel's hometown. Someone will take the lad in and raise him like Zel would want."

In a single motion, Diggy tucked Dafyth into the crook of one arm and drew a dagger with the other hand. "No!"

"Sakes, Diggy!" Mor shouted.

"Diggy!" I cried. "Put that away! You're holding a baby, for stars' sake!"

She looked startled. No doubt her mind was catching up with her instinctive reaction. She sheathed the dagger, but the pained storm cloud on her face didn't break. "Mor, we can't just give him away."

Now it was Mor's turn to look startled. "What do you mean?"

"Well . . ." She looked around the room, first at me, then to Father, then back to Mor. "We're a family now. We belong to him." She nuzzled Dafyth's head with her chin. "And he to us."

Mor looked at me for help, but I shrugged. "Sorry, Mor. I think she's right."

"You want to just . . . keep him." Clearly this idea had not even occurred to Mor. "But how? How will we raise a child while we—" He hesitated.

"While we what?" I almost smiled. "Have you been making plans for the future without the rest of us?"

He shot an annoyed look my direction. "Not *plans*, exactly. But I had some ideas. I thought we might travel. If you wouldn't miss your hearth and your many pillows, that is."

"Oh?"

"Aye. The *Lysian* is still docked in Physgot. I asked Queen Braith, and she said it's mine, since the *Cethorelle* sank. She said she might be able to use us for the crown's business but that we would still be able to . . ." His gaze darted to his boots, and I could swear his ears turned pink.

"Be able to what?"

"I thought we might travel around and tell stories."

My eyebrows shot up. "You want to be a story peddler?"

"Not like how you were with that mountainbeast, Riwor." He peeked at me. "But the right way. Stories of our own making. With a little something extra thrown in." He slid a glance over to Diggy.

"Me?" She tilted her head. "But I'm not a weaver."

Mor snorted. "Diggy, to be perfectly honest, I have no idea what you are. But you're not *not* a weaver."

"'Not not' doesn't make sense."

Mor sighed and turned to me. "Help?"

I thought for a moment. I recalled the one time I had seen Mor tell a proper story, not use his gifts in the other ways we knew how—the tapestry story he had woven in Meridione.

And suddenly, my mind began to churn with ideas. The different ways my strands might be able to bring a little sparkle to Mor's tapestries. And what if he and I linked, then told a story together? We hadn't tried that before—actual storytelling while using our linked gifts.

And then adding Diggy and her wild, unique gift into the mix?

"It would certainly draw a crowd," I said at last.

"It would be more than storytelling," Mor added. "Almost like a show."

"And you want to travel on the *Lysian* and do this all over the world while carrying out the queen's business?"

"Aye. Some of Ven's crew said they would turn legitimate. Join the navy and sail with us. Jule has his own fleet, of course, but some of our crew from the *Cethorelle* would come. War and Aeron want to join. Dylun, too, as long as he's allowed to continue his research on ancient strands. I think he and Insegno have planned a lifetime's worth of research trips."

I crossed my arms and scowled at him. "Did you talk to everyone in Tir about this before me?"

And for some reason, I glanced at my father. Who looked... guilty. Sheepish, even.

My jaw dropped, and I rounded on Mor. "Him? You asked my father before you even mentioned it to me!"

Mor held up his hands. "I wanted to be sure before I got your hopes up."

"Fine plan, Captain Bo-Difflesnout."

"Hey, it's proper to ask first."

My stomach backflipped. "To ask . . . ?"

Mor grinned. "Don't worry, Tannie. When I propose to you, it's going to be on a sandy Spice Island beach while we sip chilled spike-fruit juice. Or on a Meridioni cliff, watching a colormastery sunset. Or maybe on a golden Haribian plain, the sun warming our backs."

When. When he proposes.

"It won't be here in a cottage while this prickle-back"—he tossed a look at Diggy—"and your father watch."

"Rude." Diggy made a face, then resumed nuzzling the top of Dafyth's head.

But Father was smiling. I knew Mor *had* asked for his permission, and I had a clear idea of what Father's answer had been.

"So, that was my plan." Some of the enthusiasm faded from Mor's expression, and now he looked sheepish again. "What do you think?"

I didn't skip a beat. "I think it sounds like everything I've ever wanted."

His grin blossomed. "Really?"

"Aye. Really." I turned to Father and noticed that Cameria had joined him. "Will you come with us?"

"No." He nodded to Cameria. "We will return to Urian to be with the queen. She needs us."

Tears pricked my eyes. I wasn't entirely sure how I would part from him now, after all that had happened. "Will you maybe come with us sometimes?"

"When the queen can spare me." His eyes twinkled. "And when my daughter invites me."

I laughed, then whirled back to Mor. "All right. My answer is yes. Of course, yes! Let's go adventuring!"

"You're forgetting something." Mor nodded beyond me, and I turned.

Diggy bounced Dafyth on her hip. She stopped and looked at us. "What?"

"Diggy, if we're going to do this, we can't take in the lad." Mor stared at me. "I mean, can we?"

Diggy didn't give me a chance to respond. "Don't be daft. Of course we can. Father raised us both aboard ship."

It was true. Mor had told me so himself. It was why, though he was from Physgot on the peninsula, he was not at all like the peninsular folk who were my kin. He'd been raised on a ship, soaking in an upbringing from all over the world.

Dafyth could have that life too.

"We can't leave him," Diggy insisted. "We can't just give him away."

"Because we belong to him." I grinned.

She was right. Keeping Dafyth with us felt right, and nothing looked as natural on Diggy as that sweet baby on her hip.

Mor nodded, and I could see the idea begin to settle comfortably in his mind. "Aye, that's right. And him to us."

Diggy burst into a smile—the biggest, truest smile I had ever seen on her face. "We're a family."

CHAPTER FIFTY-FIVE
TANWEN

My shoes clacked against the stone floor of the palace, and I bit back a curse at the throbbing in my feet. What I wouldn't give for a soft pair of grazer-hide slip-ons or even my sharkskin sailing boots, which had barely left my feet for the past ten moons aboard ship.

Who had invented high heels, anyway?

I paused in front of one of the corridor windows. I could just barely see myself in the reflection on the glass. I probably would have once been embarrassed by the tousled, wind-blown look of my curls, but somehow, it suited me now.

I was just missing my tricorn hat.

The shadowy reflection of Mor's face appeared over my shoulder. His mouth twitched. "Stop fussing. You look beautiful."

The deep-purple, crystal-beaded gown had been a gift, sent straight from the palace, along with our invitation. Braith must have known my traveling trunk was full of trousers and blouses and leather waistcoats now—nothing suitable for a special occasion such as this.

I wheeled to face him. "I'm not fussing. I'm just . . ." I smoothed my hands down the front of the corset and didn't finish my thought. Instead, my gaze fixated on him. He was decked out in the dress uniform of a queen's navy captain.

His smile grew. "We're going to be late."

"Well, that's not my fault. A girl can only make so many wind strands, you know. A ship lives and dies by the wind—isn't that what you always say? I got us upriver as fast as I could."

"Are you two sniping again?"

Mor and I turned at the sound of Diggy's voice. She strode down the hall toward us, wearing a navy-sailor dress uniform that had been fitted to her tiny frame. She adjusted the fire-haired toddler on her hip.

"Didi." Dafyth played with Diggy's long black braid. He giggled and tugged. "Didi!"

Diggy unlaced his tiny fingers from her hair, then kissed his hand and bumped noses with him. "Aye, that's Didi's. And it's attached to my scalp, if you don't mind, little sailor."

Dafyth giggled again.

Diggy looked back at Mor and me. "We aren't late yet, but we will be if you two stand out here arguing much longer."

We allowed her to lead us toward the throne room. But before we reached it, a young lass with blonde braids rounded the corner, a bucket in one hand, a mop in the other. She jerked to a stop to avoid crashing into us, but then her eyes went wide.

"Oh!" Her bucket and mop fell.

Before either could hit the floor, Diggy reached out and grabbed the mop with her free hand. Mor shot an invisible strand of . . . air? I wasn't sure. But it caught the bucket of water softly, creating a cushion for it to land on without spilling a drop.

"It *is* you!" the little lass cried. "Oh, I wanted to come to your show yesterday. I really did. We'd all heard you was downriver. But I was working. Couldn't steal away." She took the bucket and mop and held them up. "Getting everything ready for today."

Mor caught my gaze and smiled.

Aye. I knew what he was after.

"Would you like us to tell you a story now?" I asked the girl. Her eyes popped even wider. "Course I would."

"Once there was a little girl," I began. A shimmering strand of blue unfurled from my palm. "She had to work very hard to take care of herself."

The blue strand circled the girl, lifting her blonde braids. She snickered.

"But this little girl had big dreams and plans," Mor continued. A strand of black satin leapt from his palm and joined the dance with my blue strand.

I smiled at it. "Somewhere along the way, while she was chasing those dreams, this girl discovered what truly mattered to her." A glittery purple strand ribboned from my hand. "Her family."

"Her friends." A green swathe of sheer fabric from Mor.

"Taking care of those who needed her." I didn't glance at Diggy and Dafyth when I said it. I didn't want to tear up right at the end.

"Standing up for what's right and serving something bigger than herself," Mor said, adding two more strands to the mix.

A whole kaleidoscope of dazzling, colorful strands swam throughout the hallway. The little lass stared up at them.

"And this girl learned an important lesson." I lifted my hand, and the black-satin strand sailed toward Diggy. "No matter what has happened in a person's past . . ."

Diggy reached up with her free hand and grabbed the black ribbon from the air. She met my gaze, then Mor's, and she jolted the strand in her hand. The black dye scattered from the fabric and disappeared into the air. The cleanest, purest white was left in its place.

A faint smile crossed Diggy's lips. She released the strand, and it rejoined the others. "There is always hope for the future," she said.

At that, the strands circled together and transformed into a crown of flowers—a whole palette of colors and a silky white bow with long ribbons down the back.

The flower crown dropped into my hands, and I placed it on the little girl's head. "There. That's for you."

She gasped. "For me? To *keep*?"

"Aye." Mor crouched down so he was at eye level with her. "Find us after this is all over"—he nodded toward the throne room—"and Tanwen will share her cake with you."

"Excuse me, Captain Bo-Lidere," I said sternly. "Are you giving away my dessert now?"

Mor shared an overly sheepish grin with the girl. "Oops. Guess I'll have to share mine with you instead."

The lass giggled.

The throne room doors opened from the inside, and a familiar face appeared. He was dressed in fine leather, his beard perfectly groomed and his hair combed back.

"I thought I heard you out here," Father said.

I rolled my eyes. "You must have been standing right by the doors, then."

The hum of many people chattering softly drifted from the throne room as those gathered waited for the main event to begin.

Father lowered his voice. "There are a lot of people in there."

Still not quite comfortable living in society. He would never settle into palace life completely.

"They're just about ready to start." Father ushered us in. "I thought you would be late. Or perhaps had decided not to come."

"We wouldn't miss this, Father."

Two guardsmen held the doors wider, and Diggy and Dafyth followed Father into the throne room, Mor and me on their heels.

But before we made it through the entrance, Mor stopped and pulled me back. He leaned forward, his hands on either side of my face, and kissed me gently.

I closed my eyes and thanked the stars we had learned how to tame the strands that flowed from our linked gifts. They were still there—I could feel them wrapping around us—but they were nearly invisible. Like bands of air.

We broke apart but stayed close enough that our noses were almost touching.

I smiled. "What was that for?"

He tucked a loose curl back behind my ear. "For being you."

"Good answer, Captain."

"Ah. May I keep my cake, then?"

"Doubtful."

We hurried to catch up with the others. Father led us down an aisle, at least a hundred people in the finest clothing gathered on either side.

The guests stared as we passed, and I tried to ignore that odd feeling I always got when people whispered our names and our deeds when they saw us. It was rather like standing on a platform in front of all the world in my underclothes.

Not like in our storytelling show, where Mor, Diggy, and I would tell wild tales to delight children all over the world. Those stories were made-up—imagined and dreamed and crafted with care to surprise our listeners, maybe teach them something new, or maybe just make them laugh.

It was different when people looked at us because of the true story we had lived. I thought I understood a little how Father must feel in a crowd.

We followed him all the way to the far end of the room—the very front of the pack of guests.

"Your places are here." He nodded toward the first row. "I'll be near." Then he slipped into a line of important folks facing the rest of the attendees—next to a stunning Meridioni woman wearing a crimson gown. I realized with a start it was Cameria. I almost hadn't recognized her in such fine clothing, but when she smiled at me, there was no mistaking her.

In the center of this line of important folks was Kharn Bo-Candryd—beaming as if he were perfectly happy.

A group of musicians began to play, and everyone turned toward the back of the room.

There, looking like she had been dressed by ice fairies, stood Queen Braith, her pale-silver gown twinkling in the setting sunlight streaming through the windows.

I still marveled at her—how she could manage the heavy gowns, pinching corsets, and miles of blonde hair pinned atop her head and somehow still look so poised. So elegant. So . . . flawless.

She smiled as she walked down the aisle. Demure, of course, because she always was. But happy—truly glad.

This was her wedding day, at last. Braith's grief—and the ten long moons of cleaning up the mess Frenhin Ma-Gareth had left behind—could be set aside today. And perhaps this would be the beginning of many days of joy and healing.

Renewal, my father had said when I'd asked some weeks ago what Braith needed to be well again.

My gaze slid to Diggy beside me. She bounced Dafyth gently on her hip as they made faces at each other.

Yes, renewal. It was possible. It was real. Braith would find it, and Kharn would help her.

Braith and Kharn clasped each other's wrists, holding their engagement bands as they spoke their marriage vows. When they were finished, they would exchange the leather bands for rings of fine gold, befitting the Queen and King of Tir.

I laced my fingers through Mor's. Our leather engagement bands touched.

A small seastone-blue strand appeared from our clasped hands—sparkling, but small enough not to pull attention from the ceremony. It wound itself around our bands and began to glow.

Suggesting a bright future—one full of hope, love, joy, adventure.

And many more stories to come.

THE END

ACKNOWLEDGMENTS

I would be remiss if I didn't first acknowledge the readers who have fallen in love with Tannie and company—those who have rooted for these characters, enjoyed the adventures of my imagining, and occasionally yelled at me on social media for writing cliffhangers or torturing favorite story people (I'm sorry!). You all make my job so fun, and it has been a delight to write this final installment of The Weaver Trilogy for you. I hope I did the story justice.

To my husband, Dave. I have never known anyone more supportive, more encouraging, or more willing to sacrifice for those he loves. Thank you for loving me so well and enabling me to pursue my dreams.

To my children, Shane, Jared, and Keira. I love you more than coffee.

To my parents, Doug and Gina, for raising me to know the value of art.

To the wonderful friends who have seen me through my years of writing The Weaver Trilogy, some of the best and hardest years of my life. Ashley Mays, who sat with me through the darkest of the dark. My world is so much brighter for you being part of it. Dana Black, who suffered through the roughest drafts of *The Story Raider* and *The Story Hunter* and saved at least one character from certain death. Jen Lindsay, who has put up with my chaotic self and helped keep me on track. I love you all.

To my Wonder Women, Avily Jerome, Catherine Jones Payne, and Sarah Grimm. I deeply cherish our friendship. Our friendship, and our tomatoes, and definitely our GIFs. Extra thanks to Avily for her critiques of all three Weaver books. If you like Mor and Tannie together, you can thank Avily and my agent, who both suggested this pairing to me. These two characters had obvious chemistry in an early draft of *The Story Peddler*, and I had somehow failed to notice.

To Chris Morris, my "big brother," my Wylie. I'm glad you stayed.

To my beloved agent, Rachel Kent, for having my back always.

To Kirk DouPonce for this gorgeous cover. It's my favorite of the series, and I'm so grateful for the vison and talent you brought to all three Weaver covers.

To my street team, my Corsyth Crew, for your enthusiasm and support, and for all the fun we have together. You guys brighten my workdays more than you could possibly know.

To the team who has worked for and with Enclave to help bring *The Story Hunter* into the world. Jordan, Trissina, Catherine, and Jamie—for support ranging from editorial to typesetting to marketing and social media promotion. I'm so lucky to work with people I truly enjoy and admire. You're all amazing and talented.

And, of course, to Steve and Lisa Laube, my editors. This amazing team only kills kittens when I put too much tea in my stories, and they very rarely throw things across the room when reading my first drafts. Thank you both for giving me a chance and for believing in me and Tannie. I'm forever grateful for your wisdom and guidance.

All glory goes to God, the Creator and Source, the maker of all good things, and the one in whom I place my hope. Winter will not last forever—he carries springtime on his fingertips.

Lindsay A. Franklin is a Carol Award–winning author, freelance editor, and homeschooling mom of three. She would wear pajama pants all the time if it were socially acceptable. Lindsay lives in her native San Diego with her scruffy-looking nerf-herder husband, their precious geeklings, three demanding thunder pillows (a.k.a. cats), and a stuffed marsupial named Wombatman.

Connect with Lindsay!

Website: *lindsayafranklin.com*
Facebook: *facebook.com/lindsayafranklin*
Twitter: *@linzyafranklin*
Instagram: *@linzyafranklin*
Pinterest: *@linzyafranklin*

SELLING STORIES IS A
DEADLY BUSINESS

Available Now!

The Story Peddler

The Story Raider

The Story Hunter

www.enclavepublishing.com